THE HOUR OF THE FOX

THE HOUR OF
THE FOX

Cassandra Clark

This first world edition published 2020
in Great Britain and the USA by
SEVERN HOUSE PUBLISHERS LTD of
Eardley House, 4 Uxbridge Street, London W8 7SY.
Trade paperback edition first published
in Great Britain and the USA 2020 by
SEVERN HOUSE PUBLISHERS LTD.

British Library Cataloguing in Publication Data
A CIP catalogue record for this title is available from the British Library.

ISBN-13: 978-0-7278-8958-4 (cased)
ISBN-13: 978-1-78029-686-9 (trade paper)
ISBN-13: 978-1-4483-0411-0 (e-book)

This is a work of fiction. Names, characters, places and incidents
are either the product of the author's imagination or are used fictitiously.
Except where actual historical events and characters are being described
for the storyline of this novel, all situations in this publication are
fictitious and any resemblance to actual persons, living or dead,
business establishments, events or locales is purely coincidental.

All Severn House titles are printed on acid-free paper.

Severn House Publishers support the Forest Stewardship Council™ [FSC™],
the leading international forest certification organisation.
All our titles that are printed on FSC certified paper carry the FSC logo.

Typeset by Palimpsest Book Production Ltd.,
Falkirk, Stirlingshire, Scotland.
Printed and bound in Great Britain by
TJ International, Padstow, Cornwall.

Some castles associated with Bolingbroke's invasion, summer 1399

ENGLAND. SUMMER 1399

I t started with the one they called the Fox during that strange,
uncertain period when King Richard took control of his kingdom
and the old century dragged everyone closer to the Apocalypse.
Insufferable heat throughout May and June was followed by scything
rains and an unexpected southerly. The weather confused everyone,
worried the farmers, and kept the ports closed to trade.

Yet the strangest events were the deaths, one after another.
Starting with the old fox himself two years previously – the duke
of Gloucester – dead. Then the earl of Arundel – beheaded. And
his brother, Thomas Arundel, losing Canterbury from his brooding
grasp, in exile – so may as well be dead. Then John of Gaunt, duke
of Lancaster, dead of venery and old age in the February.

Finally, to put the cap on it, for the last six months Gaunt's son,
Henry Bolingbroke, and his crony, Thomas Mowbray, Earl Marshal,
were in exile. And – ominously as it turned out – not yet dead.

Despite all this, during May, in the raging sun, the entire City of
London flocked to witness King Richard II set off for Ireland at the
head of a vast army.

It was a day of unrivalled splendour as he rode out of London
astride his magnificent, high-stepping, white destrier, Barbary, with
the roar of drums and shrieking sackbuts shaking the walls and
all the flags flying. Armour glittered. Pennants snapped. Cavalry
horses caparisoned in gold and silver tossed their heads with pride.

The deafening cheers of the crowds lining the narrow streets
sounded all the way to Ludgate and beyond. A tumult of well-wishing
followed. Children ran alongside shouting the king's name until
they were breathless. Flowers were strewn under the hooves of the
horses. Garlands draped the necks of the men-at-arms.

No one would have guessed how it would end although rumours
began to shake through the City with the force and brevity of summer
storms as soon as the last man disappeared down the road.

The first thing to hint at trouble was when ships were sighted in
the Narrow Seas. People ran panicking to arm themselves against

the French, believing them to be massing their warships again. Shirts of chain mail were ordered. Swords sharpened. Gangs of lads flocked to the butts to perfect their skills. Merchants stockpiled whatever they assumed would be in short supply. Fights broke out for no reason.

Then the rumours abated and everything returned to the normal squalor of buying and selling and getting by that made up the usual life of the City.

The Prophecy of the Six Kings was repeated, of course, and embellished with dire warnings. The Day of the Lamb would give way to the Mold-Warp. The realm would be split in three. The dragon, the lion and the wolf would bring havoc.

It was commonly agreed that the mystery of the death in a Calais prison of the Fox was the dark force that drove this uncertainty but you might have imagined that the great joust to settle the truth would have brought an end to speculation.

Clearly King Richard had not known who to believe in the argument that sprang up between his cousin Harry Bolingbroke and Thomas Mowbray, hereditary Earl Marshal of England.

Before he led the royal army to Ireland he tried to settle the thing. Accusation and counter-accusation flew back and forth. Gages were hurled down. Neither Bolingbroke nor Mowbray would accept blame for the accusations being touted. So the king, friend and contemporary of both men, settled the matter as best he could by clearing them both out. Exile the best solution. Give them time to cool their heels in foreign courts.

With both of them out of the way he must have felt he had established a cordon of safety from assassins if what they said had a grain of truth in it. He probably felt he had given fair warning to others not to threaten him in like manner. Yet it settled nothing.

Another rumour circulated as soon as the king himself was absent. Who started it no one knew but it caught hold and went like this: it was King Richard himself who had given the order to have his troublesome uncle put out of the way.

The king!

His uncle, the duke of Gloucester!

The duke – the rumour went – could not have died from natural causes, it passed all belief.

A hale and hearty fighting man in his prime? Dying for no good reason? . . . except that he was cooped up under Mowbray's supervision in a cell at Calais . . . Impossible!

And – the rumour-mongers continued – look what happened to Gloucester's ally the earl of Arundel, lured to his death by King Richard who, to be fair, had resorted to the law to make sure the man was punished for his treason. And it was treason, no doubt about that, came the rejoinder. The conspirators had dined at Arundel's castle to discuss their grievances and later it was Bolingbroke himself who told his father what Mowbray had said and Mowbray, calling Bolingbroke a liar to his face, vowed that it was Bolingbroke all along. And then came the joust that-never-was – followed by exile.

What was sure, the cynics pointed out, was that by getting rid of his warlord uncle Gloucester, the Fox, the way was also cleared for young Bolingbroke's advancement. What about that?

When there was no answer, they pressed the point. Who, they asked, stood between Bolingbroke and the throne? Apart from his cousin King Richard of course there was only the Mortimer child whom nobody reckoned and, added with a knowing wink, the duke of Gloucester, a foxy prince of the blood still young enough to harbour ambitions to be king.

It was obvious what a hopeful nephew would do, they said. He would get his uncle with the annoyingly similar ambition out of the way. Quick sharp.

The joust to prove the truth of these suspicions was announced. Crowds flocked to the jousting ground at Coventry to see how God in his wisdom would arrange things. The jousters, accoutred and helmed, steeds pawing the raw earth, four hearts beating and eager to engage . . . And then what? King Richard calls a halt!

One of the jailers was dragged over from Calais and forced to take the blame for Gloucester's death. Shouting his innocence and that all he did was hold the cell door, he was quickly hanged after a perfunctory trial.

But the rumours persisted.

Fuel to the fire, enter Thomas Arundel, Archbishop of Canterbury!

Veiled accusations thundered from his Canterbury pulpit, warning of hell-fire and the eternal damnation to befall any who did not side with him. When his brother, the earl, met the executioner he himself fled into exile despite the fact that, as Archbishop, nobody would touch him.

At least, with King Richard on the throne, it was unthinkable that anyone would deal physical harm to an archbishop! They were not living in the bad old days of martyred Becket, were they?

But that was then.

Three enemies of the king in exile: cousin Bolingbroke, his friend Mowbray, and the archbishop.

King Richard himself overseas with an army.

And the summer broiled on.

Times of a darker hue than anyone would ever suspect lay ahead. In truth, no one was safe, not even a king.

ONE

Chandler checked himself in at the Tower gatehouse, was briefly wearied by their deference when they noted Henry Bolingbroke's seal on his letter of admittance then, bowing his head so as not to look up at the corvids flying in sinister clouds above his head, he made his way across the bailey in the lengthening shadows to the White Tower.

The guardroom was crammed with armed men, brutish fellows who communicated in grunts. One of them was delegated to lead him deeper into the prisoners' quarters. The guard's steel boots echoed in the narrow stone corridor and when they reached a door at the far end he muttered, 'He's all yours, brother, God help him,' and Chandler was abruptly left on the threshold.

He hesitated with his hand on the door. There was a sensation of movement on every side like rats gnawing through the stonework, a susurration of prisoners weeping, of ghosts, their sighs and whispers, the sounds of terror accumulating over time and repressed.

Bracing himself he turned the ring-bolt and found himself in a chamber no more than eight feet by six. There was no window. Light from a single flare propped in a bracket on the wall revealed the body of a man stretched on the rack in front of him.

Three others were in attendance. Two hid their identities under leather masks. The third, a young priest, white-faced, dark-robed, was mumbling nervously through his Latin with his head down.

So powerful was the concentration of the three on their victim that a moment passed before they became aware of their visitor. Chandler moved further into the chamber until he was standing over the racked man and, himself suddenly attentive, found he was staring directly down into his face.

He searched it for a familiar sign but he had never seen him before.

The prisoner lay on his back, manacled limbs extended, a rag thrown over his genitals. Best not to ask, thought Chandler. Sweat began to trickle down inside the neck of his undershirt. He took a cautious step forward.

The only sound apart from the priest's mumbling was the creak of the screws as the rack was tightened once more.

'You work late, lads,' he murmured as a prelude. There was a shift beside him as his words were acknowledged.

The prisoner was a shaven-headed fellow of about thirty, his own age. His lips were drawn in a rictus so that he seemed to be smiling at some fixed and private pleasure. The stench of human ordure was strong around him. Chandler resisted the urge to cough up the foul fumes from his throat.

'Not said anything then?' he asked the priest.

The youth's head jerked up.

His skin, already pale, seemed to blanch even more when he shifted his attention to Chandler. A bead of sweat on his upper lip swelled, burst, and ran down to his ill-shaven chin. 'Nothing, dominus . . .' Mumbling. Fear in his voice.

Chandler brought one ear down to the prisoner's lips. They were moving, but scarcely, a sound no louder than the flutter of a moth's wing starting, ceasing, then starting again.

Life, he observed to himself. The frail breath arriving from who knows where and as mysteriously departing at its appointed time.

It never cased to fill him with awe and dread.

He breathed in the fumes of the man's terror and in Latin whispered, 'We are here to help, my friend. Give me your name and who sent you and we can set you free.'

The man's expression was revealed suddenly as he opened his eyes. The pupils were dilated. They were staring over the edge of the abyss into the pit of hell. His lips tightened. A gesture to the rack-man made the screws turn again. An inch. Half an inch. Less than that.

A long-drawn breath followed. The prisoner's throat strained to withhold a scream of agony. His ribcage trembled. The sinews under the sweating skin danced of their own volition.

Chandler raised his hand. 'Stop. We don't want him dead.'

In the silence that followed he bent close again, murmured sweetly to the man in French, in Flemish, in Castilian and then, noticing a tremor, like a hound in pursuit he returned to the trail, speaking again in French, reminding him of all he was losing, his loved ones, his kin, his freedom, the sweet fields of home and all the beauty therein.

The prisoner's eyes, open again, began to water. He was dissolving in tears and sweat under Chandler's gaze.

His skull had the fragile beauty of an eggshell, infinitely touching to one who is still living. Chandler waited as if with tender patience and when it seemed the man would never speak his lips began to move.

It was a curse. It floated into the air, decayed swiftly . . . leaving nothing.

Chandler stepped back, distancing himself from the stench of fear. He gave the curse no weight.

With a feeling of relief he acknowledged that the whole thing had been quicker than expected. The broken words told him what his masters needed to know. He turned to the torturers. 'That's Orleans French all right. We must have a spy on our hands.'

'Then we'll make him wish he was in hell.'

'No.' He moved towards the door.

'Are we not to continue, dominus?' Eyes glittering behind his mask, the rack-man lifted his head with indifferent ease.

'I want you to give him chance to recover his wits. Feed him. Give him wine. Find somewhere with a fire. Make him comfortable until I come back and try to get some names. Who picked him up?'

'Constables came across him after curfew outside the house of a Sire de Shen. Quite a chase he gave 'em but they cornered him by the side of Dow Beck.'

Chandler made his face impassive. Dow Beck. And the fellow would mean Chienne. It would be le Sire de Chienne, a wine importer from Aquitaine. He had a wife. Two or three children. He had lived peacefully in the Vintry for years. Chandler ticked off these facts, memory never failing, and prayed that the fellow had an explanation ready to prove his innocence.

When he left he gave the men a brief nod for their diligence. The priest's face was streaming with tears.

Haunted by the image of the man being racked, Chandler left the Tower and crossed the bridge into Petty Wales to make his way towards Seething Lane where his contact lived. He wore his hood up and pulled it further over his face so that he looked like any other mendicant friar as he turned off the main thoroughfare. The house he wanted was halfway down the lane.

The morning fish-market always left behind its stench that not even the hours of the day could mask. Everything stank of herring. Obedient to the latest ordinance the street had been cleared leaving only smears of silvery scales, a forgotten head or two, eyes, sightless blobs of jelly, and the smell which was something not even the mayor had been able to legislate against.

Why his contact lived in such a foul-smelling quarter Chandler could not fathom. He was wealthy enough to live anywhere he chose.

He stepped fastidiously from one cobblestone to another to preserve his leather boots from contamination.

It took him only minutes to pass on the information needed then he returned the same way, glad to be done with it.

TWO

The first I know anything is up is when I hear somebody thumping on the street door and a lot of men outside shouting to open up. I'm transfixed. I don't know what to do. I don't want to let in anybody who shouts like that! Somebody who sounds as if they're armed!

The mistress is in the kitchen feeding the baby. I go to call her and then run back to the door. I'm in such a turmoil. I shan't open it!

And I run back to the kitchen but then I decide it's best to open up before they kick it in and I panic back just as the mistress calls, 'What is it, Mattie?' and I begin to ease the bolt but before I can even finish, the door bursts open and a man-at-arms shoulders his way inside, nearly knocking me flying.

'Where's your master?' he bellows. Not waiting for an answer he shouts into the hall, 'Le Chienne? Come on out, wherever you are!'

The mistress runs in with the baby in her arms. 'What is it? What transpires, masters?'

'Where's your man, lady?'

'He's—'

Even I can see in all my fear the formation and rejection of lies on her face. Poor mistress. Hoping to protect le Sire from these bully-boys.

The first ruffian grips her under the chin, backing her against the wall, and grunts, 'Don't even think of lying to me, mistress. Where is he?'

At that le Sire erupts from his little study, his sword half-drawn. 'Who wants me?' he demands. 'Speak to me and leave my wife alone!'

'We want you, le Chienne. Orders of the Captain of the Tower.' The man-at-arms nods to two fellows behind him and before le Sire can move they swoop on him, one on each side, while a third appears and yanks his sword from his grasp. Almost before he can take another breath he's bundled outside where they rope him and march him off down the street.

It all happens so quickly I'm simply standing like a sot-wit with my mouth hanging open. Madame goes to the door and looks out. She's crying and the baby's crying although it doesn't know why and I'm dry-eyed with shock until the little ones come running in from the yard and I crouch down, taking them both in my arms, telling them their father is only going off on business with some men and that he'll be back soon and then I start to cry as well despite myself. Inside I feel like ice. I cannot understand why militia should suddenly swoop out of nowhere and take my master away and cause my dear mistress to stand in the middle of the hall with a face as white as death.

I stand forth and say firmly, 'It's a mistake, madame. They're foolish men. They know nothing. They have mistaken le Sire for someone else.'

The little ones scamper off, reassured now the nasty men have gone, and I go to the door to look out into the street to see them already forcing le Sire round the corner. A friar in a greyish robe is standing nearby gazing after them. Across the way Master Chaucer, disturbed by the commotion, I doubt not, has come to his door. The friar turns to stare at our house. He notices the Master opposite and they both have a good long look at each other before Master Chaucer goes back inside and slams the door. The friar moves off after the prisoner.

I close our door but do not bolt it. Too late for that now. I regret having drawn the bolt in the first place. I say, 'I'm sorry, madame, I should not have let them in.'

'Idiot girl, how could you stop them? They would've put their boots to it. You did the right thing, Mattie.' She's in a state of forlorn indecision, rocking the howling baby and pacing back and forth, as if in a dream.

I go into the kitchen and bring her a beaker of wine and persuade her to sit down before she falls down with the shock of what has happened and I'm about to take the baby from her but then we both freeze as another knock at the door reverberates round the hall.

'They're back! I won't open it!' I whisper.

'See who it is.'

I should have done that before, lifting the little flap to peep outside, maybe giving le Sire time to get out through the back and over the wall but it's too late to think of that now and it might have made things worse. When I peer outside I feel an enormous sense of relief. 'It's only Master Chaucer.'

'Then let him in! What are you waiting for?'

As the door swings back he stares at me as if unsure who I am then gives a quick glance down the street before stepping inside. 'Why have they arrested him?' He doesn't wait for an answer but goes over to madame and takes her by the arm.

She shakes her head. 'He does nothing wrong. Why would they take him?' She begins to wail again.

'Who were those whoresons?'

'Their captain mentioned the Tower,' I chip in.

Chaucer frowns. 'Make sure you look after your mistress properly.' And to madame he says in a strong, reassuring, light kind of voice, 'I shall be back. Fret not. I know someone. This cannot be.' With a squeeze of her shoulder he goes to the door, peers down the street once more, then crosses to his own house.

I'm in the doorway with the baby in my arms when I see him emerge a little later wearing his cloak and his smart capuchon. Accompanied by Adam Pinkhurst, his scrivener, he goes off down the street in the opposite direction to the militia and their prisoner.

The sky seems to be weeping with tears of summer rain. As it becomes heavier I pull my hood over my head. The market is the place to pick up news and the mistress wants me to find out if anyone saw her husband being dragged off to the Tower and if so whether they've heard why. I visit a couple of stall-holders I know who always have the latest gossip. Rain drums on the waxed canopies over their trestles of produce with a sound like thunder and the awning gives off a smell of pig fat.

I must look worried because Izzie immediately draws me under the shelter and asks, 'So what's what, lovey?'

I tell them that le Sire has been taken to the Tower for questioning.

She and her neighbour Annie try to put a good slant on it. 'So long as it's not that friar who tracks down heretics,' they re-assure me.

'That's hardly likely!'

Izzie: 'Don't worry then, duck.' Annie: 'It'll be routine.'

I go out into the rain again. I feel sorry I don't have much comfort for madame.

On the way back I happen to pass a crowd standing on the bank of Dow Beck where it flows into the Thames. Despite the rain they're all gawking and jostling to look at something in the water. I try to see what it is between their heads but can make nothing out. It's mainly men shoving each other so I assume it's a strange fish in the wrong channel and somebody's trying to drag it out.

THREE

B rother Chandler had noticed Master Chaucer standing at his door when all the commotion of dragging le Sire from his lair had been taking place. He wondered why the fellow had shown himself at his door and cursed him for his curiosity. He hoped there was nothing in it. He liked poetry. But judging by the man's writings there was much that would not go down well in certain quarters. He marked him down, wishing that he was no longer involved with any of it, but what was done was done. Chaucer was probably already on somebody's list but even so it would have to be mentioned next time he reported in.

His attention was caught by le Sire's maid but when she saw him watching the house she hurried inside and slammed the door.

He wanted to be back indoors out of the rain himself but as soon as he reached the door to the chambers he rented above the gate-house a lad sprang forth from against the wall as if waiting for him. 'Brother Chandler! I have a message!'

Rain beating on his hood, Chandler bent his head. 'From whom?'

'From Sir Arnold Archer. He asks would you attend him at Dowgate below the bridge.'

'When?'

'Now, if you will, brother. I've only been waiting a little while. He'll still be there, I shouldn't wonder.'

Sighing Chandler thanked him. 'I'll go along now.' He handed a coin to the lad for his trouble.

'I'll walk with you, if I may,' the lad replied as he stuffed the coin in his pouch. 'It's a body,' he added. 'He would like you to have a look at her.'

'I see.' Chandler showed no emotion. The child was ready to let fly with rumours and speculation no doubt. It would be unseemly to encourage him. 'Death is a sad business, lad. I hope you've said an Ave for her?'

'I have, brother. It makes me sad to think of her coming to such an end.'

When he looked down he saw that the streaks of wet on the youngster's face were not rain as he had at first imagined but tears. 'Trust she is now in a better place than this vale of sin,' he remarked. 'Come, lead me.'

When he reached the bank of the Dow there was quite a crowd despite the weather. He was noticed at once and people nervously stepped aside to let him through.

Archer, one of the City coroners, came over. 'Look at this, Chandler.' He led the way towards the edge of the brook.

Together they stared down into the rain-pitted water. There was a body in it. A young woman. She must have been immersed for only a short time as there was no bloating or discoloration of the flesh. On the contrary, her beauty was unspoiled. Not a bruise or a blemish showed on her naked limbs. She had fetched up on a shoal of refuse in mid-stream where she lay like a sleeping water nymph.

'She was untouched, dominus.' A voice spoke in his ear. Turning, Chandler saw the grimy face of the parish gravedigger at his shoulder.

'The lord coroner,' he nodded to where Archer was being questioned by a group of aldermen, 'has already examined her.'

'Then why is she still lying naked in the beck?'

A prurient crowd were jostling to get a better view.

The gravedigger ignored his question. 'They're saying she's a novice in the house at All Hallows.'

Chandler knew him, a familiar figure around the parish of Portsoken near the Tower. He tried to move his arm from the man's grasp but the black fingernails, staining the pristine whiteness of his sleeve under his cloak, would not be dislodged.

'Why is she still lying here?' he demanded again in a louder voice.

A guildsman in the colours of his fraternity turned to appraise Chandler as if overseeing a piece of gold offered by a Lombard and asked harshly, 'What's it to you, Brother Chandler? Do you know her?'

There were sniggers from some of those standing by.

'For decency's sake,' Chandler replied, removing his cloak and stepping down to the water's edge.

All London's rubbish flowed here.

The Dow was clear when it set out on its journey from the sweet heights of Hampstead to the point where it entered the City at Clerkenwell but from there it flowed down through the close-packed, rat-infested streets to spew out into the Thames all the collected detritus of the inhabitants, the shit, blood, offal, dyes, waste, effluent, name it as you will, of a thousand lives.

It gathered in the trampled mud puddles on the bank, caught in the struts of a wooden landing stage, and sailed round the feet of the coroner's men as they dragged the body out of the water to carry her onto dry land.

Unnameable bloated things curled round the tresses of the girl's hair, settled on the white skin and crawled over the dead flesh. The open gash in her throat swam with tainted river water.

When the men laid her down Chandler stepped forward and, ignoring complaints from the crowd, threw his cloak over her. A scuffle broke out behind him and was only quelled when he gave the brawlers a cold glance. Recognizing him, frightened of the look that said they had been noted, they fell back, one of them crossing himself, another scurrying off with his head down for a reason known only to himself.

Chandler waited for the coroner to wade back to shore. He spoke as soon as he knew Archer could hear him above the gossiping onlookers. 'So, my lord coroner, this is a sorry business. What happened?'

Sir Arnold Archer came up and stood beside Chandler on the bank as if comparing heights. It was a game he and most other people would lose. Chandler's father had given him height as well as his Castilian hauteur and from his mother he got his cool, grey, Plantagenet eyes, although as far as anyone knew, there was not a drop of royal blood in her veins.

Sir Arnold on the other hand was short as well as sandy-haired and, after a life latterly given to self-indulgence, carried what looked like an ale barrel in his belly in the manner of any good Saxon.

'My dear Chandler,' he began in an undertone, 'what are things coming to when a harmless novice can have her throat cut in broad daylight? Is there no respect for her calling? The times we live in, eh?'

Chandler stopped what might become an all too familiar rant with a hand on Archer's shoulder. 'While your men take her to the mortuary may I offer you a stoup of ale in the Fleece – maybe you can tell me about her there?'

The crowd was dispersing now everything was over – some, perhaps, to compare their wives to the unclothed novice, others, women, to grieve for the destruction of their own youthful beauty by incessant child-bearing, the brutal attentions of their men, and the destructions of time. The destitute, homeless and unrecognized were left to grub amongst the effluent for anything of the smallest worth discarded by those more fortunate than themselves.

FOUR

When I arrive back from market I tell madame that there was no talk of le Sire but, I add, 'There was quite a crowd looking at something in Dow Beck.'

She puts her head in her hands. 'My poor husband.' The little ones snuggle up to her and stroke her hair to comfort her.

In a while she lifts her head. 'Please, Mattie. Will you go back to find out about the crowd gathered near the Dow? I'm convinced it has something to do with le Sire.' She is shaking with nerves. 'Maybe they have arrested someone else? Maybe he's been drawn into a plot? Maybe that's what this is about? I'm in a fever to know why they've taken him. Please run along there and find out what you can.'

'Worry not. I'll go right away.'

And now here I am again standing on the bank in the pouring rain when the mendicant from the street earlier and an important-looking fellow in a fancy capuchon brushes by as the crowd disperses. I remain where I am for a few moments, staring down into the sewer of the beck. So a body has been found. A novice from one of the nearby priories. I wonder about the life of this dead girl. Someone I shall never know. The crowd surges past with their sharp eyes and fantastical ideas about how such a one came to be murdered when she had the protection of a wealthy and powerful Order behind her but they show no sign of sorrow other than a few pious crossings and murmurings.

All crowds are the same, I think, as a brief image of Nijmegen flits across my mind. Even at home in Guelderland there would be the same gossiping and shaking of heads. The novice has broken the Rule, the rumours would go, and could expect no other fate.

At least madame's fears are unfounded because even though I discreetly ask around no one mentions le Sire. They mention other fellows picked up by the Tower guards but they have nothing to do with us. I always wonder why things happen the way they do, and whether it's God's will, or fate, or blind chance? Maybe the answer is written somewhere. I wish I could read. There'll be notices put up about the arrests outside the Guildhall.

FIVE

Chandler, made melancholy by abstract questions about the death of beauty and other mysteries he could not answer, strolled towards the tavern with Archer by his side. They could already hear people saying that the novice must have deserved her fate, roaming outside the precincts of her priory, disobedient, unaccompanied, flaunting, perhaps, an expensive silver cross, coral beads or other lures for the desperate and the starving.

Chandler's austere features turned one or two heads as he picked his way over the muddy, turd-strewn ground, some with fear, one or two who did not know his trade, in admiration, and as he followed Archer into the welcoming cavern of the Fleece he was aware of being noticed and assumed it was because of his tawdry reputation as always.

The place was full.

Smoked hams hung from the blackened timbers. Chandler had to bend his head to avoid them. A fire-pit smouldered under the pent roof at the back sending aromatic woodsmoke curling into the secret folds of garments and mingling with the scent of ale. As usual apprentices were gulping down as much ale as they could swallow despite the ordinances against drunkenness. Some of them Chandler recognized from the scene outside. A heated discussion was going on about the novice and the word murder added a frisson of excitement to an already febrile mood.

It was like the time when the death of the duke of Gloucester was announced. Nobody could stop talking about it. And later when the accusations started to fly between Bolingbroke and Mowbray everybody thought fit to voice an opinion then too. It didn't seem to matter that nobody knew anything about either incident. They thought they knew. Fights were inevitable. Well, Chandler decided, that's what apprentices did to show their mettle. They fought. Anything would serve as an excuse.

With mugs of ale in their hands, he and Archer found space on a bench against the wall. 'What's going to happen next,' somebody close by was demanding, 'when a novice can't walk outside her precinct without having her throat slit?'

'I'll tell you what's next!' An old fellow took a stance in the middle of the crowd, his voice booming through the noise. 'The Apocalypse is next, my friend! These are the End Days!' Jeers greeted this although one or two surreptitiously crossed themselves.

Archer raised his eyebrows at Chandler. 'I thought this was the Apocalypse. Does he mean it's going to get worse?'

The doom-sayer overheard him and dragged himself over. 'I know you, Sir Arnold Archer. And you—' He gestured towards Chandler but seemed reluctant to name him as if it might bring bad luck. 'You may scoff, you clever fellows,' he continued, 'but there's more of this ahead. A novice with her throat cut is nothing. Not when dukes are murdered in their beds. The lamb of peace will be usurped by the Mold-Warp. Mark my words! Horror on horror to come! Father against son! Women and children raped and murdered! Bodies piled in the streets! And this time it'll be a thousand times worse than the Black Death! Worse than the Hurling Time! The Mold-Warp will rule! It is written, my friends! Repent!'

'I'll do that,' replied Archer easily. 'We all need to repent our sins. Isn't that so, dominus?' He turned to Chandler, who nodded with a tired smile.

The old prophet had more to say. He leaned into their faces and the stink of his breath made Chandler draw back. 'The devil is coming from across the seas. No man, woman nor child will be safe from his hell-fire. Mark my words. When his house is built England will fall.' He lurched off and Archer, gazing after him, asked, 'What was that about a house?'

'These ale-quaffers hear all kinds of stories,' Chandler suggested. 'I've heard that about the house before. It makes no sense. After a few drinks words get snarled in their brain pans and come out as gibberish. Prophets!' he added in derision. But his glance followed the doom-sayer and he watched him closely while he announced the coming-true of the old prophecy of the Six Kings to another group who seemed more willing than themselves to give him the time of day.

The Six Kings story was well known. The fifth king was held to be King Richard, the lamb. The sixth? Who would it be? All anybody knew was that he would be bad news with his skin hideous and rough with leprous sores. A usurper with no right to the crown. The Mold-Warp. A bogeyman with which to frighten children and the superstitious.

Sometimes, thought Chandler, even liquored-up old men hear rumours that turn out to be true. Did he have anyone in mind for the devil's role? A recent rumour of ships sighted in the Narrow Seas had not been confirmed or denied. If his own contact knew anything he was giving nothing away.

'They do say some signs of the Apocalypse are here,' murmured Archer. 'Comets. This incessant rain – unless it's a foretaste of

St Swithun's prediction coming true? Then there's the collapse of trade with Flanders. The absence of fish in the Thames. And they say a woman down in Essex gave birth to a baby with a pig's head.' He smiled. 'And finally and most worryingly there's the exile of those two. One of them must be lying if not both. I mean, somebody had Gloucester murdered. Which one was it? Do we really know?'

'No and probably never will.'

'So do we leave it there?'

Chandler had his own views based on certain logical suppositions. He thought it prudent to keep them to himself.

Mowbray was Captain of Calais. It was unlikely he had acted on his own initiative – so who had given him the order? Was it King Richard? Surely it wasn't his style.

The question to ask was: who gained from Gloucester's death? Richard, yes, without doubt. To be rid of the uncle-duke who had been ringleader against him from the day of his coronation and later throughout the terrible blood-letting of the Merciless Parliament ten years ago – who would not want a man like that dead and his death threats with him?

On the other hand, there was another obvious beneficiary. Someone for whom the death of Gloucester would clear the ground before him and lead directly to the throne. Ambition had been instilled in him from birth. Where his father had failed to gain the crown of England, the son might prevail. It fitted the prophecy as well.

When Archer seemed to be waiting for an answer he eventually murmured, 'The question to ask about any murder is, *qui bono*?'

'If you look at it without bias it's clear who gains.' Archer took him by surprise by leaning forward and saying in an undertone, 'And you must know the story going the rounds in the Mysteries? They're asking, who stands in Bolingbroke's way now his father is dead?'

'In the way of Bolingbroke?' Chandler's face was a complete blank. He did not wish to hear seditious talk from Archer.

For Archer's own sake he did not wish to hear it but the coroner went on in the same undertone, echoing his private thoughts on the matter. 'We all know what Bolingbroke has hankered for all his life. The desire for the crown was instilled in him with his mother's milk. With his father out of the way to keep him under control who is there to stop him? In fact, it's worse than that. He not only has no one to stop him – he has someone actively urging him on.'

When Chandler still said nothing Archer continued, 'Well, do you not agree that Arundel is a dark influence on him?'

'I am not listening to this, Archer. You know I can't.' He looked away over Archer's shoulder into the milling throng.

To give him credit Archer took the hint although he couldn't help adding, 'And then there was that fellow they pulled from the sea off Dover, speaking in tongues, they said. Fallen from the sky, they said.' He tried to make a joke of it.

'Yet none of them predicted the Black Death,' Chandler felt forced to point out.

'To be sure, if they could get that wrong they're not likely to get anything right. Soothsayers? Agh! Have any of them dared name the earl of Derby or Lancaster or however we are prudently to name Bolingbroke these days and say he will flout the law and return before his period of exile is up?'

'Have they?'

'He risks a judicial execution if he does so. You don't need to be a soothsayer to predict that.'

'Archer, are you saying you think those ships sighted in the Narrows are his? Where would he get them, for a start?'

Archer gave him a quizzical glance. 'Surely you know more about it than I do?'

Chandler didn't bother to answer.

'If it is him breaking out of exile, let's hope he stays safely in his own lands in the north.'

'I'll drink to that.' Chandler tilted his mug of ale and drank down a good third before putting it aside for the moment and asking, 'About this novice, then. Murder by persons unknown?'

'Yes, unless she escaped from Barking Abbey and slit her own throat at the thought of the long years ahead.'

'A most sacrilegious view of the monastic life, coroner, if I may say so.' His light tone gave way to a sudden sharpening. 'You're not suggesting suicide, are you?'

'Me? I'm suggesting nothing until I've had a good look at her.'

'I was informed you'd already done that.'

'Don't believe everything your informants tell you, my dear fellow.'

The warning was not lost on Chandler. He gave Archer a glittering smile that adequately concealed his thoughts. He often felt that his old boyhood friend guessed the name of his pay-master. But he had the tact never to ask outright. Not that Chandler would have told him. Knowledge could be dangerous. Ignorance could turn out to be the best protection he could offer his friend. Chandler was not unheedful of the value of his own reputation either. It had kept him safe so far.

Nobody dared touch him for fear of the retribution that might follow. He believed it might keep Archer safe too.

'Let fools believe what they like,' he murmured now. 'That gravedigger said she was from All Hallows. Which is it?'

'The Abbey of Barking. Mother-house. She was sent on an errand with an escort to All Hallows and intended to return today so I'm told.'

Hearing whispers from further along the bench as Archer's words were picked up, Chandler turned his head in time to see a couple of apprentices quickly throw some dice and make some comment about chance.

To Archer he said, 'That was a terrible gash at her throat.'

'It looks like the cause of death but we won't jump to conclusions until we get her cleaned up.' Archer frowned. 'They picked up a foreign fellow close by. It was probably him but if it was theft it's strange he didn't take her ring. It was the one thing that made it easy to say straight off where she came from. Almost as if somebody wanted her identity to be known.'

'Maybe he was disturbed by somebody and left the job half done?'

'Why remove her clothes? To make it look like rape?'

'Thieves can lust after virgin flesh like any man. One crime does not preclude another. Nothing is definite or absolute.'

'Now who's being heretical? I thought we were enjoined to believe in the Absolute?' Archer tapped him on the back of the hand. 'If you wouldn't mind I'd like you to come to the mortuary when you've finished your ale. Or do you want another one?'

'Let's go after this. Your men should have prepared her for you by the time we get there.'

SIX

In the Fleece there had been a simmering excitement, not all of it connected to the fate of the novice from All Hallows. A rumour was increasingly going the rounds that Bolingbroke, in comfortable exile at the court of the duc d'Orléans, had in fact broken its terms and was on his way home.

What? everyone was asking. Has he or hasn't he?

They all knew the risk, hanging followed by beheading as the law decreed.

But the rumour soon grew to a certainty, he was sailing about in the Narrow Seas, allegedly with two hundred armed men, as brazen as you like, as if trying to find a place to land. Lookouts, more used to watching for French ships along the south coast, were mystified. They were forced to report that the ships bore Lancaster's colours of red and yellow clear enough. Somebody surmised that he was probably making for the Baltic, where he had friends among the Teutonic knights.

Others shook their heads in the belief of a more nefarious intention and suspicion ran riot. Chandler and Archer went outside and it was then, just as they were walking into West Cheap, that a dishevelled courier appeared.

Riding up to the steps of the Guildhall he threw himself from his horse, bellowing, 'News! I have news!'

Somebody ran forward to take his horse and another ushered him into a privy chamber where the lord mayor, Sir Drew Barantyn, must have given him some hurried questioning because almost immediately he appeared with one hand resting importantly on the shoulder of the courier as if to present him to the citizens. His crier, ringing his bell, brought all market trading to a halt.

Archer put out a hand to stay Chandler. They both turned to watch.

Into an uncanny and unforeseen silence the mayor, decked in scarlet with his mayoral chain of office glinting on his chest, began. 'It is my duty to inform you, the good citizens of London, that the earl of Derby, or, as some may say, the duke of Lancaster, Harry Bolingbroke, a prince of the blood, to whom many held allegiance despite confusions over the challenge from his contemporary, Thomas Mowbray, Earl Marshal—'

'Get on with it,' somebody in the crowd heckled. 'We know all that. What's happened?'

'Despite confusions,' continued Barantyn, used to the hustings, 'the duke, or earl, if you will, has now seen fit to leave his place of exile in France and has been sighted off North Foreland.'

Immediate uproar followed.

'Is he sailing up the Thames then?' somebody shouted.

Nobody knew. The mayor ushered the courier back into the Guildhall. Several made slitting motions across their own necks.

As the crowd broke up into opinionated groups the question everybody was asking was where did he intend to make landfall? Was he going to come storming into London? Two hundred men wouldn't get him far. Or would he take possession of his ancestral lands in the north?

'Gaunt inherited dozens of castles up there,' somebody pointed out the obvious. 'And now his son is going to make use of them!'

Arguments broke out and for some reason punches were thrown.

Chandler and Archer freed themselves from the roiling crowd with a bit of justified pushing until the bailiffs bustled forward to clear a path. It began to rain more heavily. Archer caught up with Chandler who was first to escape the crowd. Pulling up his hood again he said, 'You're looking thoughtful.'

'So are you.'

'Are they right this time?'

As they walked towards the mortuary Archer made a remark about the Lancaster inheritance, forfeit on Bolingbroke's exile but held in trust for him until he legitimately returned. 'Has he come back for it? I hear it's wild country north of the River Humber. Most will think he's welcome to it if that's where he intends to reside.'

One or two, overhearing this, wondered if King Richard, away in Ireland, had heard that his cousin had broken the terms of his exile. It was agreed that he could not have heard anything yet. Others wondered what he would do about it when he did.

'Wonder all you like,' the bailiff announced more loudly, sending his men in to break up the knots of bystanders defying the rain. 'But do it in your own time. Let's get this market open again. We've money to earn.'

SEVEN

When I return to the house later in the day I've no sooner taken off my summer cloak and spread it out to dry when there's a knock at the door. I peep out through the flap. It's Master Chaucer, also dripping wet. His little beard is sodden. I let him in.

He gives me a brief greeting but seems preoccupied. I show him into the mistress's solar and am surprised when she dismisses me.

I linger outside the door for a moment. I desperately want to know what has brought him here with that serious expression. I pray that le Sire is not being maltreated and wonder for the thousandth time whether prayers work or not and whether I'm a sort of Lollard after all, to doubt them. I pray for deliverance from heresy then wonder who is listening to my prayers, whether the Lollard God or the other one, and who will give me preference when it comes to judgement day? I step away from the door. It seems base to listen at it like a sot-wit bawd.

After a good while the mistress comes out looking as serious as the Master but with a lightness in her step that was not there before. She smiles at me but does not see me. The Master leaves. Shooing the little ones away she turns to me.

'Come into my solar, Mattie. I have something to say to you.'

EIGHT

The mortuary was brightly lit by rows of clerestory windows on three sides. The cold light illuminated with remorseless indifference the trestle set up on the flagstones in the centre of the chamber. A group of men were clustered round a sheeted body.

Chandler watched the coroner push his way through and pull back the cover to reveal the novice's face. After a moment he set to work. The clerk, writing tray open, made notes as Archer murmured his findings, the quill flying over the vellum.

When they had done Chandler stepped out of the shadows and went to stand beside him.

Archer looked up. 'It seems a clear case of murder,' he told him superfluously, moving aside to allow him a closer look. The wound at the girl's throat was black with dried blood. An artery had been severed. The blood would have pumped out, bringing a quick death.

'But why remove her garments with no attempt at carnal intercourse? Were they disturbed by someone?' Chandler asked.

'Not that we know of. Yet.'

'To leave the ring . . . If you were a thief it's probably the first thing you would take . . . It's almost as if somebody is using her death as a warning.' He frowned.

Only the silver ring with the insignia of her Order pressed into it had given a clue to her identity. It was as clear as a label. A messenger had been dispatched to All Hallows and another to the Abbess herself at the mother-house at Barking. Maybe they would be able to provide an explanation although he couldn't imagine what.

'This is going to bring down a cartload of ordure on Mayor Barantyn and his aldermen.' Archer grimaced. 'I'm not concerned for myself. I'm not responsible for the armies of criminals cluttered within the walls. It's the mayor and aldermen who'll take the brunt of the criticism in the alehouses and markets. Barantyn might even be brought down by it.'

'It's true, All Hallows isn't some impoverished chantry like mine. It's sheltered by the Benedictines and its mother-house has royal connections. Does anyone know what she was doing outside the priory precinct yet?'

'No,' replied Archer, 'but we will. You want to ask around for me to see what you can find out at this end?' He paused to let the idea settle in. 'For a consideration, of course.'

Chandler gave the offer brief thought. He was retained by his lord for a comfortable sum. There was his chantry living as well. Money was of no consequence. The novice intrigued him. Many of the sisters residing in the mother-house were of royal blood. Commoners were not invited without a considerable dowry. It made him wonder even more who she was and what her affiliation might be, not that it would matter to her now.

And there was something else. He gazed down into the young face with its flawless skin, the dark lashes curling on the soft cheeks as if she slept. He almost believed he saw the blue-veined lids begin to open, the lips tremble in the beginnings of a smile.

'Well?' Archer asked testily.

'Yes, yes, of course,' he replied, abruptly turning away. 'Anything I can do to help. You don't have to pay me, you old fool.'

'Then come back here when the abbess arrives and you can listen to what she tells us yourself. I'll send the lad to fetch you. It'll be after tierce, I expect.'

'I'll be ready.'

Chandler returned to his rented chambers above the gatehouse at Aldgate. As he went up the outer stairs he had to pass the guards and he was aware of the silence that fell as his shadow crossed the open doorway.

The Keeper of the Heads, an ugly, unimaginative little man, and his crouch-backed servant inhabited the lower floors of the gate-house. They hated him. He knew that. But there was nothing they could do about it. Nobody could touch him.

A babble of voices rose in his wake. The Keeper evidently had some cronies in, drinking and carousing. Night and day, it usually went on until all hours. Women too. He didn't know how he managed that. By paying them well, he supposed.

For a moment, as he climbed up towards the fourth floor, he regretted the austerity of his life. But then, he had had no choice in the matter. He could have entered the service of some magnate as a secular, worked his way to a position of power, for he did not doubt his ability, but instead he had chosen to remain loyal to his father's dying wish. It set him outside ordinary life. He remained within the cult of St Serapion – celibate and true to the strict discipline of a saint he only half believed in.

When he reached the top he pushed open the door into his chambers with a sense of home-coming and called for his servant. 'Beata! I'm back!'

She appeared at once, hands covered in flour, her outdoor boots making wet prints on the floor, and beamed a welcome as if she had been waiting for him. Then her expression changed and she burst out, 'Chandler, isn't it dreadful! You must have heard what has happened at Dowgate?'

'I have indeed. I've just left Sir Arnold and shall return when they send for me.'

'That poor girl,' she added with tears in her eyes. She pushed a strand of brown hair into place with the back of her hand. 'She was scarcely more than sixteen, they say.'

'They say all kinds of things, Beata. What else are they saying?' He flung himself into a chair and waited while she hurriedly wiped her hands on her apron, poured him a beaker of wine and set it beside him within reach.

Her brown eyes were round. 'They say she was in love with a young man with no land and never wanted to be a nun at all. She was a nun, wasn't she?' she asked, looking for confirmation.

'So we believe. A novice at any rate.'

'She killed herself for love, then?'

'Very likely,' he remarked dryly, 'but what other theories are they considering?' He knew there would be more.

'Well, another story is that she repulsed the bishop and he had her murdered out of revenge.'

'Which bishop have they chosen for the villain this time?' he asked.

Beata returned his smile. 'No name has been mentioned yet.'

'At least Duke John of Gaunt cannot be blamed these days, rest his soul.'

Beata grimaced and crossed herself. 'That's true – but they can blame his son instead.'

Chandler frowned. 'I hardly think Henry Bolingbroke is going to start visiting nunneries in order to slake his lust.'

'They have mentioned him, Chandler.' Even now she could not bring herself to call him Rodric as he had suggested some time ago.

He gave her a searching glance. 'Go on.'

'His stepsister is a nun at Barking Abbey. Some say the novice came from there.'

'They know that, do they? Or think they do. Go on.'

'The nun is one of the daughters of Duke John of Gaunt's adultery with that woman,' she pursed her lips.

'You mean Katharine Swynford? In fact,' he gave a short bark of laughter, 'you mean the dowager duchess of Lancaster.'

Beata looked prim. 'Who is she to call herself duchess? There is no justice in the world when adultery is rewarded above fidelity.'

She crossed herself and he noticed the little figurine of a saint on a silver chain that she always wore and how it glinted between her breasts. She was a comely young woman, narrow-waisted, with long, glossy hair and . . . He stood up with a suddenness that took her by surprise and she stepped back in alarm, her eyes widening, at his tone.

'This has nothing to do with Gaunt's widow Swynford. You should know better than to gossip about things you know nothing about. Who have you been talking to? Those tittle-tattling market women again?'

She had stepped back when he rose so abruptly and now she replied, 'I haven't been out yet. I don't know what they're saying. It was the fisher's lad, when he brought your fish to the door – I've been making a fish pie for you all morning and scarcely taken a glance outside . . .'

He glanced at her boots and the wet prints they had made. Suddenly he felt stifled. 'It's damned hot in here. Why do you never open the shutters?'

Beata was sometimes useful with the gossip she picked up from the marketplace but often it was like this, idle tittle-tattle with no foundation in fact. The name Katharine Swynford divided the world into those who supported her and those who wished her in hell.

Unable to bear the closeness of the chamber he went outside and climbed two at a time up a short flight of steps to the roof where he could look out above the thatched houses inside the walls and see clear down Corn Hill and the junction with Lombard Street. The thoroughfare was seething with crowds going down to West Cheap.

He kept his back turned against the outer wall where the heads were spiked. There were three decapitations at this time. A trio of young men of his own generation with lives cut short. They gazed sightlessly east over the marshes towards the chapel of the white friars and the rising sun. Even turned away with his back to them he could sense their presence. They had been there ten days. Their blood had dried to crust. The cumin-soaked flesh had hardened.

Even so the crows had made short work of their eyes, pecking them out and leaving only the sockets.

Chandler was most appalled by their hair. It was long and as abundant as his own. Strangely, when the wind ruffled through it, it shone as in life as if still attached to a living skull.

He glanced briefly, crossed himself automatically, but could find no words of comfort for them. Even so, since the Keeper had triumphantly put them up there he did this same ritual. A prayer for their souls. A brief, shaming crossing of himself to a being he did not believe existed.

Now he stared determinedly down between the crenellations into the street, grateful that his own eyes were not black pits in their sockets, and tried to make sense of things. There was much on his mind: his work at the Tower, the brutal murder of an innocent young novice and, more importantly, the rumour about his master, Bolingbroke, threatening to creep back into England.

There was also the minor and more immediate problem of Beata.

She was beginning to be a problem. He did not know why. She could not know he worked for Bolingbroke. Her own opinion about all the Lancasters was too forthright if so. If she guessed the identity of his paymaster he could not imagine her holding her tongue. And now she was lying to him.

His awareness that three severed heads were within a few feet of where he stood turned his thoughts to deeper confusion. The worst thing about renting chambers at the gatehouse was this. He could not harden himself against the sight. There was nothing he could do for them, they were dead. But so was the novice. He could at least help Archer hunt down her killer. Besides, there was that little rub of disquiet, the ring, the royal connection. Was it a sign or a warning? If so, from whom and why?

He should not have snarled at Beata just now. His moods were a sin, he knew that. It was *accidia*. His purpose, his zeal, his belief in the essential goodness of mankind had been eroded and he doubted that the saints had ever had the power to intercede on anybody's behalf. It was wishful thinking. Everyone was helpless. Everybody's destiny was set down from the beginning of time. He had to accept it and get on with what little he was fated to achieve.

Intending to make amends he took himself back inside.

NINE

S he was standing beside his chair where he had left her and when he appeared in the doorway she stopped crumpling the edge of her apron between her fingers and glanced up with a start. Her brown eyes held a yearning look which mystified him. He gave her a quizzical glance.

'Chandler, I'm sorry if I said anything to upset you . . .'

'You didn't. I'm an ill-humoured brute. Take no notice of me.'

He couldn't tell her about his task at the Tower and how it weighed on him. Nor how the executions cut him to the soul and aroused such a profound revulsion in him. And now the innocent little novice, victim of a plot hatched at court, maybe, caught like a butterfly in a net.

Instead he told her the story she wanted to know about the finding of the body in the water.

'I arrived as they were about to pull her out. She looked so young. A candle and prayers will do nothing to bring back all that lost loveliness.'

'It's heartbreaking.'

'Yes.'

'But you do your best.'

'Do I?'

'You're a good man, Chandler.'

'Ha,' his lips tightened, 'that's the last thing I am.' How could he be good? He profited, despite himself, from the failings of others in their plotting against the House of Lancaster. Come to that, it's what brought him profit from his chantry too. People's sense of sin. Paying their last penny, some of them, to be forgiven. Good didn't come into it. He was the fortunate recipient of their silver, that was all.

'Whatever you say,' Beata repeated, 'I believe you are a good man in an evil world.'

Such a weariness overtook him when she said she knew he would find the killer that he went back to his chair and picked up his wine again.

He had until tomorrow to get something from another prisoner, something to satisfy Bolingbroke's lackey, Thomas Swynford, and he would have to see if the fellow from Orleans had come up with any actual names. Maybe he would put it off until the morrow.

Before she left to resume her kitchen chores Beata hovered for a moment near the door and when he glanced up she said, 'Chandler, I know what they say about you. How they fear you. But they don't know you as I do. Just remember – I'm here – if ever you need – well – anything. Even if I can only listen . . . I am here for you.' With a sudden embarrassed gesture she turned and hurried out.

The rumours. Yes, he knew about those. He was indifferent. The believers still came to offer up their prayers despite what was in their hearts. They paid him well for his intercession with the great Master of All. Or whatever it was they thought held everything together. What caused him sadness was what they thought about Beata.

They assumed she was his whore. They had a lascivious desire to believe that the holy brother was no better than themselves. What he and Beata were supposed to get up to would make a pardoner blush. It meant she was treated with less respect than she deserved.

A well-born widow, she had come to him in distress shortly after Gaunt had offered him the living in the chantry. Her husband, a merchant who favoured St Serapion, had recently died and she wanted to pay for a mass for his soul. They had no children.

When it became obvious she was being swindled out of her manor holdings by her brother-in-law, he had taken her in as housekeeper, initially for a short time until the law could restore her rights but when the case dragged on for more than three years she became a fixture in his household. He told her he would not know what to do without her. She was grateful. He knew she would come to his bed if he asked her. But he could not ask. He was bound by a vow whether he wanted to be or not.

With nothing needing his attention for an hour or so he sprawled in a chair with a flagon of wine and wondered how he had allowed himself to get into this whole sorry business and how he would ever get out.

TEN

In a roundabout way it had happened innocently and accidentally through one of the Bohemians, a cheerful young fellow called Petrus. He had stayed behind in the English court after Good Queen Anne died and most of his compatriots went back to Prague. It was suspected that he remained at the English court to keep an eye on anything that might be of interest to his master, the Holy Roman Emperor, Wenceslas, Queen Anne's brother. Fair enough, was the general opinion. Every man of substance needed spies. Forewarned is forearmed and all that.

Those close to King Richard had encouraged the Bohemian presence. It had been considered civilizing. They were concerned with music and dancing, cards and chivalry, and their clothes set the high fashion that prevailed among the peace faction at the English court and the rest of the royal courts of Europe. It had been a sad day when most of them left.

He called for Beata to bring him something to eat, thinking how simple it had been to recruit him. As easy as hooking a fish in a pond, he thought now. He had made it easy. Gullible as he was then and pleased to be chosen.

For a reason he had now forgotten he had been present at Sheen – the palace still stood in those days. It was before the great fire when King Richard had burned it to the ground in the fury of his grief at the death of his beloved Anne – and it was probably an event to do with seeing Gaunt off, seeing him back to Spain maybe, because by then the ambitious fool was calling himself King of Castile.

Most people thought Spain was welcome to him. It was good riddance. Everybody laughed at Gaunt's desire to be King of England in preference to his handsome and cultured young nephew so they weren't going to be impressed by this foreign title. You didn't have to be a paranoid boy of nineteen to suspect that your uncle wished you dead so he could put your crown on his own head. His naked ambition was obvious to everyone – and everyone hated him for it.

This hatred Gaunt aroused was what eventually put a stop to his

ambition – nobody trusted him, they never would, not with the poll
tax and so on and the stories that circulated about his poisoning of
anyone who got in his way – but his son, young Harry, had rescued
the name Lancaster from the pit of hell where most people had
consigned it by the simple remedy of showing some prowess in the
lists.

Everybody liked a sportsman and he always made sure he
looked the part, tinselled and clad in his colours, with lots of show
and cheap glitter when he strutted onto the field.

The fact that Richard and his cousin Harry were of an age made
the frisson of mutual dislike an interesting sideshow. Richard, tall
and blond and cultured and as fresh as anyone straight from the
scented waters of the bathhouse, against thickset young Harry, red-
haired like a fox, stinking of blood and sweat. It took the mind off
the daily squalor of London life. As it was then and no doubt would
be till the end of time.

Chandler recalled how Petrus, on this occasion, was standing
beside him when Gaunt began processing towards the royal dais
where the king had yet to appear. Lancaster's herald made a fair
attempt at silencing the guests but even so his announcement was
lost in the noise that broke out even before he finished speaking
when the musicians struck up a lively estampie and the floor filled
with revellers.

The Duke had scowled at this reception and lurked awkwardly
at the foot of the dais, impatient for his young nephew, his liege
lord, his king, to make his entrance before he could be seated.

'He'll soon be gone and good riddance,' said a foreign-
sounding voice in Chandler's ear. 'Is that how you say it, dominus
– riddance?'

'I say nothing that can be construed as treason.' Chandler turned
with a smile.

Petrus was laughing up at him and with a knowing wink said, 'I
see you enjoy the dancing of the lady Agnes de Lancekrona, friar?
Is that treason, do you think, or merely sin?'

He deliberately followed Chandler's gaze and the two men fell
silent as they watched the lady Agnes dancing flirtatiously with de
Vere, one of the English courtiers and King Richard's oldest ally,
while de Vere's wife looked on with a sour face as well she might.
This was, of course, before the disaster at Radcot Bridge and de

Vere's exile and death. 'I enjoy all the entertainment Queen Anne's retinue provide,' Chandler had replied lightly, dragging his glance anywhere but back to the bosom of the Lady Agnes.

To Bohemian courtiers like Petrus, coming from the capital of the Empire in Prague, England must seem dull and unsophisticated, he thought then and still did. England at that time, ten years ago, was nothing more than a backwater full of uncouth militiamen and mercenaries. He remembered saying, 'We are but savages, Petrus.'

The Bohemian disagreed but they both knew he was being polite.

They watched the duke of Lancaster pacing below the dais. As usual he had a face like a thundercloud.

It was military men like him who in those dark days were turning the realm into a recruiting ground and draining money from the pockets of ordinary, hard-working folk to finance their military exploits. England had become a place held together only by an arbitrary and vicious sense of law and order imposed by those in possession of private armies. To Chandler they seemed like nothing more than licensed thugs. Loyalty was something that was bought and sold. Taxes were what the warlords demanded so taxes were what ordinary people were forced to pay. Or else.

Petrus, he now recalled, had lowered his voice. 'When the duke eventually sets sail for Spain, King Richard will rule in his own name at last. Then things will change, dominus. Do not be downhearted. England will be England again.'

Chandler had eyed him with scepticism. The name Woodstock as Gloucester was known at that time and the name Arundel ran through his mind even then. 'Do you really believe that?'

He had not been able to tell by the way Petrus widened his eyes whether his surprise was genuine or whether it was a ploy to entice him to say more. There was no way of knowing who was friend or foe even in those days. The best protection against a knife in the back was silence.

When Chandler did not continue Petrus had lowered his voice further. 'I have heard it asked, which of the duke's brothers will try to take his place when he is gone?'

'You mean who will snatch the duchy from Harry Derby?' he asked, deliberately misunderstanding to see which way the Bohemian would jump.

But Petrus shook his head. 'I mean the greater prize Gaunt has always yearned for.' He watched him carefully. 'Is it so outrageous?'

The crown, he meant. Chandler ran through the obvious candidates: Woodstock – Gaunt's youngest brother and the king's youngest uncle – not much more than a decade between him and King Richard; also the duke of York, not that he showed much ambition to rule; and, of course, Harry Derby . . . like father, like son. Were any of them capable of treason?

Yes, of course, he had believed it even then and later events had come close to proving it. He had heard them put it in reasonable terms: all they wanted, honest, was that the country should be governed well. They would make any sacrifice to ensure that it was so – even to the point of ruling the realm themselves, they said. The only problem – and Richard's safety – lay in the fact that they could not agree who should make this sacrifice and allow himself to be crowned.

Chandler had been about to make some noncommittal reply along these lines when the steward appeared beneath the dais and banged three times with his white staff for silence.

At once the music stopped. The dancers stood in the awkward pose of people frozen to a halt. De Vere's hand remained round the Lady Agnes's waist.

Old Sir Simon Burley smiled genially round at everyone, took a breath and raised his voice. 'Make way for King Richard and Queen Anne!'

There was a flurry of doffed caps and bent knees and Gaunt, with exaggerated dignity, dropped to his knees with everyone else. Chandler watched him lower his head like one, he thought then, nervous of the axe.

The great double doors at the far end of the hall were flung open and in came the king's herald decked in cloth of gold. He played a few intricate and faultless notes then stepped to one side.

With a plain gold band gleaming on his equally golden hair Richard entered. He was dressed in a dark-blue houpelande glittering with tiny harts worked in silver thread. Anne clung to his arm. Even at twenty she was no less royal in bearing than her young husband. Pale and slender she wore a magnificent crown made of gold filigree studded with pearls, emeralds and rubies that had recently been made for her in Bruges.

The young and glamorous pair proceeded into the hall and progressed with leisurely grace between the kneeling courtiers towards the dais where two painted thrones were waiting.

It was true what they said at that time, Chandler had observed dispassionately, Richard had the face of an angel. He had been nineteen then and still the beautiful boy of popular repute. And yet, even then, Chandler had noted a change in him.

He had cast his mind back to the coronation nine years previously – he remembered it well, being not much more than a child himself at that time – and he thought the king's eyes held a different look – world-weary, suspicious, disillusioned, guarded, fearful even? All these words had gone through Chandler's mind then but he had been unable to choose one above another.

At ten the child king had been the summation of everything good and innocent. The London crowd had responded to him. It brought a blessing to them. It was heaven's covenant that all would be well, all things would be well and the realm of England would prosper.

Now his thoughts loosened themselves. Aware of this at the time, how had he himself come to his present predicament?

He had seen the truth then, but he had not known that the worst had yet to come. It was a fact, then as now, that Richard's life was under threat. Mostly, it had to be said, the threats came from his own kin. But at the palace of Sheen that night when Petrus had sounded him out it should have been a time to celebrate: the most dangerous of the king's enemies was leaving the country.

He remembered the close formation of the bodyguard that stood between the king and his guests. He remembered the food-taster at his side, how the old man offered something he had proved to Queen Anne and Richard did not lift his goblet until the contents had been assayed.

Petrus, he remembered, had watched the whole scene with close attention but then he turned to Chandler and drew him behind a pillar. 'See what I have here?'

After a glance to make sure they were unobserved he opened his palm. In it rested a small silver talisman. It was in the shape of a white hart with a chain round its neck. 'The queen has had them made to give to her followers,' he explained.

Concealing it in his palm he held out his hand. 'Take it, Chandler.'

Chandler did so. He gave it a close examination. 'It's very finely made.'

'It's yours if you want it.' The Bohemian was watching Chandler's expression while he said this, his dark eyes flickering over his face so as to miss no nuance of his thoughts.

Chandler let the piece rest in his palm for a moment then with a sudden smile he flicked it in the air and slipped it into the money pouch on his belt.

Of course it was known that Petrus was an agent of the queen's brother, Wenceslaus, who would naturally have some regard for the safety of his sister, but why had he seen fit to offer the talisman to Chandler then? During the great Rising those who favoured the king wore little pewter badges as a token of their allegiance. The queen wore a similar one herself, made of diamonds. Then the silver ones were being given out. Chandler had had no idea why he had been invited into the charmed circle. Hadn't Petrus known who his master was? Or had he believed that he could be turned, like any other spy?

To conceal his puzzlement he had taken two goblets from the tray of a passing servant, handed one to Petrus, then raised his own in a toast. 'Your health!'

Petrus clashed his goblet with Chandler's. 'To Richard, Anne – and what you say? – to the true Commons!'

It was that same evening, later, but the same night, when Petrus had said something about popular uprisings and that they would never truly die as long as injustice thrived. He had added, 'And do we live in paradise? . . . No. Ergo – injustice continues to thrive and all right-thinking people continue to resist it.'

Chandler was thoughtful as Petrus's purpose began to dawn. Cautiously he asked, 'Are you telling me that England's heretics might be welcome in Prague?'

John Wycliff's followers were being continually harassed by the Church just as now. Even then calls were being made to have them excommunicated and imprisoned until they mended their ways.

'As long as the freedom to think and pray as one chooses exists in my beloved country all will be welcome whatever they believe.'

As if something had been established Petrus moved into the open. And then it happened.

While they were having their goblets refilled at the bowl being brought round, a page came up and bowed before Chandler. 'My lord wishes to have a private word with you, dominus.'

Before he could move two men-at-arms appeared, one on each side, and without any fuss hustled him from the hall.

Petrus apart, nobody gave him a second glance.

ELEVEN

C handler drank deeply and lay back with his eyes shut and saw the corridor they had marched him along and how he had expected the men to step aside and offer an explanation for their actions – but they forced him swiftly along between them and he remembered with alarming vividness how his heart had lurched. 'Am I being arrested?' he asked trying to make his voice sound jovial.

'Carrying out the duke's orders, brother,' one of them replied, avoiding his glance. They led him into a small stone chamber with only an arrow slit for light.

Tensing in expectation of the first blow from a mailed fist, Chandler just had time to notice that they were burning braziers in the courtyard outside and that night was falling when to his surprise the two guards left him and went out.

He could hear them on the other side of the door. He went over intending to demand his release before changing his mind. He knew they would be standing with their swords at the ready. Not much point in losing a hand over it.

He leaned against the embrasure and watched the fires in the courtyard and wondered how long he had left.

They could kill him. He had no weapon of any sort. Nobody would know. What the hell was it all about?

He tried a prayer but nothing came. He was useless as a friar. His faith had gone long ago, if, indeed, it had ever really been more than a boy's infatuation with martyrdom.

With no time to muse on his shortcomings he heard the stamp of the guards as they came to attention. This was it. The door flew open.

A tall, worried-looking man entered. It was Gaunt. Chandler had the brief impression of a bustling washerwoman before the professional soldier's attire of mail shirt, steel-shod boots and the dagger at his jewelled belt drew his glance. He wore the blazon of the House of Lancaster on his surcoat.

The man himself was angular and dark-haired with a straggly pepper-and-salt beard kept untrimmed, rendering his features even more lugubrious. That he was a vigorous swordsman everyone knew. That he was tragically unlucky in battle was also something that hung round his name like a bad smell.

He made up for professional shortcomings by the grandeur of his manner backed by such enormous wealth he was said to be the richest man in England – including the king himself.

'Bow when I enter.'

'Am I under arrest?' Chandler asked, not moving.

'Don't be so bloody witless. What have you done?' The duke's glance was suspicious.

'Nothing, your grace. It's often not necessary these days to have—' He stopped, noticing Gaunt's expression and just in time bent his head and counted to three. When he looked up again Gaunt's eyes were boring into his skull.

'You sometimes forget yourself, Chandler.' He strode further on into the chamber, boots ringing out, steel on stone. 'This is the only place I could find to have a private word with you. Our lord king—' the word sounded like a curse, 'fills the palace with hangers-on. If they got the chance every man-jack would report back to him all I have to say to you before you could scratch your arse.'

Chandler waited to hear what he had to say. The little white hart badge was burning in his pouch.

The duke paced about. 'I'll be out of here by morning and down to the fleet at Southampton. I'm leaving young Harry in charge. I want you to swear your allegiance to him just as you've sworn it to me. Is that clear?'

He remembered how he had smiled to himself at being called witless. If he was witless, what was Gaunt's eldest son?

Chandler opened his mouth to say something foolhardy, along the lines of his allegiance being sold when he was fifteen and having no choice in the matter, but Gaunt was saying, 'He'll have things he'll want you to do. And you'll do them. Understood?'

'My lord.' Chandler thought it prudent to bow his head again to show his acquiescence. He would not kneel. Never. His friar's robe should save him from that humiliation.

Gaunt, having no sword after being in the king's presence, unsheathed his dagger. It was the one he used for eating with but was jewelled, impressive, and could do much damage, judged Chandler, eyeing the blade with misgivings as Gaunt waved it in front of him.

'Place your hand on this and say after me, "I, Rodric Chandler, friar of the Order of—" What the hell is your order anyway?'

'Mercedarian.'

'Never heard of it.'

'Not many people have. It's a Castilian cult—'

'You never told me that.'

'The question never arose—'

'You could have come with me.'

'I doubt, my lord, that the Castilians would have welcomed me. Our founder, St Serapion, was considered somewhat subversive and—'

'Don't bother me with all that now. Just say the words.'

'I, Rodric Chandler, friar of the cult of St Serapion, do solemnly swear—' He paused and looked to Gaunt for guidance.

'To protect and guard against all ills to the best of my human endeavour, Henry, known as Bolingbroke, earl of Derby, eldest son of John of Gaunt, duke of Lancaster, and to inform the said Henry, earl of Derby, of anything and everything pertaining to the good order of his household, his welfare and his life.'

Chandler mumbled his way through this wondering how binding it was and whether Harry Derby would want the protection of a mere mendicant with no power, wealth or influence of his own. He doubted it.

Gaunt punched him on the shoulder when he came to the end and forced him to kiss the hilt of the dagger. 'I'm relying on you, Chandler. We've picked somebody up.' He sheathed the blade. 'He's in the Tower but the boys can't get a word out of him. They've tried everything their imaginations can suggest but he's as close as a clam. I want you to go over there and persuade him to tell us the names of the others. They're Lollards. Or French. Or some such. Whatever they call themselves, they're spies and traitors. We have it on good authority. We want them all.'

'My lord—' Chandler bowed his head to hide the horror in his eyes. He had been so young then. The same age as Richard, as Mowbray, as Bolingbroke.

The Tower was a hellhole. He knew that even then. Bloody deeds were done there which kept any sane man awake at night or else screaming in terror through his dreams. The threat of damnation could not instil greater fear.

This, with Gaunt, had been his first test. It had resulted in several beheadings on Tower Hill. The entire City agog with blood-lust. Everyone satisfied by the sight of justice being done and seen to be done.

In the decade following he had been instructed to attend many similar interrogations but nothing would erase the memory of that first one. It wasn't the most barbaric by any means. Much worse had followed. But it was the first and it was significant for that reason.

His darkest thoughts loomed to the surface at times like today, when his mind was emptied of everything but the need to sit and wait. It might have been filled with prayers but it wasn't. Far from it.

The bells for tierce had yet to ring out.

He finished the flagon but resisted the urge to demand another one. Beata was singing in the kitchen. Rain began to patter against the shutters again. For some reason and only for a moment he felt fortunate.

Now, Gaunt was six months dead. Of the king's enemies from those bloody days of the Merciless Parliament, when the five knights who called themselves the Appellants had linked arms and marched in cloth of gold down Westminster Hall to outface the young king, three of them, Bolingbroke, Mowbray and Arundel, were banished.

Fair enough, but he felt that a three-headed snake had been scotched, not killed. And his feeling of good fortune evaporated.

Take the Lollards for a start. Arundel had been unforgiving of any deviation from the orthodoxy he himself preached. In those early days he had Wycliffe in his sights. He put out rumours that Wycliffe was the Antichrist. Challenged him to defend himself at St Paul's. Unbelievably there was the earthquake. God has spoken in Wycliffe's defence, everybody said, believing it. An earthquake in London, though. It made you think.

Arundel persisted.

He had Wycliffe's Oxford school closed down and homed in on his prey, revenge his motive. But the old fellow thwarted him by the simple method of dropping dead after high mass in his church at Lutterworth before he could be arrested. Wycliffe's followers had not been daunted by his sudden death. They remained. Their ideas thrived. They completed their master's work, translated the Bible and flourished. Not only thoughtful commoners but many knights with no particular religious instinct supported them in a spirit of the free speculation King Richard encouraged.

They were a hard bunch, the Lollards, thought Chandler, and now, ten years later and with Arundel in exile, they flourished and would probably do so for another ten years.

He tried to turn his thoughts to the present situation, to le Sire de Chienne, and wondered how he was being treated at the Tower. It was bad luck that the spy from Orleans had been caught outside his house. It didn't prove a connection. It was entirely circumstantial like so many things that sometimes seem like incontrovertible evidence when you're looking for it.

The bells began to ring at last. First one, close by, probably All Hallows, then St Mary's, then others, each vying to drown out their neighbours by the energy they were putting into it. He needn't move yet. Archer had said after tierce, not during it.

Before he allowed him to leave his presence, Gaunt had given him his final instructions, 'Report back to my son by means of the usual contact.'

He had stared hard at Chandler to let his words sink in and added, 'You'll address Harry as the earl of Derby.'

'Will his grace be staying here at Sheen?' Chandler had asked, damping down his rampant fear with a practical question.

'He will.'

He certainly won't be staying at the Savoy, thought Chandler, private irony being the only defence he had against the future Gaunt decreed.

Lancaster's palace on the Strand called the Savoy was the most fabulous in the land. Or it had been until it was burned to the ground by the rebels a few years previously. Gaunt had vowed never to have it rebuilt as a reminder to everyone what the rebels were capable of doing.

But somehow, contrary to his intention, the charred ruins had become a symbol of the people's fight against the great wrongs done to them by Gaunt himself and the rest of the barons on the boy king's council. It was impossible that the blackened ruins would not remind everyone of their covenant with the murdered leaders of the Rising. It was a symbol of their resistance against their Norman rulers who treated them as slave labour. Held as bonded workers on manorial lands, they were worked like dogs. Forced to get permission from their lords to marry or to leave the manor and to suffer many other controls over their freedom and that of their wives and children, the only thing that held most of them back from resisting was fear.

Tyler, Ball and the other leaders had paid the price for their courage in the full horror of their public executions and the multiple hangings that followed.

Chandler saw flowers left outside the ruins of the Savoy even now, nearly a couple of decades later. There was buckthorn, known as the purging berry, its symbolism not lost on anyone, and yellow broom, King Richard's *planta genista.*

They showed that many still clung to the belief that the king had been on their side during the Rising and, but for Gaunt and his royal brothers, he would have continued to support the bonded labourers in their wish for freedom from enslavement. The dark aftermath of Corpus Christi when so many had been martyred would always be remembered by those who remained in fealty. Chandler knew then, in those days when life seemed simpler, exactly where his allegiance lay. He still possessed Petrus's little emblem.

'Come back into the hall, Brother Chandler,' the duke had grandly invited him. 'I saw you talking to one of the Bohemians. Is he useful?'

'He could be.'

Chandler bit his lip now.

He should have bitten off his tongue.

Not long afterwards Petrus had disappeared. No one knew where. Enough.

There was no point in brooding over what might have been but it was at times like this he could not control his black thoughts.

He rose to his feet and opening a gap between the shutters stood looking down towards Corn Hill. People were hurrying to find shelter with cloaks over their heads.

He recalled one further remark of Gaunt's on that occasion.

'Never forget, brother. I have spies and spies who spy on them . . . and so will my son. Remember that.'

Now he stood for a long moment thinking that if there had been a turning point for him it must have been then. He had innocently started on a road that had only one end. And here it was.

Suddenly the little Guelderland maid he had noticed at the house of le Sire de Chienne appeared as if from nowhere. She had a hood pulled over her head against the rain and was splashing down the road in wooden clogs like a child. Well, she was a child. What was she, fourteen, fifteen?

He wondered if she would be useful. She had the manner of a little gossip. It would be as well to befriend her.

Not in this rain, though, no matter how pretty she looked.

He watched her cross the street.

Then his glance sharpened. Instead of going into le Chienne's house she darted over to the other side and banged on the Master's door. He watched as she handed something to the servant who answered it. Was it bread? Did Chaucer have no cook of his own? Or was it a gift of some sort and if so, from whom and why? He watched as she skipped back across the road and vanished inside le Sire's premises.

Rain continued to pound the streets.

Chandler leaned thoughtfully against the window embrasure. She was strikingly pretty. But what was she up to?

TWELVE

The boy from Sir Arnold Archer had still not arrived. It looked as if he might not turn up after all.

He told Beata to have him wait if he arrived before he managed to get back then went down to the street, crossed to the chantry and went in. His duties were light: to keep the holy offices, to say mass once a day, to hold an annual vigil in front of the effigy of Serapion on his saint's day, and to pray for the faithful.

His sacristan was already lighting the candles. For a moment, out of habit, he knelt before the effigy of the saint and after a sufficient pause rose to his feet and set about the familiar task of maintaining the souls in his charge in the best heaven they could afford.

'Who brought these candles in, Martin?' he asked when they met up beside the tall candelabra on the altar steps. It was the most precious thing they possessed, five feet high and made of brass. Now it bore seven long tapers. He breathed in their perfume. Best beeswax. He closed his eyes with pleasure at the sweet scent. The gift of a wealthy donor hoping for a remission of sins, he supposed.

When he opened his eyes Martin was grinning. The candle he held cast a golden glow over them both until he snuffed it out between thumb and forefinger. A wisp of smoke trailed into the air between them.

'You'll never guess, Rodric.'

'I won't try then.'

Martin chuckled. 'It was a servant wearing Lancaster's livery. A servant, more specifically, to Sir Thomas Swynford.'

Chandler gave nothing away but asked lightly, 'And what does Sir Thomas require in return for this largesse?' The fool, he was thinking. Why does he show himself here?

'The quid pro quo has yet to be revealed. He sends us warning of his arrival after his business at Eltham is concluded, so his servant said.'

'That's to let you know he's important enough to be a guest at court.'

'Aye, with the king absent in Ireland! But I tried to look impressed.'

'I'm sure you succeeded.'

'He added that Swynford is anxious to ensure the safety of his master and himself in these uncertain times.'

'Don't they have more powerful fellows in Yorkshire to see to the matter?'

Martin threw back his head and roared with laughter. Wycliffe was a Yorkshireman. But it was even better than that. 'It's ironic if Bolingbroke is really headed there as they're saying in the streets.

What's he going to do? Challenge the king to a pitched battle of words?'

Chandler smiled. It was a welcome relief to feel the muscles of his face relax after the last few hours.

'You have to laugh,' Martin continued. 'His master's black soul saved by the lighting of a few candles?'

By this time one or two worshippers were scuttling inside and, still smiling, Chandler went through into the sacristy to prepare himself. Martin was one of the few people he could share a joke with and not be accused of being a Lollard.

'It's sobering when you think about it too much,' he said when Martin followed him through. 'Men whose whole lives are dedicated to greed and ambition asking for remission of sins so they can feel free to carry on in the same old way? And what's this about breaking the terms of his exile? Is that why he's suddenly bothered about his soul?'

'It's only a rumour.'

'Is it?'

'Do you think it's true?'

'I know no more than you.'

'Swynford's got a cheek,' Martin murmured. 'Candles, indeed. What does he think we are, pardoners in the pay of the Pope?'

Over the white tunic Chandler always wore, he pulled on a chasuble, thrusting his head briskly through the opening and letting it fall in soft, voluminous folds to his feet. It always reminded him of the one adorning St Serapion's effigy, the kind of garment he was said to have worn when he was martyred. It was perfectly plain. Martin kept it clean always and now he helped arrange the garment to its maximum effect before placing the gilt cross on its chain round Chandler's neck.

'A bishop couldn't look more impressive, Rodric, but you'll have to ask Beata to cut your hair again.'

Chandler's thick, black, Castilian mane reached his shoulders. He had a fleeting image of Beata running her fingers through it as she cut it for him. Then came her comment about his eyes. My mother had grey eyes, he had told her. We are both outsiders, she replied in the tone of one who imagined it made a bond between them.

When he was ready he composed himself for the ritual incantations he was about to utter and, bracing himself, stepped through into the public space.

Martin, thrown out of his Oxford college for supporting Wycliffe, had found a safe haven under Chandler's protection, paradoxical though it might seem. Fumbling to ignite the censer he followed him into the nave in a billowing cloud of incense that Chandler regarded as entirely ironic.

THIRTEEN

Serapion's was a fairly young cult as he had explained to Martin when they first met. Surprisingly, the saint himself was an Englishman, a mercenary fighting the Saracen in Spain. Chandler had been brought up on the story because of his uncle.

What started the cult over eighty years ago was when a Christian merchant trading down in Catalonia had been captured. Knowing that the Saracens would try to force him to recant, Serapion had offered himself in exchange. His faith was firm. Whatever they did to him he would never renounce his lord Christ. The deal was done. The merchant was released and Serapion was taken into captivity.

Of course he was tortured as expected but he refused to recant, also as expected. An attempt was made to buy him back but the Saracens refused to accept a ransom. Serapion was therefore martyred in a way that does not bear repeating and the Pope at once elevated him to sainthood.

Nowadays his followers lived mainly in Castile or Catalonia but there was this small cell in London. Over the years other men had followed the saint's example. One of them was Chandler's uncle, also a victim of a Saracen torture chamber. His fate had made a deep impression on the boy Chandler and when his own father lay dying from the plague after it had claimed his mother, he vowed to follow in his uncle's footsteps and dedicate his life to Serapion.

On his deathbed his father had given his young son into the keeping of an old friar who suggested he change his last name to something more English, taught him to read and write in Latin,

Norman-French, Castilian and English but then he too died. Chandler was fifteen years old. Alone in the world. And it was only then that he discovered that he had a patron. It was the duke of Lancaster, John of Gaunt.

As Gaunt's vassal he was given the choice of becoming a shield-bearer for him or taking holy orders. With an education that set him apart from a love of arms he chose to continue his learning in honour of his father, his uncle and the friar. He had no wish to kill anybody. He would follow in his uncle's footsteps and dedicate his life to the saint.

It had seemed a good choice at fifteen, and, only a child in those days, he felt bound to it because of the beliefs of his father and his guardian.

Things were different now. To place your trust in anything these days was asking to have your entrails pulled out whole while you watched, knowing that your body would be hacked into quarters and sent to every corner of the realm.

London itself was like a mortuary. From the Merciless Parliament onwards the Appellants had viciously beheaded or forced into exile every one of the young and powerless king's supporters. They had even felt no shame at having Sir Simon Burley, King Richard's elderly tutor, beheaded on Tower Hill. For what? For his support for the king.

It had been a horrifying event. The young queen, Good Queen Anne, as the citizens called her, had begged them on her knees to pardon Burley if he had caused offence. Everyone loved him. He was a hero of Poitiers and the loved and respected ally of the Black Prince, King Richard's father.

It was inconceivable to anyone that such a man in his final years could be subjected to a summary execution merely for following his prince's dying wish to tutor his son and safeguard him during his reign.

Arundel, a high-up in the Church from a young age because of the strings his wealthy family had been able to pull, refused him mercy.

Point blank.

He raged and refused.

It was like King Richard's own father being condemned.

The Appellants turned Parliament into a blood-bath. They said nothing to halt Arundel's vicious judgement. Bolingbroke and Mowbray had been of the five who condoned this barbarity.

Now Chandler considered the nature of forgiveness and came to his usual conclusion that sometimes it is not humanly possible. He had known Burley. A more affable and kind old fellow it was difficult to imagine.

When Gloucester, the leading Appellant known then as Edmund of Woodstock, was later suffocated at Calais, it would not have been outrageous to imagine that it was the king himself who had given the order. Who would not want to hunt down the murderers from that terrible time? Was ten years, or ten thousand years, long enough to learn to forgive them?

Chandler tried to force his thoughts away from opinions such as these. He was retained to work for Bolingbroke. That was the irony. It would be madness to harbour doubts about him. As heir of the vast Lancastrian estates, now his father Duke John of Gaunt had died from the effects of his immoral life, he was not to be played with. Good nature had never been an element in any of his dealings so far and he was a force in the realm even now in his absence.

While he disrobed in the little vestry at the back of the chantry and wondered if Archer's lad had bothered to turn up, Chandler forced himself to think of something less likely to drive him to deeper melancholy. He felt he would never clamber free of the situation he was in no matter how his thoughts twisted and turned.

But look at it, he told himself, as he pulled on his cloak ready to go out into the rain. He had skills. He should not feel trapped by his current situation. If he gave up his living, rejected his fealty to Lancaster, he could survive.

But would they allow him to defect? Did they think he knew too much?

As well as languages his foster-father had trained him in something else. As assistant to the renowned Dominican herbalist Henry Daniel, the old friar had willingly passed on his compendium of knowledge to his ward.

It included a practical knowledge of poisons. Archer, for one, found Chandler's knowledge useful when faced with unexplained and killing fluxes. Few knew more about poisons than Brother Chandler.

*   *   *

He waved a hand in farewell to Martin and stepped outside. At once he was accosted by a small boy grabbing his sleeve. Recognizing him he gave a nod. 'Not before time. Did Sir Arnold forget to instruct you – or have you been playing about the streets with other bad lads?'

'No, brother, honest.' He looked terrified. 'I came straight over this morning as instructed. Your servant told me you were here and I was waiting for you as I should.'

'I believe you, lad. Let's go.'

The child led at a brisk clip through the bustle of Aldgate and down Minchen Lane to Tower Street. On the other side of the stinking gutter running down the middle was the mortuary for All Hallows by the Tower. They crossed the stream running with night soil and made it across without anything too unpleasant getting inside their boots.

'God's teeth!' Chandler swore when he met Archer at the door. 'Can't you get the City to do anything about the state of the streets?'

'No cash. But they've promised a clean-up within the next couple of weeks—'

'Useless losels.'

Archer led the way into a snug room off the death chamber and settled down in a well-worn wooden chair with a gesture to Chandler to find a seat on the bench opposite. He offered wine.

Chandler accepted despite the stink of death that almost put him off. He didn't understand how Archer could appear oblivious to it. Habit, he supposed. It armours us against so much, he thought, remembering the severed heads above the gatehouse and the bloody sights he saw on his own too frequent visits to the Tower.

'The abbess herself cannot or will not attend.' Archer came straight to the point. 'She is sending a deputy.'

'I would have thought she'd be burning to find out what had happened to one of her novices,' he exclaimed.

'The girl might have been an orphan. Her dowry paid up. They won't be expecting any more money from that quarter. They'll be wondering why they should put themselves out.'

'Poor child. So how did it happen that she was wandering alone outside the priory?'

'A runaway or so the abbess claims. She broke the rules. She's paid the price.'

'And that's the end of it?'

The coroner shrugged. 'I've given you the gist of this note she sent.'

He handed it to Chandler who scanned it and handed it back. 'It says nothing, does it? Why was she running away?'

'They're fobbing us off but I'm the coroner round here. It's up to me to ask questions. And I will.'

'Where are we going to start?'

Archer refilled both their flagons. 'I was hoping you'd say that. Now, listen.'

FOURTEEN

I leave madame's solar with a frightened fluttering in my stomach. What I've just been told terrifies me. If it turns out badly we'll all be done for. What is it like to be executed? Maybe I'll hang instead as I'm not noble enough for a quick death. What is hanging like? I can't help fingering my neck. It would be horrible. It would be undignified at the very least. How wretched to die in shame for everyone to witness!

But it won't come to that. It mustn't.

I wonder who I can ask about the stars and what they predict. I need an astrologer. Even the king has one. The fellow told him to fear nothing except the toad. So the king, they say, had a celebration in joy. Arriving last came his cousin Bolingbroke attired in a houpelande embroidered all over with squat green toads. Imagine it!

I discard the need for an astrologer – especially like that one who had probably been paid to frighten the king – and pick up the baby from its cradle to dandle him on my lap. I stroke the top of his little head feeling the warm silkiness of his tufty hair beneath my fingertips. I press a little kiss against his fat round cheek and a tear falls onto his little face making him arch backwards with a trusting gurgle. He topples forward to rub his face against my neck and laughs with delight.

The two older children cluster at my knee, applauding his little tricks. One of them hands him a tiny woollen ball then snatches it away to hide it in her sleeve until he finds it with a cackle of triumph.

I try to put my arms round all three at once and the eldest whispers, 'Why are you crying, Mattie?'

FIFTEEN

C handler and Archer talked for some time. First one then the other in an attempt to tease out the logic of the novice's movements shortly before her murder.

Her grey habit had been found some way downstream near the mouth of the Dow where it flowed into the Thames. It had caught on the warp line of a barge where a sailor had fished it out, imagining it was something he could make a penny or two from round the taverns. When he saw it was a holy garment and being as superstitious as most sailors, he showed it to his ship master who had in turn passed it over to a constable of the watch and so on up the line until here it lay in Sir Arnold Archer's chamber.

Chandler went over to have a closer look. He rubbed the material between his fingers like a cloth merchant. It was dry now after its immersion and gave off only a faint stink of sewage. Made of coarse weave it was dyed a colour close enough to pass as black when wet. He held it up as if about to put it on. There was nothing to notice about it. He rummaged around in the sleeves.

'I've already done that,' Archer commented, watching this performance. 'Nothing. No lover's note if that's what you're hoping for.'

Chandler folded the garment and replaced it on the chest where he found it.

'Standard wear. No blood.'

'Stripped before they slit her throat?'

Chandler was shocked by the callous way Archer spoke but then, he reconsidered, this was the nature of his daily life, corpses and their condition when they reached him.

'Any signs of struggle? Bruising and such?'

He shook his head. 'We'll find out if there's anything important we need to know about her when the deputy arrives.'

'When's she due?'

Archer sniffed. 'Before vespers. She's staying at All Hallows this night. I fetched you early because I thought you might like to take another look at the body.'

Chandler followed Archer through into the mortuary. 'I was expecting something more. That she comes from the royal abbey is cause enough for interest but I guess you have something else. What is it?'

Archer went over to the body that lay where Chandler had seen it that morning. The light streamed in, harsh and brilliant. Every fold and crease of the shroud was lit and when the coroner pulled it back the body of the girl shone like pearl.

She had stiffened, he assumed, and was now softening again, her expression as calm as someone having a rest on a silken pillow. When Chandler bent close he nearly gagged at the foul stench of seeping body fluids mixed with river water. The girl's robe had reeked with the stink of human ordure from the open sewer of the Dow. But this was worse. It was the beginnings of putrefaction.

Archer seemed oblivious. He reached forward and picked up one of the girl's hands. 'Look at that under her nails. What is it?'

Forcing himself to move closer Chandler stooped to take a look. Small seeds of some kind lay under the nails of the middle three fingers. 'Are there any on the other hand?'

'No. Just this one.'

'Was she left-handed?'

'We shall have to ask and assume somebody noticed.'

'May I?'

When Archer nodded he took out a small plant knife from his pouch and carefully scraped the seeds into his palm. He could not name them. But he would. 'If it's relevant,' he murmured half to himself.

'It might be.' Archer eyed them with suspicion. 'Had she been gardening maybe? . . . Picking herbs for the kitchen. Something like that?'

Chandler stowed them inside a small glass jar he used for transporting the ingredients for his cures and rammed the stopper of oiled linen back into the opening. 'I'll take them to Master Daniel. If anybody can identify them he will. Maybe we'll have to sow them and wait for them to grow!' He doubted they were important.

'I'm wondering,' Archer announced as they made their way back into his private chamber to wait for the abbess's deputy, 'where she was knifed. We're assuming it was in the spot where we found her. But how would it be possible with so many people around? That place is never empty.'

'And to remove her habit. It's busy even at night. Whores and their clients. When did she go into the water?'

'About prime. At least, that's when she was found. Hadn't been in long.'

'Who found her?'

'The gong-master, on his rounds.'

'Anyone who can vouch for him?'

'About half a dozen passers-by and the rest of the fellows in his team. They were arguing about who was first finder, bless them. It's about the only time they'll ever concede first place!'

'They'll no doubt fight it out. And they say none of them saw anything suspicious?'

'It is just about possible it could be done if the murderer concealed himself under the struts of one of the houses with jettied balconies overhanging the water. But she would have to be lured to a place like that. No one in their right mind would willingly clamber over the piles of stinking refuse that builds up along the bank under those houses round there.'

'Somebody will have seen something.'

Archer took him by the arm. 'I'd like us to take a walk along the lane beside the Dow, if you can stomach it?'

Chandler made a face to show he was gritting his teeth but he nodded. 'If you think she hadn't been in the water long she might have gone in just a little further upstream from where she fetched up. Is that what you're thinking?'

'Yes, but not as far up as where it's still called Walbrook,' agreed Archer. 'Somewhere closer to the Steel Yard.'

Chandler tried to calculate the speed of the Dow. After heavy rain it became a torrent pouring down from Garlick Hythe. The novice was not the only one to meet death in its polluted waters. Only a few weeks ago a young lad had fallen in and been swept down past the helping hands of those standing on the bank side, past the poles they held out for him to catch hold of until he had fetched up against a wagon wheel near the outflow, dead.

At present it was running slowly as the recent rains had not yet built up but the banksides were wallows of mud and excrement. People dumped anything they wanted rid of in there. Just as someone had dumped the body. It would be a wonder if she had been swept much further down from where she had been put in.

'The tanners and the dyers use it as a drain for their craft,' he remarked. 'The sort of place we're looking for will be more private than a craftsman's works.'

'We're narrowing it down already. Let's go up as soon as this fluting nun takes her leave.'

'Assuming she's ever going to arrive,' began Chandler impatiently just as, at that very moment, a loud knocking on the door echoed round the building.

'Lo! It is she!' Archer grinned. 'Let her in, boy!' he shouted to his servant.

SIXTEEN

Fluting was the wrong word Chandler realized as soon as the nun, shaking rain off her cloak, began to speak. She had a low musical voice, true, but more like a vielle played very gently and seductively, flowing melodiously through the lower registers. He could not take his eyes off her. I must be ill, he thought. His stomach had fallen, it seemed to him in this sudden wild state, and now lay in pieces at his feet. He was emptied and at the same time filled with a feeling of languor, if not downright euphoria.

She had entered with a small, neat page in tow. The child had looked round quickly for a seat for his mistress but Archer, with what for him was alacrity, jumped from his own chair and offered it to the visitor with a sweeping bow. She sank down, supple and slender, arranging her robes in artless folds, all languid alertness, as it seemed to Chandler, now confused into paradox.

Pushing back her veil a little she turned far-seeing eyes on them and both men were swept, exposed, and thoroughly scrutinized by eyes of such a remarkable luminosity that their colour was obliterated. Chandler, if asked, could not have said whether they were blue or green or grey, or in fact any colour at all. But they pierced. They pinned him where he sat. They saw straight into the depths of his dark soul.

With difficulty he wrenched his glance away and stared ferociously at the floor while Archer, more obsequious than Chandler had ever seen him, introduced them both, explained briefly what they had found and, almost breathlessly, suddenly became aware that he was still standing, and sat down abruptly on the bench nearly spilling them both onto the floor.

'I see,' the nun said after a thoughtful pause while they righted themselves.

'If I may make so bold, domina, to beg leave to pose a question or two – purely to complete my records,' Archer gabbled.

The nun gave him a penetrating stare. 'You may, sir, of course. It is my great pleasure to help you in any way.'

'We – that is I – and of course my – and the friar here – we wondered what would bring the novice outside the priory – and whether she was accompanied or not – if I may make so bold to ask? I understand she was visiting All Hallows and had shortly arrived from her mother-house at Barking?'

The nun made a small curve of her lips that only made Chandler tear his glance away again and stare more stonily than ever at the floor. They were subjected to another burst of music as the nun said, 'She was, indeed, and was to stay overnight before returning to us on the morrow. I'm told she went up to the dortoir with the other novices after compline. By the time the girls came down for prime she had gone.'

'She left in the middle of the night?'

'So it would seem.'

'A runaway, as your abbess suggested in her letter, with perhaps an assignation? Do forgive me.' He bowed his head.

The nun was unfazed. 'So it would seem,' she repeated. 'Sadly we know nothing more.'

Chandler pulled himself together. 'What was her work at Barking Abbey?'

'The usual work required of a novice.'

'Which is?' He faced her and for a moment thought he detected a faint look of surprise at his persistence.

'She receives instruction in our ways. She cleans, she prays, she runs errands.'

'For whom?'

'The other sisters, of course.' The nun leaned forward and a swirl of perfume, subtle, ungraspable, floated towards him and enveloped him in its embrace. 'Let me explain, brother. We have many elderly though distinguished nuns in our abbey who are unable to do all the little things they were used to doing for themselves. We try to make their lives as comfortable as possible. It is the least they deserve after the lives of service they have given.' She gave him a cool glance as if he had been about to query their lack of independence and added, 'They are well-born, some with royal connections.'

'And she too?'

The prioress gave an almost imperceptible shake of the head.

'And did she work in your gardens?' he asked.

The nun frowned. 'I suppose she did. Why do you ask?'

'Just to get a picture,' he replied without blinking. 'And what do you have to say to the idea that she had an assignation with someone here in the City and therefore fled All Hallows in the night at their behest?'

'I have nothing to say. It is conjecture. Nothing more.'

'Thank you.' He sounded as if she had told him something momentous. But suddenly he asked, 'So you have no idea at all why she would leave the safety of the priory at dead of night, in the full knowledge that it was forbidden both by her calling and by the ordinances of the City Watch to be out after curfew?'

The prioress drew back. 'Mysterious are the ways of novices, my lords.'

She flatters me, thought Chandler. I'm no lord. Now why would she do that? I'm nothing to her. 'How could she get out?' he asked abruptly.

The nun widened her luminous eyes. They were silver, he decided. Impossible. But true. 'I would imagine she crept past the porteress and unchained the door and so set forth.'

'Is the door not locked at night?'

For a moment her eyelids dropped down, extinguishing the blaze of light, and when she opened them they were colourless. 'I expect she managed to remember where the key was kept on its hook inside the lodge of the porteress,' she explained in a tone that said he was a dolt.

'I would expect that. But I would also expect the porteress, if she's up to the job, to have been awake and seen and heard her exit.' He met her glance.

'It seems that did not happen.'

'We would like to talk to the porteress and to the novices who knew the girl best both at Barking and at All Hallows.' He ignored Archer's sudden flurry of movement and his indrawn breath. He turned to the coroner. 'Isn't that so, my lord?'

Archer nodded but without any eagerness. He ignored the sarcasm.

The prioress seemed affronted but could hardly obstruct them. She could make things difficult, however, and her tone showed that she knew exactly who Chandler was and what his function.

She said, 'I will have to ask permission from my lady abbess. It is not our custom to have men in our precinct.' She rose to her feet in another faint cloud of perfume. 'Thank you, my lords. May I see her?'

Taken aback, as if he had not expected a woman to wish to view a corpse, Archer got to his feet and led her with much bowing and scraping into the death chamber.

Chandler hung back. His first reaction confounded him but now he had chance to observe the nun he could not help but see her as an opponent.

Strange, he told himself, watching her and watching Archer too, in the blaze of light from the high windows. The abbess had made sure she sent one of her most seductive nuns and in that lay a question. Was there something hidden behind her haze of glamour?

SEVENTEEN

When all that remained was the faint scent of attar of roses, Archer turned to Chandler. 'God's teeth, what do you make of that? It must be something in their food to give them skin like that.'

Chandler rested a foot on the bench and leaned thoughtfully on

one elbow. He gave Archer a narrow glance. 'These rumours about
a lover – I notice she didn't deny the possibility. Conjecture, she
said but with enough ambiguity as if stating the opposite.'

'Is that what you think? She certainly froze you out when you
tried to follow that line.'

Ignoring him Chandler said, 'So she meets the lover, landless,
as rumour has it, they quarrel, and he, hot-blooded, murders her in
a fit of rage . . . Or, he's a good lad, thoroughly worthy of her, but
is waylaid by robbers and fails to turn up. Believing herself rejected,
she kills herself in despair . . . Either way it lets the abbey off the
hook.'

Archer grunted and gave the bench a kick which seemed to do
nothing to relieve his feelings. 'These are just stories invented to
cover something up. Is it time we went to have another look at the
place where she was found?'

'It is. Let's go.'

The nun had rustled out after asking Archer to write up his report
as he saw fit. She would approach her abbess for permission to
continue their questioning if they deemed it necessary. She had
given them both a dazzling smile at that point as if to say they were
sensible men and would probably grasp the futility of taking the
matter further.

Meanwhile, she continued, if Sir Arnold would release the body
the priory could take steps to arrange the poor child's return to the
abbey for burial.

'Unshriven,' commented Chandler.

'Unshriven,' the nun agreed. 'We shall of course say a mass for
her poor soul.' Her face bound by its dazzling wimple was serene.
It was a perfect oval, judged Chandler, finding a sudden interest in
geometry. Her cheeks were tinged with the palest pink that in no
way detracted from the pearly sheen of her skin. Her perfect
colouring was enhanced by the black robe she wore, made of finer
stuff than that of her novice.

Chandler watched, fascinated, as the garment floated gracefully
behind her as she turned, long sleeves rippling when she glided over
the flagstones towards the door. The small page bobbed in her wake,
rushing forward only to push the door and conduct her into the
porch.

There she gave them both, Archer and Chandler, a valedictory smile and, it seemed to Chandler, allowed her glance to linger on his face as if she would like to say more.

'As for skin,' he remarked as they went out, 'maybe it's down to alchemy?' He raised one eyebrow but Archer was not to be teased.

Instead he grasped Chandler by the arm, urging in a low voice, 'There's a meeting of the chapter after compline. Come with me tonight?'

'You know I won't. Things are as they are. They're not transmutable into something else, gold least of all.'

'There's more to it than that. You know there is.'

'What, then?'

'Come along and find out. You'll meet people. You'll be surprised by who comes along.'

'Anyone I need to know? Tell me their names.'

Archer shook his head. 'Not useful to you. I've told you that. We meet to share a pursuit for the truth not power. And anyway, you know I can't break my oath.'

'Can't? Won't? Daren't?'

Archer looked irritated. 'Let's have a look at the banks of the Dow, if that's your attitude. Let's see what we can see.'

'Then maybe we should start asking who this lover might be if he exists.'

'If, yes. If.'

EIGHTEEN

I am being sent all about to make some purchases for madame but have to do it with as much secrecy as I can muster. The baby is our problem. Dear, helpless little thing. We must take every care to find whatever he can possibly need for the hazards that face him.

While I'm out I notice the same friar who has been about recently and that portly City father, an alderman, maybe, who accompanies him. They're followed by a servant and are walking briskly along Cousin Lane by the Steel Yard. Nothing to do with me. But I can't help noticing the friar. He makes me shiver. It's well known that, if you want rid of somebody, tell him and he'll find a reason that satisfies the executioner.

NINETEEN

As they made their way through the crowded streets Chandler, in a spirit of mischief, made light of the sort of gold Archer and his fellow alchemists hoped to create but all the time his mind was busy going over their meeting with the prioress.

Eventually, in response to some claim Archer made, he shelved that and said, 'The one big flaw in your endeavours, my friend, is that if and when you produce this gold you'll know it's not real. So how will it weigh against the real thing? If too dissimilar then you're wasting your time. But if indistinguishable from real gold then a glut of the stuff will bring down the price of the genuine metal. Have you thought of that?'

Archer refused to discuss the matter.

'Your best course of action,' Chandler continued in a jovial tone, 'will be to waste no further time trying to produce the artificial stuff – miraculous though its production will be – but to stockpile a little mound of genuine gold then destroy all the rest you can find. That way you'll increase the value of the gold you own.'

A lively discussion ensued as they made their way through the streets to Dow Beck and Archer compared Chandler to a fishmonger and said he should join the guild where they liked anything to do with price fixing. Chandler said Archer would be running for mayor next and giving even more subsidies to foreign traders so that the Londoners would be priced even further out of their own markets.

And before they reached any conclusion either way they had reached the beck and were standing looking down into the sewer it was.

TWENTY

I follow madame's instructions and return with everything she asked for but before I can pack it away I hear someone at the door sending me to the peephole. Master Chaucer. He enters.

'She has told you?'

'Yes.'

We have a short conversation.

Finally he looks me in the eye when I raise doubts. 'Trust me, Matilda. It's called *corpus pro corpore*. The only one to lose would be me. But I know I can trust you. We shall all trust each other.'

'Will you tell me one thing, then, Master?'

'What is it?'

'Was it the duchess you went to see? I know her son is Thomas Swynford and that those men who took away le Sire were under Sir Thomas's orders.'

'Let me tell you something, Matilda, my dear child. Here now in this chamber must be the last time you ever say such a thing.'

'But I am right?'

'You are and you know it. But I have a regard for your safety and beg you to be cautious in everything you say from now on. You are to be an empty slate. Understand?'

'I understand.'

TWENTY-ONE

There were the usual crowds slithering in the wallows. A man was knee-deep in shit, pulling a half-submerged barrel towards the bank. It had a hole in it but he evidently thought he could make good use of it and carried this trophy off with a smile of glee. Others poked with sticks among the fetid jetsam at the leavings of people better off than themselves, searching for something, anything they could put to use or profit. An old woman gathered wood, shoving dead branches washed down from open country into a sack, water-weed, excrement and other things still clinging to the stumps. Another man had a line cast far out into the middle of the stream and sat huddled under his cloak waiting for a bite from fish struggling up against the current.

Chandler stood with folded arms. 'God's bollocks,' he said at last, 'to be hoped she was dead when she landed in this.'

Archer strolled over to talk to the man with the fishing line. When he came back he shook his head. 'He knows nothing. He wasn't here yesterday. Let's walk upstream, see what we can see.'

The Dow ran in a flood from Walbrook towards the old Watergate where it entered the Thames. They walked a path called Cousin Lane that ran along the top of the bank between the beck and the high wall of the Steel Yard. Both banks were crowded with workshops and in most places there was no access to the waterside at all without trespassing in somebody's yard.

'We could go up as far as London Stone,' observed Archer, 'but we'll be no nearer finding a likely place to put a body in without being seen. This is the most likely place you could do it.'

The houses were more substantial than lower down and one or two had their own yards for stabling and deliveries.

'Might she have been in the water longer than you reckon?' Chandler hated questioning the coroner on his skills.

Archer shook his head. 'She would have started to puff up once her lungs were filled. I looked for that.'

'So it must have been be round here . . .?' He stopped. 'Look there!'

He pointed across the beck to one of the buildings with an upper storey jutting over the water. A man was leaning out to tip some refuse into the beck. Various bits of household waste cascaded down and fell with a splash before being swept away.

'Could she have been thrown from one of the houses?'

They gazed upwards. Some of the upper storeys had shutters, others had open balconies festooned with plants, strings of washing and bedding set to air. The one that had caught Chandler's eye was a large, important-looking house and probably belonged to a merchant of comfortable means. It had a balcony.

Archer glanced up. 'I don't believe she could have been thrown from a height but let's cross over and knock on a door or two.'

So saying they walked up to the wooden bridge that linked both banks and went across into the Vintry.

It was ear-shatteringly noisy. Wine barrels were being rolled down the hill one after another towards the wharf. Empty, they bounced and clattered with a roar like thunder until they piled up against the heap of those already thrown down.

With hands over their ears they reached the door of the house that had caught their attention by counting backwards from the bridge. It was opened straightaway at Archer's knock by a gnarled old servant.

'Maister's out.' He eyed them suspiciously, taking in Chandler's white mendicant's habit under the rough grey cloak without a word.

Archer edged forward. 'You know me,' he began. 'I'm one of the City coroners. Can you tell me when he'll be back?'

'I don't know nothing,' the servant said and shut the door.

Or he would have if Chandler hadn't already had his foot in it. 'Not so fast, friend.' He smiled. 'We're looking for a master William Reeve. We were told this was his abode.'

'Never heard of him.'

'So who does live here?'

'I don't know nothing,' the servant repeated with stubborn insistence.

'What? You don't know who your master is?'

'I told you—'

Affably, Chandler bent his head so he was more or less on a level with the man. 'I'd like to get this straight, my friend. You don't know who you're working for? Is that right?'

'Well, I might do,' the fellow grudgingly admitted after a sidelong glance, noting how broad-shouldered Chandler was, then shrugged. 'He ain't here, as I said. He's away. He's at his manor out Essex way. Been there this last month. All right?'

'So who is in residence here?' Archer demanded.

'Only me. Keeping it aired.'

'Don't bother trying to remember your master's name, fellow.' Archer took Chandler by surprise by suddenly turning away. 'I can find out anything I need to know through the Guildhall.' He nodded, the man stared, and Archer began to walk rapidly away.

'Is that true?' asked Chandler when he caught up with him.

'He'll pay his taxes like everybody else.' He was frowning. 'We're on a wild-goose chase. Or,' he glanced at Chandler, 'shall we knock on every door along the beck and be told a pack of lies?'

'I'll leave it with you, then, coroner.'

Archer grimaced. 'No need to be sarcastic. I just had the idea that somebody might have seen something.'

'I'll come with you to the Guildhall, shall I?'

Archer hesitated. 'I have things to do. Maybe later. I'll send the boy to fetch you.'

Chandler could not help showing his astonishment at being fobbed off by Archer.

'What's up?'

'Some things are best left as mysteries.'

When they were almost back at the bridge Archer spoke behind his hand. 'I know whose house that used to be, Rodric. It belonged to bloody John Comberton. So-called John of Northampton. Though what the hell he's ever had to do with that benighted place I don't know. He was one of Lancaster's men. Let's just leave it, eh?'

Chandler refused Archer's suggestion of a quick visit to the Fleece and made his way back in the direction of home.

What a thoroughly wasted morning, he thought. First, the fragrant prioress telling them nothing, then the servant like a stone wall, and now Archer with his peculiar reaction as if he was frightened of where the trail was leading them. He himself knew very well. If it was still Comberton's property then it led to his own paymaster. Did Archer suspect?

Everybody knew of Comberton unless they were living under a stone.

Prominent in the City some years ago, he had fallen foul of Mayor Brembre before Woodstock, as Gloucester then was, had brought the Merciless Parliament to its bloody climax. The two merchants had had a long-running feud. Its virulence was due to Brembre's massive financial loans to the king and Comberton's jealousy over the privileges such largesse bestowed.

Before the dark days of the court purge and the beheadings of the king's allies, the event that brought Comberton down was over some alleged underhand dealing in the City. His Lancastrian protectors had been unable to help him, or unwilling. The consequence was he was sent down to spend some years in a cell in Tintagel Castle, all the while pleading his innocence, as what prisoner did not. Although he was retained by Gaunt, the duke had done little to have him released. Later King Richard had pardoned him and he had kept a low profile, amassing another fortune but making no attempt to get back into public life.

As far as Chandler knew he died a couple of years ago. Perhaps the house had gone to the son, who no doubt followed in his father's footsteps. Archer wouldn't want to be seen taking sides in any way. The travelling show of internecine rivalries among the City fathers was too complicated to be understood by anybody not in on the latest quarrels.

He was just walking up Dow Hill when le Sire's maid came dancing out of one of the alleys on a short cut from her employer's house. Evidently she was being sent to market as she had a large straw basket slung over one arm. His glance followed her as she plunged in among the crowds and disappeared towards Cheap.

Then, with Archer effectively calling an end to their investigation into the murder, and thoroughly dissatisfied, he reached Aldgate and home and a few moments later he was in the sanctuary of his chamber with a jug of wine beside him and Beata cooking something in the kitchen.

TWENTY-TWO

He took the opportunity before she brought his food through to reach into his pouch and bring out the glass phial he had used in Archer's morgue earlier that morning. Noticing that Beata had pushed aside the blinds and opened the shutters after his criticism yesterday, he went over and by the light of the westering sun inspected the contents.

He had no idea what the seeds were but they looked familiar. With his duty to the dead completed for the day he debated whether there was time to ride out to Stepney and catch Henry Daniel in his lair for his opinion on the matter before he turned in for the

night, or, he sighed, whether it was worth going back to the Dow
and having a snoop on his own as soon as supper was over.

Indecisively he rose to his feet. Something was gnawing at him
but he couldn't work out what it was. He called through to the
kitchen. 'Beata?'

She hurried through, 'Yes, Chandler?'

'Look.' He ran both hands through his hair. 'Martin thinks I need
to have something done to it to preserve the gravitas of my calling.'

'Oh . . . I'll get my scissors, shall I?'

'If you will.'

She was back in an instant and he sat in a chair while she draped
a cloth over his shoulders.

'Have you been out today?' he asked as he leaned back and
looked up into her face.

She gave a nervous little laugh and avoided his glance. 'No,
where should I go?'

'I just wondered what you'd been doing.'

She changed the subject. 'Food will be ready soon.' She held up
thumb and forefinger about two inches apart. 'About so much?'

'Whatever you say. You're the expert.'

While she snipped at his hair his thoughts returned to the
Tower and the hideous sight of the French spy on the rack, and
the counterweight of his contact's house, opulent with blood
money, and then watching le Sire wrenched from the bosom of
his family and dragged off in chains to God knows what hell
and then the novice.

But for the whim of Fortune, it would have been the spy living
in the large and comfortable house and his contact stretched on the
rack.

He lifted his head when Beata's scissors came to a stop. 'What?'

'Someone at the door.'

He reached for the small oval of polished silver he used as a
mirror as renewed banging on the door drew him to the window
slit and he managed to angle a view to the foot of the tower.

A group of horsemen were milling there. Then a high voice
called, 'Dominus! Open up if you're within!'

Swynford already. He went over and pulled the door wide to find
a page standing on the threshold wearing the scarlet and gold of
the duke of Lancaster. Scarlet for blood. Gold for gain.

'Sir, my lord brother,' he piped, 'my master waits below. He wishes to have private words with you.'

He stooped to the page's level and asked as if he didn't know, 'And who is your master, young sir?'

'Sir Thomas Swynford,' came the reply.

'So send him up.'

Not for the first time he asked what the hell Swynford wanted with him that could cost the price of a set of candles and why he chose to make their connection so obvious by coming to his dwelling. It could not bode well. He preferred to be left alone. To do what he had to without anybody breathing down his neck. That's how he liked to work. Why else would he resign himself to the obscure life of a chantry priest? Why couldn't Swynford stick to the arrangement? Had Knollys complained?

His ill-humour at being run to earth in his own abode did not abate when Swynford himself appeared in the doorway. He stood there for a moment, looking in, his eyes raking every corner as if expecting assassins.

Chandler made a half-hearted welcoming gesture with one hand. 'My lord,' he said, gritting his teeth. 'An honour.'

Reassured, Swynford came inside without having to duck his head under the lintel. Chandler marvelled. Then he walked round the chamber with a swagger that sat ill on his squat frame. After he had had a good look round he jerked one thumb towards the kitchen where Beata's pots and pans could be heard. 'Who?'

'My servant only.'

'Servants have ears.'

'Indeed they do.'

Swynford gave him a narrowed glance as if suspecting sarcasm. 'Is there anywhere more private we can talk?'

Chandler nodded. Without explaining he led the way back outside and went two at a time up the steps to the roof. He made no reference to the severed heads. The lift and fall of their wind-teased hair could clearly be seen between the crenels.

Swynford noticed, affected not to, and turned his own head that for the time being sat safely on his shoulders to peer out in the opposite direction towards the teeming streets of the City. Chandler took up a position with his back against one of the buttresses. Down below, Swynford's men were visible. As well as the page he had brought a groom and two henchmen. Patient, obedient, they stood close to his horse chatting quietly. They were armed.

Chandler turned to Swynford and waited for him to explain. He did so with no preamble.

'I have here a list of things I wish you to obtain on behalf of my lord.'

'He is in France still?'

'Of course. Why do you ask?'

Chandler wanted to say, *Because of the parboiled cauldron of rumour that he has broken his exile and left France with a small army, my lord*, but he held his tongue.

Instead he replied, 'There are always rumours, you know what the City is like.'

He took the piece of vellum on which someone with an educated hand had written the names of several plants. He scanned the names then gave Swynford a sharp glance. 'Why does he not acquire this stuff from an apothecary himself? They have this sort of thing in France, surely?'

Swynford scowled. 'It is not our position to question the wishes of—' he stumbled over the choice of words, was it duke, now Gaunt was dead? But Bolingbroke was supposed to be in exile. He could not yet take up his dukedom. Backing away from that problem Swynford finished lamely '– of my liege lord.'

Chandler handed back the piece of vellum without a word.

Swynford refused to take it. 'We are told that you have some knowledge of cures and simples, that you have a source for these things. My lord wishes to make a private purchase. He wishes you to be his go-between. You will of course be well paid.'

They keep offering me money, Chandler registered, remembering Archer when he asked for his help with the murdered novice. Of course, if he did not comply with the earl's whim he would find some other means to get what he wanted – and Chandler would gain a black mark against his name that might at some time in the future prove fatal.

'When does he want these?' he asked.

'How soon can you get them?'

'By tomorrow?'

'That will be good enough. I shall return at this time then. Of course,' he added, flinching at the sight of the heads as he turned,

'I need to stress the importance of discretion. Should any hint from any source reveal the nature of his request you will pay.' He reached the top of the steps. 'I may tell you, the duke acknowledges your ability to keep silent – from your work at the Tower. He does not expect you to let him down.'

With that, unsmiling, he descended the steps to the street. Chandler stayed to listen to the echo of diminishing footsteps until the street door slammed shut. He watched Swynford being hoisted onto a black horse by his groom. His men-at-arms walked one on either side of him with the little page following on a pony as they disappeared towards Corn Hill.

Chandler reread the list of purchases he was supposed to make. It was almost sunset now. Soon the curfew bell would toll. No time to get out to Stepney to the garden where such things could be obtained. He placed the list in his scrip beside the phial containing the seeds from under the novice's fingernails ready for the morrow.

Swynford's remark about the Tower burned him to the soul. *My work, my work.*

TWENTY-THREE

Next morning, after a restless night, Chandler pulled on a thick woollen cloak against the dawn mist, and as soon as the gate was opened, set out on a hired ambler from the stables on the corner to make the short ride to Stepney.

The road was empty. Most people forced to stay outside the City walls had not yet dragged themselves out of the ditches where they had spent the night. He passed no more than a couple of carts bringing produce to market and a pardoner striding optimistically along with a bulging bag of relics.

'A phial of Christ's tears for your lady, good sir?' he called out as he approached, then, noticing Chandler's white habit not unlike his own, apologized with a wave of his hand. 'God be with you, brother!'

'Good sales to you, frater,' replied Chandler as he rode past.

He was soon there and a servant conducted him into the gatehouse cheerily telling him that the master was already busy in the gardens.

Rousing a lad to see to Chandler's horse he led the way along an aromatic path to a deeper part of the garden where the friar was working alone beneath the waxy overhanging leaves of juniper.

He looked up with a smile on seeing Chandler. 'Well, Rodric, this is an unexpected pleasure. You must have shot like a bolt from a crossbow this morning when they opened the gates. What brings you out so early?' He wiped his hands on his habit and came towards him with both arms outstretched.

'Two things, Henry,' he replied after an equally warm greeting. 'Both in their way are matters requiring some discretion.'

'As are many requests made to me.' The friar picked up his spade again and leaned on it, shrewd grey eyes almost invisible in the creases of his face. 'You know I cannot guarantee my help, Rodric.'

'I know that,' Chandler replied. 'But what I tell you may help you to offer it anyway. First, there's this.' He fumbled the glass phial out of his pouch and held it up.

Briefly describing the circumstance and how Sir Arnold Archer believed it might be relevant to his inquiry into the death of the novice, he placed it in the gnarled palm saying, 'I cannot identify them. They look tauntingly familiar. But if anyone can tell what they are it's you.'

'Your faith is most touching.' The bright eyes of the ex-merchant were alight at the challenge Chandler offered. He shook the seeds out and peered closely at them, turning them over and over between finger and thumb. He seemed puzzled. Without saying anything he beckoned to Chandler to follow him and pushing along a path bordered by tall plants to a thatched hut leaning against the high wall that surrounded the entire garden he invited Chandler inside.

The shed was lined with shelves and on every one stood rows of glass phials much like the one Chandler had brought along. They were labelled in an abbreviated form of Latin but Chandler was unbothered by that as he knew most of the contents by sight anyway.

He watched the gardener take one down, compare the seeds, then return it to the shelf. He looked perplexed. Taking down several more he eventually gave up.

'I had to check first just to be sure but this is no cure. I believe it's something quite common which we would not even dream of classifying. I believe it's dried marsh grass, the kind you might strew on any floor. It's nothing out of the ordinary.'

Chandler was disappointed. 'Marsh grass? I hadn't thought of that.' He pondered the matter. Someone lying on the floor of a house might reasonably clutch at what was beneath them. 'I'm afraid our coroner has walked up a blind alley and I with him. Never mind.' He returned the phial to the pouch. 'We were intent on finding something significant.'

'Now, what about this second thing?'

Chandler gestured towards the shelves. 'I see you have monkshood.'

The old friar looked startled. 'I will need good reason to give you that, Rodric.'

'You may charge it to me,' he replied. 'I'm merely the servant in all this and can say no more about the purchaser than that he is a man of some wealth.' He handed over the piece of vellum. 'This was given to me by my client's vassal.'

Brother Daniel took the vellum, read it, then gave a shrug. His genial manner now frosty he got to work to find the plants on Chandler's list. Mist still lay over the garden. The old man began to search about among the wet leaves to find what he wanted and Chandler, seeing how infirm he was, bent down to give him a hand.

Daniel murmured, 'This is not a good business you're in, Rodric. Your foster-father and indeed your own father were men I admired.'

'Then they should not have sold me to Lancaster,' said Chandler more fiercely than intended.

Daniel straightened. 'I dare say your father thought it the best thing to do at the time. He wanted you to have protection from your lord and Gaunt was head of the king's council at that time. None of us knew how things were going to turn out.' He pushed the leaves of one of the herbs into Chandler's hands. They were innocuous looking, close-formed on the stem, the buds not yet in bloom. 'You know what to do with it?'

'Not my concern. That's their problem.'

When it came to labelling them back in the hut Daniel scrutinized Chandler's expression and said, 'Something is causing you a great deal of bitterness. We often have to ask ourselves where our responsibility starts and ends.' When Chandler made no reply he added, 'I hope you know what you're doing, my boy. Is it too late to back out?'

'I fear so.' He gazed stonily outside. 'I'm putting my trust in the

hope that my client suffers from sleeplessness, hence the need
for henbane. The monkshood?' He shrugged. 'As for spleenwort, I
hear his lady used to conceive once a year after her husband's annual
visit to her. Now she is dead and he is satisfied that his house is
secure he will not want further complications.'

Daniel gave him a long look. 'His house? Is it who I think it is?'

'I expect so.'

'Have you heard anything?' He lowered his voice and put his
head on one side.

'I'm sure he simply wants what he says he wants, the restoration
of his lands and title.'

'You put a good light on it, my boy. Let's hope your trust is
justified.' He paused then said delicately, 'There were extraordinary
rumours coming from the ports. Then a story about ships at Ravenser.
I find it difficult to believe that he would break the terms of his
exile. Surely he would understand that the king is merely keeping
his possessions safe until a sufficient time has elapsed to allow
for his lawful return? King Richard has not parcelled his lands out
to anybody.'

'He did so with Gloucester's land when he handed it to York's
son and made him duke of Aumerle.'

'It was only held by Gloucester as a vassal of the king. Richard
had the right to give it.'

'Another interpretation is that the king hopes to humble
Bolingbroke and dangle his inheritance before him as a sign of his
own power.'

'That sounds like the voice of Arundel.'

'It's what's being said.'

'What are you going to do if this story about him making landfall
at Ravenser is true and he marches on London?'

'Am I to put my life in jeopardy on the basis of rumour?'

Friar Daniel gripped him by the forearm. 'But you think it could
be true?'

'I believe I know it could.'

'Then God help us all.'

'God help King Richard.'

Comfrey was the least ambiguous of Swynford's requests and
Chandler assumed it had been added merely because by buying it
in bulk from its source he would make most profit from it. In fact,

apart from the monkshood of such ill repute, there seemed no reason whatsoever for Sir Thomas Swynford to have made such a mystery about these purchases. Perhaps, Chandler told himself as he rode slowly back towards the City, he was a man who preferred the drama of mystery to the mundane clarity of things as they often are.

TWENTY-FOUR

It was still mid-morning and was going to be hot after the rain. When he rode back from Daniel's earlier the mist was already being burned off. Now the clanging bells from a hundred steeples deafened everybody walking down Corn Hill. He had been instructed to keep an eye on the le Sire household. As far as he knew the fellow was still in the Tower. He took up a position outside the brick yard. It was busy today but none of the passers-by had the courage to question him.

Almost at once he saw the door open and the maid came out carrying the baby wrapped in a blue shawl. She was followed by the mistress and the two older children. They were not carrying baskets and were dressed as usual, madame in a yellow gown, the children bright in parti-coloured hose and little smocks. The maid had pushed back her coif to let it dangle down her back where it tangled with a lustrous mane of gold-blonde hair. It was as well, he thought, that she usually kept such profane glory out of sight.

Lured by the vision he followed at a distance, only letting it go when he halted at the corner to allow madame to reassure herself that they were not being followed. Maybe he would cross the lane and observe them from that side until he found out where they were going. On a neighbourly visit, he assumed, unless they were less innocent than they seemed and were going to meet a contact on behalf of le Sire.

They continued in the general direction of the Tower but it was unlikely that they would try to get in to see him there. Someone would have warned them it was impossible.

When they reached the corner he let them out of sight and, glancing back, was in time to see Master Chaucer emerge with his scrivener and set off in the opposite direction as if heading for La Reol. The streets were busy. The sun was shining. It was as if everybody wanted to be out after the previous days of rain. With the feeling that Master Chaucer deserved a break from Knollys' interest, he headed for the corner as soon as he felt it safe to do so. He crossed the lane at the junction.

Her hair blazed forth like a beacon. They had not gone far. The children lagged. He could see the maid say something but was too far off to hear her. They continued down the lane towards the river.

Maybe they were taking the children to the sands, he considered. Below the bridge it was almost coastal with the tide coming in and depositing enough sand to make a narrow beach at low tide where children liked to play.

When they reached the tavern at the top of the slipway he saw them walk a little way down and the two women stood to watch as the children scampered down to the water's edge, screaming with joy as the incoming tide lapped at their feet, only to come shrieking back up the strand to the safety of the grown-ups as the waves pursued them. Her hair was lifted by the breeze and streamed around her causing heads to turn. Laughing, she tried to push it back inside her coif without success.

Several large merchant cogs of the Hansa league moored at the quay outside the Steel Yard were preparing to sail on the next tide and further along at the wool wharf the English ships and a few French and Italian cogs were doing likewise.

It was a scene full of activity and noise, with the shouts of the mariners reedy on the vast openness of the river, the splash of oars from the lighters as they plied back and forth to the larger ships anchored in deep water, the melodious singing from a crew working a windlass, and close at hand, from the direction of the tavern, the noise and bustle of kitcheners about their chores.

Madame le Chienne bent to kiss one of the children then together the group strolled towards the tavern and went inside. So that was the purpose of their excursion.

He felt sure it was mere chance that the Frenchman had been picked up outside le Sire's house. There were many foreigners living in the parish. They could have arrested him anywhere. It was down to Fortune that he had been picked up there. He had not named le Sire. Only the curse in French had revealed the racked man's origins.

The nervousness with which Swynford and his ilk regarded the French was almost comical. The king had made his peace with them. His little French child-bride Queen Isabella seemed delighted with her uncle-husband and whenever Chandler saw them in public he noticed how Richard treated her like a delightful doll, teasing her and petting her and showering her with gifts. The latest had been a little white dog that she fed at the table from her own plate to everyone's amusement.

Most thought it a good idea to make peace with the French by such an obviously dynastic marriage. An end to war. It was common knowledge that Richard would never contemplate a real substitute for his beloved Anne. The general view was that he might as well be a monk, celibate like his chosen saint, Edmund the Confessor. To Chandler there was something deeply melancholy about his fidelity to his dead wife. It was as if he carried a wound that would never heal.

His glance sharpened as the maid came outside. Her hair blazed in the sunshine. She was still carrying the baby in its blue shawl. He watched her find a seat on the bench near the door. She was cooing at the baby and he could see its arms waving and its little legs kicking out. They sat there for a while until somebody brought out a hunk of bread and a wedge of cheese. She began to break small pieces off and put them to the baby's mouth. Then she finished the rest herself.

By now the tide was at its height. It brought more noise and excitement. And then, with the imperceptible change that happens deep down in the depths of the water and only later transmits itself to the glittering surface, the tide turned. The Hansa merchant ship threw off its lines and began to nose out into the beginnings of the ebb. The gap between the ship and the quayside filled with swirling river water. Foam churned in its wake and ran up the stretch of beach to lap onto the path.

The drawbridge between the central span of the bridge was slowly winched open as the ships were rowed into mid-river. The bows of a cog slid from behind the tavern building and, low in the water, bearing a full cargo, began to make way into mid-stream to prepare its passage through the bridge. Others followed. It was a sight. He went like a child along the bank to watch.

It was a scene of great power and movement as the river filled with ships under sail. Spray dashed over their canted decks as they made for the sea. Like a great swan the cog from the tavern quay breasted the choppy waters below the bridge and as the deck tilted something caught his glance. It was a flash of yellow. In the blink of an eye it vanished.

He returned to where he could see the maid with the blue shawl. She stood up. Did not look in his direction. Did not join the crowd on the bank watching the ships leave but instead set off the way she had arrived, walking slowly back towards the house with the baby in her arms. Out of curiosity he followed.

They could not have duped him? They would not leave without le Sire? But yellow? He was not mistaken. And the shawl? The baby? He increased his speed.

TWENTY-FIVE

At the sound of his voice I look back. I freeze. I know what they say. I clutch the blue shawl as if to protect myself. What am I going to tell him?

'Mistress, I—' He hesitates as if suddenly unsure of himself. Unsure? I cannot believe it. It must be a ploy to put me off my guard.

For a moment that seems to stretch for ever we stand staring at each other in silence. I register the lines round his eyes where they crinkle at the corners as if he spends much time gazing into the sun. I notice the small wooden cross on a leather lace at his neck. His thick black hair. Somewhat ragged. His lips. My gaze is drawn back and back to his lips, to his mouth, to its look as if it says he will risk anything. I force myself to stare deep into his eyes to read his thoughts. They reflect only myself. I try to say something but can find nothing needs to be said.

The shawl cannot be hidden. I bundle it under the other arm. He gives a sort of resigned smile and reaches out.

He pulls one end of it but I refuse to give it up so it hangs between us, empty, traitorously empty. He lets go and I bend my head to concentrate on refolding it.

When I glance up again he is smiling in a way that makes me shiver with fear. 'It's Matilda, isn't it?'

No point in denying it.

'May I walk with you a little way?'

I could not stop him anyway and we fall into step going on in silence until we reach the house.

I am still shaking.

We stand for a moment in a drift of incense from his garments.

Before now I have only seen him at a distance, walking to the chantry or emerging after mass with his curate. Always churchmen about. Always the bells from the high steeples calling and demanding, always someone setting an eye on us.

I am shaking with fear and wonder how we could have imagined we could get away with it. I imagine the cog being boarded at the mouth of the river and le Sire and madame and the children being thrown down into a small boat with armed men on board. Tears of loss start from my eyes. They cascade down my cheeks in a boiling stream with the sorrow of losing them.

I dash my hand over my face before he can see but he does see and there is no expression in his eyes as he puts out a finger to wipe them away.

I sense the danger in him, aware of the way a wild animal circles its prey before making a leap for its throat.

O, dear God in heaven, preserve my good master and his innocent family. Preserve the baby and the little children.

Blindly I push at the door and there are people within, the cook, her brother, the scullery maid, others, and when I turn back, he has gone.

He has simply vanished.

I fall into their arms with a cry and we howl like orphans at the harshness of fate.

TWENTY-SIX

'Beata!' He took a step forward throwing down his cloak but stopping himself before making any gesture that would change things.

She was drying her hands on her apron with a stricken expression.

'What has happened?'

'Nothing, brother,' she whispered. 'Nothing and everything.' She made a sound halfway between a sob and a laugh.

'Do you want to talk about it?' he asked, unsure how wise it would be to probe further.

His mind was still dwelling on the look in Matilda's eyes. She had dangled the blue shawl from between two fingers as a taunt. She was telling him clearly, as blatantly as could be, *We fooled you!* He cursed himself, wondering if he was losing his ability to see what was before his eyes. It could be fatal. He would need to watch his step.

Wiping her tears! Why did he do that?

Beata was staring at him and he brought his attention back to her. She was saying, 'I spend so much time in this chamber, up above the street watching the crowds living their lives, and with that terrible Keeper of the Heads below—'

He tried to give her a cheering smile. 'Look, why don't you go down to the Cheap and buy some ribbons?' He reached into his pouch and held out a palm full of silver coins.

She was reluctant to take them and he doubted that mere ribbons would assuage her sorrow but he would not involve himself.

She took them and went out.

The problem was he was both her rescuer and her nemesis. He had taken her into his household and saved her from destitution but he could not stop the slanderous remarks that followed her through the parish. They were all on his account of course.

Eventually he was left to nurse his humiliation at being bested by le Sire. The bright eyes and blazing hair of the vintner's maid, the Guelderland girl, Matilda, taunted him. He tried to rearrange his thoughts. She was a child. Fifteen. No more than that. Sixteen then. Maybe seventeen. No more than that.

TWENTY-SEVEN

I hope I never have to live through a day like today ever again. I'm still terrified. My hands are still shaking. What if I'm dragged away to the Tower for questioning? I will never tell them anything! Never! No matter what they do to me!

I was sitting outside the tavern with the blue shawl bundled up to look like the baby and sweat was running down my back. I kept my head down as if I was talking to it while that friar skulked about, going to look at the ships as if he had never seen one before, pacing about near the strand, then coming back and praying at the little shrine on the corner of the street, then standing about as if he wanted alms. He didn't fool me!

I was thinking, does he imagine I don't see him? I'll give him something to spy on if that's what he's looking for! How patient is he? And then I thought better of it and what would happen if he decided to come over and snatch the shawl away before the cog sailed?

It makes me shiver just to think of it.

So I kept on pretending I was talking and goo-ing to it, feeling like a sot-wit whenever anybody passed too close.

They must have seen. They must have known. *Goo-goo.* The idiot maid from le Sire's, talking to a blanket.

Now it's all different.

I got up to go as soon as I thought they were safely away. And to my horror he followed me. He must have known all along. He followed me and he spoke to me!

Up close he's a confusing sort of fellow. I didn't expect that. I felt some strange power coming from him, like when you go into the nave of a church and the light sparkles in through the high windows and falls in shafts of coloured sunlight across the tiles and you don't know where it comes from and you feel it hints at something beyond your reach, something beyond anything any of us know. To something maybe we can never know.

It's the mystery of all the things we do not know.

I do not know him.
He is the mystery of what I do not know.
He is all of it.
I'm not sure what I mean now.
I'm too frightened to think.

TWENTY-EIGHT

There was another body on the slab this time. It was a young man, probably no more than eighteen. A large knife wound in his chest. It was obvious the loss of blood had done for him. This time there was no mystery. His murderer had been caught with the bloody knife in his hand outside the tavern where the brawl had taken place and half a dozen witnesses were standing round. He was now residing in the Fleet.

'Apprentices,' muttered Archer pulling the sheet over him. 'What an insult to their mothers' labour-pangs.' He gazed despairingly at Chandler.

'Things could be worse. We could be at war with the French.'

'We would be if this lot could stop arguing among themselves.' Despite his lugubrious expression he gave a sudden chuckle. 'Remember when old Brembre ordered the City to build up its defences during the invasion threat ten years ago? And the abbot of Westminster ordered suits of armour for his canons? Dear old Peter Lyttlington. I applauded his courage. But how potent is a seventy-year-old abbot in armour or out? Although Knollys could still knock hell out of anybody, or so I—' He broke off.

Chandler gave him a questioning glance.

'Or so I hear,' he murmured. 'Pushing ninety for Heaven's sake and still going strong.' He continued swiftly as if what he said meant nothing. 'Maybe our misfortune as a country is to be ruled by children and old men?' He turned away with something unsaid hanging in the air.

'Archer,' Chandler adopted a conciliatory tone, pretending he had not heard the subtext of what his old friend was saying, 'remember, we are no more than mere pawns in a royal game of chess. All we can do is play it the best we can and hope to survive from day to day.'

'Aye, hope and maybe pray?' He cocked an eyebrow and added, 'You should have come to the meeting last night. Your name was mentioned.'

'In what context?'

'In the context of the Tower.'

Chandler made no response.

Archer continued. 'And also in the context of your subsequent report to a certain knight of this realm.'

'That's what this is about. Go on.'

'Do I need to?'

Chandler inspected his fingernails. There was mud underneath them from when he had helped Henry Daniel pull up the herbs for Swynford.

'Let's drop it. What I came to tell you,' he said, 'was that those seeds we found under the girl's nails are ordinary grass seed. The sort of thing you find on any floor.'

Archer rubbed one ear.

'Henry Daniel identified them for me. There can be no doubt about it.'

'I'm sorry about that. I don't know what I was expecting. Something. I suppose I'll have to release the body as soon as they send for it. There is something strange though. Let me show you.'

As Chandler followed him down into the subterranean chamber where bodies were kept for burial, Archer said over his shoulder, 'I mean it about the chapter. They have questions to ask.'

'If it's about anything that's happened at the Tower, you know and they know I'm as much under oath as you are yourselves.'

'If I mention the name Knollys again will that change your tune?'

He came to a stop at the bottom of the steps and looked up at Chandler who affected to be unmoved by the name.

He had often wondered how long it would be before somebody talked. An icy trickle slid down his back.

'What do you want to show me about the girl?'

It was cold underground. Water slid down the walls and in places slimy algae covered the stones. Archer put the cresset into a sconce making the shadows leap like black phantoms.

'This,' he said, pulling the sheet a few inches off the corpse. It was an unpleasant sight. The bloom had faded and her skin had acquired a leprous quality. The face muscles had sagged. The bones stood out, flesh draped over them, making her look like an old woman. Without thinking, Chandler crossed himself. He was oblivious to Archer's surprised glance.

'Do you see this colour here?' The coroner pointed to a tinge of brown, like bruising, along the girl's jawbone. 'It suggests to me that she was forced to take something into her mouth.'

'Saints—'

'No. Maybe not what you're thinking. My mind is travelling along the lines of food or drink. Something she did not want, however. Hence the use of force.'

'Do you mean poison?'

'Maybe. A paralytic for instance.'

'Henbane, monkshood?' He frowned.

'Something like that. Something that might not kill her if the dose was right but she would be helpless to resist whatever they wanted to do to her. Fortunately they were not of a lustful nature or God help her. My theory for what it's worth is that she was drugged to make it easy for them to take her to the Dow Beck, maybe to ensure that she was found almost at once. It was there her throat was probably cut to make it look like straightforward murder and she was dumped into the water. It's the only way it could have been done without anybody noticing what was going on until it was too late.'

'They removed her garments.'

'Yes. But why? No idea. If they hoped to conceal her identity then it was remiss of them not to remove the ring also. They could have removed her habit after they bundled her onto a cart – people are unloading rubbish all the time in there as we saw the other day. Maybe they threw the habit into the water so somebody would find it? Well . . . what do you think?' he asked after a pause.

Chandler could add nothing to Archer's theory. It sounded plausible enough. It solved the problem of privacy which had bothered them. If she was paralysed she would not have been able to struggle and draw attention to what was happening. Maybe she had fallen to the floor in whatever place they had administered the poison and had clutched at the dried grass in her efforts to remain conscious. If so it had availed her nothing.

'Why?' he asked abruptly. 'A warning? . . . "Look what we can do." Something like that? She could easily have been swept out into the Thames and her body never found.' He furrowed his brow. 'Or was it simply the nearest place to dump the body, as we first thought?'

'No idea. What I do know is she was an orphan, dowry given to the convent as I guessed. No connection to anyone important. The nuns at All Hallows knew nothing. What the prioress from Barking told us about her sneaking out in the middle of the night was a pack of lies. She'd never even set foot in All Hallows!'

'Unless they're lying through their teeth as well!'

Before he left, Chandler asked, 'Is it possible to tell from a corpse what poison has been taken?'

Archer shook his head. 'Only if the guts are opened up. We might find something we recognized, chopped roots for instance, but it wouldn't tell us anything if the poison had been administered as a tisane or in some other liquid form. Our knowledge does not stretch so far.'

'When are they coming to fetch her?'

Archer gave him a thoughtful look. 'I don't have to release her.' There was a long pause. 'It's my decision when or whether I do so or not.'

He accompanied Chandler to the door. 'Why don't you come back later this evening?'

'I have a few chores that will not be put off.'

When Chandler walked away he was feeling sick. Poor corpse. He could no longer see it as a girl or a novice and surmised that this must be because the soul had flown from it. The idea made him melancholy and confused.

It was as if their words had finally killed her.

His other remarks about the Tower and Sir Robert Knollys troubled him on a different level. He reported to Knollys. No one was supposed to know this. If Knollys was talking far and wide they would both be in danger soon enough. But Knollys would not do that. He was a wily veteran of the French Wars. He knew the value of silence. So how had the rumour arisen?

Chandler himself was too far outside the circle of the royal court to be aware of most of the malicious gossip that flickered and died on its rounds. It was laughable really. He was supposed to be the one with the privileged access to secrets. What worth had they if they were in common currency? Maybe Knollys was at the bottom of it after all. Maybe he had decided to throw him to the wolves.

Fingers of ice played up and down his spine. They could not get him on the grounds of treason. It would be against all sense. But he knew they could say or do anything.

If they could read his mind they would have him in the Tower like a shot.

Arundel could probably have him taken to Saltwood Castle.

He shut his eyes against that. Only once had he been asked to question a prisoner there. He hoped never to go there again.

Yes, they could certainly lock him in the Tower. Who was to stop them? Once in there he would never come out.

TWENTY-NINE

I'm sitting safely on my bed in Master Chaucer's house after he explained about *corpus pro corpore*. I am now bonded to him for one year. Down below in the solar the men are talking but I can't make out their words. The Master, my new master, doesn't say much. Others do. One more than the others, as always, one fond of his own voice. Rumbling away.

Adam says nothing but I suppose he's writing. Does he write down their words when they speak? Is he a clerk as well? It's strange here. I've never known a household like it. Even the cook is a man. A grizzled old fellow who has, so he says, fed armies in his time and so will find no hardship in feeding me.

I should go to sleep but I cannot when my heart is so full of grief and fear. I loved my little family, the baby, the children, madame who was always so kind and gentle to everyone, and le Sire, too, kindly and full of good will. And I grieve that I shall never more see them or hear their voices. They dared not tell me where they were going. Nor why le Sire had been dragged to the Tower. Nor how he came to be released.

When I remember him as I last saw him at the tavern, his face so white, like a piece of bleached linen, his wrists bruised from the manacles, and his eyes saddened beyond belief and anxious about whether they would get away to safety or not, I wanted to cry for us all. I am crying. I have never cried so much as in this last terrible day. I'm not sure anybody can set things aright. It's a mystery why it's God's will that we suffer through all time for what men do when their rage is let loose and their ambition is unfettered.

That friar, will he have me interrogated? I've done nothing wrong. What can he prove? He can't prove anything against me, can he? He would have to have some reason to drag me to the Tower. Of course he would. I'm not a heretic.

And now they say the duke has landed. They say his army is marching towards London. Some say it will be a new golden age when the duke, if he is a duke, marches in under the walls with his men. Others say that women and children will not be safe and we shall have to keep within doors. We are warned to barricade ourselves in our houses and pray to God. And our men are doomed to die in blood. I cannot believe Master Chaucer will let such things happen here.

It's the sixth king of the prophecy come to wreak havoc on the realm. The Mold-Warp will rule unto the seventh generation!

THIRTY

Chandler was no nearer making a decision by the time the bell for vespers started to toll. He hurried across to the chantry. A quick mumble through the words, a prayer or two, candles lit and unlit, the cope donned and doffed and then, telling Martin he would meet him in the Fleece an hour before curfew, he added as his parting shot that he had a visit to make as well as one to receive.

Pulling up his hood he hurried down Aldgate, turned off into Mark Lane and eventually came to a halt outside the mansion in Seething Lane. There was a wooden foot-bridge across the street from the first floor balcony. It had been his habit, in the days of his wooing by the devil – as he thought of his invitation onto Knollys' payroll – to stroll across there to the secret garden on the other side. It had been some time since he had been invited into the pleasance there.

At his pull on the bell rope Sir Robert Knollys' manservant opened a flap in the door and peered out. Without replying he caused the door to swing open a crack to allow him in. 'In his solar,' he grunted. 'I'll take you up.'

Their footsteps made shuffling sounds on the stone floor and then they were creaking up the wooden stairs to a room on the inner side of the house facing east.

Old Sir Robert was sitting in his high-backed settle placed, unbelievably, in front of a roaring fire. He turned at the sound of their entrance. The servant did not need to announce him. He merely nodded and went out, closing the door quietly behind him.

Sir Robert beckoned with one be-ringed hand. 'My dear Rodric, did anyone see you come in?'

'I doubt it. The streets are pretty empty at this time.'

'So what have you got for me? Is it something new?'

'That's for you to tell me, my lord. It's new to me.'

He paused after he sat down on the stool on the other side of the fire and watched Sir Robert lean forward. The firelight burnished his shaggy eyebrows and deepened every line on his sagging yellow cheeks. It always seemed astonishing to Chandler that anyone could have fought at Poitiers and still be alive to tell the tale. That is until he came face to face with Sir Robert.

Watching him at close quarters his immense age was not in doubt but his brain was not dulled by years, it was sharpened by experience as Chandler well knew and his life force was undiminished.

Knollys waited for his visitor to come to the point.

'I have heard,' Chandler plunged in with a shot in the dark, 'that certain alchemical gentlemen are bandying my name and yours about their coven.'

'Ah.' Knollys sat back and folded his hands in his lap. Two fingers of his right hand played with a ring on his left which bore a large ruby. It gleamed like fresh blood. With an effort Chandler tore his glance from it and tried to read the expression in Knollys' features but the task was impossible. He was as enigmatic as a wood carving. 'Who speaks thus?' he asked at last.

His lips were thin and bloodless. The white hairs of his soldierly beard are as sparse as wool on a sheep's arse, observed Chandler as he replied, 'No names that I know of, my lord. Just general hints.'

'You must mean Sir Arnold Archer and his cronies.'

Chandler remained as stoic as Knollys himself.

'They talk wildly, casting out lines to see if the fish bite,' declared Knollys. 'I trust you did not?'

Chandler shook his head.

'Of course they must be stopped if we're to be of any use to our patron. You agree?' He lifted his glance, eyes twinkling in the firelight.

Chandler gave a slight nod. If he was asking him to betray Archer he was going to have to tread carefully indeed. He let that go and replied, 'If they are linking our names I want to find out where such rumours come from.' He added, 'It will not be Archer. He knows nothing from me. Among these fellows, I understand, is one we both know. Indeed, the whole world knows him.'

'Ah, yes. And does he say anything we might find more interesting than the bookish talk of such poets?'

'I have been invited to attend but have never accepted.'

'Until now?'

'If you so wish.'

Knollys chuckled. 'Invited into the lion's den,' he said vaguely, reaching for a small bell on a cupboard beside him. The servant appeared. 'Wine for our guest if you please.'

The servant disappeared and returned so swiftly he must have already had the wine prepared outside.

Knollys settled himself more comfortably. 'And I imagine you are also here to confirm that a certain guest of ours has left the country?'

Chandler gave a small nod. So that was it. It had been planned. The question now was, who had been pulling the strings?

Knollys didn't enlighten him but merely commented, 'He was no use to us. I heard you were down there. Well done, brother.'

Gaunt's words: we have spies who spy on them.

A set up then. He gulped his wine. Knollys was staring into the fire, the ruby ring winking, flame-light shining through the dark red of the goblet he drank from. Some said he drank from clear glass so that he could see if anybody had added poison to his wine.

Chandler, in the lulling hiatus when neither of them spoke, thought briefly about the little novice and how even a glass goblet would not have saved her. He decided to cast a line of his own.

'It's strange you should mention Sir Arnold. I was present when his men dragged the body of a novice from the Dow. No doubt you heard about it?'

'A terrible waste of human life,' remarked Knollys, barely moving his lips.

'I think so too. Especially as she had so virtuously dedicated her life to our blessed Virgin.' He paused. Knollys appeared to have fallen asleep. Chandler was not deceived. He continued in a casual-seeming voice, 'I believe All Hallows is under the protection of the royal abbey at Barking, itself under the patronage of the House of Lancaster?'

He stopped talking then and eventually Knollys opened his eyes and turned to fix a severe glance on Chandler. 'A most prestigious abbey. What of it?'

'The earl of Derby, the lord Bolingbroke, despite his temporary absence, must be worried for the safety of his kins-women, nuns in such a place.'

Knollys raised his brows. 'You mean Margaret Swynford, Harry's cousin? You know, Rodric, my boy, sometimes curiosity can get the better of common sense. Remember that. And remind your friend Archer of it. I suggest you keep to the path laid out for you, do not deviate, do not dawdle. Keep straight on as instructed and you will come to no harm.' He smiled then reached for a bell. 'I'm an old man. I need my sleep.' When the servant appeared he said, 'Show this young fellow out then help me up to see my wife.'

As Chandler was ushered towards the door the old commander added, 'Let me know if you hear any interesting poetry on your rounds, dear boy.' He raised one hand in farewell. His ring flashed.

Stepping outside, his pay already in his pouch, Chandler pulled up his hood and set off towards Aldgate with Knollys' warning ringing in his ears. It confirmed what he had suspected, that Barking Abbey and its nuns were not as innocent as they appeared. It also seemed to confirm the rumour going round the City about Bolingbroke having already landed, or why the warning to keep out of his affairs? It might also mean he was not sitting idly by in Yorkshire but was gathering men, the ones who owed fealty to the House of Lancaster, and as many others who could be enticed onto his payroll. As for his intentions nobody yet knew. It was all speculation. Knollys, like others of a Lancastrian persuasion, might be as much in the dark as everybody else. His warning might, therefore, have been merely general . . . or it might be specifically intended to keep Chandler out of things.

He could hardly do that, he thought, as he threaded his way along Seething Lane, when he was due to meet the exile's stepbrother in a little while. He was in the thick of it.

THIRTY-ONE

C handler ran two at a time up the outside stairs, noticing as he went that the Keeper of the Heads had his door shut and the sounds of ribaldry inside were muted. When he burst in through his own door he caught Beata with something crooked in her arms. She was singing softly.

Cynically he registered the fact that silver coins and ribbons had been enough after all. But then he saw her nervous glance at the thing in her arms. A paw appeared.

'Please don't be angry,' she whispered. 'I couldn't resist her. When she's properly trained she'll be a great help in keeping down the mice.'

'I didn't know you liked cats.' He went over. It was a kitten no more than three or four weeks old and when it yawned it revealed sharp little teeth in the cavern of its mouth.

She was still looking anxiously at him. 'Is it all right? I may keep her?'

Chandler was overcome by a feeling of shame. 'No need to look so worried,' he said gently. 'I'm not such a monster I'd prevent you having a cat if you want one. I think it's a most charming little creature.' He reached out and tickled it behind one ear and was gratified to notice that the kitten stretched with pleasure. It nestled back against Beata's bosom and he added, 'It seems at home there—' and then he let his hand drop.

Beata seemed to think it was the wrong thing to say too and stepped hurriedly back. 'May I fetch you something?'

'Not yet. I'm expecting Swynford any minute.' Taking a key from his belt he went over to his chest and unlocked it. Removing the

pouches Brother Daniel had filled for him he lined them up in the
window niche.

As he did so he asked casually, 'And did you have to use much
silver to obtain the little fellow?' He lifted his head to glance across
the chamber and was in time to see a blush spread up her throat.
Flustered she replied, 'Oh, she was given to me – rather than let
her be drowned – I . . . Would you like the return of your coins?
I'll get—'

'Not at all. They were a gift for your own pleasure, to spend as
you will.'

She scurried back into the kitchen with her head bent, talking
nonsense to the kitten, leaving him staring after her with a puzzled
expression. He had seemed to catch her out in another lie. Over a
kitten?

There was a sudden commotion outside. When he went to look
he saw that Swynford was at the end of the street. He approached
at a trot with his men-at-arms running noisily alongside him. The
little page came last on his pony. He waited for them to alight and
for the boy to come up as before.

This time Swynford followed at his heels and strode in with no
greeting except, 'Well?'

Chandler waved a hand towards the sill.

He watched as Swynford went over, picked the pouches up one
by one, loosened the cords and peered inside, being careful to tie
them up again. Chandler could tell he had no idea what he was
looking at. 'They are labelled as you see.'

Swynford ignored that as if he had no need of labels. He reached
inside his jerkin, pulled out some coins and placed them on the sill
in the exact places where the herb pouches had rested. 'What did
you tell the gardener?'

'That I had need of cures.'

Swynford raised one brow.

'He knows me.'

He did not bother to add that Brother Daniel had known him all
his life. Swynford drove him to a fury. It was everything about the
man. His ignorance. His arrogance. His pretence. His sense of
entitlement. His lack of – what would he call it? His lack of soul.
Did he believe in that? No time for theology now. The man was
grunting something about returning later for more supplies and then

he was going down the outside steps to join his men in the street.

Chandler stood at the window and watched them return along Aldgate the way they had arrived.

Now for a drink at the Fleece, he thought, when they were out of sight. He felt he had earned a drink but was not sure how.

He had lost a suspect without finding out anything more about him – not that he had been responsible for le Sire. The Frenchman must have been permitted to leave – which meant he had friends of some influence. And he himself had received a grudging, 'Well done, brother,' for being a witness.

As a corollary, the maid's derisive glance when she held out the shawl continued to rankle. She believed him to be a fool. What's more, she must know who her master's contacts were.

So, what had he learned today apart from his own lack of sense? That Knollys was aware that Archer was involved in alchemy. That the group was believed to be a front for those of a Lollard persuasion. That he had been instructed, obliquely, to find out the names of the others involved – to be passed on to Arundel and his henchmen, no doubt. That meant that they probably did not have a spy inside the group yet.

And he had also learned that he should let the matter of the murdered novice rest.

In addition he had also incidentally learned that Bolingbroke wanted a contraceptive for some French woman he had met while in exile. But then, did he know that? Why did she not do as other women did and use a douche of mint or honey or whatever it was they preferred these days? The only advantage with spleenwort was that it could be added to meat or drink and no one would be the wiser.

Thoroughly dissatisfied with his day's work and himself he set off, head down, hood up, for the Fleece.

When he pushed his way inside it was heaving. Martin had already downed a couple of flagons by the look of him. There were four states of intoxication. By now everybody was in the state they called pig-drunk. Curfew was approaching and that's why they drank so fast and furiously.

'There should be a degree of drunkenness called curfew-drunk,' he observed, sitting down next to Martin with a flagon wedged in his fist.

THIRTY-TWO

I've made up my mind. I'm going to learn to read.

The scrivener's real work is down at Paternoster Row but he has a special arrangement with the Master. It means he's here nearly all the time these days.

When I mentioned to him I wanted to read, our conversation went like this.

'What d'you want to read for?'

'So I can see what those marks mean on that piece of parchment you've got.'

'I'll read it to you.'

'How do I know you'll tell me what it really says?'

'Would I lie to you, silly duck?'

'You might. How would I know? And anyway, I might want to read other things when you're not around.'

'Don't bother your head. It'll be no use to you.'

'I'll be the judge of that.'

'You'll have to learn the alphabet first.'

'I know about that.'

'Say it then.'

'I can't say it. I just know about it.'

He shakes his head and walks off.

THIRTY-THREE

The tavern-keeper took a broom to the last of them. 'You'll get me fined if you don't make yourselves scarce and you know who'll be paying the fine in the price of their ale, so get out! Go!' He shooed them out like dogs.

Martin reeled off down the street. 'See you tomorrow, brother!' He started to sing the bass voice from the Agnus Dei.

Chandler rested one hand against the wall and watched him stagger off round the next corner. Probably going to the stews, he thought. Maybe I should go with him. He rubbished that idea and decided to take a short cut through one of the yards to get back onto Aldgate and his chambers.

He had just started down the alley when he heard a shout behind him. Before he could fully turn round somebody loomed from out of the night and he had a sense of three or four figures closing in before he was suddenly seeing stars and staggering back against the wall.

There was a thump in his belly that pumped all the air from his lungs and then a fist was in his face, blood in his mouth, a grinding like broken teeth and after that he felt himself sliding down the wall as his legs gave way under him. A kick crunched his ribs. The sound of running footsteps followed. Then silence.

The next thing he knew someone was bending over him. 'He's opening his eyes,' came a voice.

Did they mean him? Were his eyes open? He could see nothing. He lifted up a hand that felt oddly heavy and pressed his knuckles into the sockets then groaned as a pain like molten iron seared through him. Suddenly he could see and he was blinking and gasping for breath as somebody started to drag him to his feet.

'Where to, brother?' said the voice again.

He managed to mumble something and it must have made sense because the voice said, 'We'll have you there in no time.'

When he came round again, he was lying at the foot of the steps outside the gatehouse. One of the night watch was bending over him. There was a greyish light penetrating his skull and he realized it was dawn.

THIRTY-FOUR

A story was doing the rounds that Bolingbroke had definitely landed and was on the march. Disputes followed, mainly from known Lancastrian supporters who denied that he would break his exile.

What? Risk a judicial hanging and all the ignominy that went with it?

Never.

Izzie leans worriedly on her counter. 'Can he have broken his exile? What can he gain by that? The king is still in Ireland. Where will that get him?'

Annie lowers her voice. 'I got this from a neighbour but I'm not saying who. The truth is, he has landed, he's got an army but he's already had trouble at Knaresborough Castle.'

'Where's that?'

'Yorkshire. Bolingbroke country. The militia refused to come out for him so he had half a dozen hanged and the rest changed their tune.'

'Who told you that?' Lizzie insists.

'A customer whose cousin lives in the north. She said they've had a fair old to-do. Militia rampaging everywhere, scavenging for vittels, burning people out of their homes. Her cousin sent a man down here to warn her. He told her the army was growing by the day on account of the pay Bolingbroke's offering. He's supposed to be going to Coningsbrough. On the way to London.'

'Is that so?' Izzie looks sceptical. 'There's nobody here to take up arms, is there, if that's what he's looking for?'

'Only the regent.'

'The duke of York?' Izzie lets loose a derisive laugh.

'He'd be as well to remember that his son is with the king,' Annie frowns. 'And he's honour bound to defend the realm.'

'Can you see that? The duke of York at the head of an army?' Izzie roars again.

'Well, how else is he going to get out of a pitched battle with bloody Bolingbroke, if that's his plan?'

'They're all rumour-mongers. I don't believe he'd be such a faithless sot-wit.' Izzie turns away to a greet a customer.

'Wouldn't it be treason?' I ask when she turns back.

The women glance from one to the other.

'I mean,' I explain, 'if Bolingbroke has landed and marches against King Richard, wouldn't that be treason, given that the king is the holy anointed one all the dukes paid allegiance to when he was crowned?'

'And York is standing in for the king as regent now he's out of the country,' adds Annie. 'If he fails to act for the king he'll be guilty of treason as well.'

Izzie shakes her head. 'Who to believe, eh? At least the uncertainty is making folk stockpile their cheeses. I'm fair sold out today. How are you doing, hon?' She glances at Annie's almost empty counter. 'Looking well.'

'I'd better make my purchases before it all goes,' I say, 'or Master Chaucer will be after me.'

When I get back to the house I tell Cook everything I've heard and later, as soon as the Master finishes work, I hear him telling him and Adam about it.

'So that's the latest?' Adam remarks.

When I take in their ale they're standing about in silence and the Master is pulling at his beard.

'Good child,' he says. 'And you heard this in the market this morning?' He looks back at Adam with his head on one side as if he has no need to put his thoughts into words.

THIRTY-FIVE

Archer was sitting beside his bed when Chandler woke up. Sunlight flooded into the bedchamber. From the sound of passing carts outside it was full day, whether before noon or not he could not tell.

He told Archer as much detail as he thought advisable about the previous evening, only omitting his pay-master's name. 'It was a warning,' he repeated. 'Something to do with the novice?'

'Why are you so convinced? It could have been run-of-the-mill cut-purses.'

'Except that they didn't take anything. They simply roughed me up. They did a professional job. They could have easily killed me but they chose not to.'

Archer leaned forward. As the older man he seemed to think he should have seen it coming. 'Are you sure it's not to do with that other business?' he asked.

'What other business?'

He looked uncomfortable. 'Look, Rodric, I don't know who you've got in the Tower just now. I don't know at whose behest you go there, that's your affair, but with all these rumours about Bolingbroke being on the move it's clear there's something up. Everybody's already choosing sides. If the rumours turn out to be true some people are going to feel very unsafe. Can't you keep out of it?'

'I do very little for a lot of pay. Look at that pouch over there that your so-called cut-purses disdained last night. Why do I do it?'

'For pay?' Archer looked scandalized.

He shook his head then winced. 'Not entirely. I simply know too much for them to let me go. All I've done recently is keep an eye on a fellow who is better off out of the country anyway.' He avoided any mention of the Tower.

Archer was more direct than before. He usually managed to keep some opinions to himself but now he said, 'Why the hell are you mixed up in all that? Think, Rodric, think. There must be a way out.'

It was the second time in twenty-four hours someone had asked him that question. 'Tell me how it's possible to live in the City without being mixed up in something,' he replied. 'You yourself—'

Archer jerked his head up. 'If you mean alchemy, I swear it's an innocent pursuit. You're invited despite everything. Come along. See for yourself. Report back. We don't care. We're a simple group of men who ask questions. We're philosophers. We enquire into the physical nature of things. We have nothing to do with worldly ambition. We seek the truth only.'

'And the whisper that you're all Lollards?'

'This City runs on rumour.'

'QED, my friend.'

'Some rumours may turn out to be true,' Archer replied. 'Some are arrant lies spread by folk who want to control the mood of the mob.'

Chandler's head was throbbing. One tooth felt as if it needed pulling. He passed the back of a hand over his face.

Archer was smiling. 'You've got two black eyes, do you know that?'

He shook his head. 'It wouldn't surprise me.'

'Better if you don't see yourself for a few days. You'll scare yourself shitless. At least your ribs aren't broken. Bruised only.'

'How do you know?'

'You were out to the world when I arrived. I thought I'd have a quick look.'

'Preparing for a new tenant in your mortuary?'

'Not yet, Rodric. Let's hope not for a long time. But listen, I'm not entirely disagreeing with you. Something happened and it could mean you may be right and it really is something to do with that poor little novice. Yesterday evening as I was walking home up Corn Hill a ragamuffin tugged me by the sleeve. I thought he was asking for pennies but before I could offer him anything he said: master says to let it drop or you'll rue it. Before I could reply he ran off and I lost him in the crowd. At first I thought it was a joke and I'd look up to see a row of grinning faces but nobody else noticed a thing. There's only one doubtful cause of death in the mortuary at present so it's obvious whom he meant.'

'What are we going to do?'

'Go out there to Barking Abbey. We told that prioress we would and we should do it. Have you got a sword, by the way?'

He nodded.

'Can you use it?'

'I used to be quite good in the old days. Gaunt made sure of that. He had me marked out for the militia until I chose a more saintly direction.' He gave an ironic smile. 'See where all roads lead?'

'Where?'

'To war.'

'I meant, where's this sword of yours?'

'Somewhere in that aumbry over there.' He indicated a wooden cabinet with two doors. 'If it's not there ask Beata.'

'Can she be trusted?'

Chandler did not reply.

Archer got up and went to the aumbry and rummaged about until he eventually dragged forth an impressive-looking scabbard with the hilt of a sword sticking out of it. He hauled it in both hands to the bed. 'You know how to use this?' He looked impressed.

'I do.' Despite his beating and the ensuing pain he reached out for the sword and drew it cautiously from the scabbard. He weighted it for a moment then peered along the blade while still lying in his bed. From the way he handled it Archer saw it was obvious he knew how to use it.

The coroner came to sit on the edge of his bed again. 'You'd better wear that, to my way of thinking.'

'Against a coven of nuns?'

Archer grimaced.

'What about you, Arnold? Are you armed?'

By way of an answer the coroner drew from inside his sleeve a lethal-looking blade in a leather sheath. 'I don't believe they'll touch me. I'm too well known.'

'Take no chances, Arnold.' Chandler was serious for a moment. He had begun to assume that his own protectors would also protect Archer but maybe it was not so. He liked Archer. He thought his alchemy was misguided but the man was good at heart. He told him again what his patron had said about curiosity and added, 'That goes for alchemists as well.'

Archer bit his lip. 'Listen. I came over here for a reason. I didn't know you'd been beaten up.'

He took a piece of cloth from inside the leather bag attached to his belt and very carefully unfolded it. He held out something dark and unpleasant-looking. 'Now's the time to test your curiosity.'

'What is it?' Chandler peered at what seemed no more than a mangled leaf when Archer held it out.

'You or Henry Daniel are the ones to say for sure but to me it looks like hemlock.'

'You opened her up?'

He stared aghast at the evidence. For a moment in his weakened state he felt sick and saw the sharp knife cutting into the pearly skin, defacing it, slicing through the tender wall of the stomach to reveal her entrails.

Archer noticed Chandler's expression.

'She wouldn't know, Rodric. She's dead. She feels nothing now.'

Recovering, he replied, 'We need to ask a lot of questions of those nuns.'

'I'll send my man to All Hallows again.'

'I hope he's up to it. He'll need to be made of stone if they're all like the one who came to cozen us.'

He recalled the scent of roses, the wild feeling that had swamped him, the unexpected feeling she had aroused merely by allowing her glance to linger over his face one moment longer than necessary. It brought the scent of treachery. It embodied the desecration of innocence.

Archer left then with a warning nod, telling him to stay put until he could lift a sword without falling over. Chandler knew he was in no fit state to go anywhere at present without being a liability. It was fortunate that his assailants had broken no bones. His cracked rib would heal by itself. Only his jaw was causing him trouble, especially when he tried to eat, and he told Beata to give him only food a baby could swallow. The rest of his body was just one agonizing ache but he had ways of dealing with that.

While he was taking a day or two to recover Archer checked the story coming out of All Hallows, saying he left the questions to his assistant so as not to draw attention to the fact that they were taking it as seriously as they were. 'As I believe we are?'

'As indeed we are,' Chandler agreed.

'There was nothing new. She hadn't even been inside the precinct. That prioress lied. They hadn't even squared the story with themselves.'

THIRTY-SIX

The City was in ferment again. News was in that the heron was up. Bolingbroke had shown his hand. It was definite now.

He had landed at Ravenser on the Humber estuary on the fourth day of July. He had marched with the few hundred men brought from Vannes to his inherited castles of Pickering, Knaresborough and Pontefract, and mustered the militia, the men who owed him allegiance.

Next, from the safety of his fortress at Pontefract, he was now known to have sent letters to everyone of consequence claiming that the king was plotting the death of their chief magistrates in order to take the law into his own hands. He also claimed that King

Richard and his ministers were planning even greater taxation than anyone had ever known before. He lied, too, about the realm's overseas possessions, about how Richard planned to sell them for his own personal gain. And, as a final warning, he claimed that the king was going to keep his villeins in harder bondage than any other Christian king before him.

When Chandler heard all this he wondered how Bolingbroke had the nerve. To Archer he said, 'One can but admire his cunning. He knows how to play every level of the populace. To muster an army as formidable as the one we're hearing about in so short a time leaves me speechless.'

Archer's response was something he would need to confess later. He added more temperately, 'And now he's on the road to London? Better sharpen our blades. Both of us.'

Factions were rapidly forming. The aldermen, with their escorts, were preparing to go onto the City walls to greet the usurper garbed in their finest regalia in order to demonstrate their support.

The belief that Bolingbroke would put a stop to recent taxation – exorbitant, unfair, unwarranted, as it was claimed – was uppermost in their minds of course. Archer reported to Chandler what had been said in council. He was giving away no secrets. 'We are our own men and no one, not even the king, has jurisdiction over us.' That was legally true as City men with their own liberties and so said Lord Mayor Barantyn many times and loudly, powerfully aware of the coming elections.

'However,' Archer continued, 'it does not follow in any logical degree that we should therefore exchange our lawful king for a usurper.'

His fellow mercer, Sir Richard Whittington, had agreed but with a caveat. Although he supplied King Richard with fabrics and regularly loaned him large sums in his transactions as money-lender, he was willing to roll with the tide.

'As he explained,' Archer told Chandler, 'it isn't the king he has issues with but the ministers he's left in charge while he goes on this fruitless mission to Ireland. Everyone agrees that Sir John Bushy, Sir Henry Green and Sir William Bagot, along with Sir William Scrope as Treasurer, are too harsh in their tax-gathering.'

'Have you heard the scurrilous little ballad about the Bush, the Green and the Bag going the rounds just now?' Chandler sang a few bars. The hatred their policies aroused encouraged the wish that they should get their just desserts, and soon.

'Whittington was looking thoughtful. He might be on the losing side if Bolingbroke takes this whole thing to a conclusion. He said, "We must be as canny as cats." It's certainly a poor show for the king.'

'Did everybody agree?'

'It's language they understand. The court's a honey pot whichever man has the crown on his head. Their only concern is to ensure that they're not the ones to keep filling the pot with honey. Instead they want to lick the sweetness from their own paws.'

Later he came back with a yard of ale for Chandler brought straight from the vat at the Fleece. 'I have to tell you this then I'll have to get back to the mortuary.'

Chandler lifted his head groggily from his pillow just enough to mutter some thanks before pouring some ale into his mouth. 'Will I want to hear?'

'Probably not but you have to. Some fellow dragged himself into the Fleece just now, half-dead and covered in dust after a hard ride from the north. He had a story to tell, the details of which I cannot doubt. Listen to this! I got it verbatim from him. He was one of the bowmen persuaded by eighteen pence a day to join Bolingbroke against his own better judgement by the needs of his sick child. I cannot doubt him. Now he's regretting he didn't merely turn to sheep-rustling to get the silver he needs.'

'Listen, Arnold, my dear old friend, much as I care for the sorrows of others I have enough of my own to be going on with—'

'I'll get to it then. This is exactly what he told us. The earl of Northumberland caught up with the main force near Doncaster and the two great armies camped together in the summer meadows. You can imagine it.' He broke off. 'Foragers ransacking the fields of the locals for their own army kitchens, laying everything to waste—'

'Go on.'

'And in his tent, shaded from the sun, Bolingbroke – sitting on his wooden chair with his legs spread as he listens to Northumberland ranting about something or other and our fellow, on guard at the door, unnoticed, listening to every word. "I can offer you something," says Bolingbroke to Northumberland. "Do you imagine I expect you to bring your men along with me for no reward?" "I would never imagine that, my lord," comes the reply—'

'What? Northumberland says that?' Chandler struggled to sit up the better to hear. 'This is a tall story, no different from any other we hear in the Fleece!'

'Northumberland was surely unable to keep the sarcasm out of his voice,' Archer agreed. 'But Bolingbroke, literal-minded, doesn't notice. "I am going to offer you a great honour," says he. "I make you Warden of the West March." He adds archly, "If you'll accept the honour." Northumberland cannot disguise the fact that he's ready to bite Bolingbroke's hand off. Yet he had just been offered something that legally lay within the gift of the king!'

'I'm aware of that,' remarked Chandler with a dry smile. 'I'm also aware that Bolingbroke is not king. Not yet.'

'His intention is obvious, is it not?' Archer sat back. 'Isn't that proof?'

Chandler spilt some ale on his nightshirt.

Bolingbroke and Northumberland? It was so astounding, so unambiguous, that he fell silent.

'Well, for once Northumberland didn't have to swallow down the words,' added Archer. 'Apparently he was speechless. His unwonted silence made it appear that he was considering the offer with undue care. "Of course, if you decline – and why shouldn't you?" Bolingbroke continues, "I'll have a devil of a job to find someone I trust as much as I trust you." You know how he rarely smiles, Chandler? He fails to smile now. His eyes pierce the earl as if he's eyeing up an opponent in the lists. Northumberland looks as if he's about to be jerked off his horse. He was a jouster of some fame himself in his younger days, remember? Now he adopts a morose expression. And this is what he says, mark this. "Let's get the business done, then, Harry. We both know what's what. I'm your man. Let's get it done!"'

Archer sat back again, expression grim. 'This is exactly what the fellow told us. Not a word of a lie.'

'If you believe him you'll believe anything.'

Chandler, somewhat beaten up as he was, felt a mixture of emotions. Despite his response he did believe Archer. But he wasn't going to admit it yet. He believed this stranger in the Fleece. His words had the ring of truth. What's more, his story made everything fall into place. Now they knew. This was Bolingbroke's game and probably had been all along. To invade while his cousin was out of the country and rip the crown from his head.

THIRTY-SEVEN

I have very little to do. He does not really need my services. I expect it was to please le Sire and to keep him from worrying about what would happen to me that he took me on. I look after his marketing every day. I bring in what his cook wants. We eat well.

Every time I go out I hear such stories, the whole City is wild with them, stories about the army, how it landed in the north and only one man in a field shouting curses – soon made to change his tune, they say – and stories about where they're going next, stories about how everybody is having their knives ground at the cutlers, stories about people taking sides, fist fights, friars standing outside St Paul's and ranting about the wrath of God, families broken apart and refusing to speak to those on the other side, children disinherited, the pushing and shoving in the queues on Cheap because of a thoughtless word. It's getting frightening. Everybody says it'll get worse the longer the uncertainty goes on.

The trouble is nobody really knows a thing. First one courier rides in, falls in the dust and yells his news. Then another, ditto, but saying something entirely different.

Is Bolingbroke coming to London to take King Richard's throne? Yes.

Is he? No, he only wants his inheritance back.

Yet it seems to me he's already got it, so why is he marching south?

He's not. He's heading to the West Country.

No. He's already in Wales.

No again, he's at Berkeley Castle to parlay with the doddering old duke of York our regent, so-called protector of the realm while the king is absent.

Somebody makes up a song about him. 'The Grand Old Duke

of York'. He had ten thousand men. He marched them up to the top of the hill and he marched them down again. Up and down the hills to no purpose.

'Playing for time?' I suggest to Adam.

He scowls in response.

'Does old York favour Bolingbroke's attempt to become king?' I ask.

'What do they say in the market?'

'Some say, no. He's sincerely trying to stop him on his march.'

'Believe that if you will. He's making a poor job of it.'

I remember what Izzie and Annie were saying a few days ago. 'They say he can't join Bolingbroke because his own son, Edward, the new duke of Aumerle, is in Ireland with King Richard. So that's why he dithers and wrings his hands and finds only a few regular militia to follow him.'

'And half of those left as soon as they could,' says Adam.

'Why is Bolingbroke going to Berkeley Castle, if he is?' I ask. 'What's there? The king's grandfather met a horrible death in Berkeley Castle. It seems an odd choice to me.'

The Master overhears us. He says it's what poets call symbolic.

'Another rumour is that he's left there anyway and is already marching into Wales. That's the latest.'

'There are notices being put up.' Adam exchanges a look with the Master then walks off before I can ask him about them. I must, I really must ask him to teach me to read. I'll be able to find out more that way.

THIRTY-EIGHT

Chandler had in his possession something Brother Daniel had given him some time ago. It had been brought in from Outremer on one of the trading vessels bringing goods from the silk route through Genoa. It was worth its weight in gold now that route was closed to them. He had never managed to find a use for it. Now seemed as good a time as any. He needed sleep. He had been told it was good for that. He had promised Archer they would go out to the abbey at Barking tomorrow. It would be a surprise visit. He would need all his wits about him.

Sleep, he muttered to himself. The great healer, that was what his father used to call it, although he doubted that it healed the wound his father suffered after the hideous martyrdom of his brother.

He eased himself over to where he kept his special cures in a locked casket. He had no idea how much of the stuff to take. It couldn't be much different to the English poppies they used so he mixed a pinch with wine, swallowed it and, satisfied that he had got it right, collapsed back into bed. At some point he was conscious of Beata bending over him and as he dipped back into sleep he thought he felt her lips press his. Then he was sinking down under the suffocating folds of a black, Benedictine robe and there were roses everywhere.

He woke with a shout.

Intestines slithered over his face. Blood was flowing like a crimson lake from under the door. He fought for breath as the tide rose over his head.

A bright light was shining in his face. It was sunlight.

'You're not ready to go, are you?'

Weirdly it was Archer again. 'I thought you left?'

'What?'

'Didn't you go home?'

'I did yesterday. Now I'm back. Today,' he added giving Chandler an odd look.

Beata came in. 'He took something, Sir Arnold. He's been dead to the world ever since you left. He was talking wildly about a nun. I was getting worried.' She shot a glance at Chandler but with a little laugh turned to Archer. 'Maybe you can persuade him to take it more often? Once he stopped talking he was a lot easier to deal with.'

Archer peered into Chandler's face. 'You're not going to be able to come with me. Don't worry, I brought a couple of men along. It doesn't need all of us anyway.'

'Give me a minute.' He eased his legs off the bed and put his feet carefully side by side on the floorboards. They were exactly the same size. The fact fascinated him for a long moment. He wondered what he might have said in his delirium and roused himself. 'I'll need a horse.'

'I've got you one.'

'Then strap me to it. Of course I'm coming.'

The abbey was an impressive array of towers and steeples with a high-roofed building in the middle and several smaller ones surrounded by crenellated walls that would have taken scaling ladders to breach. They, however, approached the gatehouse in good order, the City coroner, the brother friar and two servants. It was a relief to get out of the City in its current fever.

As soon as they entered the gatehouse Archer produced documents with legal-looking seals to prove his authority to ask questions on behalf of the mayor and justices of the City of London. The porteress gave him a scowl, closed the flap in the door through which she had examined them and went to inform the abbess of their arrival.

A good while later the flap was reopened. Chandler imagined he could discern the scent of roses but when the door was grudgingly dragged back it revealed a little nun no younger than seventy who let them in with the warning, 'You may enter the visitors' chamber. Those you wish to question will speak to you from behind the grille. On no account are you to look at them directly.'

There was a scuffling from behind the wall and Chandler guessed they were being watched. He still felt light-headed.

Having agreed that they would go along with the prioress's story in the hope of lulling the nuns into carelessness, Archer crossed over to the grille and peered inside. 'Sister?'

'I am listening, my lord coroner. How may I help?'

Chandler crowded Archer out of the way. It was a voice he did not recognize.

Archer took over again and explained that they needed to understand how the novice had communicated to her lover.

There was a flurry of agitated movement behind the grille. 'Lover?'

'I'm told by your prioress that the novice received a message from a young man and slipped away from the priory to meet him . . . I know,' he added in a conciliatory tone, 'it's quite scandalous and we shall do whatever we can to apprehend the fellow as he is clearly guilty of murder.'

The novice, they were told, without evident irony, was named

Eloise. As for a lover or indeed of any young man they were in complete ignorance and moreover thought it most unlikely that such a person existed.

Chandler muttered, 'Not following the Abelard route then.'

A series of novices who had known her was paraded behind the grille and with downcast heads muttered their replies. No, she had not said anything to warn them of her intention to abscond. No, they did not know who her lover was. No, they knew nothing. Nothing.

'Nobody knows anything,' said Archer turning away for a moment.

Chandler was staring in over his shoulder through the grille trying to see who was pulling the girls' strings. There was a vague figure at the back of the cell but he could make nothing out.

They sent the last girl in. Unlike the others she came right up to the grille and, elbowing Archer out of the way, he was startled to find her eyes meeting his. She held his glance so boldly and with such a provocative expression he was glad for the sake of his vows that there was a wall between them. He asked how long she had been a novice and she told him she had arrived on the same day as Eloise, six months ago.

'So you knew her as well as anybody?'

'I would say so.' Her glance locked on his and would not leave it.

'Was there a lover?' he asked bluntly.

There was a sudden movement from deep in the cell and the girl brought her top teeth down hard on her bottom lip, making a face only he could see. Eventually a voice from behind her whispered, 'You may answer.'

Staring directly into Chandler's eyes she muttered, 'I know nothing, my lord.' Deliberately she closed one eye.

Aware that they were being overheard and praying that the girl was quick on the uptake, he asked, 'Tell me about her. What did she like? Did she ever work in the gardens?'

When she said yes he added, 'And no doubt enjoyed being there until the bell for vespers dragged her back indoors?'

Her eyes flashed. 'Yes. She liked being in the garden.'

'Was she right-handed or left-handed?'

'I don't know.'

The voice from the unseen figure behind her said, 'That will be all, Mercy. Go now.' And then, louder, 'My lords. Is there anyone else you wish to speak to?'

Archer pushed his face against the grille, like Chandler ignoring the warning not to peer directly inside, and said, 'We are most grateful, sister. We shall now leave you in peace. Will you make arrangements to fetch the body or shall I do that?'

'We will attend to the matter, my lord.' There was a short pause followed by a snap as a door closed inside, followed by the sense that the room was empty.

Outside they got on their horses and rode off a little way up the road until they came to a stand of trees. Riding in among them they eventually came to a stop where they would not be observed by passers-by.

Archer was looking dissatisfied. 'I don't know where that's got you. You can't get inside their gardens, if that's your idea.'

'The river flows inside the precinct. I can get in that way.' They did not discuss who was to breach the security of the abbey grounds. Despite Chandler's beating he was still the fitter of the two men and certainly the more foolhardy. He took a phial from his pouch and swallowed the contents with one gulp, hoping he'd got the measure right this time. Archer had brought more prosaic sustenance, bread and cheese, which he shared with everybody.

A wind was springing up. Leaves were eddying. Soon the trees would have bare branches. For the last week storms had been battering the coast although in London they had been unaware of it except by hearsay. Every day weather reports were sent up from Wales, prophets claiming that the winds would stop within seven days. The king would then make landfall on his way back to mend his broken kingdom.

'It means England has seven days' grace before it falls to Bolingbroke,' said Archer with a sharp glance at Chandler. 'Old York is still hiding out in Berkeley Castle. What does he think he's going to do from there?'

'Don't they say Bolingbroke is in Bristol?' chipped in one of his men.

'That was last week. He moved on after putting a few heads on spikes. It's unprecedented. The king's ministers? Beheaded without even a trial?' Archer looked as shocked as he sounded.

Chandler let it slide off him. He felt odd. Very relaxed, powerful enough to do anything he chose. He told Archer he was going to make a reconnaissance of the territory to find the best way inside.

When he eventually stumbled back he said, 'It's easy. I'll wade along the river. It's quite shallow near the bank. I'll go in under the watergate. The gardens come right down to the river and there's only a low box hedge at that point. If she's got any sense she'll work it out.'

They settled down to wait for a time they judged would be shortly before vespers.

The high winds would be a help, Chandler expected. The sound of the thrashing branches would conceal any sounds he might make as he splashed along the river for his meeting with the novice.

THIRTY-NINE

Inevitably he slipped in the mud once or twice, felt his feet sink into it so that he had to pull them out one by one with his hands. Each one made a glugging sound as it was released and once he slipped to his waist but the cold revived him somewhat and he was soon pulling himself up the bank to the little hedge that kept the tame plants in order.

He lay full length for a while before remembering what he was supposed to be doing.

Leaving a trail of water he clawed his way up the last bit of the slope and sat behind the hedge to wait.

It was someone singing that alerted him. Moving one leaf at a time he found a small gap through the box hedge that allowed a view of a segment of the garden on the other side. A grey robe suddenly blocked his view.

He whispered into the hedge. 'Are you alone?'

The grey robe was displaced by the face of the novice her guardian had called Mercy. She peered through the hedge at him then bent as if pulling weeds. 'Do you know you've got two black eyes?'

'I'm not here to hear about myself.'

'Listen to me, then, brother. This is all wrong. For some reason they're lying to you. I don't know why you thought she had a lover. Eloise had no lover. She was most pious and I have to say, forgive me, brother, for speaking so of the dead, she was dull and correct. Perfect material for these women here.'

'Go on,' he urged when she paused.

'The thing is, she heard something that terrified her. Something she was not meant to hear . . .' She stood up with her arms full of weeds.

Chandler saw her go over to a wheelbarrow and deposit them inside it. She called a greeting to someone and a few moments later was back again, kneeling behind the hedge. Whispering, with an occasional glance over her shoulder she said, 'What happened was, she overheard a conversation – something to do with the king. She was frightened because they saw her in a corner of the cloister and knew she must have overheard. My belief is they got rid of her. It's as simple as that. But it was needless. She would never have spoken out, no matter what she heard.'

'Have you any idea what it was about?'

Through the interlacing twigs he noticed a look of doubt cross her face. To give her time to reject the idea of a lie he asked, 'Who was involved?'

'The abbess and two visitors from outside.'

'What visitors? Your patron, one of the Lancasters?'

'No. I don't think so.'

'Did you see them?'

There was a long pause and through the screening of the foliage Chandler could see the doubt on the girl's face. 'You must tell me,' he urged.

Slowly she replied, 'One of them was a man I've never seen before.'

'And the other?'

Again the slight hesitation before she said, 'We're imprisoned here. If I knew where to run to I would abscond. Eloise never would have. Look, I must go.' She turned away then bent to say quickly, 'I hate it here.'

So that was her price.

'I cannot rescue you.'

'I'd never seen one of them before.'

'Perhaps there might be a way if—'

But the girl had gone.

*   *   *

Archer was pacing back and forth across the clearing when he saw Chandler coming through the trees. He gave a cry of relief. 'I thought they'd taken you in.'

'God help me if they had done.' He told him what the novice had said. 'So you're right. There is something to it. What now?'

'The abbess must be in it up to her neck – but we can't touch her, she's appointed by the king's council – one of the four abbesses to be so honoured, she the most powerful.'

And, as well as that, thought Chandler, Bolingbroke's stepsister, Margaret Swynford, is a nun here. He kept quiet.

On their way back to town while Archer ruminated over various strategies they might adopt Chandler considered who best to approach in order to discover the identity of the visitors and what they had discussed with the abbess that was so dangerous. By the time they parted at Aldgate, however, everything was still hanging inconclusively before them. Archer's parting shot was, 'I suppose you noticed what was strewn on their flagstones? Marsh grass!'

FORTY

I t was the next day. Mid-afternoon. The Aldgate chambers.

A night's heavy drugged sleep had brought Chandler no sudden enlightenment to make sense of what the novice had told them. When he came in later from the chantry Beata hurried through from the kitchen at the sound of the door. Her expression hardened. There was no welcoming smile. He briefly wondered what he had said in his earlier delirium to make her look at him like this.

She pointed to something lying on the table where his flagon of wine usually stood. 'Someone brought that for you.'

He went over to have a look. It was a red rose in bud.

'Who brought it?' he asked without turning round.

'A young page. He had a message.' She waited as if willing him to turn. He obliged.

She gave him another cold glance. The little medallion of her saint glinted between her breasts. Who was it? St Zita? The saint of domestic servants. She must have resigned herself to her position in his household without announcing the fact.

When he shifted his glance she was still staring at him.

He hardened his own expression and with an impatient jerk of his head asked, 'And the message was?'

'Urgent. To go now.' She turned abruptly and went into the kitchen shutting the door with a bang.

Chandler twirled the rosebud between his fingers. Even he could see Beata was jealous. But it was not what it looked like. Sometime soon he would explain and they would share a laugh together. Or would they? There were still one or two things she needed to explain.

Without even taking off his cloak he went over to the shelf and shook out a minute pinch of the cure from Outremer, crushed it quickly in the mortar, dropped it into a beaker of wine, downed it and went out with a shout over his shoulder to say he did not know when he would be back and not to bother with any food for him.

He would go to a pie shop on East Cheap if the sender of the rosebud failed to offer anything better.

As he hurried along he fingered the bruising on his face. The Saracen cure had numbed him so that he felt nothing. But he was aware of one or two interested glances thrown his way as if speculating what sort of fight he had been in and who had won. Let them think what they like, he thought. If he had been warned, or armed, or not outnumbered and taken by surprise he would have made sure his assailants regretted their advantage.

At Seething Lane he pulled his hood up and went down to the big house halfway along.

This time he was shown into the solar at once to find Sir Robert leaning out of the casement looking down into the street. He must have seen him arrive. As Chandler entered he pushed his hood back with a flourish, just to observe Knollys' expression.

It was one of unmitigated concern. 'My dear, fellow, what have you done to yourself? Did you fall off your horse?' He hobbled forward on his stick and peered at Chandler's face.

Taken aback by the old man's ability to dissemble he shook his head and merely remarked, 'The lads deserve a good reward from their master. They did a very professional job. I had no warning.'

'You mean you were attacked?'

Chandler gazed at him in disbelief.

Knollys frowned. 'Who did it?' he demanded on a different note. 'Is it something to do with us?'

Chandler stuck his hands in his sleeves. He didn't know what to make of it. If he had seen Knollys without suspecting he was behind it he would have had no hesitation in believing in his astonishment and concern now. But it had to be him. Otherwise it made no sense.

'I came as soon as I received the rose.'

'Good fellow. I knew you'd understand.'

Lady Knollys' red roses were famous. Everybody knew what they meant.

The old soldier flexed his shoulders. 'I've always thought you should go armed. Friar or not, none of our streets are safe these days. You owe it to yourself to carry some weapon. But come. We need to talk on another matter.'

Leading the way he started out over the wooden footbridge towards the garden on the opposite side. 'Constance is delighted with her roses this year,' he said conversationally as Chandler followed him. 'Come and have a look.'

Chandler stamped down his impatience as he was given a tour of the small garden on the other side of the street. Lady Constance, Sir Robert's wife of many years, had had the building demolished opposite their own so she could create a garden. And when the smells and sights of Seething Lane became too much for her she had a footbridge built over the street so she could visit her garden in peace.

Of the lady herself there was no sign today.

Her red roses bloomed in all their usual magnificence, however. It was a strain that had been introduced by Queen Eleanor as a gift for her second son, the first earl of Lancaster, to complement the white rose she had bestowed on her eldest son, the duke of York. Knollys referred to his wife's red roses as the Apothecary's Rose and Chandler assumed this was to appear non-partisan.

Now he led him to a chamomile seat facing an ornamental fountain that was supplied with fresh water from an underground spring. A water jug stood on a parapet next to it.

Knollys offered a drink but Chandler declined.

'I assumed it was urgent—'

Knollys cut in. 'And so it is. The constables have picked up a man. He's refusing to talk. Consequently we have no idea who he is or where he's from. Particularly where he's from. Go over. See what you can find out. When you've seen him come straight back here. Understand?' He added before Chandler could reply, 'Do you speak Welsh?'

'Only a little but I can always get help if need be.'

'There's this fellow Glyn Dwr. A potential troublemaker. Lying low these days but you never know. See if there's a connection. It's urgent.'

His words confirmed that Bolingbroke's army, after Bristol, was heading for Wales. His faction would fear civil war more than they feared anything else. It meant that so far the king was safe. But time was running out and public opinion was hardening into two implacable camps.

'Are you feeling all right?' Knollys laid his hand on Chandler's shoulder. His ruby ring glinted like a drop of Christ's blood.

'They gave me a bit of a beating but I'm taking stuff for it,' he said groggily. 'It makes me a bit slow on the uptake. I can't see the connection between things. Nothing important.' He added, 'I think I would like some of that water you offered. My lord.' He could not have risen to his feet to get it himself. He let the old man do it for him. It seemed to amuse Knollys to be waiting on a much younger man.

He creaked across to the fountain and filled the jug. When he returned he growled, 'Cup your hands and splash some of this on your face. Don't you have any idea who did this?'

'I thought I did,' admitted Chandler, doing as Knollys suggested, 'but I fear I may have suspected the wrong party.'

Knollys patted him with his horny old hand. 'If you need help, say the word.'

FORTY-ONE

The Tower then.

Something was going on. It meant that they had to keep him waiting until sufficient decorum could be reinstated. They brought a stoup of ale and then took it back and asked him if he'd prefer wine. Their manner was velvet but he still had to wait.

He tried not to think about what was going on down the corridor. The pain in his head was like a sledgehammer. He had to report back to Knollys after this. He doubted whether he could keep going long enough. Then he thought of what was happening elsewhere in the building and forced himself to stand upright.

He went to the door. He looked out. The sledgehammer continued its work. Someone offered him a bench to sit on. He let his mind wander.

Back when he first started on this path he had had to go to Eltham while the king was in residence.

It was some piece of information either genuine or planted, designed to put fear in the king as he later understood. They were always doing it. Coming up with stories to force the young king into fear. Out of malice. Out of a misguided sense of fun. Horseplay of a cerebral kind. Bullying. They fed stories of assassins caught and punished. Creating first fear then gratitude. The king was played all ways. He did not know who to trust. It made him dependent on anyone who smiled kindly, never knowing from which direction the enemy would approach.

It was said he always sat with his back to a wall.

He had been kept waiting then as well. It was the theme of his life it seemed. De Vere was alive in those days. He came up to him and asked, 'Have you reported this to Sir Robert Knollys?'

Chandler shook his head. 'There are reasons I cannot do that. There's – nothing I can prove,' he faltered. And suddenly he had no idea what he was doing here. It was all a mistake. He had no proof of anything. He had talked his way inside the palace, sure he was doing the right thing. Young, so naive in those days. It seemed important. When he was about to stand before the king himself he felt like a fool.

Nothing but words whispered behind a hand and his own surmisings.

'Who sent you?'

'No one, your grace. I am acting alone.'

A tall, fair man emerged from the shadows where he had been listening and came towards him.

De Vere dug him in the back. 'Kneel, sot-wit,' he hissed. 'It's the king.'

He fell to his knees and stared at a pair of pale kid-skin boots within inches of his face. 'Thank you, Rodric Chandler,' said a voice above his head as if to remind himself of the name. Then a hand reached out and encouraged him to his feet. He felt the king take him by both hands and hold them for a moment. Checking for knives, he imagined. 'You followers of St Serapion have a strong belief in the value of self-sacrifice. A soul for a soul. I admire you and thank you for your loyalty. Your information has been noted. You may go now. Make sure they feed you before you leave.'

He had been about the same height as King Richard and for a moment they had looked unguardedly into each other's eyes. The king's had alertness that had nothing to do with what he was saying. Chandler had an overwhelming feeling that he was a man who knew he was cornered but had no resources to deal with the more brutal forms that treachery could take. He was too fine. Too gentle. His safety lay in vigilance and the loyalty of his closest companions.

For a moment he had longed to put out a hand in brotherhood but then, unlike Wat Tyler, he remembered who he was. Making a deep bow he backed from the royal presence and de Vere followed him, slipping some gold coins into his hand as he ushered him out. He found himself somehow or other in an outer courtyard looking at the sky.

There was a crescent moon. He stared up at it for some time. He could hear a choir singing in a distant cloister with a faint, elysian sweetness that made him want to sob.

'You did bloody what?' Archer was aghast when he told him what he had done. 'They let you in?'

'I sent my badge in first.'

'What did he say to you?'

'Not much.'

'At least they let you out again.'

'Except that now I think there's somebody following me.'

'What do you bleeding expect, you gormless sot-wit?' Archer, slimmer in those days, got up and began to pace back and forth across the tavern floor and one or two people glanced up, expecting a fight. Ignoring them he went to the door and peered out. When he came back in he said, 'Cove in a fustian cloak?'

'Might be. A boat set out just after mine when I crossed back to this side. It pulled in at the same quay. I thought I saw somebody coming up the hill after me. Keeping well in under the eaves of the houses. When I stopped, so did he. Instead of leading him back to where I live I sent you that message.' He had found a ragged boy who was willing to seek out Archer for the price of a coin.

'At least you didn't let him trail you to my Guildhall. I thank you for that.' Despite his words he had given Chandler a reproving look.

Now he had no idea why the memory should flood back in such vivid detail. Was he making the same mistake all over again, only this time pledged to the opposing side? And, most pressing question of all, who had sought to knock a warning into him – and for what purpose?

He jerked to his feet when they called his name. Then he followed the guard to meet the prisoner.

FORTY-TWO

The Master is sitting at the table near the window where he likes to work. He greets me as I go through with the basket of produce from the market.

'I got a good price today, Master.' I stop in the doorway and look back. 'They're selling things off.'

He gets up from his chair. 'I trust you always to get a good price, Mattie. May I call you Mattie, Matilda?'

I curtsey. 'You may, Master.'

He reaches out and pretends to pull an egg from behind my ear which he produces with a great flourish. It's not a real one. It's one of those heavy marble ones you can get and I say, 'You heard me coming in. You already had that in your hand,' and he says, 'There's no tricking a Guelderland girl, is there?' And then we both laugh. He's such a sweet old fool. I believe he's flirting with me. I know it's just a tease and a kindness to show he likes me. I tell him about the latest rumours going the rounds and he shakes his head.

Adam is standing at his desk and looks across. He makes no comment.

FORTY-THREE

They were keeping him in a small cell, more of a crossing place between two adjoining corridors, but same stone, same echoes, same sense of pain and death and punishment as ever.

Chandler greeted the prisoner in what little Welsh he knew and he raised his head and replied in border English. It soon became clear that he could tell him nothing about Glyn Dwr. He spat at the name. It transpired, or so he would have him believe, that he was on the road to visit his kin, wool suppliers living in Petty Wales down by one of the quays below the bridge. He didn't know why he had been dragged from his horse and brought here. He didn't know anything. Yes, he had seen a huge army going in the opposite direction but it was nothing to do with him and he had carried on his journey until he had been picked up by a group of fellows in red and gold.

'Do you not know whose colours those are?' Chandler asked him.

He jigged up and down with nerves. 'I didn't then but I do now, brother.'

'So you saw Lancaster's army going towards Wales?'

'Did I?'

'Didn't you?'

'It's nothing to me,' he said, trying defiance but without much conviction. He was in terror of what was about to happen to him.

Of course he knew Glyn Dwr. He might not know of his immediate plans but he surely knew something. Bolingbroke might be leading his army into a trap. The Welsh would support Richard. What if the whole of Wales rose up?

He saw at once why his master was worried. Chandler turned to the guards and when he was out of earshot said, 'Free him. Escort him to the house of his kin and if they vouch for him, leave him there.'

A watch would be set to note who went in and who came out. Soon the Welsh supporters of the king would all be known.

He went back to tell him they were letting him go. 'The lying churl couldn't thank me enough,' Chandler remarked to the guards as he left.

FORTY-FOUR

I was chopping cabbage in the scullery with its squinted view into the garden and must have been singing under my breath because when the Master comes in he asks, 'What is that ditty you're singing, Mattie?'

'It's one I picked up in the market.' I turn to face him and sing it again, as much as I can remember.

"*A heron is up and took his flight*
And in the north he did alight
And thus what every man do say—
The steel colt with him he brings—
There is but wonder and everything
To see him thus to play . . ."

'I haven't quite got the words and there's more but it doesn't make a lot of sense anyway. Something about a fox.'

'Do you know what it means?'

'It doesn't mean anything. It's a nonsense rhyme. It's about a colt and a king heron and some other creatures.'

'The fox,' he says, 'and other fowl many and more.'

'I didn't think you'd know it.'

He gives me an odd look. 'Do you know what an allegory is, Mattie?'

I shake my head.

'It's when one thing is talked about as if it's something else. The horse or colt means Thomas Arundel and the heron is Henry Bolingbroke.'

'And the fox?'

'It used to mean the duke of Gloucester, Edward of Woodstock, because of the fox's brush he used to hang from his lance, but sometimes it means a heretic and we are enjoined to hunt them down . . . or so it is held in some quarters.' He gives me another odd look and goes out.

I think, once I can read, I'll know about allegory and foxes and herons. I'll learn about the secret meanings in things.

FORTY-FIVE

Archer was sitting in the Fleece when Chandler left the White Tower. 'Where were you last night?' he greeted him. 'Your housekeeper turned up on my doorstep. She was going out of her mind. She said you hadn't come home. She feared you'd been attacked again.'

'I had something to do. It's none of her business.'

Archer gave him a thoughtful glance. 'Was it something to do with you-know-what? We have to end it now. You must know that.'

Chandler did not reply.

Archer continued after a pause, 'There's more to it than we suspected. You're right about that.' He leaned forward. 'We have to let it go. I've been told to tell you so.'

Chandler couldn't blame Archer for wanting out. He had a lot to lose. More than Chandler himself who, to be honest, had nothing.

After weighing his words he didn't ask who had warned Archer off. He knew he wouldn't tell him anyway. Instead he tried appealing to his sense of chivalry. 'Don't give up on her, Archer. She can't die in vain. Those brutes can't be allowed to get away with it.'

The coroner gazed across the table for a long, pensive moment. Then he said, 'I see death every day. It means everything and nothing. In the end it doesn't matter how it comes. Come it will. For us all. Ashes to ashes.'

He cupped both hands then spread his fingers as if ashes were falling unseen from between them to earth.

Now I am truly on my own, thought Chandler, with a jolt. He wondered who had put the fear into his old friend. It was not like him to give up on anything, especially if he suspected the dark despoiling of innocence.

He called to the ale-wife to refill their mugs. They clashed them in brotherhood but he knew now it meant nothing.

FORTY-SIX

Adam is copying with his head bent, sitting so still he might be asleep apart from the careful movement of his hand. Sunlight slants into the chamber but he works in a wedge of shadow.

'Can you see well enough there, Adam? Would you like me to help you move your things to another corner?'

'I'm all right as I am.' He does not look up. 'The Master is still out.'

'So he is.' Head bent. 'Adam?'

A small sigh. 'What is it?'

'I want to ask you something.'

A bee buzzes into the chamber from outside, circles twice then buzzes out again. 'Adam?'

At last he lifts his head. 'What?'

I go right up to him. 'I really want to ask you something.'

'So you said.'

'Oh, I won't bother. I can see I'm disturbing you.' I drop him a curtsey. 'Forgive me.'

'Mattie,' he calls before I reach the door. 'You have disturbed me now. You know you have. You've got my attention. The least you can do is tell me what's on your mind. I don't promise to answer but if it's a reasonable request I'll try.' He lays down his sharpened quill on its little wooden rest, places his elbows on his knees and gazes at me with a touch of irritation. 'You've got two minutes.'

'Promise you won't laugh?'

'Certainly I won't promise. I laugh when I choose.'

I pull a grotesque face at him for his meanness and he grins. Emboldened I say, 'I want you to teach me how to read.' I fold my arms across my chest, daring him to mock.

Instead he frowns.

'I heard the Master talking about a Frenchwoman called Madame de Pisan. He sounded in awe of her. I thought if he can be in awe of a woman she must be important. She's not a queen or a duchess or anything. She must be important in her own right. I want to find out why.'

'She's a writer at the French court. The daughter of an astrologer to Charles V. A widow. She sent her son to the earl of Salisbury's household as his ward. He's twelve or so, I believe. She doesn't write chronicles as such but more the sort of thing the Master likes. And she makes a living from it. That's what gains his respect.'

He puts his head on one side. 'So you want to impress the Master?'

'You think I'm mad.'

'Somewhat.' But then he smiles again. 'I can deal with young madwomen. I assume they're all like you where you come from?'

'I don't know that. It's years since I was in Nijmegen. I can scarcely remember it. My cousins are there. I can remember them. But the point is I really want to read.'

He turns back and picks up his quill. 'I still can't imagine why.'

'I'll tell you why. Another reason. This is the second. The Master called me Pertelote the other day. I want to know why. Is she good and clever?'

'She's a hen.'

I can't believe I've heard him aright. 'With feathers?'

'They usually have feathers, except when they're ready for the pot.'

I must look bewildered because he roars with laughter. 'Do you still want to read?'

'More than ever!' I retort. 'How dare he!'

'No, no, it's good. It's a compliment. They were real people only being written about as if they were poultry.'

'You mean like an – an allegory?'

He looks startled. 'Yes, if you like. Pertelote was queen of the yard. A sensible woman. One the vainglorious cock of the walk ignored at his peril. It nearly cost him his life—' He broke off then and said, 'You must never see too much in what you read. They're stories. They're written to amuse.'

'The Bible is written to instruct,' I say, stung to hear him talking to me as if I'm a child.

'Well, it's not written in English much so we needn't think about that.' He looks annoyed and bends his head over his quarto of vellum and I'm cut off from him. Back to the kitchen for me.

I mutter something like, 'So will you or won't you?' Not waiting for the humiliation of no answer I go back to my chores and snatch up a knife.

I'm heating up with rage. Am probably still like that when he comes in behind me and says, 'Here. Copy this. You can use the ink on my table but don't spill it or I'll take your head off. Find a place well away. I don't want my work spoiling.' He holds out a piece of much-scraped vellum with a curly shape at the top. The ink is still wet. 'It's called an "a" and you'll learn your ABC before you go further.'

I take it in a dream. 'You are strange, Adam. I thought you—'

'Shut up.' He turns and goes back into the other chamber.

I watch him for a moment from the doorway as he settles at his sloping desk and sets to work again and then I too set to work.

FORTY-SEVEN

To Archer's question he could have admitted that he had gone out to Barking Abbey again and had deliberately not mentioned this to Beata. He had hobbled his horse in the little copse as before and walked on into the village where he lurked about wondering how he could get in to speak to Sister Mercy again. He was more than half-convinced he was on a fool's errand.

Sitting in a corner of the alehouse with a view of the abbey gates he made himself inconspicuous enough to find out that one of his fellow drinkers supplied firewood to the abbey. Some pleasantry got them into conversation. He found out that the nuns paid up promptly but that he, like all the other suppliers, was never allowed any further inside than the outer court of the farm buildings.

'We've no idea what goes on in there but we can guess!' He gave a knowing laugh. 'It's run as a prison for them young lasses. But what's their crime? Being virgins? Waste of good maidenheads. They keep 'em till their spirit breaks then they're no use to nobody.

And what's it for? So they're pure enough to offer up a few useless prayers for the souls of men rich enough to buy a place in heaven?'

'You'll get yourself done for Lollardry, mate.' The men laughed.

'I'll supply the wood not stand in the middle of it whilst it burns,' the first man said.

'It'll never come to that. Not here. Not in England. We don't burn folk for their ideas,' said somebody else and another round was bought.

The conversation turned to other matters and Chandler let it flow round him as they didn't seem to mind him and he even contributed an anecdote or two himself. And then his ears sharpened when one of them, a carter by trade, harked back to the first point about the abbey being run like a prison. It was something that plainly troubled him.

'At least they pay over the top,' he told Chandler when he noticed his interest. 'Take the other night,' he continued. 'All I had to do was drive into the City after curfew. They had a pass or summat and we were let through even though I told them I doubted we would be.'

'Were you taking something in?' asked Chandler. It was probably untaxed fish from down river.

'Flesh,' replied the man succinctly.

'Beef?'

'Human.'

The others jeered.

'It's this young lass he had to take in to one of their priories,' his companion explained to Chandler. 'I reckon he fancied her! He won't shut up about her.'

'What happened?' Chandler asked in as lacklustre a tone as he could manage.

'Nowt happened,' somebody jibed.

'That's what's narking him!' somebody else remarked amid further derision.

Chandler bent his head towards the man who looked shame-faced and muttered, 'They may be right, I won't deny it. Pretty, she was, about sixteen maybe. She was lovely, like a little angel, but she was in a terrible state. I had to drive her and two other nuns – like prison guards they were – and one of them, a big bruiser, gripped the young 'un by the arm all the while, half-carrying her out to the cart and getting her settled. "She's sick," she explained. "We must get her to the City as soon as possible." So I drove like a fury and they opened the gates for us and I left her there in one of them yards near the priory.'

'Do you know which priory it was?' Chandler asked.

'All Hallows. Everybody knows that place. It's part of this one. I thought, she'll be all right there.'

He did not look convinced however and Chandler risked asking him, 'What makes you doubt it?'

'Their manner,' he said at once. 'She was only half-conscious, eyelids fluttering, giving little moans now and then but they were rough with her to my mind, pushing her to shut up and keep quiet. No kindness in them. I drove fast but as soft as I could.'

'I'm sure she would appreciate that,' murmured Chandler.

A few more questions told him little more. The novice had been left at All Hallows. A porter, a monk maybe, a man certainly, with his hood covering his face, had come out at the sound of the cart. One of the nuns had paid the carter off then, and reluctantly, he had returned to Barking clutching a special pass to hand to the gatekeeper on his way.

'At Aldgate?' asked Chandler, to have it confirmed.

The carter nodded.

Keeping his thoughts to himself he wondered how he would manage to speak to Mercy.

In order to get inside he chose the direct approach. Finishing his drink he strode across the street to the main gate and pulled the bell rope. To his astonishment the porteress allowed him into the entrance lobby and went to fetch someone. A wizened old nun was brought out. She gave him a suspicious look through eyes embedded in a nest of wrinkles but when he showed her a replica of Swynford's seal that usually got him into places she gave him a frightened glance and went to fetch someone else.

Before he could make himself comfortable he was invited into the cell where guests were received. The grille flew open.

A dark shape swathed in black stood in silhouette on the other side. It could have been anybody.

'And you are?'

He told her.

'Sister Mercy will be allowed to speak to you in a moment.' He did not recognize the voice. The anonymous figure disappeared and the grille closed again.

In little more than a minute it opened and Mercy was standing there.

Chandler went right up to the grille and spoke in a low voice, not that he imagined her keeper would not be able to hear, but to reassure her. 'Last time I was here with the City coroner Sir Arnold Archer you told us that you had entered the abbey on the same day as the murdered novice Eloise.'

Mercy, biting her lip, murmured, 'That is so.'

'For that reason we believe you may be able to help us further. Can you tell me what you know about her family?'

'Only that she was well-born and brought a considerable dowry to the abbey.'

'Like yourself?'

'I'm the fifth and youngest daughter of a shire knight. Eloise had different connections. She was friendly with Sister Margaret, daughter of the old duke of Lancaster . . .' She leaned closer, 'You can find all this out through our novice-mistress.' Her eyes held his with a suggestion of a meaning she could not utter.

'You've planted a useful idea in my mind.' He stressed the word planted and hoped she was alert enough to pick it up.

'I'm glad to be of service, brother.' She withdrew. A hand came out to shut the grille.

As before. The wade through the water. The thick-set hedge. The pale face.

'We are no nearer tracking down her murderer. You have more you can tell me.'

She lowered her glance. 'Somebody might overhear us.'

'Can't you get out? What are the others doing?'

'It's our free time. They're resting, mostly, or praying.'

'Crawl through the hedge. I'll move off a little way down river towards those trees.' He turned away and soon heard somebody slithering down the bank. He went to sit by the water's edge where she joined him. The first thing he said was, 'I do not promise to free you. I fear it is beyond my power. It's for your family to buy your freedom.'

To his surprise she slipped a hand through his arm and edged a little closer. 'I believe you might rescue me and I have no fear of becoming a vagabond nun if it comes to it. I haven't taken my vows yet. My family will not buy my freedom. They want me to stay here. It is to their advantage to have me remain. We are no longer on speaking terms because of it. My mother is dead and my father has remarried a woman who thinks only of the status I bring by being here at one of the royal abbeys. I have renounced them utterly.'

He turned to read the truth of this in her eyes. 'So, is freedom your price for telling me what you know?'

She dropped her glance, in shame, as he might have imagined, but he suspected it was to give her time to work out her reply. A long silence followed during which she stared down at her fingers, twisting them in her lap, and Chandler turned to stare stonily across the river towards the far bank. Nothing could be heard but the gurgling of the outgoing waters and a blackbird singing in the thicket.

Eventually she said, 'You could easily tell me you already know who our visitors were and put my words at naught. This might be a trap to find out if I know what Eloise feared.'

'If it is and I'm not to be trusted you're already in it up to your pretty neck. What do you imagine your abbess would say if I informed her you'd begged me to help you break your vows?'

'She'd beat me until the blood ran.'

To his astonishment tears began to trickle down her cheeks. He took hold of the hand she had looped through his arm and stroked the back of it. 'Was the visitor sent by Bolingbroke? Everybody knows the old duke, Gaunt, used to be the abbey's patron—'

But she was shaking her head with tears still sparkling in her eyes. 'No, it was not a Lancastrian. It was someone who wore no blazon—'

'Secret, then?'

'Yes. The Lancastrian couriers are well known to us and always make sure we know who sent them so we know how privileged we are.'

'Are you going to tell me who it was?'

She looked away. 'I don't know.'

'Don't know who it was or don't know whether you'll tell me?'

'He wasn't a Lancastrian.' She set her lips a little. 'I'm fairly sure about that.'

He waited and when she failed to reply he said, 'Is this all you have to tell me?'

Again the shaken head but she added, 'The Frenchman was here and I believe their meeting was contrived.'

Chandler looked away and then, almost as an afterthought – a fact that later amazed him – asked, 'I suppose you didn't recognize this Frenchman?'

'Of course—'

'Of course?'

'It was the usual fellow from Orleans, from le duc, unmistakable by the splendour of his garments and the harness and pedigree of his horse. He often comes.'

Orleans again.

The court of le duc d'Orléans was where Bolingbroke had chosen to spend his exile. He was a French aristocrat on a par with Aumerle in his proximity to his country's crown. Unlike the English sons of King Edward III who had, one by one, been eliminated by death except for the duke of York, the French duke had several brothers to contend with should he have designs on the French crown.

'There can be no mistake about him then.'

'None. I was standing behind a stable door about as far from him as I was from you when you came into the guest chamber and spoke to me through the grille.'

'Did he see you?'

'I took care to make sure he did not.'

'And had you leave to be in the stables?'

'You know I had not!' A pause. 'I like horses. I sometimes assuage my grief by going to talk to them and decide which one will help me when I decide to escape to freedom.'

'Mercy,' he murmured, more as an exclamation than a name. He unlinked their arms and put one of his own round her shoulders. What the hell was Orléans' man doing nosing round Barking Abbey? It would not be to say his prayers. And who had he come to meet? 'Did you get any idea why he was here, this unknown fellow?'

He felt Mercy tighten her grip on his arm. 'You must take me with you.'

'I made no promises.'

'You must! If you don't I'll . . .'

He gave a derisive smile. Eloise must surely have told her what had been said during this secret assignation. He decided to attack. 'You have something to learn in the art of bargaining, Mercy. To make sure you get what you want you must have something worth offering in exchange.'

'If you don't help me I'll . . .'

'You'll what? Make up an even more outrageous pack of lies to tell me, about another mystery man?'

'It's all true and if you don't help me I'll throw myself in the river and my death will be enough to consign you to the flames of hell for ever!'

He could only give her a sardonic smile at such a threat and when she pushed away his arm and rose to her feet he did not restrain her.

'I mean it!' she threatened through clenched teeth.

'Can you swim?'

'No.'

'Then I don't advise it, not even as a gesture, because I have no intention of getting wet to fish you out.'

'You think I don't mean what I say? You're wrong! I shall drown myself because I have nothing left to live for!'

He watched without moving as she stumbled down the sloping bank towards the water's edge. When she did not stop at the brink he stared in astonishment as, with only a small whimper, she spread out both arms as if to embrace a lover, then, with the billowing folds of her habit lifted by the air, she flung herself into the water, hitting the surface with a little scream then sinking from view under a surge of foam.

He watched for her to rise to the surface and strike out for the bank but nothing happened. The waves subsided. With a sigh he rose to his feet and went to look into the depths, expecting to see her floating under the surface while she held her breath to frighten him. Instead he saw the bundled-up robes caught by the current floating swiftly downstream.

She rose to the surface for a moment, gasping and spluttering but making no effort to swim or help herself. He caught a glimpse of panic on her face before she sank again.

The thick wool of her habit was becoming waterlogged, he noticed. Instead of buoying her up it was dragging her under.

Forced into action he pulled off his own robes down to his

under-britches and with a deep breath plunged into the water. It was surprisingly warm and he struck out to where she had disappeared. There was no sign of her. He dived underneath and opened his eyes into a green world of swaying weed. Nothing. No girl floundering and gasping for breath. Nothing but an undisturbed forest of trailing weed growing near the bank and further out only darkness.

He swam around for a moment, came up for air, then dived down again, following the current with strong strokes until, staring through the misty water, and almost out of air, he spotted something drifting beneath the silver surface.

He came up for air again, swam a few strokes to where he had caught that glimpse then sank under the water. His groping hands at last closed over something, fabric, flesh, was it an arm? A leg? He grasped it and dragged it to the surface.

Her face was white and her eyes were closed but as soon as the fresh air reached her she gave a gasp and started to struggle. 'Keep still. I've got you.' He swam back with her to the bank and gripped a handful of grass to hold them steady until she recovered enough to scramble ashore.

'You really can't swim?'

Between coughs and splutters she said, 'I told you so.'

When they were sitting safely on the bank he said, 'You'll have to tell them you fell in while picking cresses for their supper.'

She was shivering so much, partly from shock he suspected, and also with fear at what she would now have to face when she re-entered the precinct dripping wet, that she had lost all her sauciness. He felt sorry that her ploy had failed and that she knew it. 'I'll do my best to get your release so you don't have to spend the rest of your life here. At least you haven't taken your final vows yet.'

'Soon! I shall have to take them soon! Time's running out!' She looked full at him for the first time since he had fished her out. Water was still running down her face. 'You saved my life. Maybe that's the most I should expect from you?'

'It's not much if all I have saved you for is a living death.'

Her glance slid to his bare chest and lower still to his wet britches. Her own garments were equally sodden with river water and slowly she began to lift her habit over her head. He could do nothing else but assist. He watched as she squeezed water from it then spread it out in the sun as if expecting it to dry. Her undershift was of the thinnest voile and clung to her limbs as she moved.

'At least I won't trail water all over their shiny tiles.'

'At least there's that,' he agreed.

She turned to him. As if coming to a decision she reached up and placed a hand on each of his shoulders and brought her mouth close to his.

'No, Mercy,' he murmured.

'I will do anything for you. But I can't tell you what I don't know. Promise me you'll come back for me? I'll wait and watch for you. I may be able to find out who the visitor was from someone.'

He detached her hands from his shoulders and folded them between his fingers, there imprisoned. Cozened by a novice? Bemused, he admitted to himself in shame, he was aroused by the idea of taking her here and now in the green shade of the woods, because she wanted him and was offering herself – and he gave a heartfelt sigh at the thought of such a bargain.

'Be a good girl, Mercy. This is not the way to seal a bargain. I'll have a word with someone I know to find out if we can prise you forth according to law and due procedure. You will not be the first young woman who fears that the convent life is not for her.'

She gave a small giggle. 'Law? Due procedure? I look at your mouth, Brother Chandler, and see that the law means nothing to you. I believe you to be reckless, a law unto yourself. One little kiss is all I ask. Then I will try to find out more and do exactly as you wish'

'You're a bad girl and no mistake.' His lips touched hers lightly and then, almost of their own accord, pressed more firmly over her own and he felt her mouth open and the tip of her tongue come out to meet his.

Before he rode back to town she said, 'I'll contrive to come out to All Hallows when they go to fetch her body back the day after tomorrow.'

'I'll be there. I'll look out for you.'

'Your black eyes are yellow now. Not much of an improvement!'

With that she had crawled back through the hedge as soon as he told her it was clear. It took only a moment then he waded back to where his horse was hobbled and rode on into the next village where he found an inn for the night. With his riding cloak over his habit there were no questions concerning wet garments. The bed-straw was clean and free from fleas.

He was back in the City shortly after prime. He went straight to see Archer. And that's when he told him Beata had been round. And Chandler had discovered he was now on his own.

FORTY-EIGHT

'**M**attie!' The Master calls me. He is sitting at his desk where he is writing as usual.

I go through from the scullery and he turns with a little frown. 'Can you go into the market and pick up a few rumours for me? Find out where Bolingbroke and his army are by now.'

'They say he's not coming to London after all.'

'Yes, but where is he going, that's the point.'

'Trust me, Master.'

I'm glad to get out and have a gossip. The Master's going to get corns on his bum if he sits in that chair much longer. Still, he has his work to do. I snatch up my basket, stuff my hair back under my coif, and am out.

First off I see the spy. He still looks as if he's been in a fight. I knew he was reckless when I first saw him up close. Some think he's a good fellow. Others pull down their hoods and make off whenever they see him. I'm not sure which camp I'm in myself. He makes me shiver but I'm drawn to him the way a blank space on a piece of vellum invites a scribe to insert some words. I'm on letter 'H' now. H for Henry. His name on everybody's lips this morning as they queue up for fish and field peas. The spy has disappeared before I reach the first stall.

'So he's definitely not coming to London after all that talk?' I ask Annie doling out the peas into my straw cone.

'That's what we hear, lass. Praise God. We don't want militia men roaming the City.'

'Wouldn't the mayor have kept them out?'

'Him and whose army?' She cackles with scorn. 'Them aldermen would be as much use as a fart in a snowstorm.'

'Maybe Sir Richard will come to the rescue with his cat,' I reply and she cackles even more as if it's the height of wit and repeats what I've said to Izzie among her cheeses who laughs so loud she shows the gaps in her teeth before passing it on to her neighbour. I like these market women. They're always the first to know what's happening and they treat the follies of men with the contempt they deserve.

'Always bloody fighting,' Izzie says with her usual sniff. Then, 'Cheese!' she bawls. 'New cheese! Tasty cheese from Kent! Come and get it!'

I buy a big hunk because I know the Master likes it when it's fresh and crumbly like this. She cuts off a piece for my own self to eat. Feeding a child. I remind her of her grand-daughter, a great lolloping girl of fifteen she tells me, and adds, as always, 'Fingers crossed she turns out like you, pretty doll.' She turns to bawl out her wares again. 'Come and get it! Don't miss out! When it's gone, it's gone!'

I notice the spy again, strolling through the crowds, his saintly, suffering, sceptical expression much the same as always apart from the fading bruises from two black eyes. I cannot help staring at him. He makes me think of a time on the edge of memory or out of a dream from long ago.

He notices me. We pass deliberately close to each other but do not acknowledge the other's presence. We pretend indifference. He strolls away. I expect he's picking up news like me. Who says what. A black cross beside their name. Death.

I start to follow him to amuse myself. The spy spied on. It makes me smile. Mistaking my smile for them one or two people smile back. Soon he will turn and our eyes will meet and I will know he knows I've been following him. He will know. And then? . . . I recall my purpose. Best place for the latest news is the Guildhall steps.

I see at once that something terrible has happened because people are breaking up into little groups talking, talking in low desperate voices, their faces stricken, unbelieving. A woman is weeping. Children cling to their mothers' skirts and become solemn. Everybody is saying they know now where Bolingbroke has led his army.

He has taken them into Cheshire, into the king's own heartland.

This is not all. Terrible stories are filtering back about a massacre. They are too vivid not to be true. I try not to hear. My eyes are watering at the thought of the little children and their mothers cut down by the sword. Their terror-stricken cries. Their vain attempts to protect themselves. It is too horrible to contemplate. Too evil to be true.

Everybody falls quiet to listen in a kind of stunned silence as a courier comes out at the top of the steps and begins to read from a scroll.

After he stops speaking he pauses for a moment, staring down at the words as if he cannot believe what he has just read out. Then very slowly he rolls it up and walks back to where the guildsmen are clustered.

Sir Richard Whittington pats him on the shoulder. The others look as if they do not know what to do. One or two turn away in a huff as if they believe he is lying. Plainly shocked, the rest of them drift back inside just as a voice from the crowd shouts, 'Long live King Richard!' A subdued cheer follows. Nobody knows where the king is at this moment. Is he still in Ireland? Or is he on the sea on his way home? When will he land? Has he landed? The recent storms have abated. He must have landed by now. Surely he's landed. Nobody knows.

'To be hoped he puts a stop to this latest – if it's true,' says one of the bystanders.

'Surely,' I say, 'if the mayor has had it read out it must be true?'

'How can we know?' somebody else objects. 'It might be a pack of lies. For Lancaster to lay waste a piece of England? To cry havoc against an entire county? To kill unarmed English folk in their beds? To burn them out of their houses? It's past all belief.'

There are murmurs of agreement.

Somebody else mutters, 'The king will weep at the thought of such woes inflicted on his people.'

When I get back to the Master, still sitting at his desk of course, I tell him all I've heard. 'Many doubt the truth of the courier who brought the news,' I finish.

'But they haven't killed the messenger,' he replies mysteriously and goes back to his writing.

FORTY-NINE

Chandler was as stunned as everybody else by the latest news concerning the Cheshire men. It must be the bowmen, he thinks, they must have refused to come out for Bolingbroke. They must have remained loyal to the king. So, simple-minded fellow that he is, Bolingbroke gets his revenge by wreaking havoc on their women and children. He is a man who reacts to events like a caged animal when loosed. Maybe Arundel can tame him?

Unconvinced that any good can come from that quarter he threaded his way through the silent and appalled citizens until he found himself near the Dow.

He stood for some time, staring into the filthy waters. Who had the Orléans fellow met? Eventually someone hobbled up beside him and tugged his sleeve. It was the gravedigger from Portsoken. They exchanged caustic remarks about the news. The old fellow took him by the arm, dirty fingernails again on Chandler's white garments.

'Listen, brother, I have something for you.' A quick glance down at the muddy waters. 'I know you want to find out who did this terrible thing.' He nodded towards the beck.

Chandler bent his head.

'No, not here. I can't be seen talking to you but there's somebody you need to meet. Come out before curfew when you've finished at your chantry. It won't take long. Meet me here.' He walked off with just one backward glance over his shoulder.

FIFTY

'So, Adam, what are we supposed to think? It's too horrible to imagine. Do you think it's true?'

'Most likely.' He is at his most morose.

'But what can we do?'

'Bear witness. That's what I shall do.' He picks up his quill and bends over his work.

Soon I shall know what he's writing because when he goes out into the yard to have a piss I shall come in here and take a look.

Bear witness? What does he mean by that?

FIFTY-ONE

'That was a full congregation,' Martin remarked as he shut the vestry door behind them after compline and followed Chandler down the nave towards the darkening street.

'No doubt everyone is worrying about whether their own house is going to be put to the torch.'

Martin looked shocked. 'Or maybe they're simply concerned for the fate of their fellow-countrymen and want to offer up prayers for their poor souls?'

'Mayhap.'

'This must lead to outright war, Chandler. As soon as the king returns we must pray that evil devil will get his final comeuppance. And amen, say I.'

With Martin's prayer in his ears, Chandler made his way towards the Dow. He had not quite reached the bank where the gravedigger last spoke to him when the old fellow appeared from out of the shadow.

'Here!' His hoarse whisper invited Chandler to follow him down a narrow alley between the houses. Aware that he had a precautionary knife tucked in his wristband, Chandler followed and found himself in a small yard where an ale-wife was plying her trade from one of the cottages. It was dark by now and flames from a smoking brazier were the only light. He was aware that three or four men were hovering near an upturned beer cask, faces lurid in the flames, but the gravedigger ignored them and led him straight inside to a back room. At once someone tailed them in. With only one candle stuck in a bottle it was too dark to see who it was but Chandler checked that his knife was where he could get at it.

'I have information you may want,' greeted the stranger. Evidently he knew who Chandler was already.

'How much?' Chandler replied, reaching for his pouch. He proffered a few pieces of silver. The man grunted, took them, counted each coin separately then dropped them into his own money pouch.

'This is the gong-master who puts the night soil into the Dow,' the gravedigger belatedly explained. 'Let him tell you something.'

'About that little novice,' says the gong-master. 'I was about to lead my team about their work that morning her body was found but somebody told us to clear off. It was scarcely light, being before prime.'

'Why did they do that?'

'They wanted the place to themselves. We all worked that out. They had something special to dump in the drain.'

'The body?'

The man gave a derisive snigger. 'That's what I'm telling you.'

'So who was this person who warned you off?'

The man held out his hand again. Chandler obliged.

'I've no idea—'

He was just about to ask for his silver back when the gong-master added, 'But I can give you a close picture of him and there'll be no mistaking him when you see him next.'

'Where am I likely to see him?'

'At the Earl Marshal's office.'

'What?'

In the gloom Chandler was aware that the man was staring at him with a look of triumph at the surprise he had created. The gravedigger at his shoulder nodded. 'You can trust him, brother.'

Chandler doubted it but he pressed further. 'What makes you think he came from there?'

'Because one of my men had already come across him.'

'He's sure of this?'

'He's got the scars to prove it.'

'So he's trying to get even, is he?'

'Ask him yourself. He's back there.' He nodded towards the yard. 'I'm as sure of him as I'm sure I've supped Dolly's good ale.' He raised his flagon, emptied it and held it upside down.

Chandler handed some coins to the gravedigger. 'And for yourself and this other fellow.' When he had gone back into the outer chamber he said, 'The Earl Marshal is appointed by King Richard. I believe young Aumerle of York is the recipient of the honour this time round. I suppose that means you're of the Lancastrian persuasion yourself?'

The gong-master looked affronted. 'Not me. Never. I'm for King Richard and the True Commons. If you can make sense of it then I've earned my silver and done my bit.'

'It makes no sense for a man from the York household to want to dump a body of a novice from Barking Abbey in Dow Beck.'

'That's what I think. That's why I thought a better brain than mine should be in on it.'

The gravedigger shuffled back inside with a younger man at his heels and a paddle of ale for them all. There was a fresh scar down one side of the youth's face. Chandler thought it tactful not to ask. 'So you recognized this fellow who asked your master to keep out of the way the morning the novice's body was found?' he began.

The lad kept his head down and seemed too much in awe of Chandler to look up. Chandler picked up the candle and held it in its bottle close to the lad's face. 'I can see whether you're lying or not. Your master will tell you I can be generous when I hear the truth. And if I don't hear it, I'm generous in a different way.'

'Go on, lad. Tell him,' the gong-master urged.

With a terrified glance at Chandler, making him wonder about the state of the boy's soul, he said, 'I know him. That's right. Bastard porter at the Earl Marshal's palace on the Strand, right?'

'Did he tell you that?'

'Trying to put the fear on him, he was,' his master declared and spat into a corner of the chamber.

'What did he look like?' Chandler persisted.

'A big, red-haired fellow. You can't mistake him. Nasty mean little eyes. Hears all, says nowt—' He broke off for a moment to search for a sign of offence on Chandler's face as it was obvious the same could be said of a Tower spy, but then, emboldened by Chandler's calm demeanour he added, 'He wears a green capuchon. A red, bushy beard. A strapping fellow as I've said. A big belly. He gave me this, knowing I was unarmed.' He fingered his scar. 'Strike first, talk later, that's 'im. A right bastard. But I'm not trying to get back at him,' he added as an afterthought. 'It's only that I saw him talking to my master,' a glance for confirmation, 'and asked him what it was about, thinking there was some follow-up to this.' He touched his scar again.

'I told you we were being pulled from our work,' added the gong-master. 'And you wanted to know if we were still being paid.'

'And you said yes because we'd be back later to finish it.'

'That's about it,' added the gong-master. 'I trust that picture is enough to aid you in your task, brother?'

'As far as it goes . . .' He added, 'There can't be many men in the City of London who wear green capuchons.'

'No need to be sarcastic,' the gravedigger reproved.

They downed their ale in silence and Chandler realized it was time to leave.

FIFTY-TWO

Remembering the gong-master's doubtful compliment about his brain Chandler left the noisome drinking hole and set off back to his lodgings with a sense that he was walking through a thick fog. He believed the youth but his story made no sense. What was a York fellow doing down by the Dow at dawn with a body to dispose of? Did Aumerle know what was going on during his absence in Ireland?

There was no fog as a matter of fact. It was a clear night. So clear that when he glanced up at the high white wall of the gatehouse as he approached along Corn Hill his gaze was drawn to the narrow slit window of his chambers on the top floor. Inside a light flickered.

He reached the outside door unable to prevent the way it ground on its hinges then passed the, for once, silent chamber of his neighbour of the Heads, mounting the stone steps and entering his own apartment with some stealth. The place was in darkness. Something came scampering from his bedchamber and he realized it was Beata's kitten. He allowed the door to swing back to reveal the rest of his shadowy chamber. Nothing moved. He glanced behind the door. No one there either. He fumbled in the darkness for the tinder in the niche and lit a candle. Shadows leaped like devils but the chamber was empty.

He knew it was here that the light had shown itself. A glance towards Beata's door revealed that it was firmly closed. There was no sound from within. The kitten scratched at the door, mewing.

Another little piece to add to her mystery, he registered. He would bide his time. Sooner or later she would make a mistake that would not be ignored.

FIFTY-THREE

Without Archer to argue with and tell him he was a fool Chandler was forced to mull things over unassisted. There was plenty to trouble him.

The porter for instance, so-called. Did he exist? If he did he clearly had more duties than merely checking who came in and out from Aumerle's headquarters. Was murder part of his remit, and if so who had instructed him? Aumerle was in Ireland. Did he know what was going on behind his back? Was the so-called porter a traitor taking orders from the Lancasters? That seemed the most likely explanation.

As a story it wasn't as neat as Chandler would have liked. He could hear Archer mocking his logic.

'It's like this,' he would explain. 'The novice, as we've learned, heard something she shouldn't have. Maybe it was to Bolingbroke's detriment – on top of everything we've already heard of course—' he would hurry on, to avoid hearing Archer say, 'I told you so.' 'And thus,' he would continue, 'she was silenced. Now we have a witness claiming the presence of a possible perpetrator, a red-bearded fellow – unless he was merely roaming around Dow Beck for the mere pleasure of it and—'

'And this theory of yours depends on a) the existence of a red-bearded porter at the appropriate time and b) that he was bought behind Aumerle's back by Lancaster?'

'You can't say the latter is at all unlikely.'

'Granted. If the fellow exists.'

'That is a flaw,' he would agree.

And they would buy another ale apiece and all would be as before.

Lacking Archer's assistance he went on to consider the reason for Lancaster's involvement at all. It would be connected to his strategy for regaining his inheritance. Archer would no doubt demolish that too.

First, he would argue, Bolingbroke has no reason to imagine that his inheritance is forfeit. King Richard has not parcelled out his lands to his trusted followers as he did with the lands of the traitorous Gloucester. The Lancastrian inheritance was safely sitting there waiting for Bolingbroke to claim it as the new duke of Lancaster now his father was dead. The fact that he had been able to call out his standing army proved that.

Second, he might go on to argue, who was the stranger with the assignation with le duc d'Orléans' emissary? According to Mercy he was not the usual Lancastrian visitor she had seen before. Could it have been the red-bearded losel, perhaps? If so, it was clear he must be playing a double game and working for Bolingbroke.

At this point he would wave his arms and exclaim, 'Rodric, you know we know nothing. Let's leave it! We've been warned off. Let that be an end to it.'

Chandler stubbornly clung to what he knew. It was a weak point as to why Orléans might tell Aumerle's man anything. If Bolingbroke had confided another purpose for his invasion to le duc's emissary he would hardly be likely to blurt it out to one of Richard's closest allies. Not even for a goodly bribe – le duc was said to be the richest man in France and probably beyond bribes – it would have to be something so substantial as to make ordinary folks' eyes water. Calais? Something in Aquitaine? It was not to be thought. So unless Aumerle's man had been bought he must've been simply nosing around to see if there was any news he need take back to his king. None of it, he concluded, could be worth a murder.

When Mercy came into town for the requiem mass – if she was able to keep her word – he would persuade her to tell him more. He suspected that she already knew full well what had alarmed Eloise so much – for surely the novices would have talked the situation out to the nth degree? Isn't that what girls did?

FIFTY-FOUR

He decided he would take a stroll through Ludgate next morning and have a look at this porter, if he existed, although he found it hard to distrust the scarred lad whatever his motive. Even his master had gone along with his story without hesitation. There was no point in making up lies. Where would that get them?

Before he went anywhere he had to appear at his chantry for prime but when he arrived the vestry door was shut and he could hear Martin snoring lightly inside. Thinking it kinder to leave him to his slumbers, he hovered around to see if anyone was going to attend but when no one appeared he made his own brief, sardonic obsequies, drawn to do so by habit more than anything else, then set out for Ludgate. Even after all this he was still one of the first to exit the City.

Soon he found himself outside the town house of Aumerle which, as befitted its owner's absence, drowsed under an air of somnolence in the early morning heat. Even the porter's lodge was shuttered up. Undeterred, he took up a spot across the street outside a usefully located inn and, after a brief question to the ale-master to make sure he was sitting opposite the right place, he let the time pass until, patience rewarded, he saw the lodge door fly open and as if on cue a burly figure in a green capuchon stood looking out, arms folded across his chest. His beard was prodigiously red and his belly unmissable.

Counting on the fact that he would be unknown, Chandler got up from his place, pulled his hood half over his face, and shambled over.

'Alms, good sir?' he began.

Red Beard snarled something offensive and Chandler asked quickly, 'If no coin for a poor mendicant, sir, mayhap you'll be gracious enough to direct me to the priory of the beloved sisters of All Souls in the City?'

'Go through yon gate and head for the Tower. A blind man can't miss that. Then ask around. Their priory's hidden among a jumble of similar buildings.' His eyes narrowed. 'What do you want with them?'

'Alms, of course. I've heard they're wealthy women. And generous with it.'

As if regretting his help but offered an explanation he could understand, he grunted something about blood-sucking friars then went back inside his lodge and slammed the door.

Retracing his footsteps Chandler waited until he was within the City walls again before casually turning to glance back down the street. He was in time to see a youth slip hurriedly into a doorway. Smiling to himself he walked on and after a few yards turned down a back alley and, knowing the snickel ways as well as anybody, was soon confident that he had lost Red Beard's lad in the maze of back streets. When he reached a narrow laup across from All Hallows he observed the youth already lounging outside. He was casting an occasional puzzled glance up and down the street but remained at his post.

It told him as clearly as anything that Red Beard was guilty of something. Now all he had to do was find out what.

He edged out of sight and, finding the pathway that would lead between the houses to the drinking den the gravedigger had brought him to, soon emerged into the yard where the gong-master and his fellows hung out. He was pleased to find them back from getting rid of the night soil beyond the tideline according to the ordinances of the aldermen and their ale jars were already foaming. A large untidy woman with arms like hams was busy filling the last one when Chandler approached the master.

'That lad I spoke to last night—' he began but the group parted to reveal the youth skulking behind them. 'It's this—' Chandler beckoned him. 'I've checked your man with the red beard. A nasty customer. How did you cross him?'

The lad looked at his feet then stole a glance at Chandler, was reassured, and muttered, 'It was all over a coif.'

'That's not much to give you what he did.'

'White linen it was. What did he want with that? It was just floating there. Somebody must have chucked it out.'

'Maybe he wanted it for his girl?'

'Him?' The youth guffawed.

'Where were you when this happened?'

'In Dow Beck near Comberton's 'ouse. It's down—'

'I know where it is. He'd no right to smack you for that. He could have taken your eye out.' He slipped a coin into the lad's palm. 'And this was just before that young novice was found, poor child, was it?'

The lad looked at Chandler suspiciously. 'Are you saying it was her coif?' He gave a shudder. 'I wouldn't have touched it if I'd known.'

Listening to this the rest of the night-soil men seemed to have arrived at the opinion that the friar was not as bad as some made out – or that he was at least worth cultivating – and a brimming flagon was thrust into his hands. He had no choice but to pass the time with them but nobody said anything more to make him change his mind about going over to Comberton's as soon as he could.

FIFTY-FIVE

All Hallows. A requiem mass for the murdered novice. *Eternal rest give unto her.*

The place was well filled with the nuns from the priory and others he assumed had travelled from the mother-house at Barking. The array of bent heads looked identical from his place at the back. He decided to stay until they filed out with the coffin. With any luck she would find a way to leave the procession and come to him then.

The scent of beeswax filled the air. He was reminded of the prioress who came to see Archer and himself. From somewhere came the mingled sweetness of attar of roses.

Sanctus, sanctus, sanctus. Light eternal shine upon us. May the angels lead us. May the holy martyrs save us . . . Spare, O God, in kindness spare us . . . Doomed to flames of woe unbounded . . .

And so forth, he thought.

Comberton's had been interesting for only one reason. It had taken him only a minute to have a look at it before coming down to All

Hallows. As he had watched from under the eaves further upstream just about where he and Archer had stood contemplating the issue, a woman had appeared at the yard gate. She had turned to say something to someone inside. Then she hurried away without looking back. From her basket poked the head of a kitten. She had started to carry it around like that whenever she went out. It was Beata.

FIFTY-SIX

've just finished getting the Master's fresh fish when I notice a procession assembled outside All Hallows. Somebody standing by tells me it's for the novice who was murdered and thrown into Dowgate sluice. 'They're taking her back to her abbey, poor lass. She can't have been much older than you,' the woman tells me.

She looks me up and down then crosses herself.

I see the spy break away from the crowd and go to stand beside one of the nuns. He has his head bent in a most devout manner. She gives no sign that she knows he is standing next to her but I feel he has sought her out deliberately and fear for her, knowing the stories they tell about him. A little movement of her head, half-turned from him, shows she is suddenly aware of him and he, staring at the ground with his hands in his sleeves, knows exactly what he is doing.

Innocence.

Pull the other one.

While the commotion of leaving, with the coffin placed on the flat of a cart and the two horses being led into the street, is going on, I see him bend his head towards her. She looks up at him then. A bonny face she has, quite young, and they are both solemn-looking and start talking at once. About churchy things no doubt. Who has sinned. What the Pope is telling them to do. I stay where I am. I wonder what's going to happen next. Will they just part, trailing mystery behind them?

In a moment they separate themselves from the procession and are back inside the church without anyone really noticing. I follow. I'm getting the habit of spying now. None of what I observe makes sense. A little scene here or there. An accidental meeting. A shake of the hands. A sidelong glance. What does it mean? The City is a seething cauldron of people watching other people. I feel that none of it has a meaning for any one of us as it is. It's only if we all share our little pieces of information that we will ever understand it. But it will take six hundred years, a thousand or more, for that to happen.

And so they reach the altar. They kneel and pray. I walk quietly along the arcade until I'm level with them, half-hidden behind a pillar, and I see she has her veil half-covering her face. I wouldn't know who she is now if she were my twin sister. They remain there for some time, side by side, heads bent, hands folded like praying saints. A chaste distance separates them. I wonder if they are lovers like Abelard and that other Eloise? The thought makes me feel sick.

Then the novice gets up without warning and hurries out. For a little time the friar remains where he is but when he shows no sign of leaving I follow her out, slipping away through the arcade to the outer doors where I cross the street to sit on a wall.

FIFTY-SEVEN

Mercy had had nothing to add when he asked her about the English visitor to Barking. From where she had been standing in the stable yard she had been able to tell that he wore no blazon to show his allegiance. He questioned her further and she said, 'Yes, he could have had a red beard,' she frowned. 'But he had a scarf wrapped across his face.'

'Like a mercenary?'

'I suppose so.'

'And his hair?'

'Inside his basinet.'

'Not a courtier, then?'

She shook her head.

'I just need to be sure. Did you hear him say anything at all?'

She appeared to think for a moment then said, 'Only to wait for him.'

Chandler nodded.

Mercy was looking hopefully at him but when he didn't say anything she asked, 'That's not enough, is it? Does it mean you won't help me?'

'I promised I would try but you must be patient. We have to be discreet.'

'What do you mean?'

'Isn't it obvious? If you're seen to want to leave your Order so soon after Eloise's murder people may ask why. They may come to an erroneous conclusion that you are implicated in the same trouble as her, the trouble that drew a murderer to her. That you know what she knew,' he added, to make it as plain as he could.

He noticed her cheeks blanch.

'But I don't know anything more. I'd tell you if I did.'

'I hope for your sake that's true.'

After a pause she said, 'You know it's true.' And after another pause, 'Thank you for saving my life. I shouldn't have thrown myself into the water.'

She rose to her feet and hurried from the church with her head down.

By the time he left All Hallows the cortège had moved off leaving the street empty except for one small figure sitting on a wall. It was Master Chaucer's sharp little maid. Her attitude made him wonder if she was older than he reckoned. He strode over to her. Aware of his first intention to use her position in the Master's household as his eyes and ears he wondered if it would still be possible. He smiled down at her.

'No baby today?'

She looked startled, then wary, her feelings flitting across her face in quick succession. Apparently she decided to humour him, as she seemed to imagine she might. 'Not today, brother. I work for Master Chaucer now as I'm sure you already know. He has no baby that I'm aware of.'

He licked his forefinger and stuck it in the air to acknowledge that she had scored against him. 'One to you, Matilda. But be sure you don't cut yourself.'

'Me?' She looked confused.

'Being so sharp, as you are.' He shook his head in admonishment and walked off.

Yes, she was older than he imagined. It was merely that she chose not to flaunt herself in the way young women of sixteen and seventeen were wont to do. It made her different and therefore intriguing. Of course, there would be nothing really intriguing about her because she had not lived enough. He had checked up. Brought to London as a child in the entourage of one of Roet's followers and destined to be a maidservant, she was less than uninteresting. Her life could be written on a piece of parchment no bigger than his thumb.

He wondered why it was only now that she had been taken in by Chaucer. His marriage to Roet's second daughter, Philippa, would have made that the obvious household to take her or she might even have been taken on by Katharine Swynford, Roet's eldest and more successful child. She could have become the personal maid of a duchess. He wondered if she ever thought of that.

Putting such nonsense aside his thoughts returned to Mercy's meagre offering. The visitor at Barking might or might not have been the same man as the one who had given the gong-master's lad a slash. If it was, as one of Aumerle's men he could have been sent secretly to check out Bolingbroke's story that he only wanted to regain his lands. But why meet le duc's man to do that? True, Bolingbroke had chosen Orléans as the place to sit out his exile and would no doubt have discussed his predicament with le duc but the Frenchman would have no reason to admit anything to one of the king's men. That would be the last thing he would do.

He frowned. Had the royal fleet made landfall yet? As King Richard's chief advisor, Aumerle would have had to act promptly to safeguard the king's interests and, no doubt warned of the extent of Bolingbroke's army, he would advise the king to re-muster his own men fresh from their triumph in Ireland as quickly as possible. The two great armies would inevitably clash. Then it would be one side or the other to be routed and every man for himself. The Welsh might be the deciding factor in any such confrontation. Maybe he was checking out the extent of the Bolingbroke–Orléans alliance and whether le duc intended to send an army to aid Bolingbroke?

Chandler was dissatisfied on all counts with these suppositions.

They were as baseless as the belief that the man with an assignation with the emissary and the one who met the novice at All Hallows on that fatal night were one and the same. Whether one man or two were involved it made no difference if the task was to keep the girl quiet, but what could she know that was so dangerous? And who gave the instruction to have her taken from the abbey?

FIFTY-EIGHT

He turned onto the street leading to the Tower. Knollys' boy had brought him a message. They had picked up a Welshman almost immediately after letting the other lying devil lead them to the house where he claimed to have kin. This one either spoke no English whatsoever or he was refusing to cooperate. Chandler was led along to see him straight away.

He was a tall, spare, grey-haired fellow with a straggly beard down to his chest. He might be a bard, thought Chandler, and stared at his fingertips to note the hardening caused by regular harp-playing.

'Are they looking after you, bach?' he began.

When he did not answer he added, 'So far from home,' and straight on, 'Where is home?'

Again no answer.

'I have a sad duty to perform. They will have explained why they have arrested you. Now I have to explain what is to happen should you refuse to cooperate. Your hands,' he said, reaching out to touch one of them where it lay in his lap. The man did not move. 'I'm sure you value them and the music they allow you to give to the world.' He sighed. 'They are barbarians here, I'm sorry to say, and have no respect for music and musicians. They sing like crows themselves and think it no bad thing. We, I include myself in this, are different kinds of men, ones who cannot live without the solace of music. I will do what I can for you but I cannot help you if you will not cooperate. So may I ask you again, where is your home?' He dredged a phrase from out of his memory of another time.

The prisoner looked at him with contempt.

'Forgive my uncouth accent,' Chandler bowed his head.

The man laughed softly. Of the two of them he seemed the more at ease. Chandler was aware that he was no ordinary street vagabond. There was a stillness and power in him that commanded respect. They sat for a long moment in silence.

Eventually Chandler asked, 'So you will not help me?'

When the man did not even look in his direction he rose to his feet and called one of the guards.

Everyone, he believed, was attached to something. Desire always had a home. It might be virtue or it might be vice. It might be a woman, a boy, an old mother, a place, land or sea, a king or a God. When he returned they had his right thumb in a screw.

Chandler asked again, sitting close, speaking softly, bringing out his barbaric Welsh from its meagre hoard, sympathizing with him, cajoling, watching intently for any change. 'Where is your home, my friend? Why are you here in this godforsaken country?'

But he saw him let go when the pain must have seared through him with meaner force, a trick he had seen before with mystics, the genuine ones. They sank away from it. They truly believed the flesh is naught. They could detach themselves and move freely in the spirit realm unharmed.

'How do you do that?' he murmured. 'How do you detach yourself from the horror of this place? I wish I knew.'

The man opened his mild blue eyes. To Chandler's astonishment he spoke a civilized English with a half-smile on his face. 'At last you're asking me a question worthy of being answered.'

'So?'

'Young fellow, I believe you know the answer in the secret corridors of your soul. You are only trying to provoke a response from me that you can take back to your master and use against us.'

'Us?'

He shut his eyes.

Chandler put up a hand to stop the screw being tightened again. 'So I am, forgive me.'

A long pause followed and then the prisoner spoke again. 'I believe not in this brute world. It is a chimera. It is an unreal distortion of what truly exists in all its glory.'

Chandler's eyes never left his face. 'What about those people we love? Have you a mother? Is she not real? Do you not love her?'

'She is dead. Out of reach of your claws.'

The screw was tightened another fraction of an inch but he lay as if on a bed of feathers. At ease. A soft smile on his lips. Transcended.

For Chandler this was the turning point. What he wanted was his secret. All the other answers could go to hell.

'Leave off now,' he told the guard. 'I'll talk to him alone.'

The guard unscrewed his toy and went out without a word.

The bard stared at his thumb without speaking and when he glanced up at Chandler there was no expression on his face at all. It was either in repose or masking a world of rage.

Chandler asked, 'Now you can tell me whatever you think I need to know.'

'About Glyn Dwr?'

'I care nothing for Glyn Dwr or any of them, Welsh or English. I want to know how you can be so certain of a world beyond this one.'

A feeling of peace seemed to fill the chamber. Chandler was astonished at himself. He was a child again. *Tell me*, he wanted to whimper. *How can you know for certain?*

The bard talked to him in a barely audible voice. This, and this, he said, beyond human understanding but as humans we strive, yes, we strive to understand. There is no easy way. You are too webbed inside their nets. They are strangling you. For your soul's sake you must escape.

FIFTY-NINE

Down Cheapside way I am listening to what the market women are telling me. It's the usual scandal about who's done what with whose husband and so forth, daily transgressions to be kept from the priests and take their minds off the bigger issues that are haunting all of them but then, just as somebody comes up looking worried with another rumour about Bolingbroke, and before they can hear more, there's a disturbance at the other side of the market and Izzie the cheesemonger is first to act.

'Hey up!' she warns. 'It's Swynford's retinue come for their breakfasts.' She swipes a couple of her most expensive cheeses under the counter and kicks a sack over them. Her neighbours do what they can, produce hidden in the pocket of an apron, leeks with a cloth thrown over them, quality fish tipped into a bucket and the lid closed.

I stand on tiptoe to look over the heads of the crowd and to see what's what as a group of militia start to push their way from stall to stall. They barge past the queues, elbowing the old and patient aside, grabbing what they want. None of them pay.

Izzie leans innocently at her stall while her foot kicks the cheeses further underneath the counter.

The men stroll haphazardly from stall to stall, with arms now stuffed with stolen merchandise. When the bailiffs' men appear they do nothing but exchange a few words and both groups move on.

When the bailiffs are close enough Annie calls out, 'Fat lot of good you lot are! Call yourselves men?'

'Now then, missus, you know we can do nowt. We're at the whim of the barons as much as you are.'

'Swynford ain't no baron!'

'No, but his lord is. And he's going to be more than a baron by the time he gets here.'

'I hope you're joking!'

The bailiff shakes his head. 'It's only what I've heard.'

'If Nick Brembre was here we'd have some action,' Izzie at the next stall says.

'Well, he ain't here. He's dead an' gone.' He looks nettled.

'And we know who murdered him, poor old soul.'

Annie chips in. 'At least Woodstock got what he deserved! Duke of Gloucester my arse! He was nothing and he proved it. Hand out titles as they like, it don't alter the fibre of the man and Woodstock was a shite through and through. We're well rid.'

'I suggest you watch your tongue.' The bailiff's man lowers his voice. 'Be patient, woman. They won't get away with it. We've got to watch our step as much as you.'

One of the militiamen reaches Izzie's stall, lumbering and sweating in the heat of the day in his mail shirt. Inspecting the cheeses on show he gives a sneer. 'This all you've got left?'

'You have to be up early in this market to get the best,' she replies.

He gives her a mean look. 'I'll make do.' Snatching one of the cheeses he takes a big bite out of it and chews, staring defiantly into her face. Crumbs of cheese stick to the fuzz of beard around his mouth. He takes another bite. Izzie says nothing. They stare at each other. She does not drop her glance. With a sneer and still chewing he walks away.

'May you eat wasps,' she says under her breath. A sidelong glance in Annie's direction shows that the counter is almost bare. She's close to tears. 'My profit's all gone,' she says. 'Now what do I do?'

Izzie feels for her. She knows she is by herself with five grand-children to feed since their parents were taken by the plague a year past. She waits until the militia have moved on then selects one of the cheeses from the sack under the counter. 'Here. I've only me and him to feed.'

'I can't.' Annie is reluctant to accept charity.

'You can and will, you sot-wit. What am I going to do with it? Sell it to some swaggering oaf whose belly's already over-full?'

I follow the bailiff's man who remarked on Bolingbroke. 'Sir,' I say, tugging at his sleeve, 'is it true about the earl of Derby? How can he be more than a baron when he gets here?'

The man gives me a sidelong glance. 'You're a pretty little maid,' he says in a gruff voice, 'but don't go fretting, lovey, it's only a rumour. He's still in Wales. Maybe he'll stay there.'

'But the king?' I persist. 'Where is he? Is he still in Ireland?'

He shakes his head. 'Some say he's landed at Milford Haven. Some say he's gone up to Conwy with his army.'

'Which is more true, the one or the other?'

'Both as likely wrong as right. We'll have to wait and see before we find out which side we're supposed to be on.'

'To be hoped on the king's side,' I reply with a look designed to shrivel treachery. He slopes off in an attitude that says, enough of girls.

SIXTY

Chandler decided he would go and have a word with Archer whether he wanted him to or not. The thought had crossed his mind that Archer might be holding out on him and failing to pass on further information. He could not have given up so definitely, could he? It wasn't in his nature to be frightened off by anyone. There must be something else behind it. Maybe it was his own habit of suspicion that now made him imagine an order had been given to block his path from somewhere within the labyrinth of City politics.

Were any of the aldermen involved? Was Mayor Barantyn? Whittington? Once he started to trawl those waters he would drive himself mad with possibilities. Only Comberton's son, as the current owner of the house on the Dow, could have a finger pointed at him but after enquiries he discovered that he was still at his manor in Essex with no plans to return to the sulphur-pit of the City, as he apparently termed it. His lack of interest in politics was apparently notorious.

Archer was in his usual place when he called in at the Fleece.

'Where have you been hiding, Rodric?' He was at his most genial and seemed to have genuinely missed Chandler's company.

'Not hiding, Arnold, merely busy . . .' He placed a brimming flagon in front of his old friend. 'I'm still not finished with that business with the novice,' he added, sitting down beside him and stretching out his legs. 'Any news at your end?'

Archer gave a swift glance round. 'I knew you wouldn't be told. Has your persistence paid off yet?'

Chandler gave him a noncommittal glance. 'Things are falling into place, little by little, as they usually do. Truth will out.'

Arnold looked uncomfortable. 'As long as you know what you're up against.'

'What's that?'

'One of the most influential abbeys in the realm and their patron. Your patron, maybe?' He gave him a piercing glance. 'Bearing that in mind I'm surprised you're still sticking your neck out.'

'It has something to do with truth. I don't care how powerful her murderer is, they're not getting away with it.' He thought of Red Beard and the evidence he would need to put a noose round his neck.

Archer sighed and the expression in his eyes changed from warning to humorous resignation. 'Still the same old pig-headed devil you've always been. You know you can call on me, don't you? Forget what I said earlier.'

'About time you recovered your moral lodestone.'

'*Mea culpa, mea culpa*, brother. Drink up.'

And they were back on their old footing once again.

Archer, however, seemed to know no more than he himself and failed to offer any useful suggestions.

SIXTY-ONE

July was the hottest anyone remembered. Fish disappeared from the Thames and the guild wars started up again with the mariners down river able to call the shots and sell cheap in the markets.

Lancaster's vassals flourished. They were heard more and more frequently in the City, often in confrontation with the City fathers who themselves, fearing a loss of trade, drew up new contracts, sold their cloth to whoever would buy, lent money to the new regime, traded and creamed off the taxes, all as before, and watched their coffers continue to swell despite this power-shift.

Chandler saw all this with a growing sense of detachment. It was nothing to him. The world was nothing to him. He wondered how they were treating the Welsh man. Now and then he remembered to keep an eye on Master Chaucer and his fellows although so far Archer had failed to follow up his invitation to one of the meetings of the alchemists. Mostly he went about his business as before despite his contact becoming impatient. Chandler told him that meetings were infrequent and that he would attend the next one without fail, sure it would be before the end of the month. His visits to the tavern opposite Red Beard's pitch on the Strand yielded nothing of any use.

When he told Knollys about the likelihood of a meeting with Chaucer's group he said, 'They'd better have it soon. We need to clean this place up. News from Wales is encouraging. He's landed at Milford Haven, disbanded his army and run off to hide in Conwy Castle. I wonder how they'll prise him out of there?'

SIXTY-TWO

A hot breeze is blowing in through the open casement of the writing chamber. The Master is preoccupied when I poke my head round the door but it's the time when he usually calls for a drink and I have to ask twice to attract his attention. 'Master, may I get something for you?'

He looks up and shakes his head. 'You're a good girl, Mattie. I doubt whether you could get me anything to ameliorate the situation.' He gives a resigned smile.

'A trouble shared and all that.'

He beckons. 'Then sit down. I have something to tell you. For once it's me with the latest news.'

'What's happened?'

'Come. It's best for us all to be forewarned. I fear the weeks ahead are going to be dangerous for everyone who fails to protect themselves.'

'That poor little novice didn't protect herself,' I say as I take a seat on his writing chest. 'If somebody living in the safety of a great abbey like Barking can be murdered in the street like the most helpless kitchen maid, none of us have much chance.'

'Remember that and make sure you go nowhere dangerous. Stay close to those who'll protect you.'

I shiver. 'Of course I will.' He's looking so serious I can think of no quip to lighten his mood. 'Has something terrible happened?'

'I'm afraid it has. It's going to change our lives . . .'

He pushes aside a neat pile of vellum and pours out a drink for us from the jug. 'The rumours you mentioned the other day are turning out to be horrifyingly true. One of the esquires has managed to escape and came straight to London to warn us. I trust him because he was travelling in the entourage of le duc de Berry for the adventure of it and saw what happened with his own eyes – nor does he have any need to lie.' He frowns. 'The long and the short of it is the king has been captured and imprisoned.'

'What? By Bolingbroke?'

'The same.'

'What happened to King Richard's army?'

'It was scattered during a storm and his men were forced ashore up and down the Welsh coast. The king himself made landfall at Milford Haven. For some reason not yet clear he set off with only a handful of men towards his castle at Conwy. He must have heard about the army Bolingbroke got up and was hoping to make contact with the earl of Salisbury and the rest of his militia.'

'So what happened?'

'He fell into a trap. Archbishop Arundel and the earl of Northumberland, the latter with a massive army of his own, summoned him to Flint to discuss the whole thing with Bolingbroke. And that's when they took him prisoner.'

'Isn't that treason, to take the king captive?'

'Of course it is. They are completely in the wrong.'

'What happened when the earl of Salisbury summoned the king's army?'

He frowns. 'They refused to muster.'

'The traitors!'

'They were probably forewarned not to support the king. They must have found out what a hideous price the Cheshire men paid for their loyalty. They'd be thinking about their women and children. You can't blame them.'

'I can!'

He gives a sad smile. 'Easy to say when you've no small child to protect. They may have already known that Bolingbroke was sending letters from the Midlands to all the magistrates repeating that he only wanted to regain what was his—'

'He's going a strange way about it! It's out-and-out treachery!'

'King Richard rightly exiled Bolingbroke for his plotting in the Mowbray affair and was keeping the Lancastrian lands intact until his return. Aumerle, in fact, as Constable, was charged with holding them on Bolingbroke's behalf. No one knew of any plan to parcel them out as the king had done legally with Gloucester's holdings.'

'I'm more and more frightened by what's happening. Is the king safe, do you know? Where is he now?'

Chaucer looked grave. 'That's all the messenger could tell us.'

'I'm going to the market, if I may, Master. My friends there will surely know what's up.'

'Are you going alone?'

'I'll hurry. No one will notice me . . . I simply can't believe the king is a prisoner. How can they do such a thing?' I'm moving in a sort of horrified wonder towards the door and turn to look back at him.

He rubs his thumb over his palm. 'This is what does it, Mattie. Gold. The truth is, Bolingbroke is the richest man in England now his father's dead and he's spending his inheritance hand over fist in order to grab the crown. The pay he's offering to good bowmen down the length of England is three times that of an ordinary archer. Not many can resist a lure like that.'

'It shows them up in the blackness of their treacherous hearts! Let them wait on the judgement of Heaven!'

'We are small fish in a vast ocean of intrigue, remember that. We must take care not to swim into their nets.'

As I hurry out I'm reminded of the novice from All Hallows again. She swam into a net. She can't have known that until it was too late.

As soon as I reach Cheap I hear a great commotion of men chanting and cheering and when I turn the corner I see the market in chaos. Stalls overturned. Produce littering the cobblestones. Swarms of men, some armed with clubs, some with swords, are baying at each other from opposing sides and rushing sporadically into those opposite to beat them up. Thinking it must be the fish wars breaking out again I push my way towards Izzie's stall. She's shovelling cheeses into wicker baskets as fast as she can as if she's leaving.

'What's happening?' I shout above the chanting.

'It's the king. He's been taken prisoner in Wales.'

'I know. I've already heard.' I help her pack away the last remaining cheeses. 'Is he safe?'

'Nobody knows. All we've heard . . .' She pauses, breathless from her exertions, 'is that he's been betrayed by the man closest to him.'

'Bolingbroke has always been his closest rival, if that's what you mean—'

'Not him. We already knew about him. No—' She stops with one hand resting on the top of a basket. 'It's worse than that.' She knuckles her fists into her eyes. 'It's his so-called right-hand man.'

'Who?' I urge.

'The cursed, benighted son of the duke of York—'

'What? Edward Aumerle?'

She spits.

'What's he done?'

'He broke his staff of office and refused to follow him. Refused!'

'Why? I can't see why he would do that—'

'Bolingbroke must have paid him off.'

'But has he had time to do that – I mean . . . I don't know what I mean. Haven't they just landed?'

She gives me a knowing look. 'Ah, yes, haven't they.'

Annie, above the noise of the fighting in the square, calls, 'He's done for. They've all been bought off. We're finished.'

A lad I recognize from Sir Arnold's office is suddenly thrust between us and Izzie grabs him by the arm before he falls. 'Did that fellow give you a cuff round the head?' She glares into the mob at a red-faced fellow in a torn hauberk. 'Leave this lad alone! He's half your age. You should be ashamed!'

'Izzie, careful,' warns Annie going to stand beside her but the brawler hasn't time for market women and pitches himself back into the melee again and begins to punch and kick out at anybody within range.

'Thanks, missus,' the lad says, rubbing the side of his head. 'He's a Lancastrian. They said they were going to beat every supporter of the king they could find and I dared them, to my rue.' He grins and Izzie gives him a reproving glance. 'Get off home, lad. They're turning bull-mad. If it's not fishing rights they're fighting over it's something else. There's nothing we can do until we hear the facts.'

She stuffs a small cheese into his hands and pushes him away in the direction of Corn Hill then turns to me. 'That's about it, lovey. Get away home yourself. They're armed. They don't care who they knife when they're in this state. It's not safe.'

'What about you?'

'We're off now, aren't we, Annie? They'd better not mess with us.'

SIXTY-THREE

Chandler heard the latest from several sources. The facts were clear. How you interpreted them would fit to your own prejudices as, in the storm of rumour, everyone was doing.

The simple fact was that Aumerle, son of the regent appointed by King Richard to safeguard the realm in his absence, paid fealty to Bolingbroke. The big question everyone was asking was had he changed sides – or had he been playing a double game all along?

Chandler knew which view seemed the more likely. Why else would his father dither in drawing up an army and marching against Bolingbroke as soon as he heard he was on the move? It was to give his son time to land and hand his king into the custody of his enemy.

To have Aumerle's allegiance confirmed changed things from top to bottom. He set to working out the ramifications for himself, for the murderer of the novice, and for the realm.

Ever since the rosebud affair, Beata had been treating him with a degree of frost and if it was meant to make him feel guilty over some suspected lover it was a failure. She clearly did not understand him at all, nor the bigger game that was being played out, nor, as was certain, did she understand the danger she herself was in now he knew she was lying to him.

Her gold cross was more in evidence. He caught her praying at a small shrine to St Zita she set up in the kitchen. It was no more than a thumb-size icon, the sort that could be picked up in the market for next to nothing and there was always a small flower or two beneath it.

That won't help her, he thought, when I eventually call her to account.

If he was meant to show he'd noticed her show of piety he failed to do so. Coldness suited him. She should not have lied to him. He sprawled in his chair while she fetched and carried and attended to his whims. It left his thoughts free but they always returned to the same question: if the red-bearded porter was Aumerle's man and Aumerle was in the pay of Bolingbroke who had given him his instructions concerning the novice while his lord was on the high seas?

SIXTY-FOUR

J uly turned to August, as hot as ever. The constant talk was of the End Days. It seemed to be the only way to understand what was happening. The people of England and Wales had sinned in a thousand ways and the overwhelming heat that shrivelled the crops and brought the threat of starvation nearer was their own fault for allowing their anointed king to be taken prisoner. The churches were full night and day. Chandler suspected that it was because they were the only places cool enough to be tolerated.

Now the bailiffs had drafted in extra constables to keep apart the two gangs fighting in the marketplace by cracking a few heads, the traders returned to their stalls swathed in veils against the sun and sweated and cursed and moved with the celerity of slugs. Water-carriers made the most of their sudden affluence. The beach below the bridge filled with squalling children. Young bloods jumped off the wooden struts and hit the water with wild shouts. The streets stank of rotting food and excrement. He briefly wondered where le Sire had taken his little family for safety. Wherever it was he was well out of it by now and no doubt living on some leafy manor near Orléans or a farm down in Aquitaine.

Now and then he saw Matilda walking by the water's edge. She looked lost and scared. Was she waiting for the family to return? It seemed unlikely but even so he always cast a glance over the river as if to catch sight of a ship returning with a woman in a yellow gown standing on deck.

The White Tower simmered in the heat under its burden of sorrow. He had not been recalled to question the Welshman. By means of buying a few drinks at the inn on the strand he learned that Aumerle's porter was called Ed Edwinson and that he had pretensions to Saxon lordship somewhere in Kent, although what that boast earned him was difficult to see. He was the sort of heavy-set man who can make smaller men wary and it seemed nobody had much to say about him either for or against.

'So you keep out of his way?' Chandler tried with one of the ale-drinkers.

'We do.'

That was as far as he got. The problem of getting the truth from him was a torment. If approached of course he would deny it and Chandler would probably finish up with another black eye at the very least.

The question of his affinity did not come up.

The coven of warlocks as he and Knollys referred to them was due to meet soon. Archer offered the invitation circuitously. It took a moment for Chandler to grasp that he was being invited again.

'I'm not sure it's appropriate,' he managed after appearing to give it some thought. 'You know what I think about alchemy.'

'We welcome sceptics. Every fact must be tested and assayed to prove its worth. I know you agree with that, with your penchant for logic. You'll feel at home.'

'Despite – ah, you know my situation . . .'

'I trust in your right thinking, Rodric.'

So be it, he decided. Knollys would be pleased.

SIXTY-FIVE

'Mattie?' The Master looks up from his writing. 'I have some friends visiting me this evening. Will you be kind enough to wait on us?'

'It will be my pleasure, Master, but scarcely a kindness as I believe it to be my duty to wait on you and your friends.'

'Are you driven by duty, my child?'

I think it a strange question. After a moment I say, 'We are told we have a duty to God. More than that it's probably up to us to decide on what we believe to be our duty.'

I'm thinking of the murdered novice for some reason. Somebody has a duty to find out who killed her. I can't get her fate out of my head. It seems so unfair. What harm had she ever done to anybody? It's like the king. What has he ever done to harm us? It seems to me we're living in a nightmare and nobody knows what to do to wake up so we mill and bite our tongues and commit ourselves to the daily round like dreamers as if we have no other thoughts in our heads than 'Has the bread risen yet?' or 'Fetch a bucket of water from the well,' or 'Early night for me in this weather, too hot to do owt.' This isn't what our duty is, is it?

I say as much, adding, 'No one should die in vain. We owe it to them to make it not so. It's a wonder to me that the angels allow it. Our anointed king to be a prisoner is bad enough! Let alone a poor little novice to die as if she has never existed.'

Master says kindly, 'I believe Sir Arnold Archer was determined to find out who took that little maid's life. Talk to him. He might set your mind at rest. Not much any of us can do about the king.' He glances down at his writing. 'After vespers then, Mattie, if you will.'

He gets on with his work.

Cook has already opened the wine. Madame de Pisan sent it along in thanks for something the Master said about her to the earl of Salisbury, ward of her son – in admiration of her ability to earn a living from her writing I doubt not.

'This wine is better than any coin you could hope to receive,' I tell Cook when we taste it.

'Yes,' he says. 'It shows the extent of the esteem she feels for him, as does the rest of Europe. He is the most famous poet alive.'

'What about that other one we hear a lot about, Master Gower?'

He smiles. 'Adam tells me you're learning to read?'

I nod. I'm quite pleased with my progress. It's different from those early days when it was all curly insects on the page. 'I'm beginning to make out proper words,' I tell him.

'Then don't waste your time with that sycophant Gower. Read the Master.'

'I'm looking forward to doing so . . . And Cook?'

'Yes, Mattie?'

'The Master said I may speak to Sir Arnold Archer when he arrives. Will you tell me which one is he?'

SIXTY-SIX

The first guest wears a hood of good-quality linen. He keeps it half over his face until he's indoors. A page follows but does not waste time with me. I wonder if the Master expects me to announce them but it seems he does not. It seems to be the custom to use no names.

Then I have a shock. When I open the door for the sixth or seventh time I find the spy standing there. His hood is thrown back and arranged loosely round his neck. Bruises healed. Hair long again. Mouth, reckless. When he sees me he laughs out loud.

'Good evening, Matilda. You look surprised. Am I the last to arrive?'

'Last but not least,' I reply sarcastically.

He grins at me in an infuriating way and waits for me to show him inside.

'Please be kind enough to enter,' I say with a curtsey.

'I am most honoured,' he murmurs, matching my tone.

I can envisage a rare old battle of words if we were around each other for long. Without adding to it I turn and lead him down a short corridor into the chamber set aside for the meeting. It's full now and they have to shuffle up to make room for him and I'm surprised by the cordiality with which he is greeted, especially by a kindly looking fellow in a scarlet hood who seems to have something to do with the City council.

Cook nudges me when he notices me glance across. 'That's Sir Arnold in the scarlet.'

While he pours the wine I hand it round. The Master does not tell me to leave so I stand near the trestle ready to keep their goblets filled and wonder how I'm going to be able to speak to Sir Arnold and what I shall say.

SIXTY-SEVEN

handler glanced out of habit along the street before he knocked. The little Guelderland maid opened the door and her eyes widened in astonishment. She could not keep her feelings off her face. He didn't know why he always thought of her as little. She was almost as tall as he was. Straight as an arrow, a long-legged child. No, not a child at all. He knew now she was about seventeen or eighteen. Old enough to be married off if anybody had cared to arrange it. To append the word little to her name suggested the need for protection but he put the thought aside. She saw too much to warrant protection. It was innocence he perceived, or honesty, which sometimes amounted to the same thing.

As he took his seat next to Archer the door received a good thumping by somebody unused to waiting and the girl rushed to answer it. When she returned she was accompanied by a heavily veiled woman. With the rustle of expensive fabrics she was ushered with some reverence to a place beside a fellow in taffeta and velvet. A touch of their hands showed they knew each other. He smiled. He knew who they were. Knollys would certainly make something of this.

SIXTY-EIGHT

I cannot believe my eyes. An esquire of about fourteen dressed in silk is banging on the door and he jerks to a stop with his fist raised as I push it open. 'Make way for my mistress!' he pipes, his voice breaking into a growl that he clearly finds embarrassing.

I step aside. A lady enters followed by a small page who slips after the others like a little mouse escaping a cat. When she appears there's a shifting and murmuring and after she takes a seat they sit down again like schoolboys in the presence of a master. She throws back her veils but I have absolutely no idea who she is. The friar is giving her a close look and appears to sink into the wall to efface himself.

'I hear,' says the fellow in taffeta continuing his conversation where he left off, 'that he refused to speak to him after greeting the king. He said: "You did not speak to me in France, Salisbury, so I shall not speak to you in Wales."'

'He always was small-minded. Cheery enough when he was winning but a morose, bad-tempered whoreson peasant when he was losing,' replied someone else.

'No grandeur, no magnanimity of spirit,' another voice added.

'They say he asked Richard to come down to him, into the bailey. Imagine it! He was in full armour, the insulting losel. Except for his basinet. He left that behind. Instead he wore that laughable black high hat to make himself look taller. He would still look like a squat toad beside the fine, fair figure of the king.'

'Alliteration won't get us anywhere,' murmured the Master. 'Let's pool our information so far. The reports coming out are conflicting. One line is that they've set out for London, and the king is willingly riding with them. Another is that he is threatening the king with unspeakable torture and is doing everything to humiliate him.'

'Like father, like son.'

He? I ask myself. Which father? Which son? They all seem to know without his name being mentioned.

The handsome young fellow with curls to his shoulders who greeted the lady takes up the theme. 'I fear for him. Maybe you've heard the story going the rounds about poison?'

I notice the friar make a small movement.

'They would surely never attempt to poison him?' The man Cook pointed out as Sir Arnold sounds aghast.

'See what you think about his chances when I tell you this,' says the younger man. And then he launches into a long and rambling story about the men likely to have been poisoned by the duke of Lancaster on the way to the throne – from the Black Prince, to his brother Lionel and on. Quite a string of them.

'It's more than ordinary chance, the way the path to the crown was cleared by the father and is now being cleared for the son,' he finishes. 'Don't you agree?'

A growl of support arises and someone says, 'All I can say is I'm glad I'm not Thomas Mowbray.'

'What? You think he's in danger down in Venice? I'd imagine he's far enough away to be in safe territory.'

'With Gian Galeazzo as a neighbour?'

'The duke of Milan is—'

'We all know his reputation!'

'The poison-master!'

There are chuckles but they are tinged with nervousness and dismay. 'He was a great friend of the father, and the son spent time with him when he was buffing up his allies abroad,' the young courtier continues.

'But Lionel? Not an ounce of ambition in his soul.'

'No, but he was the second son, next in line to the throne, as healthy as you like, marries Galeazzo's daughter, the aptly named Violante, and dies from a stomach ailment on his wedding night or close enough!'

'To be hoped he enjoyed something of it,' another fellow quips.

'Indeed. But better to ask how he died. Coincidence or what, but Gaunt's paid and illustrious mercenary, Sir John Hawkwood, was sent to Milan at the same time. Did he carry a secret message to Gaunt's ally: get rid of the prince? Was Hawkwood carrying a chest of gold to Milan as the price of a poisoning? We shall probably never know now Hawkwood himself is dead.'

'Most propitious for Gaunt.'

'True, and but for dear little ten-year-old Richard, the way was then clear to the throne of England, don't you see?'

'It's an interesting theory but what went wrong?'

'His other obstacle was his gross unpopularity among those he swindled over property and whose wives and maidservants he bedded. But for that we might indeed have had a king called John.'

'The very thing the populace resisted during the Great Rising.'

'"*We want no king called John.*" Yes, they knew what he was even then.'

'I can see your theory takes you further,' invites Sir Arnold.

'The logic is most persuasive. Listen. Thwarted by unpopularity, he turns his attention to an easier target, the throne of Castile, has himself crowned, and bides his time. His son, fed on the milk of ambition, decides to learn from his father's mistakes. He makes himself popular by the only way that appeals to the mob, by prowess in the joust!'

There are rumblings of agreement.

'In fact, his winnings there are more to do with the show he puts on than his skill but let that pass for now. He makes the most of it. He acquires a following. With the vast resources of his father's ill-gotten lands he can also afford to buy the loyalty of men not impressed by his activities in the lists. Now we need to ask, who stands in the way of the son?' He glances round the chamber to invite an answer. Half a dozen voices readily supply one.

'Richard!'

'Yes, his popular cousin, the king everybody loves. And one other. Go back a year or so.'

'You mean his black-hearted uncle—?'

'Edmund Woodstock – so-called Gloucester!'

'But don't forget Richard's chosen heir to the throne should he have no issue,' someone interrupts.

'The Mortimer lad is only seven or eight, isn't he? I doubt there's appetite for another child-king.'

'And there'll not be another heir now the king's beloved Anne is dead.'

'That was mysterious in itself,' Sir Arnold interrupts. 'The plague, they told us. But it can't have been because nobody else caught it. It was as quick as poison.'

There's a pause while everybody thinks about it. Then the Master says, 'Let's get back to Gloucester—'

'Yes, the king was ill-advised to send him to prison in Calais when he could as easily and justifiably have had him executed for treason.'

'The king's main failing, if I may say so, is that he's not brutal enough. Tot up the beheadings by his enemies from the time of the Merciless Parliament over ten years ago to the present day, including the score in this current adventure, then compare it with those the king himself has had executed in his entire reign. No contest.'

'That's true. Have you made a list?'

'Not yet but I intend to.'

'Are we getting off the point here?' The Master draws them back once more. 'You were saying, the king did not have Gloucester executed when he could have done?'

'And the theory going the rounds is that it must have dismayed Bolingbroke to find he'd indicted his rival but the king failed to get rid of him; his main rival alive if not free. Why not tip the word to his jousting mate Mowbray that Gloucester would be better off dead?'

'The job is done but the guilt remains?'

'And that's why Mowbray blurts the truth. Unfortunately he chooses the wrong ears.'

'And it's why I still say I wouldn't like to be in Mowbray's shoes, wherever I was hiding.'

Murmurs of agreement follow.

'When Duke John informed King Richard what Mowbray was supposed to have said,' the courtier continues, 'he expected to gain support for his son. But the king was unable to believe that his one-time friend was plotting against him. And, unable to behead either of them as traitors, decided that the fairest thing was to let them fight it out like knights. Let God decide! It would've been a battle to the death, which is why people flocked to see it. But then the king made another mistake. With bloodshed abhorrent to him he calls a halt before the first blow's struck. Banishment is the compassionate choice. Let them cool their heels abroad for a while and then return with apologies on their lips.'

'An optimistic prospect if not naive.'

'And sadly not to be.'

'I'm telling you, I, for one, wouldn't like to be in Mowbray's shoes now.' The same man repeats what he said earlier and looks round at the others for corroboration.

I'm listening with my mouth open, I realize this and shut it. Why do they not name Henry Bolingbroke, earl of Hereford, Derby, Lancaster and no doubt elsewhere, when it's obvious now who they mean? Is it something to do with the law of treason? Are they merely being cautious? Or do they not want to summon the spirit of Bolingbroke to menace us?

I glance sidelong at the friar and notice that he has picked up a vielle from a side table and is bending his head as if to tune it without disturbing anyone. His long fingers caress the strings sending silent music into the world.

The men continue to talk and the lady joins in, is listened to and heeded, and I wonder if she is this Madame de Pisan the Master reveres, and yet she doesn't sound French but speaks in a very forthright manner in plain English. Her disgust is directed at someone she vehemently calls a betrayer, an out-and-out traitor, she says, one she should have bought poison for long ago and why ever did she not? She throws up her hands as if to beseech Heaven for an answer.

More wine is poured and the friar, that ambiguous presence, begins to play faultlessly until a final chord brings a sigh from those sitting by.

Sir Arnold Archer calls, 'We'll make a courtier of you yet, Rodric.'

Chuckles of amusement follow.

The talk turns to alchemy and my eyes begin to droop. *Rodric.* He is as attentive to the conversation that follows as to all the rest of it.

Afterwards I say his name to myself. It seems miraculous to hear it. I don't know why. I hug his name to me like a personal secret. I feel I have learned something momentous.

Rodric, I murmur later in bed as I drift off to sleep.

And then comes the thought as hard as marble. I forgot to speak to Sir Arnold so it means I shall have to pay him a visit.

SIXTY-NINE

Chandler flexed his fingers. It was an age since he had played any instrument but it had come back to him with an unexpected sense of joy.

The hunt is up, the fox beware,
Whoop whoop, the hunt is up!
Let the lark sing and the sun shine,
But whoop whoop the fox beware!

The words might be a warning to any who imagined they were safe. It was St Bernard who had called heretics foxes, to be hunted down and killed. What else were these alchemists? If not heretics, Lollards, everyone, then clearly they were on the side of the king which was just as culpable in these disjointed times. There was no

safety for kings or commoners now, just as there was no safety for
novices inside a convent.

Despite her vehemence, the lady Constance had said nothing of
any use to him about her turncoat brother Aumerle.

SEVENTY

I'm out early. Because I have no idea what hours Sir Arnold
keeps I'm waiting outside the mortuary when he arrives shortly
before lady mass. He doesn't look as surprised to see me as I
expected and I guess that the Master has mentioned me.

With a swift glance up and down the street he mutters, 'Come
inside.'

In a trice I follow him into a small chamber cluttered with scrolls
and he turns to me. 'I hear you're worried about the death of the
novice from All Hallows and believe that nobody is trying to find
her murderer?'

'That sums it up, Sir Arnold.'

'I can assure you I am doing what I can. The first problem is
that no one saw anything that would give rise to suspicion. The
second is that there is no murder weapon.' He sits down behind a
desk and steeples his fingers. 'Did you know her?'

'No—'

'Then why do you want to involve yourself in something that
might be dangerous?'

I give him my speech about the angels and how in this case it
seems as if they need help from one or two mortals. He smiles.

'The way you can help is to bring me the murder weapon. And
if you come across anybody who saw anything suspicious that
morning it would be a bonus.' He's mocking me. I do not return
his smile. He falters slightly and adds, 'My best advice to you,
young maid, is to keep out of it. Get on with your own life. There
are powerful forces involved you can know nothing about. If they
have murdered a novice from one of the royal abbeys supported by
the House of Lancaster they'll not stop at murdering a maid employed
by a man whom they already regard with hostility.'

When he rises to his feet it is with the air of a fellow who sees himself making an end of the matter. Just because I follow him out with an appearance of meekness does not mean I agree with him.

SEVENTY-ONE

As Chandler made his way down East Cheap next morning he decided that all in all it had been a successful meeting the previous night in that his presence had aroused no comment. He would be invited again. They had certainly betrayed themselves, however. He couldn't understand such lack of restraint. It puzzled him. Didn't they know about his contact with Knollys? He thought everybody knew by now. No one would retain their heads on their shoulders if their sentiments were repeated in the wrong ears.

Aumerle's sister showed that there was no love lost there if she was truly speaking her mind and not merely putting out a trail to see who followed. Others often about the City were present, merchants, an alderman or two, others from the court circle, scions of impetuous youth, and all seemed to take on trust that Chaucer's guests were of a single mind in their support for King Richard.

Or, he considered thoughtfully, in these times when no one could be trusted, had he been invited in the hope that word would get back about the strength of the opposition to Bolingbroke's plan? Arundel at least must be aware by now that they needed a way to counter the loyalty the king aroused. Many remembered with fondness the little golden boy in white silk on his coronation day being carried on Sir Simon Burley's shoulders from Westminster Abbey, and his bravery at fourteen when he saved the peasant army from certain massacre at Smithfield after Wat Tyler was killed before their eyes.

And yet it might already be too late to stop Bolingbroke's rebellion surging to its conclusion, courtly opposition or not, while the *poraille*, as one might call them, were being blatantly cozened by Arundel's organized rumour-mongering. It was obvious that the truth about Bolingbroke's murderous ambition would be kept from everybody until it was too late to object.

Suddenly a thought struck him with such force it made him stop dead in his tracks.

The novice? The secret that led to her death? Was that it?

Had she overheard about Bolingbroke's plan to seize the throne?

What more likely than that the emissary of the French duke had met one of Aumerle's men in secret at the abbey to discuss Bolingbroke's true intentions? It had taken place before he landed at Ravenser and mustered his no-expense-spared army. Even then was it his intention to buy the crown of England?

In a flash he saw what would happen next. Objectors would be swept aside as had happened after the Great Rising. Mass hangings would be the order of the day. The populace, whatever they wanted, were landless, with no vote, no power. Able to do nothing against the ruthless ambition of a man intent on grabbing complete power – and the resources to carry his desire to a conclusion – they would simply be ignored.

If the realm was now divided it was because the most vociferous saw their future wealth more likely to be secured by the would-be warlord Bolingbroke, commander of the largest army the country had seen for decades, than by his peace-loving cousin, Richard. Chandler walked in a daze.

Could she have known? Had she known?

Well, well, he thought, such is life.

With little regard for secular power himself the rumours had never struck him as likely. Now he saw how blind he'd been. The unfortunate novice had surely overheard some reference to Bolingbroke's secret intention. Terrified out of her wits, she had kept it to herself. And paid the price. Certainly Orléans would not want his role of money-lender to the usurper bruited about the courts of Europe. And his co-conspirator at Barking? He had been right before, it had to be a Bolingbroke supporter. And so it was. It was the duke of Aumerle, of all men.

What he understood now was that if she had confessed the truth to anyone and if it had reached the ears of King Richard he would have been able to summon an army and prepare a trap that would catch the traitors – and Bolingbroke would now be a dead man.

He suddenly found himself at a stall selling musical instruments but was too preoccupied to put his mind to buying one and strolled on in deep astonishment at the power of ambition and his own blindness.

SEVENTY-TWO

'**M**attie? Are you going out?' Adam, working late, stands in the doorway.

'I'm going to compline,' I fib. 'To pray to the angels,' I add more truthfully.

He steps aside with an odd look on his face and I get outside without having to explain further.

The long summer nights are still light enough for what I intend to do and this early in the evening most people are snug in their houses or in church so there is nobody around near Dowgate Beck to see me slip off my boots and step into the water. As the mud squishes round my legs I make a solemn request to the angels. *Please, let me find what others have overlooked. Please, O you mighty host, grant me this wish so that I may do your will for the good of your poor fallen sparrow. Amen.*

I grit my teeth as the scummy water reaches my knees and dead creatures brush against my skin. Something grips one of my toes and I lift my foot with a repressed shriek but it turns out to be nothing much and I shake it away. More defiantly I wade out daring anything to touch me and begin to dredge along the bank to where they found the body.

They must surely have looked for the murder weapon themselves, I think as I poke among the debris washing up among the mounds of mud. That coroner, despite his high manner, seemed a thorough type to me. When he uttered his challenge – as I see it – he did it with the confidence of a man who had already made a thorough search of the place and was certain of my failure.

I grip my talisman, a little figure of St Edmund, and offer up another prayer. *For King Richard,* I mutter, *and the True Commons,* although I don't know how it could have anything to do with the king but he has problems of his own so I add him in. *O great angels of justice,* I whisper, *I'm sorry to bother you but please let me find it, amen.*

By now I've reached the big house along the bank and so far

nothing at all. I urge the angels on. Poking a stick into a mound of rubbish below the overhanging balconies I wonder why people have to throw away such useful stuff. I come to a halt. I can't go any further than the sluice. The current is too strong here and anything that fell into it, or was thrown, would have been washed away ages ago.

They have let me down. I daren't scold them. I'm sure they're doing their best.

Thank you, I whisper, thinking it prudent to treat them with angelic gratitude.

I go back a little way then climb out of the stinking water near Comberton's house and go to sit on the muddy bank and wonder what to do. I ought to trawl back again to see if I've missed it. It seems a vain quest. I suppose Sir Arnold thinks as I do: why would a murderer throw away the weapon he did it with? What a sot-wit he'd have to be.

Just then I hear voices above my head as somebody comes out onto the balcony. I cringe back into the shadows under the struts and hope they don't look down.

'So,' comes a man's voice. 'You can talk freely. He's still away in Essex sharpening his sword.'

'He went to the meeting as you said he might but has said nothing about it.'

'Nothing at all?'

'No. He was in a black mood and went straight to his bedchamber.'

'Didn't you join him?' There's a long pause then he adds, 'I'm not getting my money's worth here, mistress.'

'I'm sorry—'

'It's no good being sorry. That won't keep me in ale, will it, nor will it keep my master satisfied.'

'I do my best but he's stopped talking to me. He's worried about something.'

'Let him worry. He should be dancing for joy or whatever it is friars do when they're on the winning side.'

I hear him give a snigger of amusement at his own wit. He continues, 'I'm dancing. We've got shut of that mincing girl-king. Now we'll have a man back on the throne. It'll be good for us, Beata.' His voice drops and I miss the next few words but then she says, 'I can't forget what you did . . .' Her voice becomes inaudible.

And then, 'Why didn't you keep her locked up instead . . .' And again I miss her words as her voice drops.

As I shift my cramped legs I dislodge a large stone and it falls into the water with a splash. To my horror I hear footsteps thump across the balcony and a voice calls down, 'Who's there?' I keep so still I stop breathing until, after an age, the footsteps return and a voice mutters, 'Cursed rats. I'll have to get that cat back to work again. How's your one turning out?'

The voices move out of hearing and I wait until I'm sure they've gone indoors and then I creep along the bank until I gauge I'm far enough out of earshot to get down into the water again.

By now the sun has disappeared behind the houses and the stream is in shadow. Beata? Who's she, I wonder? The name rings a bell. I'll ask Izzie. She'll know. It's so dark when I reach the street I can't tell what horrible things are sucking at my legs but I flap my hands and, carrying my boots, begin to run barefoot towards home.

By the time I get in I'm still wondering what they were talking about up there in private. A cat? You might lock a cat up if it was in a new place and you didn't want it to return to the old one. Then why did the woman, Beata, sound so horrified? Over a cat?

My angels have been a dead loss. Familiar doubts return and I say, *What a sot-wit you are, to be sure, Matilda Nijmegen. No wonder Adam gave you that funny look before you came out.*

SEVENTY-THREE

News comes in about a massacre of a dozen men near Oxford. Their bodies were piled up beside the king's highway where they were discovered by some townspeople. It's rumoured that they had set out with the intention of rescuing the king from the clutches of his captor, Henry Bolingbroke.

Several attempts had already been made by different, somewhat uncoordinated groups but they had been beaten off. These would-be rescuers, it is discovered, came from Hampshire and places further west. A fellow called Richard Swalbe, a minor knight from the New Forest, put up a valiant fight as did the others but he was noticed especially because he managed to take three or four of the attackers down with him before he was himself brought down.

There is a sense of mourning throughout the markets when the news comes in, many people having kin in those more southern parts of the realm.

Everybody is bewildered by it. Why, they ask, is the duke of Lancaster, if that's who he's now calling himself, waging war on his own folk? Why kill Englishmen in their own country? Others begin to ask questions about the duke taking King Richard captive. 'Is it true?' they ask. The duke abducting his own anointed king? It makes no sense.

Another piece of news comes in and again it shakes everyone.

Sir Peter de Legh of Chester has been beheaded without trial, for not showing enough support for Bolingbroke.

People look askance. Beheaded?

What can you do?

At least now they know where they stand.

Beside this bloodshed and betrayal the death of one lowly novice seems unimportant to say the least and speculation around the markets about her killer fades. Chandler registers, too, that her secret is common knowledge now. They must all know what Bolingbroke wants even though he continues to deny it. Strangely it makes him even more determined to bring her murderer to justice.

The duke's cavalcade of several thousand has been spotted stretching back along the lanes for many miles. It moves in a continual bruit of horns, kettledrums and buisines.

Stories from eye-witnesses flood ahead into the City. There is no room for doubt. To some it is almost a relief to find their worst fears confirmed. Now they can stockpile what they might need in the coming weeks when battlelines will be drawn up, or flee to the country to seek sanctuary with kinsfolk. Nothing is worse than uncertainty. Now they are certain.

It is being said that the cavalcade is expected to be on the road for a fortnight but it jogs along at such an eager pace many assume it will arrive in London sooner than that.

The continual roar of so many men passing by draws peasants from the fields and entire families from the nearby villages. News of its coming flashes along the country lanes and hollow ways to swell the ranks of those already standing wide-eyed to watch a show of military power bigger than anything they have ever seen before. It sends them up trees for a better view or to flock along the cleared verges when the army reaches the great highway. Townsfolk come out just as eagerly from Nantwich, where there is another failed rescue attempt followed by summary hangings, and from Stafford, Lichfield, Coventry, Northampton, St Albans, the same, and so it goes all the way to the gates of London.

There Lancaster's military harbingers, ready with pikes and swords for any kind of action, line the route to keep back unarmed crowds. Trouble-causers are picked out and dealt with before the army comes in under the walls and now and then an over-zealous horseman rides his caparisoned mount deliberately into the thick of the crowd to show them their limits.

But nobody cares. The cheers are deafening as the cavalcade rides in. They are under the illusion that the king is back!

SEVENTY-FOUR

Mattie is standing with Adam and the Master's cook in the press round the gateway near the Tower. Despite the arrival of the Lancastrian army everybody believes that Bolingbroke, riding a big white destrier, Barbary, the king's own horse, his favourite, and decked out in gold and silver medallions that tinkle when he moves, is seen as the herald for the arrival of the king, even though few can understand why he is the one astride the king's own horse.

It is like the coronation all over again, they say, when Harry, a mere child the same age as his cousin, both no more than ten years old, carried before him the great ceremonial sword Curtana with its inscription 'justice without rancour'.

So they cheer. They cheer to high heaven. Eventually when the king does not appear their cheers falter. Where is he, they begin to ask?

Meanwhile a bewildering stream of militia march by. After the duke on his borrowed horse come battalions, regiments, arrays from all over the country, an endless army of mercenaries equipped for war and accoutred in Lancaster's colours of red and gold, steel breastplates glittering, gauntlets, greaves glinting, followed by vizored men astride restive war horses with brightly coloured saddlecloths, a thousand polished hooves thundering in the narrow streets on the approach to the Tower. The crash of the steel boots of the foot soldiers on the cobblestones almost drowns out the kettledrums, the trumpets, the pipes.

Somebody at an upper window shouts down. 'Here he is! It's the king!' But the voice is lost in the noise echoing from below.

Without anyone noticing the king has indeed passed by. Still dressed in the grey, threadbare garments of a Minorite friar, he is sitting astride a small pony with the earl of Salisbury similarly mounted beside him. The two men are escorted so closely and by such a large mob of militia riding their powerful war horses that the crowd, crushed against the walls of the houses, do not notice the two men in their midst. They have to be told later.

'He's a captive, all right,' Adam mutters as somebody points out the close-packed men-at-arms in the middle of which the king rides into the awful, unknowing, faltered silence of the crowd.

'Is he in chains?' Cook asks.

'I can't see from here.'

'Are you sure it was him? I didn't see him.'

'Nobody's cheering,' says Mattie.

'They are up front. Listen!'

'That's because they think he's about to appear.'

'They don't know it's him, already gone by. Nobody can see.'

'Well we're still waiting. It can't have been him. He won't go by without us knowing.'

'My little lass has a posy of flowers for him,' says a woman standing by.

The silence of the crowd must seem unforgiving when it's no more than confused. Mattie feels like weeping. She has a memory of a tall, kind, fair, smiling man she once saw in a procession near the Guildhall. Now they're saying he is reduced to grubby friar's robes and a pony. But nobody can see him. Nobody knows whether he's there or not.

'He will not know we are here to cheer him.' She takes hold of

Adam and the cook by the hands. 'Long live King Richard!' she shouts at the top of her voice.

One of the guards lining the route turns and gives her a hard stare. She shouts again. One or two murmur their agreement but are cowed into silence when the guard reaches out with his mailed fist and hits Mattie in the mouth.

She stares at him in astonishment, too shocked to feel any pain. Blood streams from her cut lips. The cook places himself between her and the guard but the fellow has turned his broad back on them, confident in the Lancastrian bands of steel that protect him.

'Come on, let's get out of this.' Cook carves a path for her through the crowd. Heads turn at the sight of blood. 'A guard did that!' he announces to all and sundry as he forces a way past them.

Adam follows without a word. When they get to the edge where they find some space he says, 'There was no cause for that.' He brings out a cloth from his sleeve and tenderly wipes Mattie's bleeding mouth.

The three of them walk back to the house in silence. There is worse to come. Now they know it. There is nothing left to say.

SEVENTY-FIVE

K nollys is in court clothes. He has just returned from the welcoming party at Westminster Hall and his stick, the one with the silver dragon's head, is resting against his chair. 'Well managed, don't you think, my boy?'

'The opposition was played successfully. A most masterly coup. Mistakenly they gave their cheers for the man astride Barbary. Nobody even knew the king was in the middle of that mob. He must be shocked to his kid-skin boots to be so slighted by his beloved Londoners.'

Knollys chuckled. 'You say well. Now, to the point. You attended yesterday's coven as I asked?'

'They are certainly no warlocks.'

'So no one sniffed you out? I hope you sniffed them out. Who should I know about?'

'I doubt there was anyone you do not know about,' he replied. 'They were the usual as far as I could tell. All names you've mentioned before.'

'Did they not question you?'

'I believe Sir Arnold's support is enough to satisfy their misgivings.'

'Is he the dolt he seems?'

'I believe his only interest is in alchemy, the search for truth. He has no interest in court affairs.'

'Very high-minded of him.'

'He has always been so. Remember, I have known him since he was a boy being beaten for his Latin.'

Knollys chuckles again. 'I take your word on trust, brother. I know you would tell me anything I needed to know.'

Chandler falls silent. Does Knollys know about the lady Constance? If he does not mention her he will lose Knollys' trust if he does know. If he does mention her and he did not know he will be putting her in danger. On the other hand, it was difficult to guess where her allegiance might lie. Maybe she was sent to spy out the enemy by whoever is this unknown master of masters? He makes a decision he hopes he will not regret.

'I suppose you know they were not all warlocks who attended?'

Knollys jerks up his head. 'A witch?'

Ah, what to say now, he thinks. How much does he really know? 'The Master' – he uses the epithet sarcastically – 'is much in thrall to a Frenchwoman—'

'Oh her. A writer. Yes. I thought, however,' he screws up his eyes, 'that she was out of the country?'

'Maybe so.'

Knollys gives him a searching glance. 'And?'

Chandler cannot answer.

'No ideas?'

'Beautifully dressed, of excellent lineage. I thought you might have sent her?'

Flattered, Knollys leans back. 'You know something, brother. I enjoy our little jousts.' He takes a sip of wine then draws his lips back in a parody of a smile. 'You may leave me if that's all you have to tell me. Bring her name next time you call.'

'I hope I've been of service, my lord, and ever hope to be.'
'You have been of service, brother. Indeed you have.'

SEVENTY-SIX

With instructions that arrive out of the blue to return to the Tower to have another talk to the Welsh bard, Chandler wonders if the prisoner has been told what happened to his fellow Welshmen when they repeatedly tried to rescue the king from Bolingbroke's soldiers on the march through the Welsh Marches.

It was barbaric by any standards.

When some of them were caught they were tied to the tails of their horses and dragged over the cobbles until they were flayed. How can he put this to him? He might know them personally. They might be his kin.

He is thwarted by the crowds as soon as he leaves the house. A subdued and confused citizenry are walking aimlessly about in the streets wherever they can avoid the militia, some from the Tower, others towards it in the hope of seeing something that will make sense of what they have witnessed. At the gatehouse the guards are busy turning people away. They even turn Chandler away. As he remonstrates, the cavalry is clattering over the drawbridge into the bailey. The event is a cross between a state funeral and May Day celebrations, except that there is no maypole and little music other than the braying of trumpets.

The colours red and gold are everywhere. He hears that the duke and his personal retinue have entered the White Tower to escort the king to his chambers. Then he hears the opposite, that the duke has taken up residence at the palace of Westminster. The king alone will reside at the Tower.

SEVENTY-SEVEN

A day or two of more wild and unsubstantiated rumours flood the City. Various dignitaries are seen arriving and leaving. Their faces are solemn. They give nothing away. Men from different parishes appear in small, defiant, disorganized bands but are soon routed by men-at-arms. The marketplace on Cheap is almost empty.

Like everybody else I make hurried visits in the hope of finding something out and make equally hurried ways home to find safety behind closed doors. There are armed men everywhere you look. The citizens are beginning to keep their mouths shut unless it's to shout support for Bolingbroke. But he is not being called that now. That name belongs to the past. He is the duke of Lancaster, heir apparent to the throne of England.

An air of mourning permeates the little house of the Master but he has a constant stream of visitors. Not his sister-in-law in person. Apparently the dowager duchess of Lancaster is living in Lincoln now but she sends him a message by courier warning him to avoid trouble.

I hear him telling Adam she has warned them to keep their heads down, 'until,' he says, 'we discover how this thing will be brought to pass.'

By 'this thing' he must mean the unbelievable crowning of Bolingbroke in place of the rightful king.

The visitors who do arrive have one question on their lips before they even offer a greeting. It is: is he still alive?

Nobody laughs out loud any longer. There are no jokes. We walk like people under the sea and wait in vain for the tide to fetch us safely back to land.

I know most of their names now. Through his court connections Chaucer seems to know everyone. Despite what Katharine Swynford has warned he cannot keep out of it. They draw him in by their constant visits. He cannot work. He sits and stares at the vellum on his desk but writes nothing. Every moment there is an interruption. The same question: is he still alive?

I do what I can to help. What can I do? Nothing much. Keep as quiet as I can and fetch him drink and make sure there is as little to disturb him as possible. In my heart I am seething with disgust. The City Fathers disgust me. Turncoats. Disloyal, greedy, self-seeking turncoats. I hate them.

A story has come out that a group of them rode out to Chester even before the cavalcade set off. Why? If you can credit it they went there in order to demand the king's immediate execution.

This is almost impossible to believe.

The duke is said to have replied: 'Fair sirs, it would be a very great disgrace to us for ever if we should thus put him to death. But we will bring him to London and there he shall be judged by Parliament.' So that is what we are waiting for. Whoresons.

'Who was in this deputation, Adam, do you know?' I hear the Master ask when the story reaches him.

'A handful of aldermen.'

'Richard Whittington?'

'Not that I know of. When he heard them he was standing by with a white face and stroking his cat, saying nothing.'

The Master makes no comment but turns back to his desk.

The lord Despenser turns up with the lady who was here before, who turns out to be his wife, Constance. She has the misfortune to be sister to the duke of Aumerle. They are the children of the useless duke of York who was probably not useless at all but simply playing for time to help his nephew Bolingbroke mass his forces to march against the king at Flint.

Adam says I am a cynic. I prefer to think I'm a realist. I have observed men. This is how they are. This is what they do. All false-seeming.

Brother Chandler, Rodric, as bad as anyone.

Walden, the ex-archbishop of Canterbury, is here. When he addresses the Master he is blank with shock. 'He has pushed me out of my pulpit!'

'What?'

'Arundel. He's pushed me out!'

'How?'

'He just marched in with a couple of armed men and told me to get out because he was archbishop and now he was back!'

'Didn't you protest?'

'With a sword at my throat?'

'What about the congregation?'

'They couldn't believe their ears. "We won't accept him," they cried. When he waved his arms about and told them the Pope had given him dispensation to return they noticed his armed men and meekly dropped to their knees.'

'And had he? The Pope, I mean, re-installed him?'

'Not at all. It was another flat lie. He appointed *me*. The Holy Father must be out of patience with us English, fighting among ourselves like savages, but what can he do from Rome?'

'He could excommunicate the lot of them, Arundel and every last one of his followers.'

'He doesn't seem to have thought of that.'

'He won't, as long as he's getting his taxes from us. He won't want to do anything.' Walden is quite beside himself with self-recrimination. 'I know I should have stood up to him. I should have. But I don't like violence. The Lord exhorts us to be peace-loving men.' He spreads his arms, gentle, and helpless, and lost.

It does not end there, for how can it? The next thing to happen is when a courier from Venice arrives post-haste with messages for the Lombard moneylenders. I am in the marketplace and hear the news as it flashes from one stall to another.

Sir Thomas Mowbray, lately exiled, is dead!

'That ends that,' observes Adam when I tell them about it back at the house. 'Now we'll never know the truth about who murdered Gloucester.'

'Actions speak louder than words. They can betray the truth more clearly by what they do than by a denial shouted from the rooftops.' Despite his words the Master looks shaken to have his fears confirmed.

I remember the conversation at the meeting of the alchemists in what seems like another era when that old fellow kept saying he would not want to be in Mowbray's shoes. He was convinced that Bolingbroke would silence him. Now he is silenced. With Bolingbroke innocently in England. Just as his father had been far away when

Prince Lionel died unexpectedly in Milan at the palace of the duke and set Gaunt a step closer to the throne.

'How is he said to have met his death?' I ask.

Both men stare at me.

'Plague,' they say.

I remember the name Galeazzo, the king of poisons, but say nothing.

SEVENTY-EIGHT

C handler tried to get inside as instructed to see the Welshman and once he knew for sure that King Richard was in the Tower and not down in Westminster he redoubled his efforts.

A mob, whipped up to a storm of hatred by the followers of the red rose, seemed to reign down there. They had rampaged through the palace, so the story went, demanding the instant death of the king and his ministers. It was nonsense. The taxes the aldermen encouraged them to object to were only imposed on those who could pay, the idle barons mostly, so it was no skin off their noses, they didn't earn enough to pay taxes, but they must've been paid to create mayhem by their masters so that is what they did.

Lancaster, meanwhile, had taken himself off to the safety of one of his castles.

When he reached the Tower a crowd stood as usual round the gate-house like dumb oxen. What were they waiting for? They must have known they would not be allowed in anywhere near the royal prison. Military men came and went without hindrance on production of their dockets. The turncoat aldermen also were let through.

Chandler informed the captain of the guard that he had a prisoner to interrogate but when he told him who it was the fellow said he had been let go. 'Freed a few nights ago, brother. Did nobody tell you?'

He knew he was lying. It was a different captain to the usual one. A Lancastrian. He wondered what had happened to the old bard. It didn't bear thinking about. He wondered whether he managed to remain serene until the end.

As he walked away he decided he would go down into Petty Wales to see if he could hear word of what had happened. He felt responsible. How could he not be? He had done little to try to get him out when he might have had a chance. He hoped there had been no reprisals against him when rumours of the Welsh bands and their attempted rescue of the king became known.

SEVENTY-NINE

Thomas Despenser is back. He brings with him an esquire of the earl of Salisbury, the latter being imprisoned in the Tower with the king.

He strides back and forth, declaiming, 'There is no way they can make his theft of the crown legitimate? Is there? Is there? Tell me what it is, if so. There is no way, not without lying through their arses.'

The Master is going through all the copies of his work, listing them while Adam writes down everything he has and he says, 'We'll finish searching through to find anything Arundel might find unorthodox later on.'

Adam gives him a look. 'Shall I burn the lot then, Geoffrey?'

Despenser laughs. 'Humour at a time like this?'

The Master shakes his head. He points to it, bald as it is, and says, 'Look, Adam, I still have it firm on my shoulders. I'd rather like to keep it this way.'

'So would I, my own I mean.'

'My scrivener, at his most lugubrious,' the Master explains to Despenser. I ask Adam how to spell it.

Despenser says he is going back to the Tower to see what's new and leaves straightaway saying, 'There is no legitimate cause to make him abdicate. You can't just rid yourself of an anointed king because you don't like his fiscal policies. Trade is at its most buoyant. It has never been so good now those incessant wars with the French are over. How does Harry Bolingbroke imagine he can improve things? Is he going to start shitting gold from his benighted arse?'

His esquire gives me a rueful grin as he follows him out.

I feel flattered that he noticed me. My face is still a mess. Every time I eat or drink my lips split open where that bully-boy cuffed me and I get blood in my food. I suppose it does no harm to drink your own blood. The thought of it makes me imagine the heads on London Bridge again. They soak them in cumin but the crows still peck out the eyes. It's like being inside a nightmare every time you venture within sight.

I get ready to go to market again. As soon as I'm out in the street I notice a strange atmosphere, a violent, uncertain, feverishness that makes me pull my straw hat down and keep my eyes on the ground in front of me. There is hardly anybody around.

When I reach the corner of Cheap I'm shocked to find the market almost empty too. A few stalls in the process of being dismantled remain but of produce or anyone attempting to sell anything there's not a sign apart from a fishmonger with a couple of what look like day-old herring on his counter.

'What's up?' I ask.

'No trade. Gates blocked. Nobody can get in or out.'

By chance I glance across to where I usually buy our cheese and there's Izzie just coming out from behind a trestle that a couple of young fellows are heaving onto the back of a cart. 'What's this?' I ask when I go over.

When she sees me she is plainly worried. 'What are you doing here, lovey?'

'Hoping to make a few purchases for the Master but I see I'm too late.'

'We're out of here as soon as we can,' Izzie replies. 'There's been trouble. I'm not staying to have my stock stolen from under my nose. I thought Swynford's men were bad enough but this lot are far worse. Annie has already left. As soon as we've got this stuff on board we're off.'

'Where are you going?'

'Back home to Kent. I'm staying there until it blows over.' She gives me a sharp glance. 'What's the matter with your face?'

'A guard lining the route gave me a swipe across the mouth because I shouted, "Long live King Richard."'

'There you are then. That sums it up. Best get out if you can. Go home.'

'I can't go home.' It suddenly hits me. 'I haven't got a home. My only refuge is with the Master.'

'I'll take you with us if you like?'

'I can't go. I'm bound by a legal contract.'

'Legal?' She spits. 'That's what I think to their legal. Have you heard what they're planning now?'

I shake my head.

'Only to make it illegal for the king to rule in his own realm.'

'They can't do that.' For once she must have it wrong.

'You mark my words. They'll tie him up all ways in their law clerk's jargon and he won't get out. Now he's in the Tower that's where he'll stay. That Arundel is still thundering worse than ever. Between the two of them, the duke and the archbishop, they're tying everybody in a stranglehold. Mayor Barantyn has simply rolled over and accepted it. Good job he'll soon be out, unless we get somebody worse if they fix the vote. Soon the realm will be ruined worse than ever it was when the king was supposed to be making such a mess of things. Legal, they say – when there's nobody left to protect ordinary peaceful citizens going about their business? What's legal about that?'

'We heard gangs shouting last night. A constable of the Watch banged on the door and warned the Master to stay indoors.'

'You keep out of it right now. If you're not coming with us you best get off back home quick and don't come abroad again without an armed man or two beside you. I'm warning you, lovey. It's not safe and it's going to get worse.'

The couple of young men helping Izzie have tied down the trestle and the awning onto the cart with ropes while we've been talking and look impatient to be off. 'My sons,' Izzie tells me.

One of them is sitting on the cart holding the reins and he turns to haul his mother on board as the other one jumps onto the tailgate and their pony begins to walk on.

I go with them as far as the bridge where I leave them with tears in my eyes. I might never see them again. Life seems to be nothing but farewells. I shout after them and wave my arms. I can't help noticing the severed head newly put up.

Apart from a few cowled figures muttering prayers a small crowd stands below it in silence. It has been sent from Bristol in a white basket. It is Sir Richard Scrope. Or was.

I do as Izzie recommends and start back to the safety of the house through the hostile quiet of the usually noisy thoroughfare. Then I suddenly remember the name *Beata* and stop short, but it's too late now. Izzie and her boys are out of sight.

Before I get to the door Brother Chandler, appearing from thin air, steps into my path.

EIGHTY

Chandler was surprised to find Mattie suddenly appear before him. She stepped away from him with a little cry.

'What are you doing out?' he asked. 'Don't you know it's not safe?'

'What are the sheriffs and their constables doing?'

'Nothing by the look of it. Is the Master at home?'

'I hope so.' She gave a little flounce. 'He won't see you. He's busy.'

He asked, 'What have you done to your mouth?'

'Nothing. It was one of the Lancaster men-at-arms lining the route who did it.'

'I have something that might heal it more quickly and leave you with no scar.'

She glared at him as if suspecting a trick.

He said, 'I'll go to my lodgings and get it.'

'I can't pay you.'

'I expect no payment.'

'Is it your act of compassion for the day?'

'Put it like that if you wish.'

EIGHTY-ONE

I stand as if transfixed until he reaches the turn in the road and disappears towards Aldgate then I hurry into the house to warn Adam that Brother Chandler intends to call and he goes to warn the Master. Next I see them passing the door, backwards and forwards, with bundles of documents in their hands.

By the time the spy is knocking on the door the writing desk is almost empty except for one half-finished piece the Master is making up while Adam writes it down. They stop in mid-sentence.

'Welcome, Brother Chandler,' I say, drawing open the door with a great flourish.

He ignores me and goes in to see the Master and when I follow I'm in time to see his glance sweep the chamber as if looking for something.

Adam glances up from his writing. 'Are we to stop here where the cook is in mid-sentence, master?'

'I'll remember how it goes on, Adam. Make another copy thus far, will you?'

He turns to the friar. 'How are the streets now? Still in turmoil?'

'For some. They seem to leave the ecclesiastics alone, however.' He glances at me. 'Your maidservant was in the street when I noticed she had a wound which I may be able to heal. If you'll permit me?'

The Master turns to me. 'It would be best to have it put right, Mattie.' To Chandler he says, 'Go through, brother. You'll need water, I expect.'

We troop through to where Cook is slopping things around and Chandler asks for a vessel of clean water with which to bathe my mouth. Cook says, 'Better in the yard and take it straight from the well.'

We share a well with a dozen or so others but it is quiet here in the sunlight. Everyone seems to be busy indoors. Chandler – Rodric – has a clean cloth in his scrip and after hauling up the wooden bucket dips it into the crystal water. I flinch as he tends the broken skin.

'Such a pretty mouth,' he murmurs. 'Shame to have it disfigured. This may sting a little but it will be worth it when you're restored to your former beauty.'

I know he's mocking me. Beauty? I give a quick dart of my eyes to gauge his expression and he touches my eye-beam with his own as the ancients describe it and our glances mesh and stay like that, knotted, his dabbing halted while his hand hovers just above my mouth. I feel my soul drawn from me. I close my eyes. I cannot bear that look.

His damp cloth comes down again as gentle as before and then, my eyes still tight shut, I feel the coolness of a salve of some sweet-smelling sort and the little sting as it touches the wound and then a warmth that takes away the pain I had almost forgotten about.

'Brave child,' he murmurs and now I know he's mocking me.

I give a long-suffering sigh and step back as soon as he finishes. 'Thank you, brother. I hope this helps you satisfy your confessor and mitigates your penance.'

He is rinsing the cloth in the bucket then throws the used water onto the ground where it dries in an instant in the hot sun. He gives that slanted look I'm beginning to know and his lips reveal his teeth as he tries to dazzle me with a smile before saying, 'You're a wicked girl, for sure, and I think it's you who might need a confessor.'

'Perhaps you'll do me the honour?' I say with a look meant to show I think he's far beneath honour and he says, 'I would not welcome sleepless nights pondering a suitable penance for you and sadly St Serapion does not allow me to hear confession either so I am saved a double travail. You'll need a priest for that.' He gives me a sudden sharp look and asks, 'Do you need a priest?'

'Of course not!' I'm incensed. 'Don't you imagine I made my Easter confession as I should?'

'I'm sure, Matilda, you do everything . . . as you should.' He turns to go then suddenly swings back. 'How old are you, Matilda?'

'I'm nearly nineteen.'

'How nearly?'

'In about four or five months' time.'

'In other words you're eighteen and a half. Probably even a little less?'

I feel affronted. 'How old are you?'

'I'm twenty-nine. In your terms I'm nearly thirty.'

'When was your birthday?'

'Last week.'

I blurt, 'Twenty-nine isn't old.'

He gives that dazzling smile again. 'Who said it was?'

I am dismissed. He is so final. I go back indoors with the cloth to my mouth mumbling my thanks.

EIGHTY-TWO

The Master tried to offer him money but he refused.

'It was but a slight thing, mayhap enough to help the child.' He was dismissive. She was too provocative. At least he had had another look inside the house. There was nothing to see. He didn't doubt that they had put away anything that Archbishop Arundel might find offensive.

He went back to the Tower. Contacts in Petty Wales had refused to tell him anything. It could have been they did not know the bard was imprisoned there at all or they did not wish to incriminate themselves by appearing to be in the know and thereby lay themselves open to further questioning.

This time it was a different captain at the gatehouse and when he showed him Swynford's badge without telling him more he let him through at once. The usual crowd were standing around outside and gave him a good glare as he went through into the bailey.

Again the scavenger birds were circling overhead. Again the rough louts in the guard room. Again the echoing corridor with its sickly smell of blood and filth.

And again, praise be, the old Welshman lying as if asleep on a golden couch in the dank cell. As soon as Chandler entered he opened his eyes. 'Back to see me, my son. I wondered if you would bother.'

'I tried before but they lied and told me you'd been freed.'

'Maybe they thought they had freed me and it's by a mere oversight that I'm still caged here?'

'I'll tell them I have a docket from Swynford to let you go.'

He sat up. 'Are they likely to believe you?'

'They're in chaos at present. Nobody knows who to believe. The king – have you heard anything?'

'Still alive, I'm told. Courtiers come and go. The archbishop has a penchant for this place. He's never out of it.'

'Maybe Saltwood is getting too crowded.'

'Is that where he tortures his heretics?'

'So they say.'

'Ever been there?'

'Once. I hope never to repeat the experience.'

'You're the wrong man in the wrong job. Why not get out and leave them to it?'

'Don't I have obligations to my fellow believers?'

'It depends on what they believe.'

Offering a wry smile he says, 'At this time in this place they believe in the Antichrist.'

'Only I am allowed to say that as only I am imprisoned for it.'

'Is that your crime?'

'Who knows in these days? Anything becomes a crime as soon as the usurper and his presumptuous archbishop decide it should be so. What is happening to this country?'

Chandler stops him and says slowly, 'You've said more than enough to have your life forfeit. Have you given up on it?'

'The Lord enjoins us to hold to the truth.'

'With a priest to intercede for you when you sin?'

The bard gives a slow, sad smile. 'I've more than endangered myself. You do not need to go further with this interrogation and exact further heresies from me.'

'I meant what I said about releasing you.'

'I will not lead you to anyone.'

'I would not expect it. Nor do I expect you to tell me where you'll go afterwards. I advise you not to stay in the City nor even in Westminster. Glyn Dwr can learn nothing to his advantage here. Go away as far and fast as you can.'

On his way out he stopped the guard on duty and held up Swynford's badge. 'Orders to let the prisoner free at once.'

'Who says?'

'Look at this. Who do you think?' He held the badge closer so the fellow could touch it. It seemed enough to convince him.

'It's due procedure to wait for my captain to confirm it.'

'It is confirmed. I told him on the way in. Here, to prove it.' He dug into his pouch and pulled out a piece of silver. 'Convinced?'

The guard was uncertain but after a brief struggle between fear and need he reached out and palmed the silver into his own pouch. 'Go on then. I'm off duty for a bit. Going for a piss.'

Chandler waited until he reached the end of the corridor and disappeared then he went into the cell and hurried the bard out clutching his few belongings. 'Go on ahead of me. Make for the watergate but don't draw attention to yourself. I'll join you there and we'll take a boat upriver. I'm guessing you'll want to go west?'

'Is this a trap?'

'No, trust me.'

He went, composed enough to meet his fate whatever it might be, with his few pathetic belongings under his arm.

As he left, Chandler heard voices raised in anger from an upper floor and wondering if it was anything to do with any of the prisoners on his own list he was about to go up to investigate when twenty or so gaudily attired courtiers poured in through the main doors and began to ascend the steps. They were soon followed by a crowd of retainers.

Curious to find out what was going on and deciding that he needed to give the bard time to reach the watergate, Chandler mingled in at the tail end and allowed them to sweep him up with them as they mounted to the second floor and entered what was evidently the royal apartment.

It was already crowded. An oak table that could easily seat twenty guests took up one end and other chairs and chests were ranged against the walls. In the middle of the chamber a bristle-bearded fellow was standing in a dominant position with his fingers tucked into the gold bands on his sleeves. Next to him a young, sharp-faced ecclesiastic in the robes of a Church high-up was standing by with an expression that showed that at any moment he was going to erupt into rage again. His large pectoral cross made Chandler look twice. Archbishop Arundel himself.

Chandler stayed near the door and tried to merge into the shadows. A third man was involved in what was clearly the middle of a heated argument. Chandler's eyes widened. It was the king. The argument had been brought to a temporary halt by the entrance of the courtiers but it was resumed as soon as the archbishop had glanced at the newcomers, observed that they were of no importance and turned back to the king. The bearded fellow with the uncertain manner was Bolingbroke, no less. Of the three he seemed the most disconcerted by the verbal affray.

Chandler put more effort in trying to efface himself. The king, he noticed at once, was a shadow of what he had been, his face haggard, all the colour gone, his hair a wild tangle of red-gold in need of a wash, and his garments far from the kingly robes he had been wearing when Chandler had last seen him – how many years ago? Ten? Fifteen? – when the palace of Sheen had been a place of harmony, beauty and innocent pleasure. Another world now in every sense.

An elderly courtier stepped forward in an attempt to insert himself into the argument but was largely ignored. The duke of York. And the fellow who now pushed his way in front to take over must be his son, Aumerle. No sign of the lady Constance.

The king now swung to face Aumerle, picking up the threads of the argument, shouting, 'Don't lie to me, you traitor, you two-faced, lying, treacherous hound! It was your advice I followed. I believed you had my interests at heart. Instead you're a lying, scheming turncoat worthy to be flayed alive!'

'I swear I had the best of intentions!'

'Stay, you said. Don't leave Ireland yet, you said. We have plenty of time, you said. The weather, "Oh, sire! The weather is against us!" I should have believed Salisbury. You must have known Harry was massing an army. You gave me false counsel at every stage! I curse the hour you were born! You liar! You traitor! You two-faced coward!'

'Then take this!' Aumerle ripped his gage from his belt and flung it at the king's feet.

Richard, raging as only he could, kicked it across the chamber. 'Traitor! I am king! I am your lord! And I will continue as king! I will be a greater king than I ever was in spite of you and the ill counsel of you and the rest of my enemies. You, Arundel, you swore on the Host at Conwy Castle that Harry did not want anything more than his lands back. You swore that he didn't want the crown! You lied on the Host. You, Edward, day after day in Ireland, knowing what was going to happen! Liars, all! You are not fit to speak to me!'

Before Aumerle could reply, Henry Bolingbroke stepped forward to restrain him. 'No, no, say nothing, Edward. You cannot challenge him. Pick up your gage.'

Richard put a hand on his cousin's arm. 'Why have you brought me here, Harry? Why do you keep me so closely guarded by your men-at-arms? You did not tell me I was going to remain a prisoner.

You said you had to protect me on the march back to London. You said nothing about keeping me a prisoner. What do you intend to do next? Am I still your king?'

'Indeed you are, my lord. This is what I came to tell you. The council of the realm have ordered me to keep you confined until Parliament meets next. That is all.'

'Confined? False traitors! I will not be imprisoned! Free me at once, if not, prove yourselves against me. I'm ready. Try me! I'm a true knight and you know it! I'll take on all four of you by my own self! Come on! I challenge you!'

He then threw down his own gage.

To the astonishment of everyone present Bolingbroke fell to his knees. 'Forgive this uproar, my lord. Do as we ask. Be patient until Parliament is called and everyone has chance to bring forward his concerns.'

Richard calmed down enough to say, 'I shall defend myself in a fair trial if that's what they want. I can answer all their false charges. Let me answer their charges! I can do it and I will!'

Bolingbroke looked up at Richard from his position at his feet with a face as guileless as a saint. 'All I ask is that you be patient. Let the council have their say. Nothing unreasonable will befall you.'

'At least let me see my dear little Isabel.'

'That is impossible. She is safe in the palace at Sonning. The council do not wish you to see her.'

Richard flung himself away. 'Get out, all of you!' The colour had come back to his features but it was the colour of rage at the knowledge of his impotence and his hands were shaking.

Everyone drifted out, some lingering on the steps, chewing over what had transpired, others leaving at once with their retinues, Lancaster, the Yorks, and Arundel and his acolytes, like men with the satisfaction of a job well done. The rest spread about the bailey in excited groups.

Chandler, unnoticed, made his way towards the watergate. He saw no sign of the bard until he reached the landing stage. There he observed him holding out his wrist to one of the ravens and when it alighted he seemed to be talking to it in an avian discourse the bird seemed to understand. As soon as Chandler appeared he let the bird fly away.

A hire boat was preparing to leave as one of the duke's barges was rowed into the narrow channel inside the gate and, hurrying the bard a little, Chandler made sure they stepped on board before it left.

He longed to explore the ramifications of what he had just witnessed with the old fellow, in the expectation of hearing some sound common sense about the deception that had been perpetrated against the king, but a boat loaded with strangers was not the place. He gave the boatman silver to take them up to Westminster with the intention of hiring another vessel when they reached the landing there. No point in making it easy for anyone who might be following them. The guard would have returned from his break long ago and might have had a sudden and inconvenient attack of conscience.

Both men kept their hoods up. Chandler was surprised to find it was still daylight.

EIGHTY-THREE

I first hear the news when I go out into the yard at the back to fetch water from the communal well in order to change the dressing on my mouth as he had instructed.

Adam reminded me to do so. 'It's looking better already,' he announced in an offhand tone after a brief glance at my face. 'You won't be able to scare anybody soon.'

Scowling I go outside. A group of neighbours are standing near the well, with the excuse that they are fetching water but in reality they are lingering to hear the latest rumours. Now it has become too dangerous to venture out to the market if, in fact, anybody had been able to bring in stock to make it worthwhile, the well has become the main place to hear the latest.

The chief bearer of news this day is a large woman from further down the street whose son was a retainer to a hedge knight who had happened to be in the group present at the Tower when an ultimatum had been given to the king.

'The duke laid down the law to him and no mistake and got him to hand over his signet. He told him he'd remain a prisoner until the citizens of London saw fit to release him. Of course a tantrum followed. He went raging round the chamber, overturning chairs and tables, kicking out at things, but there was nothing he could do. They're going to bring him to trial when they please which might not be for some time. So there it is.'

'What charges are they going to bring against him?' a young maid from one of the houses asks.

'Aye, I don't see what he's done except displease a few idle greedy barons,' a groom from the same house assents.

The large woman gives him a dark glance. 'Are you saying you think the duke has overstepped the mark?'

'Maybe he has, maybe he hasn't. I wasn't there so I don't know the truth of the matter. We've only got your second-hand word for it. All I'm asking is what are the charges they're bringing against him? Did your son say?'

The fat woman dismisses him with an angry shake of her head. 'I'll say the same to you as the duke said to him.' She gives a smirk as if she has special knowledge. '*Be patient.*' She begins to wind up the rope with a full bucket of water dangling on the end. 'Patience is a virtue, master. Isn't that what we're told?'

Heaving her filled bucket over the parapet of the well and slopping it somewhat over her skirts as she dismissively hauls it back across the yard to her house she leaves a momentary silence behind her until I venture to say, 'It's still a good question. What are the charges against him?'

'If you ask me the duke hopes to make him look guilty so he can depose him and set the crown on his own head. But how's he going to do it? That's my real question. There's no real precedent.' The groom is frowning. 'King Richard is the anointed king. It's a holy bond with God himself. How can a mere duke break that?'

'King Dickon could choose to abdicate like his grandad.'

'Aye, call that choosing! We all know what happened to King Edward the Second!' There are shifty glances until one of the men says, 'By, that must have been a painful experience! What a way to go!' He shivers and pulls a grotesque face and a few nervous sniggers follow.

'The duke would never do a thing like that, would he?'

'They were barbarians in them days. Things are different now, Mattie. He'll be asked to step down and if he agrees that'll be the end of it.'

'Don't we get a say?' the groom asks.

When I eventually go back indoors I tell Cook what has been said. 'God help us all,' he murmurs and leaves it at that.

EIGHTY-FOUR

C handler had worn his sword underneath his friar's threadbare gown most of the time since Archer had suggested he did so when they rode out that first time to Barking Abbey. He was glad of it now although nobody actually threatened the two men but Westminster was descending into anarchy as quickly as the rest of the country. It reminded him of the Rising when people had called it the hurling time with good reason. Bits of broken masonry were scattered everywhere along the strand, now as then. Pots. Tiles. Brick. Broken bottles. All kinds of debris used as missiles.

There were still-simmering fires from the night before when incomers had slept rough on land near the gates of Thorney Island, sending curls of smoke melting into the summer haze. The towers of the abbey rose behind them floating in the sky and looking as frail as spider webs.

Away from the City the air was fresh. The Thames, wide and serene, brought two promises with it, one of rich inland meadows full of flowers and the scent of sweet hay, and another of salt winds and the wide-open sea leading to foreign shores.

The bard thanked Chandler for bringing him to the threshold of safety. 'Only in my wild Welsh mountains among my own folk shall I feel truly safe. I take on trust what you have done. May you go well in the coming weeks. May the king prevail against his enemies.'

Chandler saw him go aboard the horse ferry and begin the river crossing to take the road on the other side into the west. Glyn Dwr was noted for his audacity. He watched him until the boat reached the other side then walked thoughtfully away.

Arnold Archer was sitting in his usual place in the Fleece when Chandler arrived. It was later the same day. He had risked getting back to the City on foot and was unhampered by the gangs roaming the strand between Westminster and Ludgate Hill, but the enigma of Glyn Dwr had taunted him every step of the way.

Crossing the Fleet and entering the City at Ludgate it was obvious law and order had broken down even here within the walls. Gangs roamed the streets looking for trouble.

Fires were started for no reason. Shops were looted. Children ran wild. Already summary hangings were taking place. The Foul Oak, Brembre's old execution tree, was in frequent use, as in the old days of anarchy when the barons first tried to oust the king. Now robberies had increased. Knifings and other killings were commonplace.

The duke had taken it upon himself to issue writs in the name of King Richard to all the sheriffs throughout England ordering them to step up their efforts to keep the peace. His orders were clearly being ignored.

He was foot-sore by the time he sat down with Archer and ordered his ale. 'So how goes it?' he asked.

'Worse and worse. They're still discussing how to depose him. It seems to be a foregone conclusion that's where it'll end.'

Thinking about what he had witnessed earlier at the Tower he asked, 'Has Bolingbroke made a declaration of intent?'

'Not yet. He's playing shy. Reluctant, they say, to take on the role of king. Him! As if! He'll wait until there's nobody else left with any sort of claim then he'll step forward in the manner of one coerced into doing us all a favour.'

'Where's the earl of March?'

'Out of it. Too young. They don't want a child again. Especially not a Mortimer.'

'And Arundel? Is this his doing?'

'Pulling the strings? We shall never know to what extent. Sure it is they met up near Paris during their exile. Was the plot formed then?'

'Arundel will go after the Lollards as soon as he can. He'll not spare them. Remember that, Archer. Remind your alchemists.'

'They need no warning, Rodric. Did you know Purvey has been dragged off to Saltwood Castle?' He named the most well-known of Wycliffe's translators of the Bible into English.

'God preserve him. When did this happen?'

'Nobody knows for sure.' He gave Chandler a cold glance. 'You have enough on me to have me sent there.'

Chandler pondered the colour of his ale for some time before saying, 'In that case, pray you get me as your interrogator.'

Archer did not stay long. That he was still hostile and confused about Chandler's allegiance saddened him. He had never felt so isolated. Hated by both sides, all he could do was follow the path where he imagined it led.

Worse proof of where his particular path might lead was when, a little later, after braving the now familiar ice of Beata's reception, a loud knocking at the door heralded Swynford's page.

'Greetings, brother. My lord is below.'

'Then bring him up.' Chandler went to the top of the steps to see Swynford astride an expensive piece of horse-flesh, garishly caparisoned. He saw the page deliver his invitation.

Swynford looked up at the gatehouse, noticed Chandler and waved him down. Reluctantly Chandler descended.

After he had given him a close scrutiny Swynford said, 'I hear you've been busy at the Tower?'

The guard, thought Chandler at once. Bribable but not bribable enough. He felt ice slide down his spine. But it wasn't that, after all. It was the other thing. 'You were seen in the royal apartments, brother.'

'I heard shouts and noticing the duke of Lancaster's colours thought to witness the event in case of the need for aid.'

Swynford, for once able to look down on Chandler, gave a kind of snarl. It could have denoted satisfaction. 'My lord the duke attended the king in order to inform his grace that he will be charged with a number of offences detrimental to his regality. But that's not our business. I now have the task of obtaining further supplies for my lord. As before.' He began to turn his horse's head and kick him on. Over his shoulder he said, 'The duke is in residence at Hertford Castle while they thrash out the legalities of the present issue. Bring them to me there.'

As he watched him ride away with his jangling entourage Chandler thought how easy it would be for Swynford to ride out to Stepney to get the stuff he wanted. He could be back before the sun went down. He, on the other hand, would have to hire a horse if he could find one and then ride out. He would have to leave his small congregation to Martin again. And after that he would have to take the road to Hertford. Was he expected to ride through the night? In this atmosphere of anarchy? Turning, he went back indoors to prepare.

Proclamations were being made as he crossed over to his chapel to seek out Martin and square things with him and he paused to listen. A small crowd had gathered. For once there was no heckling. They stood like mutes.

The crier stood on a box to ring his bell. 'I hereby give notice that this proclamation is issued on the advice of Thomas Arundel, archbishop of Canterbury, Henry, duke of Lancaster, Edward, duke of Aumerle, Henry, the earl of Northumberland, and Ralph, earl of Westmorland along with other great princes of the realm, in order to let it be known that the current disorders are contrary to the duke's intent and the king will in nowise endure the same. Anyone caught committing the following crimes and misdemeanours will bear the full brunt of the law as exercised by . . .'

Noting the order of precedence, Chandler's thoughts turned to Martin and when he met him in the vestry he mentioned Arundel straightaway.

'I'm hearing all kinds of rumours,' Martin admitted. 'It's bad news about Purvey. What's his crime when all's said and done? It comes down to a matter of opinion. Wycliffe translated the texts to prove his point. There is no mention of the Eucharist in the Bible. The bread and wine are symbolic. It's the sharing of it in fellowship that's intended by the last supper. The Christian fathers wrote down everything they wanted for our guidance. Anything else is opinion only.'

'My question, Martin, is do you have a safe house you can run to if necessary?'

He shook his head. 'Oxford will not be safe.'

'A temporary measure will be my chambers at Aldgate. We must think about somewhere more long term.'

Martin laughed. 'I don't intend to hide away. I intend to put the case for Wycliffe and the rest of them. It's too important a question to allow Arundel to choose the terms of the argument. He must accept that scholars better than he will ever be have reached different conclusions. The truth is what's at issue here. Not blind orthodoxy according to some self-appointed authority like him with only self-interest on his mind.'

Chandler had no reply. He said, 'The other matter I wish to mention is that I shall be grateful if you will stand in for me until I return. I have business that will take me away overnight.'

EIGHTY-FIVE

The herb gardens at Stepney. Brother Daniel in a straw hat. A summer drowsiness filled with the contented humming of bees about their work. Only faintly could the sounds of brawling in the streets be heard beyond the walls.

'Come and sit with me awhile,' he said when he met Chandler at the gate.

He led the way between banks of rosemary, lavender and fennel, breaking off leaves and sniffing them with pleasure as he went.

'I'm here on a similar errand as before,' Chandler told him at once. 'I have to ride out to Hertford Castle as soon as I have them.'

'But not before you sample an elixir I'm proving.' Brother Daniel smiled. 'Try this.' He poured a honey-coloured liquid into two small cups and handed one to Chandler. 'My dear boy, what times. Is there something I can do for you?'

He told him about the scene he had witnessed at the Tower and how little hope there now was for the king. 'But it's this business of the novice as well. I fear her murderer will go free.'

The old herberer sighed. 'Have you no ideas?'

'I know the probable motive, given the timing.' He told him why he thought the novice had been silenced. 'This latest proves it, don't you think?'

'To keep the secret of Bolingbroke's invasion plan.'

'And I was puzzled about Aumerle's involvement. He was still on the high seas with the king at the time, to all intents his trusted advisor, but he must have known what was expected of him before he sailed – unless he has a most talented astrologer in his entourage.'

'So it was his man who killed her?'

'It looks like it—'

'If so he's untouchable.'

'Except for a knife in his back.'

Daniel gave him a sharp glance.

'Not my way.' Chandler fingered the small wooden cross under his shirt. 'And what evidence is there it was his hand on the knife?'

Thoughtfully, Daniel added, 'The Mold Warp has planned this coup with a subtlety I know he does not possess.'

After a pause the old friar held up his small tasting pot containing the elixir. 'Your verdict, Rodric?'

'Like a piece of heaven distilled by God himself.'

Daniel struggled to his feet. 'Come on, let's get these cures. I fear that novice's death goes far deeper than either of us can guess.'

He led the way between the flowering herbs and when Chandler's pouch was full he took him to his store. He turned to him. 'I have something special for you, Rodric. You may need it given the dangerous territory you inhabit. Handle it with great caution. Use only in the most extreme situation.' He gave him a long look. 'My dear boy, do your duty, but have a care at the court of the sixth king.'

EIGHTY-SIX

'Master, I'm troubled.'

'What is it, Mattie?'

'They're saying something that strikes fear into me.'

'What have you heard now, my little spy.'

'It's this. They're saying that Archbishop Arundel wants to burn heretics. But it seems to me that if we say or believe something wrong then God will punish us and reveal our wrong-hood to us. There's no need to add to the misery of life by setting fire to us. It's too horrible to contemplate.'

'Who tells you he wants to burn us?'

'It's what I've heard. It's a sin to gossip, I know, but at times like this when everything seems upside down we have to grab at what news we can get in order to understand what's happening.'

'Both popes, the one in Rome and the one in Avignon, are for burning heretics too. It's not just Archbishop Arundel.'

'But King Richard doesn't agree. You all say he encourages new ideas. He doesn't burn people for their thoughts. If some ideas run counter to the rigid beliefs of the popes then surely we should allow them an airing so we can put them to the test and make up our own minds?'

'That's what I and many others believe. I fear it's obvious from my writing over the last twenty years. What do you think Adam and I are doing with all my stories? We're looking for anything that Arundel might construe as heresy. Gower is busily rewriting his offerings. I hear he's already rededicating his books to Henry Bolingbroke and scrubbing out any reference to King Richard that praises him.'

'Have you been doing that?'

He gives me such a look that I hang my head.

Coming up to me he rests a hand on my shoulder. 'Dear little Mattie, I have no desire to burn in flames at Smithfield – or anywhere else come to that. We must hope for three things: that the king will not be deposed; that Arundel will not get any statute through Parliament that will result in the burning of heretics; and that poets and philosophers will be left free to get on with what we do best.'

He returns to his sifting and sorting but after a moment or two calls to me, 'Have you seen Adam?'

'No, master. Not since yesterday.'

He frowns then continues his work.

Soon I shall be able to help in his task. Reading isn't all that difficult if you follow the rules. Before he gets too deeply into it – when he won't hear me even if I shout in his ear – I say, 'Master?'

'Yes, Mattie?' He doesn't lift his head.

'This is one last time then I won't disturb you again. It's this. Who is Mistress Beata?'

'She's Brother Chandler's housekeeper.'

'She visits a house on Dow Beck.'

Raising his head he gives me a sharp look. 'How do you know?'

'I was under one of the balconies when she and a rough old fellow came onto it.'

'Do you know which house it was?'

'It was that large one with the yard beside it up near the sluice.'

'Are you sure?'

'I was searching in the beck for the knife that poor novice was murdered with and sat under its balcony long enough.'

'That's Comberton's old house. His son has it now. Was he there?' His eyes are suddenly needling into me.

'The fellow I heard speak referred to somebody being in Essex sharpening his sword.'

'Ah.'

He seems satisfied by this and is about to return to his work when he asks, 'And did you find the knife?'

'Of course not. Sir Arnold knew I wouldn't.'

Adam has been taken in for questioning. The Master is informed by chance from one of the gossips who saw him being marched down Paternoster Row where he sometimes worked.

He says to Cook within my hearing, 'This time I fear I cannot do anything to help. It's not as if la belle Katharine has any sway over Arundel.'

'If she's any sense she'll fear being called a witch, the way things are going. She's best up in Lincoln behind her convent walls.'

'Where are we best, my friend?' He goes back to his writing.

EIGHTY-SEVEN

Chandler arrived at Hertford Castle in time to hear the discussions about how to get King Richard out of the way.

The great hall was crowded with the retainers of both Lancaster and Northumberland. York and his son were present too as if to confirm their change of allegiance and other more minor knights were in attendance with their own retinues. The kitchens were kept in constant busyness in an attempt to feed such a huge crowd of hungry men.

Chandler was directed towards a table where he shared his dole with a pardoner who appeared to have no affiliation to either king or usurper but instead had a lively interest in the rights and wrongs of legal procedure.

As soon as greetings had been exchanged and he discovered that

Chandler had just arrived, he said, 'Let me put you in the picture, brother. It's been quite splenetic at the top table.' He gestured to where a few men were still sitting. 'The archbishop is leading the debate. Understandably he's hoping to keep quiet about the oath he and the earl of Northumberland swore at Conwy – that Duke Harry had no intention of trying for the crown. You can see his point of view!' He sniggered. 'Instead he's saying Harry has to persuade the king to name him as heir and then get him to abdicate, legally and above board.'

'That's a tall order. How is he going to persuade King Richard to do that?'

The pardoner sniggered again. 'A repeat of the famous event at Berkeley has been suggested as an inducement.' He gave Chandler a knowing wink. 'Imprisoned in the Tower, Richard's not going to have much say, is he? They can do what they like to him. Who's going to know? I'd be worried if I were him, wouldn't you?'

'I certainly would,' Chandler replied without emotion.

'The duke's argument, on the other hand, is that he should claim the crown by right of conquest and if that doesn't convince everybody he's going to claim it by right of descent from Henry the third.'

'What? From Crouchback? I thought that old story had been laid to rest.'

'So did I but desperate needs need desperate remedies. Who of us,' he glanced widely round, 'can say that Crouchback wasn't the first-born and should therefore have been king?'

'If it were true it would invalidate every king since Henry III himself. Even good King Edward III would have been illegitimate. I can't see that going down well.'

The pardoner reached for another hunk of bread and wiped the platter that had contained fish in an almond sauce, finishing off by eating the last of the wastel. He poured wine into his own goblet then thought to offer the flagon to Chandler who nodded and asked, 'So which plan will prevail, do you think?'

The pardoner scratched his chin. 'Difficult to say. There's still Edward Mortimer on the scene, even if he is only eight.'

'I was told he was out of the succession by general agreement. Nobody wants a child king again.'

'In my opinion,' the pardoner leaned forward, 'Arundel will lose this one. Harry's a man of action. He won't want to delay long enough to risk giving the king's friends a chance to get over their shock and muster against him. Look at it, at the moment Harry's got the City on his side, trade being more important to that lot than right or wrong. He's got an army, over-paid and as loyal as that makes them – though he can't go on paying them for ever. He's got the fealty of the militia from a dozen or more castles placed strategically up and down the country – by courtesy of his father, admitted. But his ace is this. He's got an unblemished record as a ruler for the simple reason he's never ruled a kingdom in his life! On the other side we've got the trial of the king in Parliament coming up. They'll drag out every misdemeanour and wrong look they can find. They won't leave him a leg to stand on. He'll be out on his arse.'

'When they see him before them in all his regality, the anointed king, arguing his case as he will, they'll see their dilemma. I wouldn't want to place bets on the outcome between those two.'

The pardoner looked shiftily from under his brows to see if anybody was listening in. 'I hear they're going to get him to sign a document confirming that he wishes to abdicate. When they call Parliament they'll wave that in their faces. Then Harry will step forward by popular demand.' He opened his mouth to laugh. 'They're sharp ones and no mistake.'

'When are they doing this, did you say?'

'On the morrow, so I hear. They're all preparing to leave for Westminster now. I'm getting back on the road as well. With luck I'll meet enough sinners carrying ready money to keep me in comfort till Martinmas.'

While Chandler was finishing his meal the pardoner, pleased to have an audience, waxed forth about the long list of holy relics Arundel kept at Canterbury.

'Do you know,' he marvelled, 'he's actually got a piece of the Virgin's under-shift?' He gave a knowing laugh. 'The young devil! It's the idea of it. Cunning! He's supposed to have the toenails of St Peter as well! All right for anybody with foot problems!'

'What about you?' Chandler asked mildly.

'Only the usual. Plenty of bones. Pig, mostly. Are you interested?'

'Not really.'

'I didn't think you would be.' He winked.

* * *

Determined to locate Swynford with his pouch of herbs he approached the chamberlain and was directed into a warren of passageways, eventually coming out in a side hall where a few men-at-arms were lounging over a game of dice. One of them went to fetch Swynford, who came puffing up a flight of steps to greet him. He took Chandler by the sleeve and guided him into an ante-chamber where they could talk privately. 'Did you mention to anybody what you've brought me?'

'Of course not.'

'Good man. I see why my lord trusts you. Bed down for the night then come back with us to Westminster in the morning.'

His excitement was so palpable Chandler guessed that the story the pardoner had told him was true. Tomorrow was going to be a big day in the deposition of the king.

EIGHTY-EIGHT

T he last day of September dawned with cloud-cover bringing the sort of fine drizzle that seeps into everything and rusts even the most well-maintained armour. Everybody was grumbling. They moved south in a jangling procession with the duke and his archbishop at its head. By the time their harbingers reached the City walls the rest of the train was still tramping along the highway between the arable strips by Stoke Newington manor.

The final stretch of the road was thick with travellers from all levels of society. Everybody wanted to get inside Westminster Hall to hear what was going to happen. Rumours were rife. They crossed the bridge onto Thorney Island and at once filled the yard outside. There was much jostling as riders dismounted and plunged through the gawpers flocking round the doors.

Chandler was lucky. He followed on the heels of a passing knight and his squire and managed to find standing room at the back of the Great Hall.

It was already crammed with parliamentary representatives and a teeming horde of citizens who had come out early from London itself and it took time before all those necessary to the legal process about to unfold had been found places to sit.

Chandler looked up at the magnificent wooden roof of carved angels recently designed and erected by Herland and pondered the meaning behind their shields bearing King Richard's emblem of the white hart enchained. It was an uncannily prescient symbol. He wondered what had led the king's mother, the Princess Joan, fair maid as she once was, to choose that out of all the images she could have chosen and why her son had adopted it for his own.

Why not an eagle? Why not a leopard rampant?

The answer was obvious.

Meanwhile, despite the hubbub, the chair of state standing in for the throne itself remained conspicuously empty.

The archbishop of York, one of the le Scrope kinship, together with the bishop of Hereford, had been appointed as proctor. With disregard for correct procedure he ignored the usual sermon by the Chancellor and the election of a Speaker for the Commons and allowed no time for the appointment of judges. Instead he launched straight into a reading in Latin of the king's letter of abdication.

After the Latin, just to make everything clear to the citizens, it was read by the clerk in English. He quickly followed this by reading aloud the accusations against the king. There were thirty-three *gravamina*, le Scrope intoned before he began.

It took some time. At least it was in English so everybody could understand but people began to shift about almost at once. Grimaces were exchanged. Eyebrows raised. It seemed that everything the king had done since the barons had executed his closest allies ten years ago at the Merciless Parliament was a grave transgression of his kingship not to say an offence against themselves and his entire realm.

Was it true the king had resorted to bribery and tyranny to punish those who had plotted against him? What were those who so plotted now doing but bribing and tyrannizing those who got in their way?

People began at look at each other out of their eye-corners. Had he favoured poor dead Mowbray over Duke Harry Bolingbroke, now present and very much alive, in the dispute between the two men over which of them had connived at the murder of the traitorous duke of Gloucester? It seemed that Bolingbroke had been given the lighter sentence of six years' exile while Mowbray, not that it mattered now, had been sent out of the realm for life. A fate ironically to come true sooner than anyone expected.

Was it a fact that the king had bled the realm dry with his personal extravagance? Trade was buoyant for the first time for decades now that the warlords themselves were prevented from demanding ever-larger taxes to finance their raids into France.

Was it true, and if it was, did it matter that the king had tricked Parliament into surrendering its powers to a committee ruled over by himself? Hadn't John of Gaunt done the same?

Hadn't Gloucester also tried it on? Had they ever been called into Parliament to explain themselves?

In fact, the whisper began to go round, where was the king? Shouldn't he be here to defend himself against these cobbled-together charges?

Before the whisper could become a roar one man stood up. It was Bishop Mercks of Carlisle. 'My lords, commoners, citizens, I beg to lay a question before you. It is this.' A hush fell. 'Is it not illegal and against all precedent to sentence the king in his absence? Even the lowest criminal is entitled by the laws of this land to hear the crimes with which he is being charged before he is judged.'

Before he could say more a scuffle cut him off. The bishop suddenly found himself surrounded by armed guards. In a moment he was being dragged from the hall. The commotion caused a small ripple on the awed and stunned silence into which the assembly had plunged. No one spoke.

To Chandler, everything seemed to speed up after that as if to forestall any further objections. An ad-hoc committee, formed allegedly to represent the Commons, pronounced their verdict. Guilty on all counts. It was decided that they would visit the man now no longer king in his prison in the Tower to inform him of their decision on the morrow.

The next task before them was to find a successor. And quickly. The realm was descending into anarchy. Who could bring back law and order?

Chandler tried to get out. He had no relish for charades. Even the most sot-witted fool could guess the answer to this one. But the crowd was so densely packed around him he was trapped and was forced to stay to witness every pre-planned, traitorous move.

On the dais where everyone could see it the chair of state, covered by a cloth of gold, was still glaringly empty.

Before he could move Bolingbroke rose to his feet. His supporters, on cue like trained mummers, bowed and genuflected to allow him to step forward. He waded between them with the gravitas of Moses parting the Red Sea. Meekly, with bowed head, he made the sign of the cross on his own forehead and chest then turned to look out over the sea of faces.

Humbly and in plain English so they could all understand he issued his challenge. 'I, Henry of Lancaster, descended by blood from the good lord King Henry the third, am sent by God in his grace with the help of my kin and friends to recover the realm at the point when it is being undone by bad government and the undoing of the law. Does any opponent step forth to challenge me?'

If any foolhardy citizen or commoner had stepped forward, their counter-challenge would have been drowned out by the vociferous cheers of his supporters. He held up his hand to reveal the royal signet and boomed over the tumult that King Richard himself had placed it on his finger himself.

Chandler closed his eyes in disgust. All around him underneath the rehearsed cheers people were muttering and casting glances round about to seek any opposition to this travesty.

Carlisle had been bustled off in chains and nobody else was willing to face up to the imposter and suffer the beating they would get as a result.

A hush fell when Thomas Arundel stepped up beside his protégé and took him by the right hand. Le Scrope followed to take the left hand and together the two archbishops led Henry towards the vacant chair of state. For a moment it looked as if he was going to resist but he only wanted to kneel for a moment at the foot of the chair as if to pray and when he stood up again the two men reverently helped him to be seated.

Unable to stomach more of this Chandler found that others felt the same way and before Arundel could launch into a sermon he joined them in a rush for the doors.

It cannot be, many were muttering in desperation. Too stunned to say much else and finding they were being hustled straight out of the precinct between two lines of armed guards, Chandler saw them quickly being dispersed in separate harmless ways off the island and out into the surrounding streets and alleys before they could regather to make any sort of protest.

Unnoticed he turned back along the side of the enclave and when he came to an unguarded stretch of wall he climbed back into the precinct and, walking as if he was on official business, went inside again.

What had given him the nerve to return was someone he had noticed just as he was leaving the hall with the other objectors. His red beard was distinctive, even in the colourful opulence of the great hall, and now Chandler noticed that he was standing with a group of militia wearing a similar blazon to himself. It showed they were part of Aumerle's entourage.

At a word from Aumerle, Red-beard, man-at-arms or whatever he was, broke away from the group and pushed through the tumult towards a side door leading deeper into the palace. Already ablaze with anger, Chandler followed without a thought, pursuing him up some steps and along several passages until he caught up with him as he entered what could have been a guard room. There was no one else there.

Chandler strode up to him and slammed him against the wall. The man, Edwin something, objected but Chandler cut in, 'I want to talk to you.'

'I'm unarmed,' he protested.

Chandler reached down to the man's boot and plucked out a knife. 'You are now.'

He laid the knife across the man's throat but had to swerve as a mailed boot kicked out with what would have been a crunching blow. He kneed the man's leg to one side and punched him in the face as he did so.

'I haven't any money on me, mendicant,' the fellow said through a bloodied nose.

'I don't want money. I want information.'

'What about?'

'The novice you delivered from All Hallows to a house on Dow Beck.'

'What about her?'

'Was she alive when you left?'

'Of course she was.'

'You're lying. How come you picked her coif out of the beck?'

'Because she was disrobed by her own nuns. I left them to it. Not my game. I was only following orders to deliver her.'

'I can vouch for that,' said a voice behind Chandler.

Before he could move two militia men rammed him against the wall and through the tears caused by the impact Chandler saw the man he knew to be the duke of Aumerle strolling towards him with a sardonic smile on his lips. He gave the slightest lift of his eyebrows and his men released Chandler and fell back.

'Now, brother, do you have good reason for attacking one of my men in this extraordinary manner?'

Chandler, aware that he was outnumbered, told him, as succinctly as possible, what he wanted to know, only to find Aumerle raise his eyebrows again. He seemed determined to smile his way out of trouble.

'So as I understand it you expect me to chastise one of my men for obeying my orders?'

'You ordered the murder of a novice?' asked Chandler, astounded to hear him admit it.

Aumerle gave a pleasant chuckle and leaned elegantly against a chair.

'I was instructed to maintain secrecy by my cousin Bolingbroke. We were informed that the girl had the misfortune to overhear a private arrangement being made and my trusted man here' – he nodded towards Red-beard – 'was ordered to take her to a place where she could be held until it was safe to release her. He'd have done the same with anyone who was likely to broadcast the truth before time.'

Chandler glanced across and noted with satisfaction that the man's nose was still bleeding.

In a muffled voice he said, 'I told you she was alive when I left.'

'Whoever killed her went too far, I'll give you that,' Aumerle continued, staring hard at Chandler. 'If the fellow to whom she was delivered had used his wits he would have imprisoned her until it was safe to release her. Sadly . . . he had his own instructions, it seems.'

When Chandler went on staring at him he said testily, 'I don't know what you expect me to do about it. It's nothing to do with me. I gave no such order. You'll have to look elsewhere . . . Or do you expect me to resurrect the dead?'

Chandler was about to put a futile hand on his sword – half-believing that he might even use it – to demand who had issued such instructions when Aumerle made a small gesture with his ring finger and his guards slammed into him again, dragged him outside and rushed him along the passage to the top of some steps with his feet scarcely touching the floor but before they could hurl him head first down them he managed to say, 'All right, lads, you win. Lay off!'

He strode back along the strand towards the City in a fury.

EIGHTY-NINE

Parliament was called for the sixth of October to confirm the king's abdication.

Sticklers for protocol sitting in the Fleece asked each other how Parliament could be called when there was no king to call it and then they discussed whether it was a king's right to call the two houses together anyway if he was a prisoner in the Tower. Could a prisoner, king or not, have the right to call Parliament and, if not, at whose behest was it now being called?

There was no clear answer although the pundits drinking ale had many opinions on the subject.

'Not,' said Archer, 'that it will make one blind bit of difference what verdict you reach, my friends. If Arundel wants to call a Parliament so he can continue to accroach the king's regality then call it he will.'

Chandler said nothing. By now he probably knew more about the matter than anybody here. The story of the king's abdication in line with what he had apparently promised Bolingbroke at Flint had spread rapidly. His enemies made sure of that. More, it was now explained that he had given up his crown with a smile. 'Glad to be shot of the burden of kingship, I shouldn't wonder,' said one or two innocents.

Somebody made a remark along the lines of wondering how it

was that if you repeated something often enough it became true. 'Mayhap there's alchemy in language, my friends?'

'Aye, black alchemy to suggest he gave up his kingship with a smile. Like some gormless sot-wit?' Archer was scathing.

He wasn't the only one. As the story began to spread around the streets and taverns it was met with incredulity. It was beyond mortal belief. So much so the story had quickly to be amended to give it some credibility.

The new version was that no, he had in fact refused to give up his kingship, 'showing his usual ill-temper of course', but had then willingly changed his mind and handed the reins of government to his cousin because he believed he would make a better king.

It was like watching a once-loved building destroyed by a raging fire. There was nothing anyone standing watching in the imaginary lane outside could do other than witness the roof cave in and the walls crumble.

The next day Sir William Thirning, the Chief Justiciar, headed the proctors to the Tower where they informed the king that he was no longer King Richard II, King of England, but had been given a new title, Sir Richard of Bordeaux.

His reply, the story went, was something like, 'Yes, well, I know you're only doing as you're bidden but I hope my cousin's going to be a good lord to me, as I was to him.' Thirning then had the duty to inform Richard that he now had to renounce all the honours connected to kingship.

It was now he baulked.

'That I cannot do. The spiritual essence of kingship cannot be renounced. It is a bond with God made at the time of my anointing with the holy oil and exists for eternity.'

'But, Sir Richard,' Thirning protested, 'you have confessed yourself as unworthy to reign so how can you claim the honour of kingship?'

'My answer to that is that my downfall has come about because my government displeased so many. It has nothing to do with the sacredness of kingship.'

When this version of events was told in the Fleece, Archer announced to the group of fellow Lollard alchemists he was sitting with, 'The point to remember is that Arundel is consumed with hatred for the king, never having been admitted to Richard's inner circle of pleasure-seekers, and, feeling that his path to advancement was stopped, his rage has festered and grown to monstrous proportions.'

'An imbalance of spleen,' somebody suggested.

'Yes. It leads him to imagine that only one thing can assuage his wrath and that's to pull down the king and destroy him utterly.'

'Spleen aside,' added someone else, 'I see it as a battle for power between Crown and Church.'

'At least the puppet-king appears humble and well-meaning.'

'Aye, in a bumbling, covetous, dim-witted, two-faced, monosyllabic way.'

Gales of laughter greeted this apt description of Bolingbroke.

'Have a heart!' the same man reproved when he managed a straight face. 'There is nothing in the ability to knock a man off a horse that encourages consecutive thought or the understanding of words.' More laughter but it was the humour of the gallows.

Chandler was still shocked at how Bolingbroke had simply waded in like the opportunist he was and lied that Richard had agreed to step down.

The Fleece nit-pickers asserted that it was a blatant admission that he was a usurper, forced to appease Parliament in this manner, even though both houses were packed with his place-men.

Chandler bent his head to Archer and warned in an undertone, 'You people don't make my life easy. What you're saying is enough for Arundel to cart you off to Saltwood.'

To his astonishment the coroner stood up and grabbed him by the neck of his robe shouting into his face, 'I no longer care, Rodric! I'm saddened to think you support this treachery! Betray me to whomsoever you will! At least then I'll have chance to put my point of view and make it heard!'

'For what good it'll do you with Arundel.' He too stood up.

So furious was the cataract of punches Archer drummed into Chandler's ribs he was gasping for breath. Everybody fell silent.

Into the hush Chandler said, 'I'm not going to fight you, Arnold.'

A punch landed hard on his chin and he turned his head.

'Fight, damn you!' yelled Archer, thumping him again. 'Traitor! Snake!'

Chandler pushed Arnold away with one hand.

It was he who should be offering himself for martyrdom, not a

City coroner dedicated only to discovering the secrets of physical matter. Maybe the time would come when Fortune's wheel would turn and it would be time to fulfil his obligation of martyrdom to his saint.

The next date of significance was the thirteenth, the Feast of St Edward the Confessor and the date on which the lord mayor of the City was elected. This year it had extra meaning. It had been decided that it should be the day of Bolingbroke's coronation. And so it followed in not much more than a week after the so-called abdication.

Beguiled by promises of lower taxes and preferment the new mayor and his aldermen fell into line at once. Trade was uppermost in their minds, of course. The wool tax, the cost of transport, wages, the safest place to put their money, the price of fish, these were set against the things they could not see nor barter, truth, honesty, fidelity, chivalry.

As the crown was lowered onto Bolingbroke's head, Whittington, his cat at home with a trusted maid, turned to Archer standing by and murmured that he was already plotting how he could transfer his money-lending to the fellow they would now have to call King Henry IV of England.

While the ceremony dragged on he told Archer that his trade with King Richard, he corrected himself, with Sir Richard, had been lucrative and pleasant, the need for fabrics from overseas was constant, together with other luxuries it had been a joy to import. 'Along with money-lending,' he added, 'our dealings were easy and without friction.'

His glance assessed the fox-coloured hair on which the crown now rested and he told Archer he was worried enough to offer up a prayer or two that if he played his hand cautiously things would come right for him in future business, adding, 'It's not the man that wears the crown but the crown that wears the man.'

Archer admitted that he had watched the ceremony with gritted teeth, especially when the anointing took place behind the gold screen. Henry's rumour-mongers had already invented a story about this anointing oil.

It was the one thing Richard of Bordeaux, still in the Tower and missing out on his cousin's coronation, had held on to in his reluctance to surrender his royalty. Something mystical had happened to him at his own coronation when the chrism oil had been used to mark his body with the sign of the holy cross. He could not renounce it.

Not to be beaten, his cousin had miraculously discovered an ancient phial of holy oil kept secretly in a cupboard somewhere. Inside this eagle-shaped ampulla, it was claimed, was the sacred oil of St Edward the Confessor.

'That's a deliberate insult to Richard,' Archer had muttered in Whittington's ear. 'He always regarded Edward the Confessor as his own sacred protector.'

'The date of the coronation is an insult if it comes to it, being the saint's own day. Are we meant to regard it as the saint's blessing on usurpers?' The merchant gave a cynical smile.

Chandler spent the day in the Fleece, where Archer and the other alchemists invited to Westminster Abbey later found him.

Archer greeted Chandler by throwing both arms round him and holding him in a bear hug. It was their first meeting since his attempt to have a fight.

There were tears in his eyes. 'I don't take back a single word, Rodric, but . . . you know . . . your allegiance . . .'

Chandler nodded. 'I know, I know.' He thumped him several times on the back.

'Let me fill that for you.' Arnold took Chandler's ale mug and when he returned he said, 'Arundel was in his element. The eminence behind the throne, ensuring his manikin is as visible as the sun in heaven. It remains to be seen whether that fellow will ever do anything on his own initiative.'

Chandler looked thoughtful. 'Do you mean that? You believe his grace has managed this entire coup?'

'Mark me down for further transgressions against the new orthodoxy, Rodric, but I won't be the first to say this. Bolingbroke's ambition has always outstripped his intellect. When his father died, enter our ambitious friend Arundel who, seeing an opening for the next move in his own faltering career, shoulders his way into the presence. Whispers in the ducal ear began—' He broke off, spreading his arms.

NINETY

I am sitting on a bench near the door of the Master's guest-chamber. Rodric is staring into space. He doesn't speak. He hardly moves. It's as if he's absent leaving the shell of his body behind. Only now and then his hand moves to allow him to lift the goblet to his lips. He could be one of those mechanical toys you sometimes see the sailors bring in from abroad to sell to the rich. When I think he's ready to have his goblet refilled I get up and go to stand beside him. I pour out the wine but he doesn't notice. He's lost in thought.

The whole City is decked in flags. Everybody is on holiday. Church bells peal incessantly, not as a call to prayer so much as a celebration. Food stalls do a roaring trade. Wine flows from the conduits for anybody to drink. Minstrels play on every corner. There are acrobats. There is a man doing tricks with fire. Another juggles with eggs. People are linking arms and dancing. Laughter and celebration on all sides.

It seems wrong. I feel flat. When I had to go out I couldn't get back to the house fast enough. And now, here sits the spy, no doubt glorying in the fate of King Richard, alone in the Tower, and over the fate of Adam who has never done anything wrong apart from blot one or two words on the Master's manuscripts and who they suspect is now a prisoner in the dungeons of Archbishop Arundel's castle at Saltwood.

And it goes without saying he is as indifferent as you please to the murder of an innocent novice. I wonder about his housekeeper, this Beata, and if she knows the nature of the man she serves or, worse, is complicit?

I pour myself a small cup of wine and swallow it quickly. The spy glances up and notices my head tilted back and I feel caught out, like a thief. I put down the cup, pick up the flagon and go over.

'More wine, brother? Or does your saint forbid it?'

He tilts his head on one side and narrows his eyes as he glances up at me. Without speaking he lifts his goblet and holds it out for me to replenish.

Rodric, I say to myself for no reason, *placing his lips to the rim.*

NINETY-ONE

The scrivener was released. Chandler did not flatter himself that it had anything to do with the remark he made about the Master missing his services.

'He is stumped for a way in which he might progress his new work,' he had informed Knollys in a tone as guileless as a green girl's. 'Poets . . . you know what they're like! He can only work with someone he is familiar with.'

A eulogy in praise of King Henry IV – 'the so-called king', as the French referred to him – was being requested by the court with greater frequency. It seemed to Chandler that it was a licence to write. No eulogy meant no recognition and therefore no payment, however small. Chaucer's begging poem drawing attention to his empty pouch was provoking some mirth but little else.

'Is there anything of interest coming from the alchemists these days?' Knollys asked before he left.

'Nothing. They're not much interested in court matters. I believe they are like most people. They accept the changes as a fait accompli. Not their business. Alchemists like to talk but that's as far as it goes. As long as they have their retorts and astrolabes and their books of numbers they're happy.'

Knollys made a sound at the back of his throat that implied derision.

NINETY-TWO

Adam, reticent as usual, opens up enough to show us his scars. 'They're healing quickly, thanks to your friar's special salve, Mattie.'

'He's not my friar!' I retort.

He covers them up again. 'What do you want me to do today

then, Master?' He stands at his copying desk and begins to mix his ink.

The Master puts an arm round his shoulders. 'We need to talk later. First let's get my priest's tale finished.'

NINETY-THREE

When did it become known that the royal prisoner had been removed to another more secret prison?

Chandler had no idea. His own knowledge came earlier than most because of his constant duties at the Tower. Recently he had been instructed to question several acknowledged Lollards but was able to report that they were happy to recant outside St Paul's as demanded by Archbishop Arundel.

Even so the first inkling he had that the royal apartments were empty was when one of the guards made a joking reference to a forester they had smuggled out a couple of nights previously. His unexpected refusal to wear ordinary black spurs when they took him out had caused ructions until King Henry had generously allowed him a pair of silver-gilt spurs in keeping with his status as a knight. The midnight exit through the watergate was mentioned in the same context. Gravesend and Leeds Castle down in Kent were also mentioned. Further information as to his whereabouts after that was not available.

NINETY-FOUR

I'm setting a watch more closely than ever. Somebody daubed a slogan in whitewash on the street door. Before the Master sees it I begin to wash it off. Inevitably he hears me slopping water about.

'What's this, Mattie, my dear?'

'Nothing, Master.'

'Then how is it you're washing nothing off the door?'

'Please don't worry. It would only be doltish lads trying to be funny.'

He comes out into the street to stand beside me and squints at the words underneath the smear of half-obliterated whitewash. 'Did it say what I think it said?'

'That depends.'

'Hm.' Making no further comment he returns indoors.

I hear him calling to Adam and the Cook. They go into his private chamber and close the door. When they come out Chaucer says to me, 'I will rescind your contract if you so wish, my dear. We have decided we shall have to move somewhere safer than this. Being so close to the Tower makes us vulnerable to prejudice . . . Only if you wish, Mattie. I shall not willingly send you away.'

'I have nowhere to go, Master. And even if I had I would refuse. If you would allow it,' I add.

'Dear creature. I thank you. Then let's stand together, the four of us. We'll start packing today and I'll go down to Westminster to see someone I know there.'

NINETY-FIVE

When Beata went to pray in Chandler's small chantry she was sometimes the only parishioner present. Martin was unsmiling, Chandler himself often absent. An atmosphere of tension prevailed throughout the City. The wise were making sure they were seen taking part in the ritual of the Eucharist at St Paul's or one of the larger churches. The affiliation of the bishops became a matter of concern.

The usual banter in Cheapside changed to hard-faced bartering. Many of the usual traders had not returned after the unrest. Stalls stood empty. Prices were hiked up. Everybody counted their change and looked shocked then counted it again.

Chandler rode out to see Henry Daniel at his gardens in Stepney. After they talked he sat in the arbour for a long time with his head in his hands.

Next day he helped Martin carry a few possessions out there. Setting off they looked like pilgrims, straw hats, hired palfreys, a couple of saddlebags, and they told anyone who asked that they were on their way to Canterbury.

Only Chandler returned, entering the City relatively unnoticed through Aldersgate shortly before curfew. The stout wooden gate in Stepney was barred behind him after he left, turning the gardens into a refuge.

A day or so later he was standing at his window while he shaved when he noticed Beata, carrying a shopping basket, hurrying away down the street. It was odd but he hadn't heard her go out. Now, instead of turning off towards the market she carried straight on towards Dow Beck. Curious to know where she was going, and remembering the mystery of her frequent lies, he wiped his jaw with a cloth and followed. Soon, from a safe distance, he watched her turn alongside the beck and carry on up Cousin Lane.

He was following when she slipped into the yard beside Comberton's house. After a little while she reappeared and, from the shelter of a passage opposite, he watched her hurrying back down the street. Instead of making any purchases in the market, as the basket over her arm might suggest, she returned to Aldgate and was soon back inside the house.

Giving her a moment or two to complete her subterfuge he strolled back, trod quietly two at a time up the stairs and flung open the door. She was just hanging up her cloak and turned with a start of surprise.

'Been to market, Beata?' he asked.

'Yes, I forgot something.' She gave him a flustered smile.

He went to the basket at her feet and upended it, tipping out the kitten and nothing else. 'It seems you've forgotten it again.'

When he glanced up, her face flushed scarlet.

'So where have you been?'

'Nowhere, Chandler, honestly. I just wanted to get out for a walk.'

'I didn't know you knew Comberton's son?'

The struggle to invent a convincing lie failed and she bit her lip.

'Who did you go to see there?' He stepped closer.

'No one, Chandler, it was no one, nothing. I just—'

'It's not the first time, is it?' He felt like hitting her. 'You've been lying to me for some time. Lying about going out, wet footprints on the tiles – other things, nothing in themselves but they add up to one thing. You're deceiving me.'

She cringed back.

Rage erupted suddenly enough to make him reach out and grab her by both shoulders. 'Who are you working for?' he demanded fiercely. She put up both hands to protect herself as if expecting a blow and he flung her back in disgust.

'It's not young Comberton because he's away. Who else is there?'

'Only his steward.'

'Who? That gnarled, lying old fellow?' He remembered when he and Archer in another age had knocked on the door of the house in their pursuit of the murderer. He stared at her. 'In God's name why him?'

'He gave me the kitten—'

'What?'

'And – and he lent me money.'

'What for?'

Again she bit her lip and he waited for the next lie but before she could find the words he gripped her savagely by one arm and forced it behind her back. 'You know who his master is? You know where his allegiance lies?'

'I don't tell him anything important, Chandler, honestly!'

'How can you know what's important and what isn't? Do you tell him about places I go to? Well, do you?' he repeated when she merely stared at him with stricken eyes. 'Answer me!' He shook her.

She was sobbing now but it was because she knew she was trapped in the web of her own deceit. 'You're hurting,' she managed to gasp.

'Not as much as I might hurt you. What have you told him?'

'I said you visit the old military commander in Seething Lane. That's all!'

So that's where the rumour had come from. 'How do you know that?' he ground out, already aware of the answer. He blamed himself for being so lax.

'I followed you,' she confirmed. 'You were in a hurry and never looked back.'

His voice was drained of emotion when he released her. 'You've been keeping him informed about my movements . . . You're a stupid, disloyal, faithless woman. I've a good mind to kick you out onto the street where you belong.'

She was still sobbing, begging him not to, saying, 'I'll never go there again. I'll give the kitten back. Please, Chandler. I haven't done any harm.'

He knew it didn't matter now. Almost as an afterthought he said, 'You must know he owes allegiance to Aumerle?'

'But so do you – we all believed he was loyal to the king . . .! That's why I thought—'

When she read his face an expression of horror dawned and she drew back, clenching her fists. 'Do you . . .? I didn't know . . . How could I?' One hand went to her mouth. 'The red rosebud . . .?'

'It's not your business. Anyway, they're allies. We all know that. You're the one to be on the wrong side.' He turned away. What had Gaunt said all those years ago: *we have spies and spies who spy on them.* To be spied on by a lackey of Aumerle!

She went to him on impulse to clutch him by the arm. 'It happened almost without my realizing it . . . then he said he would tell someone and I'd finish up in the Dow with my throat cut, just like her . . . I was frightened, Chandler. I didn't know what to do, how to escape—'

'Why didn't you tell me, if you thought we were on the same side?'

'I was frightened. He warned me not to.' Glancing up at him, her eyes were wide with the fear of what he might do.

'Tell me about this steward and what else he said to you.'

'He said he wanted a fortune so he could live comfortably in his old age.'

'What did he mean?'

'He was selling information to whoever would pay . . .' Her throat constricted and she was unable to go on.

Noticing her stricken expression he asked, 'Is this about the novice?'

Her voice was a whisper. 'You know it is.'

'Go on.'

'They brought her from the abbey to All Hallows . . .'

'I know that. And?'

'And the nuns had given her something to make her sleepy . . .

and – and then, he said, they paid off the carter and got another man to bring her to Comberton's—'

'And he was waiting for her. Did he use the knife against her?'

'I don't know!'

He didn't believe her. She began to sob again and he wondered if even her tears were genuine. Even so he put one arm round her shoulders. He knew their webs and how they spun them so tightly it was impossible to free oneself. What comfort that was for the novice, alone, drugged, with the steward leering over her with his knife, only the angels knew.

NINETY-SIX

I n the days that followed as the new reign settled into a pattern of repression Chandler thought constantly about the novice and who had given the steward his instructions. Of course he had used the knife.

After a long talk with Beata, an interrogation if you like, came proof. She admitted that, after a few drinks one day, the steward had boasted about his need for haste, the way her ring would not come off her finger, and how his master had paid him a fortune for a job well done.

'And this generous master?'

'He showed me his seal . . .'

The look of horror on her face was enough to tell him that this time she was not lying. When she described the seal his own suspicions were confirmed.

She moved like a ghost round the apartment after they talked and both spoke only when necessary. There was no way of bringing such a man to account.

The new century was imminent. The realm seemed balanced on a knife edge as if anything might happen. The soothsayers had a clear field for dire warnings on everything. A bestiary of outlandish creatures put fear into usually rational adults as well as children and the overly superstitious.

The next Parliament brought in statutes to confirm Henry's power. Heresy was stamped on and the Lollards were scattered or imprisoned or decided that it was wiser to recant in public outside St Paul's as demanded. The streets became less rowdy as law and order was reasserted and the Fleet prison filled up with rebels and miscreants waiting for the hangman. Of those who fled the City for safety many did not return.

Out of necessity, produce from the countryside began to seep back into the markets and the merchants began to trade again, but slowly. Trade had slumped but optimists believed it would soon recover.

One day in December Chandler had an unexpected encounter.

It was St Lucy's Day. The saint's eyes, exhibited on a silver patten in front of her effigy, winked blue and blind. Entering All Hallows with a large and voluble retinue of seculars and nuns was a figure he recognized. Or was it the perfume of attar of roses that aroused his attention first? Whichever it was he drifted in its wake.

Lo, it is she, as Archer would have put it.

He followed the group inside. Stood unobtrusively at the back. His opportunity to speak arrived afterwards as everyone lingered in the porch. The December rains had turned to sleet. Gusts scudded across the fore-gate, making everyone jostle and hold back. Servants were sent to fetch a canopy for the illustrious. In the hiatus before departure he stepped forward.

She certainly remembered him. In fact she went so far as to thank him and his colleague Sir Arnold for their tact in dealing with the matter. 'It might so easily have become a disaster!' she fluted.

The sickly perfume of dead roses tainted the air as the meaning of what she was telling him sank in. The novice, it seemed, had overheard a private conversation, exactly as Mercy had told him. It was between one of Aumerle's men and an emissary sent over from France to finalize a few details about a war loan from le duc.

Henry had spent part of his exile at the court of Orléans and been given a loan to buy ships and men. When he reached England he planned to use his family fortune to pay for the army of foot soldiers and bowmen he would need. The presence of his emissary proved without doubt that Aumerle had been in it up to his neck, playing both sides until it was time to reveal his allegiance.

Chandler did not follow her explanation in detail. It fitted with what he now knew. He heard only the gist, the betrayal, the planning and the traitorous intentions that the unfortunate novice had accidentally overheard. He could well imagine her terror when she understood what it meant and who was behind it.

'It was, of course, as I'm sure you will appreciate,' fluted the prioress, 'of paramount importance that she was stopped. Determined to go her own way and reveal the truth, she brought her fate upon herself.'

Chandler's silence encouraged her to add, 'It would have been a calamity if she had let slip a word of what was about to happen. King Henry would have been in great danger . . . ' She spread her elegant arms. 'Our abbess decided we could not risk that. Secrecy was of the utmost importance for King Henry's mission. York and his son Aumerle understood this.'

She spoke with the righteousness of one who has chosen the winning side.

'So although the duke of Aumerle was in Ireland with King Richard, he knew what was afoot through his father, the regent—' murmured Chandler.

'And aware of the thinking of the king's counsellor, we of course took the necessary steps to deal with the danger.'

Chandler was aware he had not asked after Mercy. Some time he would make moves to find out where she was and tell her how brave she was to confess the little she knew.

So that was that. Or almost. He felt he had everything but a signed confession, for what good it could do.

Archer was right to keep out of it. After all, there was nothing to be done once they found the body in Dow Beck except to speed her flight to heaven.

NINETY-SEVEN

Chandler is crossing the street to the chantry, a place diminished by Martin's exile, when he notices the maid, Matilda, walking back from market. It is a while since he has seen her and he is aware that Chaucer himself has not been seen about the City recently either.

As he is about to hail her two horsemen ride up and rein in their horses one on each side of him. Their mounts are so close he wonders if they intend to crush him and if so, why, when one of them gets down. He is joined by two other men on foot. They are all armed and wear Lancaster's colours. He is surrounded.

The one sitting astride the horse grunts, 'We want to talk to you, brother.' Chandler weighs things up.

He decides to make a point. 'May a poor mendicant not go about his business unmolested these days?'

Two of the foot soldiers draw their swords with awesome speed.

Chandler stands stock-still and then steps from between the horses and begins to fumble under his cloak.

NINETY-EIGHT

I am walking down the street on my way back from market when I notice a group of militia drawn up close by the Mercedarian chantry. It takes me a moment to understand that they have a man in their midst. It is the spy, Chandler. *Rodric.*

I see the whole encounter from the beginning. Brother Chandler. The men-at-arms. The horses on either side keeping him kettled up in one place. One of the riders alights.

The other one calls down to him and Chandler makes some reply which I am too far off to hear. The men-at-arms draw their swords.

To my astonishment Chandler, reaching inside his cloak, drags forth a sword of his own. He holds it as if it is something he has never seen before and one of the militia sniggers and begins to swagger towards him. He pokes the point of his sword at the spy the way you might tease a child with a toy. Then he makes a feint or two and steps closer. Both men have moved away from the horses.

For some reason Chandler is smiling.

The next minute the military man's sword is lying on the ground at his feet. Chandler puts one foot on it.

For a moment nobody moves.

Then a second man steps forward and his sword goes flying away in like manner and the point of Chandler's sword is suddenly at his throat. He is holding it like a dagger. He takes a step towards the man who falls to his knees with his arms outstretched begging Chandler's mercy and saying, 'I surrender, brother.'

The others have been watching so silently I've forgotten they're there but now I look across to where they're bunched beside the horses and I'm in sudden terror that they outnumber him and my hair stands on end. Now they will cut him down as sure as anything.

I shout, *Rodric!* And begin to run forward.

The first man who lost his sword is already shouldering his companions away and the horseman remounts and moves off. The man crouching at Chandler's feet is abandoned to his fate.

Chandler picks up the sword. I'm close enough to hear him say, 'Better not have this until you learn how to use it.'

He gestures for the man to go then stands with two swords, one in each hand.

He looks bemused.

I can't help myself. I shriek again, *Rodric!* And find myself running right across the road to throw my arms round his neck in sheer relief. He cannot stop me. His hands are full. But he accepts my embrace, his skin warm, his hair brushing my face, his body taut against mine, vibrantly alive! Embarrassed I let my arms slide from around his neck and step away. A small crowd has gathered.

Very carefully and without looking at me he replaces his own sword in its scabbard with touching clumsiness then removes his cloak to wrap round the blade of the one he won.

When he's finished he looks up and gives me that slanted look. He raises his eyebrows a fraction. 'Rodric?'

I fight a blush that races up my throat into my face, trying to hide it in vain. Still looking bemused and ignoring the onlookers he puts down his cloak with its bundle and reaches towards me. The crowd are beginning to disperse as he pulls me against him then he takes one of my hands and kissing my palm with great slowness and thought places it against the side of his neck where he holds it under his own. I can feel his pulse strong and steady beneath my palm.

I lift my head to say something but there is nothing to say as so often with him and his mouth is so close I cannot help being drawn . . . but then he bends to pick up the sword at his feet, places one hand on my waist and begins to walk with me along the street. We ignore the remaining bystanders and their comments, and drift in silence, blindly, in a strange dream where everything is changed.

NINETY-NINE

As always her feelings were written on her face. Dragging the extra swords along, Chandler walked her towards Aldgate and his lodgings as if it was the most natural thing. She did not object but stared straight ahead. He stopped before they reached the gatehouse. 'I will have to send my servant out on an errand . . . Then maybe you will come up . . .?'

They were outside the chantry already. The door was never locked and he pushed it open. 'Will you wait for me here?'

She wore an entranced look like the Virgin at the Annunciation but there were no angels. The stone chamber had only its martyred saint and the carving of his mangled body to remind them of the true nature of things.

As he was about to leave something made him reach out to untie the string of her coif. It allowed her hair to fall around her shoulders in all its secret abundance, red-gold tendrils crazily falling to her elbows, and she looked even more like an angel. He couldn't resist lifting a strand to press his face into its beguiling honey-scented silk.

After a moment he murmured, 'Always wear it down for me.'

She leaned against him meltingly and whispered, 'Am I to wait here for you?' She was in awe of the meaning of the place despite the simplicity of Serapion's ungilded cross fixed to the plain wall. The only concession to orthodoxy was the faint perfume of candles and incense. But the light fell around her and such innocence made him want to weep.

'I hope you'll always wait for me.'

'You think I'm too young but it's almost like Lady Constance and Thomas Despenser and they're married—' She broke off in confusion.

He said helpfully, 'But it's the other way about. Lady Constance is the elder of the two.'

'What does age matter? The duke of Aumerle is married to a lady thirty years older than himself and she's not even an heiress. And anyway, I'd feel—' He watched her think a moment and then with the kind of courage that disarmed him he heard her whisper, 'I'd feel like this if you were one hundred and twenty-nine.'

It made him smile and hold her closer.

'I doubt it. And I'm glad I'm not because otherwise I wouldn't be capable of doing what I want to do next.'

She widened her eyes. Her beguiling honesty undid him.

'What do you think I mean?'

'I don't know,' she bluffed, suddenly losing courage.

'You do know. I want to make love to you.'

'You're a friar.' She did not pull away.

'So?' he murmured, taking her into his arms more decisively.

'I thought . . .'

'You thought you were safe?' His eyes danced. 'You must know our terrible reputation!'

'I do now.'

ONE HUNDRED

When he reaches out to untie my coif I feel stripped. I am naked beneath his gaze. He lifts a lock of my hair to his lips. For a long time we stand like that . . . his mouth in my hair linking us and when he raises his head to look at me he draws me with his recklessness and I am willing to do anything for him. Nothing is between us but the thin fabric of our garments and I yearn for his skin, his body, for every part of him.

Slowly and never releasing me he ushers me towards a little door at the far end of the nave opening into the vestry. An embroidered cope hangs from a peg, bed-straw fills one corner for when he stays over for the night offices, and he, as I ask, am I to wait here, turns to the door to wedge something in it and then with no break in the seam of our being we are lying on the bed-straw and he asks in a strange voice unlike his own, may I remove your clothes and then it's me, tugging at the lacing on my bodice and my shift sweeping

over my head and thrown to one side and he, whispering, if I ask
you if I'm about to take your maidenhead will you rage and cut me
to shreds as you sometimes do? And me, shaking my head saying
it is yours, Rodric, take it, and feeling ashamed at being so green
and he says nothing, not in words, but only in the movement of his
hands over my skin and as the bliss begins to rage I know that
his touch is an allegory just as words are and it is an allegory for
our shared desire.

ONE HUNDRED AND ONE

A s the shadows were filling up the nooks and crannies of the
chantry he said she should go home. 'What will your Master
say when you return so late? Will he whip you?'

She giggled. He kissed her but not on the mouth and she arched
a little sighing with bliss and saying, 'Rodric! . . . I didn't know
you were allowed to do that.'

And he said, 'We're not. It's forbidden, as all delight is forbidden
by the Church.' He raised his head and stretched up to reach her
lips to kiss them next. 'I want to keep you here for ever . . . but
then I don't want you to be punished for being late either.'

'He's away,' she murmured. 'The house is empty.' She sat up,
languid at the thought.

He lifted his head. 'For how long will it be empty?'

'Two or three days.'

'And where is he?' he asked in as casual a tone as he could
muster.

'Calais.'

'What?'

She looked confused and the thought crossed her face that she
should not have told him. Quickly he asked, 'Am I invited to stay
with you in this empty house?'

She relaxed. 'If you so wish.'

He took her in his arms again and lay full length over her and
murmured, 'It is my only wish.'

ONE HUNDRED AND TWO

My glance falls on the carving above the little door into our paradise, angels and strange monsters, and I suddenly see that they're letters of the alphabet. I spell out the letters then tell him, 'I can read.'

He kisses me and says, 'I like a girl who can read.'

He always teases me. It makes me cross. 'You don't believe me!' And he says, 'I believe every word you utter.'

'Over the door it says,' I reply lifting my hand from where it was resting, 'St Serapion, martyred for God.'

'So it does.' He turns to look at me and asks, 'What else can you read?'

'I'm reading the Book of the Lion,' I tell him. 'But slowly at present until I learn to pick up speed.'

'And what's it about, this book?'

'It concerns a king who is beloved by his people and a man who is jealous and plots to win the crown from him. It's an old French story the Master is translating.'

He kisses me again and says, 'Put your hand back where it belongs.'

'I've never touched a man there before.'

'I should hope not.' He sighs and stretches. 'Matilda . . . Matilda . . . my dear sweet Mattie, my lover, my leman . . . We need only the alphabet of our bodies to read anything worth reading.'

ONE HUNDRED AND THREE

And he turned his head to smile into her eyes, saying, 'I'm devastated . . . All the while I've been in paradise you've been reading the wall!'

They wrestled for a while, exchanging small bites and nips, she running her hands through his thick hair, he trailing long strands of gold between his teeth until it was time to don their garments and re-enter the outside world.

The Book of the Lion was one they did not have on their list. The scrivener had failed to mention it even under torture. With a narrative like that he now knew why.

ONE HUNDRED AND FOUR

Twilight has already softened the look of the streets when we leave the chantry. He insists on walking back to the house with me to protect me, as he says, from night-hawks. He promised to return after compline and after attending to a few other duties at Aldgate. It is now long after compline and he has not yet shown up.

Cook and I rattle around in the house and it seems too big without the Master and Adam taking up so much space but most of all it seems empty because he is not here. How can absence be so like a physical presence? It envelopes me. I breathe it in. My entire being is full of him not being here.

When I go to stand at the open door and glance down the street it is hauntingly empty. I try not to be down-hearted. I know he has duties to fulfil towards the followers of his saint but I am still awake when the matins bell tolls. The sky is heavy with stars and still no sign of him. I resign myself to a sleepless night and begin to wonder if he ever intended to return.

ONE HUNDRED AND FIVE

After leaving her he felt bound to call on his contact. It was dark by now. Curfew. Only felons and those such as himself abroad. Torches were blazing outside one or two of the larger houses. The shadows they made were as black as widows' weeds.

The spyhole snapped open and two eyes peered out. 'Oh, it's you.'

'Is he abed?'

'Aye. Come in.'

The door creaked open.

He is indeed abed. His wife is a snoring mound beside him but he, spry as usual, is sitting up and demanding, 'Calais? What the hell's he doing there? We'll have him followed when he gets back.'

'I'll do that. I've found a way to be at the house more often.'

'That won't be necessary. You may be needed elsewhere.'

The old man insisted on keeping him talking for some time. Of an age where sleep will not easily come, he seemed pleased to have found some diversion and questioned Chandler about all manner of things to do with events over the last few days. He even mentioned Arundel.

Eventually, dissatisfied, eager to get away, and without mentioning the Book of the Lion, Chandler left the house in Seething Lane and took the route towards Aldgate past the poet's house. It lay in darkness now. He imagined her in the high attic, slumbering in hot sheets with her wild hair spreading like molten gold across her pillow. Undecided, he thought twice then turned for home, walking back in the shadow of the eaves.

Abruptly Swynford on his high horse emerges out of the darkness before he reaches the gatehouse. His men appear carrying cressets and the smoke streams between them, black coils in the garish light.

Swynford wears a basinet. It glints as he moves. 'I hear you gave my men short shrift earlier?'

Chandler stands his ground. 'Did those fellows come from you?'

'Did they not tell you so?'

'Not that I remember.' He indicates the chantry. 'I may have weapons belonging to one of them.'

'Keep them. You earned them.'

'Will they not need them?'

'Not where they now reside.' He does not explain. Instead he says, 'You're to come with us. That's what the sot-wits were trying to tell you.'

He doesn't move. 'Where are we going?'

'You'll find out.' He adds, 'It's King's business.' Glancing over his shoulder, he shouts, 'Somebody get this man a horse.' Turning back to Chandler he says, 'You'll be away some time.' He gestures towards the gatehouse. 'Is that your abode?'

Chandler nods, in doubt of what will come next. The man knows it is.

'Get your things for a lengthy absence.'

'Are we going overseas?'

Swynford looks mystified. 'No, why should we? We're going north, brother. That's all you need to know.'

While a horse is being brought, ousting its rider for the sake of the new one, Swynford, at his most genial says, 'Maybe there's more to you than milord suspects?'

Chandler says he has to go inside the chantry to make sure all is well. He has everything he needs with him. He's a friar. 'We travel light,' he explains.

When he emerges he closes the door and instructs one of Swynford's esquires to take a message to his housekeeper. It may be the last chance he has to set things right. *Use the small key to open my casket. What is there is yours. Use it with care.*

'Repeat after me,' he orders. When the boy is word-perfect he scampers off.

And so Chandler is forced to take to the road. He travels, not like a Lollard, on foot, but riding a well-shod destrier and carrying his saddlebag and his scrip of cures. He is accompanied along every heavy mile by Swynford and his retinue of militia.

ONE HUNDRED AND SIX

I stand looking down into the waters of Dow Beck for a long time, remembering the novice who drowned herself for love. The current swirls towards the Thames where the two waters meet and although I know the story isn't true because she was murdered, I want to lie down in the stream, filthy as it is, and die like her.

Slowly it has begun to dawn on me that he is no different from any other man. He is as they all are and I wonder how I could be so wrong about someone. I believed in his alphabet but it has turned out to be only the jumbled-up letters of lust. He was doing what they all do, and I have thrown myself away on a worthless liar, and I feel like a fool.

The way to Aldgate is no distance but it might be a thousand miles for the time it seems to take. If he has merely slaked his lust with me then I want to hear it from his own lips. How can lust feel so deceptively holy and transform the world if it means nothing? When I see him face to face I wonder if I shall strike him or not. I debate the matter with myself and am still unsure when I reach the gatehouse. One thing is certain, I will not fret and moan for someone who is not worth a farthing.

An old, evil-looking fellow nods me towards the steps inside and retreats to his lair without another word as soon as he understands why I battered on the door.

A musty smell of decay and damp stifled between thick stone walls hems me in as I begin to climb. The walls are so armoured against attack they cut off every sound from outside. Only the whisper of boot-leather on stone, desolate and doomed, accompanies me to the door at the top. It is shut and I bang on it with all my force.

It flies open at once and a woman stands there. Her face falls when she sees me. She must be his housekeeper. I don't like the look she gives me. Ignoring it I say, 'I wish to speak to Brother Chandler. Will you tell him someone wishes to see him?'

'I can't,' she says.

I'm about to object when she adds, 'He's not here. He did not come back last night.'

'Not back?'

She shrugs in a helpless sort of way and I realize she is as anxious as I am when she adds, 'I'm afraid something terrible has happened to him.' She hesitates as if she wants to say something else but instead says, 'I'm sorry I can't help you further.' She is about to close the door when I slam it back against the wall.

'What do you mean?'

She looks astonished at my rage then a new expression comes into her eyes. 'Come inside. You're the Master's maid, Matilda, aren't you?'

We sit facing each other in a chamber filled with his presence. This is where he lives. These are the things he touched in his everyday life, the life kept secret from me. My eyes well with sudden tears – whether of anger or sorrow or something else I cannot tell.

She says, 'I fear an evil has befallen him. He would not be warned off and now they have taken their revenge.'

'Warned off? What revenge?' I ask like a sot-wit.

'About the murdered novice.'

'The one whose body was found in Dow Beck?' I gape as if there might be others.

She nods. 'He was determined to find her killer and bring him to justice . . . he didn't care who warned him off.'

'I didn't know,' I reply, wiping my hand across my face. 'I thought he didn't care.'

'He did care. He always cared. I said once, "Not a sparrow falls but the good Lord mourns," but he felt justice should apply in this life too.'

'And who,' I ask after this has sunk in, 'did he wish to call to account?'

'The steward – but his real master is not who you might think. Chandler has no way of proving anything.'

'So?' I urge.

'Aumerle was secretly trying to secure favour at the usurper's court. None of us knew that at first.'

'It's common knowledge now. It explains his father, the regent, to-ing and fro-ing during the invasion.'

She looks surprised. 'Yes that would be so. It was Aumerle's man-at-arms who was instructed to leave the novice with the steward at Comberton's.'

'Did he murder her?'

She nods.

'Did Rodric know that?' I burst out.

She looks startled. 'You call him Rodric?'

'Don't you?'

I hold my breath but she shakes her head.

'He was kind to me when I was widowed and at my lowest . . . I repaid him by disloyalty . . . being who he was he forgave me. I have vowed to make amends.'

'I'm sorry,' I say, as if it's my fault. We sit in silence for a moment. I see we are allies of a sort, though probably rivals too. Eventually I ask, 'So where do you think he is?'

'In a ditch with his throat cut.'

'Never! I know he's still alive!'

She smiles sadly at me and takes me by the hand. 'I pray to St Zita and the angelic host that your faith is justified.'

Gripping her hand in response I say, 'His mission cannot go unfulfilled whether he's alive or dead. The murderer must be brought to account.'

'I vow he will suffer. Trust me. Come with me now. I have to go out.'

She goes into a kitchen where some bread is cooling on a tray with a casket of herbs next to it. She takes down a basket from a hook on the door, pops a kitten inside and, wrapping the bread in a cloth, places it carefully in the basket and pulls on her cloak. We leave together.

Out in the street I make my useless prayer to the angels again. *Please, please, punish the offender by your divine grace. And please bring my beloved to safety and not let him dwell in sorrow and pain, amen.*

ONE HUNDRED AND SEVEN

Some three or four days pass. No sign that the angels have heard me. The Master returns from Calais when he said he would but says nothing about his purpose in going there. Together we finish the packing we started before he left and, with Cook and Adam carrying the heavy stuff, we pile everything onto a cart and prepare to set off for a new home within the safe purlieus of Westminster Abbey.

'Better there than in this ship of fools,' the Master remarks as he joins us.

I scarcely know what I'm doing. I'm living in a never-ending nightmare but somewhere in the depths of my mind I know he is safe despite what Beata said. He will one day turn up with an elaborate story about where he had to go and why he has only just thought to come back to me. And I will wait as he asked me to.

ONE HUNDRED AND EIGHT

Meanwhile the man the French insist on calling 'so-called' King Henry IV or the Usurper is staying with his four sons over the Twelve Days of Christmas at Windsor Castle just as his cousin Richard did the previous year when he was king. This time the rambling, magnificent old place is seething with the red and gold of Henry's faction. Everyone is in festive mood. The music, the dancing and the feasting show no sign of letting up.

The Apocalypse, much feared, was only idle talk, after all. Where are the Four Horsemen? Where are the mighty waves supposed to drag cities and mountains into the sea? Where the endless fires? Where the comets? Where the dragon, the lion and the wolf who are to divide the realm between them?

Young bloods, disregarding talk like this, are fretting about more mundane things, their physical fitness, the state of their armour, their horses. They are even now preparing for the great joust that always occurs as the Twelve Days come to an end at Epiphany. Favours are already being bestowed. Esquires drilled. Mounts groomed to make their coats glow like molten metal. More importantly, lances are measured and assessed.

When Swynford's retinue arrive the halls are already decked with holly, the berries as red as king's blood, and mistletoe, white as death, winding round the green branches of the host.

Long tables arranged down the length of the Great Hall are steeped with every kind of meat and fish you can imagine, all arranged with enough artistry to show off the conjurations of the royal cooks. They make a gaudy and brutal display. A jelly-eyed sturgeon, tail in its mouth, a roasted meat edifice, turrets of spices and almonds, a castle with miniature men-at-arms manning the walls and a tiny king on a glazed throne poised under a gold-leaf awning, all amaze and astound the senses.

Servants in a never-ending stream heave in great salvers loaded with fruits and exotic imports from Outremer, lifting them high above their heads to force a path between the riot of guests. Heralds play a flourish for every new dish brought forth. Not only endless amounts of food appear but barrels of ale and wine are stacked along the walls. In the middle of the hall is a never-empty space for dancing and musicians in their loft take turns to keep the music constantly playing.

Swynford, noticing Chandler sitting to one side and not eating anything, strolls over. 'Surely you're permitted meat during the Twelve Days, brother?'

'I choose not to. My cult is quite strict on such matters.' This is not true. It's something he would not admit to Swynford but the barbarism of the present self-indulgence offends him.

Swynford picks up a snipe cooked to a crisp in a coating of batter and says, with careful casualness, 'Tell me, is there a remedy to stifle a man's appetite? If anyone knows, it must be you.'

'I know not, my lord.'

'Come now, surely?' He scowls and bites off the head of the snipe. 'If you don't know you'd better find out for me from someone who does.'

Chandler sighs to himself. It sounds like a threat. But why does Swynford want to know? Henry might be somewhat heavy in the arse but is surely not bothered by that now he's got the crown to keep him happy? He replies, 'I will bend my mind to the question, my lord, but may I suggest you try bladderwrack and see if that works?'

'I've got a better remedy for putting you off your food,' a nearby courtier pipes up, his lips greasy with fat.

Swynford, with the last of the snipe halfway to his mouth, asks, 'What is it?'

'This,' says the courtier.

He purses his lips and aims a gobbet of spittle into one of the heaped platters before them. It lies there glistening and wobbling among the jellies and the meats but plainly and undisguisedly what it is.

Despite their rough manners everyone draws back. Swynford looks sick.

Later someone hands Chandler a vielle and he fingers the four strings but the sound is lost in the thumping beat of an estampie. Only when everyone collapses with laughter and exhaustion is there sufficient quiet for solo singers to take the floor. When his own turn comes he chooses the ballad about the three ravens. There is an ironic edge to his voice, a double meaning that is hard to pin down. Silence falls.

'*I saw three ravens sitting on a tree*
Down a hey down down.
They were as black as night, all three,
With a down,
Then one of them said to his mate,
"Where shall we our breakfast take?"
With a down derry, derry, derry down down.'

Urged to continue he tells the whole story, about the slain knight, his faithful hounds, his noble hawks and, finally, the fallow doe who kisses his wounds and carries him to the bank of a lake to bury him – then dies from grief by his side.

For a reason that surprises him he sings the last few lines in a sort of wonder at the idea of such devotion:

'*May God send every gentleman,*
such hawks, such hounds – and such a leman . . .
with a down, derry, derry, down, down.'

Murmurs of approval break out as the last note dies. He puts the instrument aside. A vision of red-gold hair swamps his memory and he is overwhelmed by a searing sense of loss.

Only one thing mars the celebrations.

Although the empty barrels are rolled away and full ones brought in as the feasting continues, an unexpected stomach pain afflicts the king and his heir. For a day and a night they have to sit bare-arsed on the privy while the court continues to raise the roof. After their indisposition, the usurper and his son, another Henry, are eventually conducted back into the feast hall. Pale and shaken, they can only drink watered wine for the rest of the festivities.

The new king's ministers feel bound to speak.

Led by Archbishop Arundel they spout warnings about the possibility of poison. Arundel claims that danger is inevitable from the folly of keeping Richard of Bordeaux alive.

He is especially vehement. 'Majesty, you will be in constant danger as long as he lives. Heed our warnings, I beg of you. Execute him!'

As a usurper, the self-styled King Henry is not unaware of personal danger. To reassure them and himself he makes a vow.

'If there shall be any rising in the country in his favour, he shall be the first to die!'

ONE HUNDRED AND NINE

Before we leave for our new home in Westminster another rumour to heighten the feverish mood goes the rounds of the market. It is that the plague has returned.

'How many dead?' is the question on everybody's lips.

It turns out that only one man has died.

When I hear that it is the steward at Comberton's house I bite my lip and, as nonchalantly as I can, I ask, 'Why do they think it's the plague?'

'Because it happened sudden, like,' replied Izzie.

'That gravedigger from Portsoken don't agree,' Annie butts in. 'He saw the body. He says it's more like . . .' she lowers her voce and mouths the words, 'something he ate.' She winks.

I think of Beata and wonder if she has heard this story and a little later after they have described with great relish the contorted blackened features of the dead man and the fact that he must have lain in agony several days and nights with nobody there to hear his death cries, I remember I have not seen her since she went out with the gift of fresh bread. I ask, as if it is of no moment, 'Where is Brother Chandler's housekeeper these days?'

'I heard she'd gone into a convent somewhere,' Annie adds indifferently as she turns to a customer.

I say nothing.

That same day the gravedigger launches a story that begins its flight quietly but soon wings everywhere in a subdued tumult until he silences it by telling us he heard it from Sir Arnold so it must be true.

It is this. When the dead man was found he was grasping something so tightly in his hands the bones of his fingers had to be snapped, one by one, to release it. What it turned out to be was a small cash box.

When Archer's lad prised the lock off they found a small amount of silver coin inside and a document. This turned out to be an IOU for an astonishing amount of gold. The seal it bore was that of Archbishop Arundel.

What his Grace was doing sending such a large sum to a mere steward leads to much speculation in the Fleece. Some forthright suppositions are put forward which, under the new repression, can only be described as seditious.

'I wonder how long Arundel is going to last,' Adam speculates in a general sort of way as we set off for the safety of Westminster. 'Still, that's that for now.'

'And so it is,' I reply. 'May flights of angels bless us all.'

Chandler left Windsor in Thomas Swynford's entourage. The latter, as the new Constable of Pontefract Castle, had urgent business in the North. It was the Eve of Epiphany. A dozen riders swept into the bailey as Sir Thomas and his men rode out.

Claude
Monet

Trewin Copplestone

List of Plates

PLATE 1
Woman from Normandy in Profile
(c. 1856–57) opposite left
Black chalk, 9⁷/₈ x 6¹/₄ inches (25 x 16cm)

PLATE 2
Young Dandy with Monocle and Cigar
(c. 1856–57) right
Black chalk with colour crayon, 9⁷/₈ x 6¹/₄ inches
(25 x 16cm)

These two examples of Monet's early artistic interest as well as of his financial enterprise, made when he was about 15, show him to be a caricaturist beyond normal expectation and indeed his drawing at that time also showed academic ability. This form of portrait illustration was popular in the 19th century and such figures as Spy achieved a considerable reputation from similar treatment of famous figures of the day. Nevertheless, the influence of Boudin soon redirected Monet to more serious painting.

The Impressionist revolution, one of the most dramatically successful and influential developments in the character of Western art since the beginning of the Renaissance, is encapsulated in the life and work of Claude Monet, recognized universally as the quintessential figure of the movement. The course of Impressionism is delineated through Monet's working life which covers the whole of the latter part of the 19th century and up to the second decade of the 20th century. Monet and Impressionism are so interrelated that it seems at times that he must be the only Impressionist, so much does he personify its characteristics and qualities. His long life encompassed many domestic and personal difficulties during which he struggled to enlarge his art. The result is a consistent if changing development which ended with a series of massive panels epitomizing his philosophy and becoming the greatest single monument to the success of the Impressionist movement.

Of course, a whole art movement cannot be encompassed in the work of one artist. The wider the accepted generic coverage of any movement or period, the greater the number of artists that may be included and appropriately identified. In, for instance, a broadly inclusive term such as 'Renaissance', many artists of different nationalities and pictorial intention over a long time span may be included, with each contributing something significantly different to the general classification. When the grouping is numerically small, spans only a short period of time, consists mainly of one nationality, and with few formative figures as is the case with Impressionism, the contribution of each individual artist will materially affect the perceived character of the movement. For this reason, it is essential to be clear which artists may properly be included before one can establish the parameters of the movement.

With Monet at the heart, we may confidently claim Renoir, Sisley, Pissarro as original participants and determinants while Degas, although always claiming to be an independent and not liking the term Impressionist, was clearly associated and contributary. It has been said that any attempted definition of Impressionism which definitely excluded him would be inadequate although ultimately it has to be recognized that few of his paintings are even approximate to the evident intention and character of Monet's work. Another artist usually included in the Impressionist net is Manet, eight years older than Monet and the recognized leader of the group of independent painters from which the Impressionists emerged. His association is even more questionable than Degas'. He did not exhibit in the first Impressionist show in 1874 but he was a friend of Monet's. His painting philosophy and practice was never close to that of the Impressionists and he is now regarded more as an influence than as a participant. Other painters are also usually included, such

as Cézanne, who through Pissarro certainly had a short connection; Bazille, who died in the Franco-Prussian War of 1870 before the first 'Impressionist' exhibition; Van Gogh and Gauguin, inaccurately, but because of their association with the group; and a number of others because of a perceived Impressionist character in their work, such as the two sculptors Auguste Rodin and Medardo Rosso, and even others because they exhibited in the first Impressionist exhibition. Thus, in attempting to identify Impressionism and its artists, it is essential to identify what it is first, and we are confronted with a chicken and egg situation; an unresolvable problem. It has usually been helpful to examine Monet's contribution as an *a priori* situation.

Claude-Oscar Monet was born in the rue Laffitte, Paris on 14 November 1840, into the *petit bourgeoisie*. His father and uncles were all grocers and ship chandlers, living comfortably without ambition or wide interests and except for one aunt, who was an amateur painter, the family had no interest in the arts. When Monet was five, the family moved to Le Havre, a port on the north coast of France at the estuary of the Seine, and his father entered a partnership with his brother-in-law, a well-to-do

ship's chandler. Monet was unhappy at school, learned little and whenever possible spent his time on the beaches and cliffs or in boats on the water. It was at this time that his interest in the movement of water began and, indeed, with all nature, which remained with him throughout his long life. Indeed, most of the characteristics that he revealed in his mature life were already evident in the child. He was independent, in little need of praise or social approbation, irreligious and concerned only with what he learned from his own experience.

Perhaps most fortunately for him, he was stimulated by antagonism and adversity, both of which he was to experience early in his working life as a painter. On the other hand, he was self-indulgent – some said he ate enough for four ordinary appetites – could be vindictive and taciturn, and was crafty and manipulative with money. When only 15, he was selling caricatures of locals for 20 francs in the small stationery and framing shop in Le Havre which had been owned by the painter Eugène Boudin. He met Boudin, who was a landscape painter of the local coastal scenery and who, importantly for Monet's development, painted *en plein-air* – on site in the open-air; Boudin quickly transmitted his love of the coast which he

PLATE 3
Photograph of Monet (1913)

PLATE 4
Trophies of the Hunt (1862) opposite
Oil on canvas, 41 x 29½ inches (104 x 75cm)

This early work, painted when Monet was still studying at Gleyre's atelier, is an indication of the academically based influence under which he produced his first works. It is painted in the traditional tonal structure and representational presentation which was the only valued approach at that time. It was against this restrictive practice and exhibitionist intention that the young painters who later became the independent group, of which Monet was a member, rebelled. The values of this painting indicate that Monet already had control of his technique and was capable of academic draughtsmanship, despite the short training that he had received. It may not be an inspiring work, but it is clearly competent. Gleyre, commenting on one of Monet's paintings, observed 'Not bad! Not bad at all, that thing there!'

knew so intimately to Monet. Boudin himself had been encouraged to paint by some of his customers, painters who themselves had an influence in Monet's life; Thomas Couture, a well known academician, with whom Manet was a pupil for six years, Jean-François Millet, a painter of *genre* subjects of peasant scenes of pathos and simplicity, and Constant Troyon, a painter of animals – particularly cattle – in quiet landscapes.

Painting out-of-doors with oil paint was not usual or very practical until the convenient means of transporting the paints in tubes was introduced in the 1840s. Boudin was a determined practitioner who convinced Monet that it was essential to capture 'one's first impression'. This was the one essential principle that guided Monet, and was perhaps the subconscious reason that he called his painting, in the first exhibition of the independent group in 1874, *Impression: Sunrise* and Impressionists became the name by which the group was subsequently known. Louis Le Roy, a well known critic, wrote a review of the exhibition which he entitled 'The Exhibition of the Impressionists', not the name that the group had chosen nor did it represent the content of the exhibitors' work.

In May 1859, Monet visited Paris, went to the Salon, and admired the work of the Barbizon painters Daubigny and Troyon. He also attended the Académie Suisse where he met Pissarro and visited the Brasserie des Martyrs, where the Realist group foregathered around Courbet.

During the winter he saw a number of Delacroix's paintings at a loan exhibition. In the autumn of 1860 he was called up for military service and chose to serve in Algeria 'because of the sky'; he was excited by the light and colour he found there. He was, however, sent home on sick leave in 1862 and his family bought him out of the army so that he never completed his military service. In the summer of the same year, while painting on the coast with Boudin, he met Johan Barthold Jongkind, a Dutch landscape and seascape *plein-air* painter who worked mainly in France, anticipating Monet's later practice of painting the same subjects in different atmospheric conditions. Thus, at the beginning of his professional life, Monet had already been introduced to the two features which became the central foundation of his art, and thus, of Impressionism.

Monet returned to Paris in 1862 and, though he had been advised by Troyon to study with Couture, joined the atelier of Charles Gleyre. It is interesting to speculate what the effect on Monet – and on Impressionism – would have been had he chosen Couture. Gleyre was a celebrated and much admired painter and teacher. Although Monet was dissatisfied with the teaching, Gleyre was actually one of the more liberal and popular masters in Paris. In his atelier, Monet met Renoir, Sisley and Bazille – all of whom became part of the independent group when later formed. Bazille was an out-of-doors painter and

an important member of the group who is not as well known as the others since, as noted above, he was killed in the Franco-Prussian war of 1870 before the first Impressionist show.

The year 1863 was seminal in the development of the independent painters. In December of that year, Gleyre closed his studio – an almost symbolic event since it established the professional beginnings of the young independent students from his atelier. Even more significant to them in its immediate effect was the exhibition at the Louvre, from 15 May for a month, of the Salon des Refusés. This exhibition was staged on the command of Napoleon III that the paintings refused by the Salon itself should be shown in order to reveal, by contrast, the superiority of the Salon artists. Among the paintings of the *refusés* was Manet's *Déjeuner sur l'herbe* (above), which was the cause of a scandal since one of the figures in the painting was a naked female, accompanied by two elegantly dressed gentlemen. She looks boldly out of the picture as if defying censure and, incidentally, uncomfortably turning all viewers into unwitting voyeurs. This was all much too real for the *haut monde* and the critics, but for the young eager artists, already excited by the work of Delacroix, it was a clarion call to revolt. Although not at all what Manet had intended, he reluctantly became the leader of the avant garde and their meeting place became his favourite Café Guerbois.

Delacroix also died in 1863 and the admiration with which he was regarded by Monet and his friends was the inspiration for a new start, an artistic revolution. The reverence for the sturdy 'painterly' Romanticism of Delacroix himself even diminished and the classical, historicist and Romantic elements of the Salon were attacked by the young independents under the new banner of Realism, inspired by Courbet, who provides another strand in the developing artistic convictions of the nascent Impressionists. Gustave Courbet was born at Ornans, studied at Besançon and Paris, but was dismissive of tuition and was largely self-taught. He chose for his subjects landscapes and the everyday conditions of poor peasants he knew in his native village. In 1850, his painting *Burial at Ornans*, and exhibited at the Salon, caused a sensation, and was attacked on the grounds that the 30 figures represented combined to give an unreal view of a village ceremony, presenting the clergy as cynical and the peasants as degraded and brutal. Courbet himself had intended to give a sincere and sympathetic view of the villagers with whom he had grown up. His opposition to the false posturing of later Romantics and his scornful view of the whole academic training process revealed an independence which was an inspiration to the whole generation of young painters.

Courbet insisted that only the actual, tangible objects which existed in a real world, without imaginative

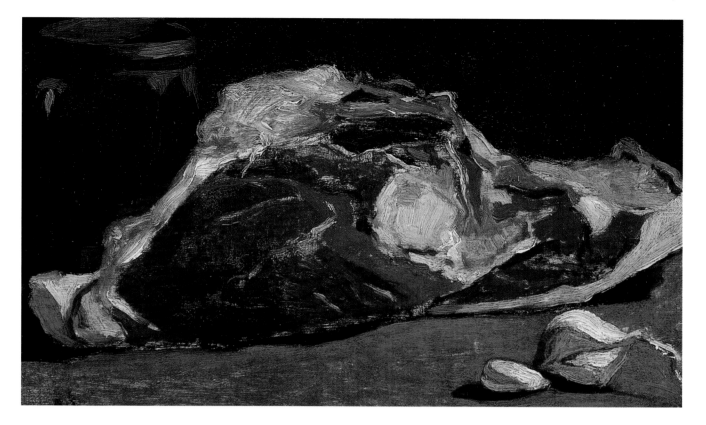

embellishment, idealization or alteration in the presentation of any subject, was acceptable. Monet and his friends from Gleyre's academy, Sisley, Renoir and Bazille were fully in sympathy with this view which was inherently part of the developing aesthetic of the age of Zola, Baudelaire and Balzac. Monet's response was, in a number of still-life paintings of the 1860s, to paint simple everyday objects, such as a single lamb chop or a couple of eggs with diligent vision and craftsmanship. Although of an inferior technical quality, Cézanne was also painting similar subjects at this time.

After the débâcle of the Salon des Refusés of 1863, which was not repeated, the Salon became the principal exhibition to which most painters, including the independents, were obliged to submit if they wished to show their work, and it is important to recognize that it ceased to be exclusively the outlet for academic exercises and began increasingly to accept the work of independents such as Boudin, Jongkind and Courbet, whose gold medal in 1849 meant that he was no longer subject to jury selection. In 1865 Monet submitted for the first time, and both his paintings were accepted and well regarded. 'The two marines of M. Monet are unquestionably the best in the exhibition,' declared one critic and when one recalls that Monet was then only 25 it must be regarded as an early success. His success was repeated in the Salon of 1866. He had painted a large *Déjeuner sur l'herbe*,

PLATE 5
Édouard Manet's Déjeuner sur l'herbe
(1863) detail opposite
Oil on canvas, 84½ x 106¼ inches (215 x 270cm)

PLATE 6
Still-Life: The Joint of Beef (1864) detail above
Oil on canvas, 9 x 13 inches (24 x 33cm)

Monet undertook a number of small studies of grouped objects, particularly (as here) of meats and vegetables. As artificially arranged objects, as nature morte *rather than living nature, they allowed him to concentrate on the intrinsic character of the objects he was exploring. The resulting work has some of the quality of surprise and originality that already suggests that Monet was not content to follow a traditional painting career. It has also been noted that these paintings owe much to Chardin, whose still-life paintings are among the most admired legacies of 18th-century French art.*

PLATE 7
The Walkers (Study for Déjeuner sur l'herbe) 1865
Oil on canvas, 59 x 47¼ inches (150 x 120cm)

The Salon des Refusés of 1863 was a watershed for the young painters of independent mind through the scandal provided by Manet's Déjeuner sur l'herbe (plate 5) and Monet was inspired to make his own version of the subject for the Salon of 1865 (plate 8). He was not able to complete it in time; he had intended a large scale work, approximately 5ft x 20ft (4.5m high by 6m wide), and in fact never did complete it. But he did make a number of studies for it, of which this is one, and did paint a smaller section for the Salon. He was in the first stages of his affair with Camille Doncieux and she modelled the female figures while a painter friend posed for the male figures, in this study, Frédéric Bazille, who was killed in the Franco-Prussian War. Monet's intention was different from Manet's. He wished to create a sense of the reality of the sunlit scene in which a picnic could properly take place.

influenced by Manet, which he intended to show but, unable to complete it in time, painted, in four days, a life-sized portrait of his mistress and future wife, Camille Doncieux, which, with others of his works, was enthusiastically received. Despite this *succès d'estime* he was not selling his work and after a serious quarrel his family disowned him and withdrew their financial support.

Astonishingly, after such success, Monet only exhibited in the Salon twice more. The authorities, in the form of Count Nieuwerkerke, the Imperial Director of Fine Arts, recognized that the new group, with Monet as a prominent figure, was a threat to the academicians' continued dominance of the Salon so that, in 1867, one of Monet's important paintings *Women in the Garden* (plate 9) was rejected. Monet never forgot the slight and many years later, when the government wished to purchase the work, he stung them for 200,000 francs.

Monet's life at this time was full of difficulties, lack of money being the cause of much of them. Although he continued to paint over the next two years, his domestic conditions were unsettled and some paintings shown in a shop window which included *Women in the Garden*, which was ridiculed by the now jealous Manet, did not sell. He was now penniless and, leaving a now pregnant Camille, went to stay with his aunt. By the middle of 1868 he was dispossessed and penniless and had become so depressed that he is believed to have attempted suicide by drowning.

Mercifully, at this time, he managed to acquire his first patron, a M. Gaudibert, who had commissioned Monet to paint his wife (plate 12), and later in the year established him in a house in Fécamp, a seaside resort on the coast of Normandy.

Monet married Camille in 1870 just before the commencement of the Franco-Prussian War. After the outbreak, and to avoid involvement in the war, he left Camille alone with their three-year-old son and went to London. In the same year Paul Durand-Ruel, a young dealer, had staged an exhibition at the German Gallery in New Bond Street, London, the first exhibition of the Society of French Artists, in which Monet had one painting and from then until 1874 showed several times with the Society. During 1871 Monet was in England, Holland and Belgium whence he returned to Paris late in the year and in December rented a house at Argenteuil, then in a small town on the outskirts of Paris. In the following spring he was in Le Havre, in the summer Holland, and returned to Argenteuil in the autumn where he painted, with Renoir, a number of riverscapes on the Seine. For the subsequent five years, Monet's house became a favourite meeting place for most of the group and the many paintings done during this period, particularly those by Monet and Renoir, were the foundation of the Impressionist pictorial revolution. Indeed, it was in 1872 that Monet painted the work he

PLATE 8
Déjeuner sur l'herbe (1866)
Oil on canvas, 51⅛ x 71¼ inches (130 x 181cm)

This smaller version of the intended large composition for
Déjeuner *indicates how Monet would have concentrated on the*
sunlit pastoral scene. Camille was almost certainly the model for
the female figures and the composition in the previous plate can be
seen on the left-hand side while the figure of Bazille is repeated
in the figure on the right, stretched his full lanky length in the
foreground and wearing a hat in the centre background. It was
clearly an important work for Monet, his first great set-piece. He
was, however, discouraged by Courbet who saw the work in
progress and made unfavourable comments about it.

PLATE 9
Women in the Garden (1866–67)
Oil on canvas 100$^{1/2}$ x 80$^{3/4}$ inches (255 x 205cm)

Monet's signature on this painting is an indication of the importance that he attached to it. It is a large painting and he submitted it to the Salon with the expectation that it would make his name known, and he made sure that it was not to be overlooked or misread. In the event, it was rejected by the Salon and for a time suffered indignities; firstly it was taken to Honfleur as Monet fled his creditors after slashing over 200 paintings to avoid their seizure; then, after the Salon rejection, it was exhibited in a dealer's shop window where it was ridiculed by Manet. In 1921 Monet eventually revenged himself for what he considered to be a slight by the Salon by charging the State, which was anxious

to obtain the picture, the extraordinary price of 200,000 francs. The painting was, Monet claimed, painted in the open-air 'on the spot after nature' in the garden of a house he had rented at Ville d'Avray. Camille was the model for all the figures and a trench was dug into which the large painting could be lowered to enable Monet to paint the upper part. For his friends this was a difficult and challenging work. It precedes the Impressionist method and shows something of the influence of Manet; but Monet's interest was in the effect of sunlight on the figures and foliage. Note the reflected light on the face of the girl in the foreground, thrown upwards from the white dress. Courbet commented that Monet had refused to paint the foliage in the background when the sun was not shining. The painting is composed in oppositions of light and dark, with spots of bright colour, and transforms Camille's hair into a strong brunette.

called *Impression: Sunrise*, a study of the docks at Le Havre (plate 20).

In 1873 another figure emerged who was to be influential in Monet's life, the well-heeled amateur painter and borderline Impressionist, Gustave Caillebotte, who became his patron and began to collect Impressionist work. His own works are not insignificant examples of the independent realism and in the broadest terms of inclusion could be termed an Impressionist.

The exhibition which established the group, introduced Impressionism and became the main outlet for their work until 1886, was held in 1874 at the former studio of the notable photographer Nadar, whose aim was to help the young and struggling painters. It was organized principally by Monet and Degas and was called the 'Première Exposition de la Société Anonyme des Artistes, Peintres, Sculpteurs, Graveurs' and opened on 15 April for one month. Monet exhibited five paintings and seven pastels.

MONET'S IMPRESSIONISM
The 1874 exhibition, now usually described as the first Impressionist exhibition, there being subsequent exhibitions (the last and eighth being held in 1886), is central to the early character of Impressionism. All the young independent painters exhibited but it was Monet who for the critics and public identified the character of

the movement as well as providing the name by which it has become known. Although they did not regard themselves as Impressionists at the time, most of them – to some extent all of them – contributed something to the perception of what constituted Impressionism. Degas did not like the name and his painting technique was very different from that of Monet. Renoir, who exhibited *La Loge*, one of his most famous works, in the first exhibition, came closer to Monet but every attempt at assessment of the qualities that are essentially Impressionist returns to Monet for justification. How closely does it actually identify with Monet?

It is important to remember that at the time of the first Impressionist exhibition, the painters were all young and their major works were still to be produced. This is particularly significant in the case of Monet whose last great waterlily paintings occupied him until his death in 1926. But it is true of all of them. The works that they showed in 1874 and earlier are those which established the name Impressionism but do not represent all the ramifications, digressions and experiments that each in their different ways, and variously influenced, incorporated in their later works.

If therefore we are to identify the revolution as that of the young painters it is to Monet, Pissarro, Sisley and Renoir that we turn. Manet never participated, Degas rejected the Impressionist name preferring independent or realist. It is Monet who offers the clearest ideas of early Impressionist work and particularly the stage at which he had arrived since settling in Argenteuil. It was here on the outskirts of Paris by the river Seine with his friends and colleagues, who in 1874 included Manet, that the best known and most closely linked Impressionist works were painted.

For Monet, water had always been a fascination, first on the seacoast near Le Havre and now on the river Seine. Capturing the movement of water, always a repetitious movement but never remaining the same, affected by light and weather, in different moods, had become for Monet, since his days with Boudin early in his development, a constantly demanding subject which, when painted in conjunction with moving foliage, demanded all his concentration. To capture the movement in an unchanging landscape was the basis of Impressionism for him. To seize what for Monet seemed the significant moment in any given potential subject was always his aim but which was inevitably frustrated by the time it took to

paint it. Each moment of significance demanded a different approach from its predecessor and perhaps many hours of painting time to realize it, during which time other significant moments intervened in a constant progression. It was necessary for time to stop which, of course, was not possible. Concentrated memory and a fluid technique, light and delicate dabs of colour where the forms lost definition which seemed almost to dissolve in light, were demanded on some occasions while on others the forms knit by tight paint application closely together gave a quickly completed image.

At this time, at Argenteuil, Renoir and the others were painting similar works in a similar technique and it is then that Impressionism speaks with its most unified voice. The immediacy of the transient moment engaged them all in their different ways, which could be considered a 'snapshot' approach but was not the case. Monet and the others did not forget or ignore the limits of the canvas or that they were constructing a picture within the long pictorial tradition of which composition was part of the

PLATE 10
The Terrace at Sainte-Adresse (1866)
opposite
Oil on canvas, 38¹/₂ x 51¹/₈ inches (98 x 130cm)

*The view towards the Channel across the estuary of the Seine at
Le Havre is taken from a window of Monet's aunt's villa and is
a family portrait group. The seated figure is his father, a dignified
and carefully modelled form; his aunt, Mme. Lecadre, is seated in
the foreground under a parasol. The young couple in the
background are Monet's cousin Jeanne-Marguérite and an
unknown man. Although Monet is painting a scene with which
he was familiar, as with Trains (plates 19, 28, 29), there is a
message in the ships in the background. Old sailing ships, one a
five-masted barque, and new steamships, their stacks belching
smoke like trains, are consciously contrived to point up the change
in sea travel and the importance of Le Havre as the chief port in
France. Monet later observed that the flags placed on either side of
the canvas were considered very daring at the time. The
composition is a strange combination of closely drawn forms and
loosely painted foliage. The water has a curiously patterned
regularity of surface and tone which flattens the visual effect of the
whole scene and draws attention to the distant ships and their
message in a way that would not have been evident in actuality.*

PLATE 11
The Beach at Sainte-Adresse (1867)
Oil on canvas, 22¹/₄ x 32¹/₄ inches (56 x 82cm)

*As a child, Monet had played on this beach and in these boats
and it remained one of his favourite haunts, full of happy
memories. It was also the place where he painted with Boudin
who must be counted as his first important influence and it was
near here that he also met Jongkind, another source of
inspiration. It is not surprising, therefore, that this work and
other scenes of this area are not so much observation as an
externalization of the pervasive presence in singularly calm and
energetic images. In this painting, the scene is casually accurate
and the drawing affectionately direct, the simple authority of the
blue boat in the right foreground being the sign of a natural
painter. There is a spatial, airy openness drawn into scale by the
fishermen in the foreground, who are themselves simply painted
– the one in black almost a caricature, a reminder of an early
interest of Monet. The low horizon, reminiscent of the 17th-
century Dutch landscapists, gives more than half the picture area
to the sky, much more than is usual in Monet's later paintings,
and is treated delicately to dominate and create the fresh open
quality of his vision.*

PLATE 12
Portrait of Madame Gaudibert (1868)
Oil on canvas, 85½ x 54⅓ inches (217 x 138cm)

This picture of Madame Gaudibert, the wife of Monet's first patron, Louis-Joachim Gaudibert, is the first of a number of significant portraits that Monet painted. It is treated as if it were a formal academic portrait, the figure dressed elegantly, and with the usual table and flowers in an interior of simple refinement. But the pose of the figure and the turn of the head gives it a sense of temporary, casual informality as if the subject is either unaware

or uninterested in the fact that she is being painted, almost suggesting, perhaps, that Monet baulked at the formal requirements at the last moment. It shows how capable Monet was at achieving whatever he wished, having reached a level of technical accomplishment that enables one to infer that whatever he does is what he intends to do, uninhibited by inadequate technique. Louis-Joachim Gaudibert was a good friend to Monet. He was a collector and bought a number of Monet's paintings, enabling Monet and Camille with their newly-born son, Jean, to set up a home together in Etretât on the coast despite the fact that Monet, as usual, was soon to be penniless again.

training. What they were trying to avoid, however, was a continuation of the static posed images of classicism as still practised by the academicians. The inherent movement of life visible in all nature was part of their goal and this demanded both a new painting technique and new visual perceptions. Instead, therefore, of defining forms with line and colour they adopted a broken non-linear paint application which suggested or implied a visual flux. So far was this from academic practice, that their vibrant colour and interfusing of forms and voids with nervous, delicate or bold dashes of paint seemed to traditionalists to be mere incompetence. One critic, in 1877, commented of Monet and Cézanne: 'They provoke laughter and are altogether lamentable. They show the most profound ignorance of design, composition and colour. Children amusing themselves with paper and paints can do better.' This is an extreme but not unique type of criticism at this time, a case of unfamiliarity breeding contempt in this instance, and it is this new different treatment of familiar subjects that underlay the Impressionist revolution.

But there was more. Monet later in his life realized that the single image painted *en plein-air* was almost an impossibility if one was searching for the single, significant moment, because light constantly changes and the time taken to make one brushstroke detracts from the accuracy of the last and next. For him (and although it was a compromise he recognized and deplored), it became

necessary to make a series of paintings of single subjects, such as the famous grain stacks, the poplar trees on the Epte, and the stream near Giverny. These works, which culminate in the great and ultimate long-lasting series of waterlilies are the culmination of Monet's personal and unique exploration of Impressionism.

AFTER ARGENTEUIL
Up to the time he left Argenteuil in 1877, Monet had already met most of the artists and supporters who had affected his career. In the previous year he had met the American-born John Singer Sargent who painted with him, the extraordinary collector Victor Chocquet whom he had met through Cézanne, and had visited the collector/financier Ernest Hoschedé at the Château de Montgeron. Hoschedé was a very wealthy man who, although he had already bought some of Monet's paintings, only knew him slightly. Also, in 1876, Monet had participated in the second Impressionist exhibition in the rue Le Peletier, showing 18 works. Remaining for the winter in Paris, he painted the well known *Gare Saint-Lazare* series (see example plate 29) in which a train engine features. Monet and the other Impressionists were devoted to nature and landscape subjects but it is interesting to note that the railway and trains appear frequently in their work. It seems that they were fascinated by the idea that the new

Continued on page 106

PLATE 13
Jeanne–Marguérite Lecadre in a Garden
(1866) below

Oil on canvas, 31½ x 39 inches (80 x 99cm)

In the mid 1860s Monet was experimenting with the various technical problems of translating natural effects effectively into paint, usually with a variety of brushes, sometimes with a palette knife or, as here, by using a brush to differentiate flat areas, such as the sky. These concerns become central to Monet's technique, leading in the 1870s to his essential Impressionism. Jeanne–Marguérite was Monet's cousin.

PLATE 14
The Luncheon (c. 1868–69) opposite
Oil on canvas, 75⅜ x 49¼ inches (191 x 125cm)

Monet's early life was punctuated by frequent crises, usually financial, and he was fortunate that M. Gaudibert came to his aid in the summer of 1868 enabling the Monet family to rent a small house at Etretât, near Fécamp. It was a time of brief happiness. He told Bazille, who was godfather to his young son Jean: 'I am surrounded by everything I love.' Manet had already painted a luncheon scene which Monet probably had in mind since he had been a model for a preparatory sketch.

This is essentially a realist composition, carefully painted and with all the visual implications of the subject. Camille attends lovingly to Jean whose toys lie beneath the chair in the foreground, the maid is leaving, having set a typically French lunch and an unidentified visitor stands watching. And the viewer, outside looking in on this domestic scene, is involved by the steep perspective, carefully constructed to focus attention on mother and child. The place-setting in the foreground is obviously for Monet himself. A sense of immediacy is established by the objects awkwardly placed over the edge of the table, the newspaper, napkin and loaf of bread. A charming, if laboured pre-Impressionist work.

PLATE 15
La Grenouillère (1868) detail
Oil on canvas, 30 x 39³/₄ inches (77 x 101cm)

The area along the Seine at Bougival and Croissy near Paris was popular with young Parisian pleasure-seekers, literary figures and the middle-rich, all of whom found something to entertain them; swimming, eating, talking and drinking. The most popular resort was La Grenouillère and its restaurant was owned by Père Fournaise. For Monet and Renoir it was an attractive painting location where they could sit side-by-side painting the same views. Renoir's comments are interesting: 'The world knew how to laugh in those days... I always stayed at Fournaise's. There were plenty of girls to paint.' The hub of the radiating composition is the circular 'camembert' and a catwalk joins it to the floating pavilion on the right. Monet's work at this time is beginning to approach the stabbing brushstrokes of Impressionism.

PLATE 16
Hôtel des Roches-Noires, Trouville (1870)
opposite
Oil on canvas, 31¹/₂ x 21²/₃ inches (80 x 55cm)

Monet was painting in Trouville with Boudin and this painting
shows Boudin's influence, particularly in the inclusion and
treatment of the figures. There is a delicacy and charming lightness
of touch in Monet's work, however, which is not evident in
Boudin. A small work, the scene is nevertheless full of a sense of
space, sunlight and an air of assurance and freedom typical of the
plein-air Impressionist approach. An observation by a visitor in
1874 describes the scene: 'The great building which seems to guard
the entrance to Trouville is the Hôtel des Roches-Noires. This is
the chief hotel, the resort of the most gaily dressed of the loungers;
it is worth seeing. There is not so much as a beggar to destroy the
illusion. Truly Trouville would have seemed a paradise to that
Eastern philosopher who wandered about in search of happiness;
and the paradise would last – perhaps till he was called on to pay
his hotel bill!'

PLATE 17
Camille on the Beach, Trouville (1870)
above
Oil on canvas, 15 x 18¹/₈ inches (38 x 46cm)

After a summer at Sainte-Adresse, in 1868 Monet painted a
number of subjects around Le Havre and only in the summer of
1870 did he go to Trouville with Camille and Jean. The influence
of Boudin is evident in this beach scene of the resort across the Seine
estuary from Le Havre, where the two painted together. Monet's
painting is much bolder than Boudin's and this small study could
almost be a detail of a larger work, so freely is the paint applied. It
was painted on the spot and grains of sand are embedded in the
pigment as evidence. The figure on the left is Camille, whom
Monet had married in June and she and Monet remained in
Trouville until September. Boudin, in a later letter, recalls the
occasion: 'I can still see you with that poor Camille at the Hôtel de
Tivoli ... little Jean plays in the sand and his papa is seated on the
ground, a sketchbook in his hand – and does not work.' In
September Monet left Trouville and fled to London.

PLATE 18
Madame Monet Wearing a Red Cape
(c. 1868–69)

Oil on canvas, 39$^{1}/_{3}$ x 31$^{1}/_{2}$ inches (100 x 80cm)

This sketch must have had a special significance for Monet which is unknown to anyone else. Is it an elaborated note of Camille's glance into the house as she passes, a momentary eye contact of great importance? We are entitled to speculate on this matter because it is the only early work that Monet kept with him for

the rest of his life. It was probably painted in Etretât at the same time as The Luncheon *(plate 14) in the winter of 1868–69 and is unfinished, broadly painted, and not designed to be an exhibition work. Nevertheless, it is an attractive work depending, necessarily, on the effect of immediacy that Monet succeeds in creating by the placing of Camille behind a grid of window panes in a relationship that is clearly not static although the broken up sharp red notes focus attention on the enigmatic expression of her face. Is it quizzical or sad?*

Continued from page 99

technology, that was increasingly cutting swathes through open countryside or causing great iron and steel bridges to be built, was impressing a new modernity on nature. It is almost as if this was evidence of their appreciation of modern change.

During the whole of the later period at Argenteuil, Monet was desperately short of money. After a disastrous auction sale of Impressionist paintings in 1875, he was forced to ask Manet for a 20-franc loan and in 1877, after a second visit to the Hoschedés, again spent the winter in Paris soliciting or borrowing money from friends and patrons. In the following January he rented a house for his family at Vétheuil, on the Seine further from Paris. The year 1878 was especially dramatic – Camille was ill, Michel his second son was born, and the rent was not paid, which resulted in a crisis relieved again with the help of Manet. This was followed by a further complication. Hoschedé, the successful financier, had disguised from his partners and from his wife, Alice, the fact that his business affairs were in grave difficulties and when his associates called him to account, a disastrous situation was revealed. Despite deprivation of his directorships and the reduction of his shareholdings, he continued to live lavishly and, rather than attempt to explain the situation to his wife, fled to Belgium where he wrote desperate letters to her threatening suicide. She, with her six children had by this

time joined the Monets at Vétheuil.

Camille's health steadily declined and she died in the following September. Monet, despite his genuine anguish at his wife's death, felt committed to showing works at the fourth Impressionist exhibition held that year in the Avenue de l'Opéra and submitted 29 paintings. After a disagreement with Degas, Monet, together with Renoir and Sisley, failed to show in the fifth Impressionist show and, in the case of Monet, also the sixth and, after a work was rejected in the Salon of 1880, did not submit again.

After Camille's death, further difficulties arose since Mme. Hoschedé was deeply religious and Monet was an atheist. She was exceedingly distressed at the irregularity of their household arrangements and, despite an increasing regard for one another, the couple could not marry since her husband was still alive. Monet was also deeply distressed at Camille's death. The result was an unhappy household and, in the hope of improving matters, they tried living in Pourville and Poissy, but unsuccessfully until, in 1883, Monet found a house at Giverny, a small village west of Paris on the Seine. For most of the year Monet travelled leaving his children with Alice while he painted on the Normandy coast, at Trouville, Fécamp, Dieppe, and Varengeville. In January 1883 he was painting at Le Havre and Etretât. At the end of April Manet died and Monet, after the funeral at which he was a pall-bearer, returned to Giverny.

PLATE 19
Train in the Country (1870)
Oil on canvas, 19²/₃ x 25¹/₂ inches (50 x 65cm)

*In the 19th century, the train was the ubiquitous symbol of
technology and progress, spreading across the countryside and
invading the life of the city. For the Impressionists, concerned as
they were with modern life, it was of particular interest and
importance and appears in many Impressionist paintings. This
characteristic landscape is divided horizontally by the speeding (in
the terms of those days) train, splitting the earth from the
heavens, smoke despoiling the sky.*

THE LAST PHASE

Monet lived at Giverny for the rest of his life (more than
40 years), visited by friends, fellow painters and, as his
fame increased, by national and international visitors. It
was the last great period of increasing security and
contentment, marred only by the eye trouble which by
the end of his life would leave him blind.

Giverny is a small village on the Seine near Vernon,
with hills on either side and two streams, the Ru and the
Epte in the valley, which divides the provinces of
Normandy and the Île de France. Monet's new house was
an unpretentious long, rather tall building, set in a garden
which, when Monet bought it, was typically bourgeois
and uninteresting. The ambience, nevertheless, was
attractive and the garden had great potential. Monet
immediately started to work on the property so that over
the years he was able to transform it into a famous and
exciting retreat, one which is now one of the most visited
properties with artistic connections. The village too, old-
fashioned with narrow streets, was delightful and the
surrounding landscape a constant attraction with poplars
lining the banks of the Epte and the fields well tended by
the simple peasants who viewed the Monets as curious,
strange and unwelcome additions to the village. Monet
was not well liked and his painting was regarded with
ignorant suspicion. The house and garden became a haven

PLATE 20
Impression: Sunrise (1872)
Oil on canvas, 18⅞ x 24¾ inches (48 x 63cm)

This painting was unwittingly responsible for the naming of a movement in art that has enjoyed the most widely based popularity in the history of Western art – no mean trick. It is actually an attempt by Monet, in the context of his developing art, to make a small study of a sunrise in Le Havre, a transient moment he observed from a small boat in the harbour. The story of how it gave its name to Impressionism is told on page 86. The painting itself is an interesting, freely executed view into the rising sun, its reflection in the water being the only solidly painted element, with the docks and their machinery, the boats they serve, and the enveloping mist. It can be no more than the dictionary's definition of an impression – 'an immediate psychical effect of sensory stimulus'. With the work before our eyes, the sarcastic words of Louis Leroy, critic of Le Charivari *and responsible for attaching the word to the movement, will be of interest: 'What freedom, what ease of workmanship! Wallpaper in its embryonic state is more finished than THAT marine.'*

of seclusion for the increasingly reclusive painter and when Monet ventured out to paint grain stacks or poplars, local peasants threatened to destroy the stacks and cut the poplars down. The family's isolation was nevertheless a protection and Monet ran his household with military precision.

He needed money to accomplish his plans but it seems hardly necessary to mention that his shortage of money still continued. This condition prevailed for most of his long life, despite his increasing fame. Of course, his plans for Giverny were expansive and expensive, but Paul Durand-Ruel had been the main support of Monet and other Impressionists in the early years. Unfortunately, the year after Monet moved to Giverny, Durand-Ruel's bankers failed and he was unable to continue his support. Monet, in desperation, went to another dealer, Georges Petit, Durand-Ruel's rival in Paris and a rift opened between the two men because of this lack of loyalty. Although never fully healed, by 1890 Monet was again with Durand-Ruel on a better business footing but with a cooler personal relationship. He had just begun his series paintings, the first being of fields of poppies, poplars and grain stacks. At the same time he was continuing the transformation of the garden and at this time began the famous water garden which would contain the waterlilies he painted in a series of enormous panels, as well as in smaller studies. Spanning the water garden, he constructed

PLATE 21
Regatta at Argenteuil (c. 1872)
Oil on canvas, 18⅞ x 29½ inches (48 x 75cm)

Painted in broad slabs of colour in high key, this scene is illuminated by the brightest sunlight and exhibits a special joy and freshness, a visual delight, which reflects Monet's pleasure in the small town on the banks of the Seine. This painting, a small esquisse, or preliminary sketch, is built of broad directional form-constructing brushstrokes with great immediacy. The flat area patterning and the luminous colour reflect the influence of Japanese colour prints which, at that time, Monet was collecting. This is one of the works in the collection of Gustave Caillebotte, a rich collector and amateur painter who exhibited with and collected the work of Impressionist painters.

the Japanese bridge which he painted many times during the succeeding years and which, in sequential review, reveals the increasing deterioration of his sight.

His life at last was tranquil, his work was beginning to sell, he was getting semi-official recognition and was being visited by great figures of the day. In 1892, Monet began his impressive and much discussed series of Rouen Cathedral which eventually, it appears, amounted to about 30 paintings although the whereabouts of some is not now known. In 1888, and again in 1891, he visited London where he painted a number of scenes along the river Thames. These paintings carry echoes of Turner's work which Monet had seen in 1870 and admired. Turner's influence is evident in his work and the two had much in common. Later, however, Monet claimed that he did not much like Turner's work. Although the time Monet spent in London during the Franco-Prussian War is frequently said to have influenced him as a result of his seeing Turner's work, there is not as much direct evidence of this in his paintings as is often claimed. Perhaps more significant was the misty London river landscape he encountered after the clear sharp air and revealing light of France. There is, perhaps, more than a touch of Whistler's nocturnes in these paintings – Monet had originally met Whistler when they were students together at Gleyre's atelier and Whistler, a notable wit and fashionable exhibitionist, was becoming an increasingly important

PLATE 22
The Basin at Argenteuil (1872)
Oil on canvas, 23²/₃ x 31¹/₂ inches (60 x 80cm)

*The bridge at Argenteuil, an important element in many
Impressionist paintings during the period when Monet rented a
house there, is seen here from the basin dock and forms a low
horizon line, reminiscent of 17th-century Dutch paintings of a
flat land. Within the land area, the horizontal banding of cast
shadows on the left makes a strongly engaging pattern with the
bridge and confirms the flatness of the whole land area. The sky,
in contrast, is full of circular cloud forms swept by a brisk wind
across the upper part from left to right. The difference between
land and sky is central to the appreciation of the painting – a
quiet land under a squally sky.*

painter, as well as being one of the finest of etchers. There
exists, however, one curious but interesting parallel
between Turner and Monet. Both were passionately
interested in the sea and its many moods. There is the well
known story of Turner observing a storm at sea lashed to a
mast. In 1893 Monet, accompanied by two friends, made
a three-week trip on the liner *Normandie*. A tremendous
storm blew up and while even the hardiest abandoned
deck, Monet and his painter friend Blanche remained in
securely fastened deck chairs to watch the storm's ferocity
with similar Turnerian sangfroid.

Monet's presence in Giverny, as his fame grew, drew
people of all kinds to the village. Many came, attracted by
its charm, but the most dramatic effect was to transform
the quiet rural locality into an artist colony. With no less
than 40 studios being created in a village whose
population had been only about 300, the change was
dramatic and since that time Giverny has remained a place
of pilgrimage for artists and art-lovers. Around this time
Monet was well advanced in his plans for the garden, and
was growing exotic trees and plants and designing walks
and vistas.

There are many stories of his visitors. Clemenceau, an
almost exact contemporary of Monet's, but who survived
him by three years, became a close friend and admirer and
a frequent visitor. Clemenceau, known as the 'Tiger of
France', was twice prime minister and presided over the

PLATE 23
The Luncheon (c.1873)
Oil on canvas, 63 x 79¹/₈ inches (160 x 201cm)

After 1870, Monet did not submit his work to the Salon for a decade, but did exhibit in the first four Impressionist exhibitions, in the first showing not only Impression: Sunrise *(plate 20) but also seven pastels, three other medium-sized oils and a large oil,* The Luncheon, *which had been refused for the 1870 Salon. In the second 1876 Impressionist exhibition, he exhibited another painting referred to as* a panneau décoratif, *but subsequently also called* The Luncheon. *The earlier painting was an interior with Camille and Jean (plate 14), whereas the second depicts a table prepared for lunch and it is this one which is illustrated here. It is an isolated example not related to any preparatory sketches. It represents Camille and another figure moving towards the prepared table, with Jean playing nearby. There is a hat hanging from a tree with a strange black ribbon and a white rose lending a startling counterpoint to the approaching figures. This charming atmospheric work, originally described as a decorative panel, has been greatly admired by a number of painters and Bonnard produced a painting reminiscent of it.*

PLATE 24
The Bridge at Argenteuil (1874)
Oil on canvas, 23³/₄ x 31¹/₂ inches (60.5 x 80cm)

This is perhaps the archetypical Impressionist painting, completed in the year of the first Impressionist exhibition and depicting what can only be described as the early headquarters of the movement – Argenteuil and the Seine. It was here that the group met and painted together, sometimes side-by-side in front of the same subject. In the broken colour now characteristic, Monet has made as careful an observational study of the scene as is possible, given the apparently casual nature of the subject. But this is deceptive: there is an ordered inevitability in the scene that is calculated and has resulted in a classical calm and balance. The boats are linked in a single solid unit and their masts with their reflections provide a stabilizing vertical. It is frequently supposed that Impressionist paintings, because they are concerned to give an 'impression', must be 'accidental' – that is to say, 'not composed'. One of the reasons why this work is representational is that it is so evidently composed. Absence of composition is not an identifying element in Impressionist work.

PLATE 25
A Corner of the Apartment (1875)

Oil on canvas, 32 x 23¾ inches (81.5 x 60.5cm)

In this strange but gripping painting, Monet has constructed a mysterious ambience into which to place his son Jean, who looks resigned as though accustomed to his role as a model. It is an affectionate study of a much-loved boy. He is placed on a highly patterned parquet floor and surrounded by outdoor plants, probably brought in for the winter, although it is a sunny day which means that the apartment is back-lighted. Monet had developed a habit of using blue in a particular way and he has used it in this painting to create the subdued lighting of the interior. Monet in fact listed the painting, when he sold it to Caillebotte in 1876, as Intérieur (tableau bleu).

Paris Peace Conference after the First World War. His influence and support were of great value to Monet. Cézanne visited in 1894 and met Clemenceau, Rodin and the critic and writer Geffroy. At the same time, the American painter Mary Cassatt was staying in the local hotel and met Cézanne during whose visit Renoir and Sisley came to dine and Cézanne, upset by their comments on his work which, though favourable, he misinterpreted as ridicule, left the house and all the paintings he had done during his stay, and he and Monet never met again. It was typical of Cézanne that he should leave his paintings behind and Monet, not believing – possibly incorrectly – that Cézanne would be much upset at their loss, sent them all on to him. Such anecdotes of the Monet ménage at Giverny abound.

After Ernest Hoschedé's death in 1891, any irregularities, as has been mentioned previously, were resolved by Monet's marriage to Alice in 1894. But the complications of Monet's family life did not end there when Jean, his elder son, married Alice's daughter Blanche in 1897 becoming both his step-daughter and daughter-in-law. Alice died on 19 May 1911 and Monet was devastated by her death, probably even more so than by Camille's as their life together had been longer and closer than his first marriage had been. All Monet's friends came to the funeral, even the near-blind Degas, and Monet seemed to lose interest in everything until autumn when

PLATE 26
La Japonaise (Madame Monet in Japanese costume) (1875–76)

Oil on canvas, 91⅛ x 56 inches (231.5 x 142cm)

Few lively and independent painters in France during the latter half of the 19th century failed to be engulfed by the waves of enthusiasm for all things Japanese which arose mainly from the import of coloured wood-block prints and subsequently from seeing the work of the great Japanese printmakers. Monet displayed this subtle influence in many of his landscapes from the early 1870s, but this painting is an extraordinary and unique homage to the Japanese style. The work is quite outside Monet's usual treatment of his subject, overtly contrived and painted in a style that he had long abandoned. Camille, looking more seductive and fey (her face in Renoir style) than in any other painting, is in a bizarre costume, probably based on a Japanese print. The robe would have been of silk but, as one critic noted, it looks more like homespun. The strongly painted samurai looks like a dwarf figure actually emerging into the scene. (Note the arms outside the line of the gown and the random disposition of the fans, jazzing the whole ensemble into a sort of visual frenzy.) A strange work but a great success – it sold for 2,000 francs. In 1918, when a friend told Monet that it had been resold for 150,000 francs, he replied that the purchaser had bought 'trash'. 'But yes, it was trash in being nothing but a caprice.' He also said the Camille was wearing a blond wig.

PLATE 27
Wild Poppies (1873)
Oil on canvas, 19²/₃ x 25¹/₂ inches (50 x 65cm)

In December 1871, after his return from England, Monet rented a house in Argenteuil which became the centre of the early stages of Impressionism. He was close to the river Seine and was able to pursue his study of the effects of water. The countryside around Argenteuil also interested him and provided another subject that he painted for a number of years – fields of red poppies – of which this is an early example. The next three years at Argenteuil was a relatively calm period for Monet and he made a number of tranquil, almost idyllic paintings often (as here) including Camille and Jean, now aged six. This one, in fact, includes Camille and her son twice, although Monet painted Jean differently attired. Camille is, however, wearing the hat that appears on the tree in plate 23. Although a casually structured work, the delicacy of touch, the fresh openness of the scene, the brilliant red of the poppies inviting the observer into the landscape, and the balancing firmness of the distant line of trees with the central dwelling to place humanity in nature, makes this a typically accomplished work from the maturing Monet.

he began to paint again. He discontinued his long painting trips, made almost every year, and became an almost total recluse, discouraging even his closest friends from visiting and rarely leaving his house and garden. He painted a number of Venetian scenes from memory and 29 of these were exhibited at the Bernheim Jeune Gallery in Paris in 1912. Monet was disappointed with his work at this time but, more seriously and like Degas, realized his eyesight was failing and was eventually diagnosed as having a double cataract for which he refused an operation, fearful of losing his vision altogether.

In February 1914, before the outbreak of the First World War, Jean Monet died and Blanche, his widow, became Monet's companion and housekeeper for the rest of his life. During the first two years of the war, within sight and sound of guns and troop movements he was immured at Giverny, depressed and without the will to paint. During this period Clemenceau, even though involved in affairs of state and, later in the war, was prime

PLATE 28
Train in the Snow (1875)
Oil on canvas, 23¼ x 30¾ inches (59 x 78cm)

Two aspects of Monet's subject interests are combined in this painting. He was interested in unusual weather effects, particularly winter snow and ice, and painted many landscape studies of the colour differences between winter and summer light effects. He was also interested in the railway and the new systems that were spreading across France. His house in Argenteuil was near the railway and the track ran through his property at Giverny without, it appears, any disturbance to him. This painting is a remarkably effective treatment of an overcast winter day in close tones of grey and shades of yellow ochre, with the sharp orange headlights surrounded by a dull warm red giving the train a welcoming appearance in a chill landscape.

PLATE 29
The Gare Saint–Lazare, Paris (1877)
Oil on canvas, 29³/₄ x 41 inches (75.5 x 104cm)

The importance of the railways to the Impressionists has already been noted and this is an important and effective demonstration of Monet's ability to find a pictorial method of translating this innovation, dominated by steam and smoke, iron and glass, with the new mechanical monsters at the fulcrum. Monet produced other versions of the subject in his last major series as commentaries on modern society. The viewpoint is one which passengers would have been familiar with, the station's terminal looking towards the Pont de L'Europe which forms a hazy rectangular block emphasized at each end by smoke or steam in sunlight. The engine is belching a delicate mauve smoke which rises to the containing broad triangle of the shed roof. To the left of the engine is a carriage while on the right, in sunlight, the waiting passengers stand motionless while sunlight pouring through the glass panels of the roof intensifies the effect of steam and smoke which swirls around them. The central line of the painting is the pitch of the roof and taken together, the whole evokes an 'impression' of the gothic nave of a cathedral which, when one recalls Monet's atheism, makes a fitting setting for the modern, secular 'religion' of industry and commerce.

PLATE 30
The Rue Montorgueil: Fête of 30 June 1878
Oil on canvas, 31½ x 20 inches (80 x 50.5cm)

Monet's last paintings of a Paris subject are the two (the other is the smaller Rue Montorgueil Decked Out with Flags) *he made at the national fête of 30 June in the year of the Exposition Universelle, the first since the Franco-Prussian War and the Commune. The scene in the rue Montorgueil is an exciting interplay of diagonals, vertical strokes and complicated*

criss-crossing of the national colours in the flags, painted with verve and enthusiasm. It is surely intended as an impression in the true sense of the word. Recalling the scene much later, Monet reminisced, 'I like flags very much. At the first Fête Nationale, of June 30th, I was walking along rue Montorgueil with my painting equipment. The street was decked with flags, but swarming with people. I spied a balcony, mounted the stairs and asked permission to paint. It was granted... Ah, those were good times, though life was not always easy ... '

minister, spent time and much trouble trying to encourage Monet to paint. He suggested that Monet undertake some large water paintings, stimulating his enthusiasm so much that he had a large studio built, 75ft long and 49ft high (23 and 15 metres) which he stacked with large canvases. This gave Monet new heart to the extent that he began to work assiduously on paintings, sketches and studies related to what became an extensive project, known as the *Décoration des Nymphéas*, which he intended to present to the State. Without Clemenceau and Blanche, this work would never have been completed. Monet was tempted to abandon it as his eyesight worsened and he overpainted work already done, almost ruining it in the process. Clemenceau once threatened that he would never speak to Monet again if he broke his promise and failed to finish the programme. Supported by Blanche who encouraged Monet every day, Clemenceau persuaded Monet to continue what was in itself a daunting task for a man nearly blind and almost beyond his powers. Nevertheless, the *Nymphéas* were eventually finished and after some discussion were located in the Orangerie of the Tuileries in 1927.

Like Degas, Monet continued to work when almost blind until, by October 1926, he was in considerable pain and his doctors diagnosed pulmonary sclerosis. He died on 5 December 1926 in his much-loved home at Giverny. He was given a quiet funeral without religious ceremony

which, as a non-believer, was his wish. The pallbearers at his funeral were Clemenceau, and the painters Bonnard, Roussel and Vuillard. There was not even a funeral oration, only flowers. 'I perhaps owe having become a painter to flowers,' he said in 1924.

THE LAST WORKS
The final decade of Monet's life was overshadowed by his steady loss of sight, despite eventually accepting an operation for cataract in 1923, which partially restored the sight in one eye. The studies he made of parts of his garden or lily pond are poignant evidence of his growing inability to control either line or colour. He did a number of views of the Japanese bridge, for instance, in which the bridge itself is, as a form, hardly discernible. These last paintings are canvases without form but reveal the potent impact of a painter for whom colour without form was not only almost the only discernible result of applying paint but also was, as it had always been, his abiding interest. For him, from the early tentative beginnings, the small searching dabs and short strokes of colour which suggested both form and moving nature had remained a constant inspiration. In the last works, apart from the *Nymphéas*, the colour is intense and unrefined as his vision only allowed him to see the strongest colours.

There was considerable fear that he would destroy the effect of the large *Nymphéas* panels that had already been

PLATE 31
Snow Effect at Vétheuil: Looking Towards the Church (1878–79)

Oil on canvas, 20½ x 28 inches (52 x 71cm)

Early in 1878 Monet left Argenteuil (and Paris) for Vétheuil where he began a period of hard work during which (although they are not given the attention of the earlier works from the Argenteuil period) he produced a number of fine calm paintings of the town and its surroundings. Vétheuil is on the Seine and Monet lived not far from the water he so much loved, near an eminently paintable section of the river with its small island and rich vegetation and tall poplars along its banks. The snow scene here must have been painted from one of the small islands or from Monet's bateau atelier or floating studio. The whole ambience of the picture and the colour key is a remarkably evocative image of the chill of the snow-enveloped town.

worked on and it took all of Clemenceau's persuasion and authority to prevent this happening. Thus the latter period of Monet's working life was a collaboration, albeit confrontational, between the great prime minister of France, the 'Tiger', Monet's closest friend and supporter, and the near-blind painter who desperately wanted to improve, as was always his endeavour, the last great paintings of the late Impressionists, the *Nymphéas* (plates 47–49). We must be grateful that both triumphed in the end. But it was a late ending to the most significantly influential development of 19th-century painting. All the great movements of early 20th-century art had commenced – and most finished – before Monet died, a legendary and venerated figure but, as it seemed then, an artistic irrelevance. Later, and wiser one hopes, we now see Monet as one of the great revolutionaries of modern painting and a founding father of 20th-century style.